THE
VIP
DOUBLES
DOWN

ALSO BY NANCY HERKNESS

Wager of Hearts Series

The CEO Buys In

The All-Star Antes Up

The Irishman's Christmas Gamble (novella)

Whisper Horse Novels

Take Me Home

Country Roads

The Place I Belong

A Down-Home Country Christmas (novella)

Stand-Alone Novels

A Bridge to Love

Shower of Stars

Music of the Night

THE
VIP
DOUBLES
DOWN

WAGER of HEARTS
—♥♣ **BOOK 3** ♦♠—

NANCY
HERKNESS

Montlake
Romance

F
Her

Published by Montlake Romance, Seattle

www.apub.com

Amazon, the Amazon logo, and Montlake Romance are trademarks of Amazon.com, Inc., or its affiliates.

ISBN-13: 9781477824030
ISBN-10: 1477824030

Cover design by Eileen Carey

Printed in the United States of America

To my treasured critique group: Miriam Allenson, Lisa Verge Higgins, and Jennifer Wilck, all wonderful writers, terrific critical readers, and great friends. You understand Gavin so well.

Chapter 1

Gavin Miller walked into the paneled bar of the ultra-exclusive Bellwether Club, rolling his neck in a vain attempt to ease the jabbing muscle spasms. Spasms that came from staring at a computer screen for hours at a time without typing a single word of the novel that was now eight months overdue. He hoped a stiff drink would offer some relief.

His friend Luke Archer had persuaded him to venture out on a sleety late February evening. Luke was the New York Empire's Super Bowl–winning machine of a quarterback. Former quarterback, as of a few days ago. Which was why Gavin was suspicious of the invitation, since he would expect Luke to be home celebrating his retirement with his new wife.

"What the . . . ?" he snapped as he spotted Luke sitting with Nathan Trainor, the CEO of Trainor Electronics. Nathan was also a friend, as well as the third participant in a drunken wager they'd made five months before. A wager on love.

Luke was dressed casually in khaki trousers and a blue-and-white-striped shirt, but the CEO was wearing a navy suit, as though he'd come directly from a business meeting. The fact that Luke had brought reinforcements increased Gavin's wariness. Stalking over to the brass-topped table, he scowled at the two men. "I didn't know we were having a convention."

"Sit down, Miller," Nathan said, the corner of his mouth twitching as he waved his cut-glass tumbler toward an empty leather chair. "And stop being so charming. We're just three friends having a drink together."

Gavin slouched into the chair, shifting as pain ripped through his neck and shoulders. He forced himself not to wince.

The CEO nudged a glass of amber-colored liquid toward Gavin. "Bourbon. Maybe it will mellow you."

Gavin seized the glass and took a gulp, praying the liquor would dull the pain. "*Mellow* is not a word found in any of our vocabularies."

The Bellwether Club accepted only those who had made their ten-figure fortunes for themselves with no help from family trust funds. So its membership was not a group that was known for kicking back and relaxing.

Nathan took a sip of what Gavin assumed was single-malt scotch, his usual drink. "Speak for yourself." A smile played around the CEO's lips, and Gavin knew the man was thinking of his fiancée, Chloe. The wedding was scheduled for October at Camp Lejeune, in honor of Nathan's Marine father. Gavin was a groomsman, much to his public dismay and secret enjoyment.

He lifted his glass toward the quarterback, careful not to move too quickly. "Congratulations, Archer. You went out in a blaze of glory by retiring after your fifth Super Bowl victory. I salute you for knowing how to make an exit. I swear several of those sports reporters were wiping away tears because their golden boy will no longer be around to give ratings-boosting interviews."

"I appreciate the good wishes, Miller." The ex-quarterback's Texas twang held the edge of sarcasm Gavin took such pleasure in provoking, since Luke's usual persona was that of a laconic, unflappable jock.

"Are we gathered here to celebrate the end of your football career?" Gavin needled.

"You can really turn an innocuous phrase into something awful," Luke said.

"That's what makes me a great writer." Trading insults with Luke was easing Gavin's tension.

"When do you take the Series 7 exam?" Nathan asked.

"Series 7, Series 6, Series 66." Luke listed an impressive battery of tests required to qualify as an investment adviser. "I start the process in two months. Miranda's helping me study." As he spoke his wife's name, Luke's eyes warmed in a way that made Gavin envious.

"And you intend to ace them all." Gavin started to shake his head but thought better of it. "Every brokerage firm in the country is clamoring to hire you without a single test to your name, but you have to pile on the qualifications from the get-go. Take a break. Stop competing for a day or two."

Luke lifted one shoulder in a shrug. "If I'm going to tell people what to do with their money, I want to make sure my advice is sound."

His insistence on all the tests was ironic, considering that Luke had made most of his fortune not by playing football but by funding a start-up that had hit big.

"Always the quarterback, aren't you, boyo?" Gavin said. "Calling the plays."

Luke flashed a grin that brought out his famous dimple. "I've been doing it since I was eight years old. Hard to break that kind of habit."

"Like standing at attention when your father walks in the room," Nathan agreed. "You don't even realize you're doing it."

Gavin scowled at his glass. Whenever his father had walked into a room, he'd hidden whatever book he was reading. Otherwise, his father would give him a list of chores that needed doing, and they were usually the dirtiest ones.

Now his father was gone.

"Hey, Miller." Luke nudged Gavin's polished black loafer with the toe of his cowboy boot. "Where's your mind wandering?"

"I was just considering whether we should thank or berate our fathers for making us what we are."

"We're getting into deep waters now," Nathan said. "Freudian and Oedipal."

"Oedipus was all about his mother," Luke interjected.

"Yet again the jock surprises us with his intellect," Gavin snarked.

Luke leveled a bland stare at him. "I had to take three gut courses a semester to play college ball. When I got bored, I listened to the professor."

Gavin snorted. Luke Archer was famous for memorizing his team's playbook. He had a mind like a steel trap, which was why Gavin had no doubt he would earn the highest possible score on every financial test.

"I'm fortunate," Nathan said. "I've been able to make my peace with my father, thanks to Chloe. But you never got the chance, Miller. That's a damn shame."

Gavin's father had died suddenly, struck down by a massive heart attack as he carried a bag of horse feed out of the stockroom of the family store. Gavin had met Nathan and Luke for the first time in this very bar right after Gavin returned from the funeral. They'd gotten drunk together and made the ridiculous wager. A wager two of them had won well before the one-year deadline they'd set. Gavin was the only one whose stakes were still at risk.

"I'm not sure there was any peace to be made with my father." Gavin's mother had bolted when he was a child, unable to bear the isolation of the rural Illinois town and the joylessness of her older husband. He remembered her turning on the radio and dancing around the living room, her brightly printed cotton skirt swirling around her bare calves while the heart-shaped locket at her throat threw out glints of light. Every couple of songs, she would try to tug his father to his feet to join her. But his dour father just shook his head and sat in his lounge chair, pretending to watch television. Gavin wasn't fooled, though. His father's eyes followed his mother's graceful, swaying figure through every dip and turn.

When she abandoned her small family, she'd left the jeweled locket on Gavin's dresser with a tiny strip of paper folded into it that read, *Love you, lightning bug. Always have, always will. XO, Mommy.* He'd never heard another word from her.

Luke cleared his throat, yanking Gavin back to the present. "We know you're still having a problem with writer's block."

He jerked, and his back muscles protested with a jab of torment. "Has my agent been talking to you?" Gavin injected a warning note.

"Only about writing my autobiography now that I'm retired." Luke's tone was a mix of amusement and exasperation.

"You told us yourself," Nathan pointed out.

"Because there's no point in keeping it secret when all my readers know the publication date has been pushed back yet again." Gavin took another swig of bourbon, trying to wash away the bitter taste of failure.

"So we want to take some pressure off you," Luke said. "We want to cancel the bet."

A boil of anger flushed sweat out on Gavin's forehead. They thought he was so pathetic that he would back out of a wager of honor made between gentlemen. The edge in his voice was razor sharp as he said, "I don't renege on my bets."

"We're not suggesting you renege," Nathan said. "We're withdrawing from the wager."

"You can't withdraw. You've won, both of you." Gavin could feel the rage tightening his already rigid shoulders. "Frankie has confirmed that you found women who genuinely love you, although God knows why."

"It was a ridiculous bet," Nathan said. "We'd had too much to drink."

"And we were in dark places," Luke added. "A bad combination."

"Don't insult me," Gavin said. "I proposed the bet."

"No, I did," Luke said. "You challenged us to find a woman who loved us for ourselves, not our money. I forced the stakes on you, both the secret ones and the charitable donation. And set the one-year time limit."

"You're really pissing me off, Archer," Gavin said. "I am capable of finding the right woman and putting an engagement ring on her finger before this October. Writer's block doesn't interfere with that."

"Simmer down," Nathan said. "Neither of us knew what you'd just been through or we never would have agreed to the bet."

Somewhere in the rational part of his brain, Gavin acknowledged that was probably true, but dark clouds of temper were overwhelming his better judgment. "You'd just found out that a woman you loved had lied from the moment you met her, Trainor," he pointed out before leveling his gaze on Luke. "And *your* best friend had just retired from football, leaving you staring at your future retirement with profound depression. My father's death was no more serious."

"We're your friends, man, so we know it was more than that," Luke said, shifting in his chair.

"Really?" Gavin gave the two men a cold smile. "Tell me what you think you know."

"Your ex-fiancée showed up at the funeral," Nathan said. "To use you for her career."

"And your stepmother wouldn't let you sit with the family," Luke added. "That's heavy stuff on top of losing your dad."

All the anguish Gavin had crammed firmly into the far recesses of his memory flooded out, sending a burn of black ice through his veins. "My friendship with you two was an unfortunate mistake," he said, before polishing off the last of his drink.

"Oh, stuff it, Miller." Luke's pale blue eyes sparked with irritation. "Friends cut each other slack when they need it."

Gavin didn't want slack. He wanted something to clear away the gray fog that seemed to hang over the world around him, muting sound and color and feeling. Strangling his ability to write. Truthfully, he welcomed the burst of anger his friends' offer had ignited. "No favors," he said. "In fact, I'm going to double the amount I have to donate to charity if I lose the bet."

Nathan shook his head. "I won't agree to that. Archer set that number high to make sure we took the wager seriously. None of us were thinking straight that night."

"Donal," Gavin called over to the bartender, "I need your boss for a little business transaction. And a pen and paper."

"Oh, for God's sake," Luke said. "We didn't record the donation amount with Frankie the first time. Only our personal stakes. She doesn't need to be involved."

"I want to make it official," Gavin said, "so you won't be tempted to *cut me some slack* later on." He put heavy emphasis on the words Luke had used. He knew he was being obnoxious, but he couldn't tolerate pity, even from his closest friends.

Nathan and Luke exchanged a look that he couldn't quite read, and he didn't like the hidden communication. He poured another drink, gingerly nodding his thanks as the bartender placed a couple of sheets of heavy vellum and a Montblanc pen on the table.

"Cheers," Gavin said, knocking back half the bourbon in one gulp.

Luke blew out a breath of exasperation. "Look, Gavin, you helped me out by convincing Miranda not to give up on me. I'm trying to return the favor."

Recollections of that day at Miranda's family farm breathed some remembered contentment into Gavin. Luke had rounded up a few football players to help out with stacking hay bales. Gavin had tagged along, partly out of curiosity as to why the superstar quarterback was dragging them all up to Nowhere, New York, but mostly because he couldn't bear to stare at his blank computer screen another day. Luke had quickly melded them into a team, and Gavin had found pleasure in the physical labor and the easy camaraderie. Of course, that was before every muscle in his back decided to clench itself into a throbbing fist.

He had also observed the vibrating tension between Luke and Miranda. So he'd offered Miranda a little pep talk, just enough to persuade her to share her true feelings with the quarterback. When Luke threw them back in her face, Gavin had told Luke what an idiot he was.

"I hope you never give me reason to regret my intervention with Miranda," Gavin said.

Luke's icy gaze dropped to glacial temperature. Gavin held up his hand in silent apology.

The big mahogany bar door swung open, and the club's founder, Frankie Hogan, strode in, clad in one of her signature tailored pantsuits. This one was dark gray, which made her smooth silver hair glint brightly in contrast. "It's déjà vu all over again," she said as she walked up to their table.

The three men stood, their height dwarfing the Irishwoman physically but not in spirit. Gavin admired Frankie for thumbing her nose at all the exclusive clubs that had rejected her and her new money. She'd founded the Bellwether Club, a place of stratospheric exclusivity that had nothing to do with your birth, only your success. Of course, now membership in Frankie's club had become highly sought after.

"You're looking lovely this evening," Gavin said, ignoring the shriek of his shoulders as he held a chair for her.

He was surprised when a slight blush added to the glow in her face. "Fresh air and exercise," she said, her voice holding both the rasp of whiskey and the lilt of Ireland. "They cure whatever ails you." Her gaze fell on the paper and pen, and she lifted an eyebrow at them. "Am I to be witness to another wager, gentlemen?"

"An amendment to the original wager," Gavin said. "You hold the sealed envelopes with the stakes that are of personal significance to us. However, we also had an extra side bet that wasn't recorded, a purely financial donation to charity. I'm sweetening the pot by doubling the amount I'm betting."

He picked up the pen and wrote twice the amount Luke had originally proposed before signing his name with a flourish.

Frankie gave a low, musical whistle. "That's a hell of a lot of money, even for one of my members."

Before Gavin could hand the paper to her, Luke grabbed it and ripped it in half.

Nathan nodded his approval, saying, "An amendment requires the agreement of all parties to the contract. Archer and I do not accept Miller's addition."

"I see." Frankie crossed her arms and turned to Gavin. "We seem to have a difference of opinion."

He should have been furious, but the sense that even here he had failed swamped any anger. He shrugged. "No one can stop me from making the donation in the event that I lose the bet."

Luke reached over to grip Gavin's shoulder with one of his big, powerful hands, making Gavin wince. "You're not going to lose."

Chapter 2

Gavin glared at the blinking cursor on his empty computer screen before he shoved himself to his feet. His back spasmed, and he kicked the chair so it banged against the desk. "What the hell good is an ergonomic chair if my back still hurts?"

He didn't even have the excuse of a hangover from drinking with Luke and Nathan the night before. The other two men had refused to join him in a self-pitying binge.

Stalking over to the standing desk once used by Charles Dickens—the antique he'd bought with his first royalty check from the first Julian Best movie—he picked up a pen and clicked it open and shut several times.

His gaze rested on the blank legal pad lying on the desk for several moments. He grimaced and wrote: *A CEO, a quarterback, and a writer walked into a bar.*

The desk stood solid under the weight of his focused gaze.

They made an insane wager. The kind you make only when you're both drunk and choking on despair. The kind that you can't begin to imagine winning.

Yet two of them won, their lives transformed by their good fortune.

"Mr. Gavin, Mrs. Jane is here to see you." Ludmilla, his house-keeper, spoke in her strong Polish accent.

With a combination of dread and relief, he tossed the pen onto the desk and turned away from the accusingly empty expanse of paper.

"Gavin, how are you doing?" His literary agent, Jane Dreyer, had followed Ludmilla into the home office on the second floor of his New York City mansion.

Leaning down, he kissed the tiny blonde woman on her perfectly made-up cheek. She threw a quick glance at the desk where he'd been standing. "No," he said. "I'm not writing the next Julian Best novel."

She sighed and sat down on the gray leather sofa, crossing her legs so he could see the red soles of her high-heeled designer pumps. Today, her dress was brilliant blue embellished with gold necklaces of varying lengths. Her gaze held concern. "To hell with the deadline and the movie. I want you to be writing for your own mental health."

Gavin lowered himself into the wing chair in front of the flickering fireplace, stretching out his long legs and giving her a half smile. "I know your motives are pure, because we could both live in high style on my royalties for the rest of our lives."

His bestselling books paid well, but it was the movie deals Jane had negotiated that made him eligible for a place like the Bellwether Club. He owed her.

She locked her blue eyes on him. "I'm worried about you, sweetie, so I have a serious proposal to make."

"No ghostwriters." He would rather kill off his fictional super spy than entrust him to another writer.

"Of course not." She waved her hand in dismissal. "I want you to buy out your contract with the publisher."

"What?" Shock vibrated through him. "I've missed a few dead-lines, but I'm not ready to throw in the towel." His book might be eight months overdue, but before this he'd never overshot a deadline, not through fourteen novels and three novellas. He had seven chapters drafted, but he hadn't written a word since . . . since all the events he had shoved to the back of his mind.

"It would take the pressure off, give you some room to breathe."

Gavin hurtled out of the chair, adrenaline overwhelming the protest of his muscles, and laid his arm along the marble mantelpiece. When he caught a glimpse of himself in the silver-framed mirror, he was shocked by how sunken his eyes looked. No wonder Jane thought he needed a rest. "We both know the publisher is the least of my worries. It's the movie producers. I don't know why the hell I let them change the movie's ending to a cliff-hanger."

"Because they were very persuasive, and it was a creative challenge for you to weave that cliff-hanger into your next novel."

He shook his head. "If the movie had ended like the book, no one would care whether I had writer's block. They could have made a movie from one of Julian's earlier novels." He huffed out a breath. "It was pure arrogance on my part."

"I'll handle the movie producers."

She would, too. Jane's small body housed the spirit of a tigress when it came to protecting her authors. The powers that be in Hollywood cowered before her.

"What about the actors and the gaffers and the best boys?" The weight of responsibility settled on his tortured shoulders. "They're counting on the next Julian Best movie."

"If you're worried about Irene Bartram, she'll be just fine." Jane's tone was acid. "I hear she's already found herself a guest role on a soap opera."

"I'm well aware that Irene can take care of herself." His ex-fiancée had made it very clear that her career interests took priority over their relationship. That had contributed to her becoming an ex. Fresh disillusionment twisted in his chest, and he straightened away from the mantel to escape it.

"Ludmilla was right," Jane said.

"About?"

"The fact that you're in physical pain, too." She leaned back against the sofa cushions. "At least I have a cure for that."

Gavin rolled his shoulders under the black cashmere pullover. "It's just tension. Nothing I can't work out with a trip to the gym." He had a well-equipped one, including a lap pool, downstairs, but he hadn't taken advantage of it in weeks.

"Well, you're getting help. I called Havilland Rehab, the best facility in the area. One of their top physical therapists just started her own private practice. I hired her to come here five days a week, starting tomorrow." Jane smiled. "And she's used to difficult clients. You can thank me later." Jane stood up. "Think about the contract buyout."

"I don't want or need a physical therapist," Gavin snapped, even as a shooting pain in his neck gave lie to his words.

Jane rested her hand on the forearms he had crossed over his chest, her gaze scanning his face. "You've been through a lot recently. Your father. Your fiancée. Your book. There's no shame in accepting help from your friends."

He forced himself to meet her eyes, even though he was afraid she might see too much. "You've always told me you were my agent, not my friend."

She didn't flinch. "I'm a hundred times tougher than you, so insults won't chase me away."

"What will?"

"Your promise to let the therapist in the door."

"Ludmilla will do that."

"Writers." Jane sighed in exasperation. "Always hiding behind words."

"My words have made us both a lot of money."

She clamped her fingers around his arm. "Work with the therapist. You've been doing this long enough to know how interconnected the mind and body are."

"For you, Jane, anything. Especially since you're cutting off the circulation to my writing hand."

She released his arm and reached up to pat his cheek. "You'll break through this, sweetie. Just give yourself time."

"Don't go soft on me. I count on you to crack the whip over my back as I slave away at the computer."

Jane wouldn't take the bait. "I'll call tomorrow to see how you like Allie."

"Allie?"

"The therapist. Allie Nichols."

He had no intention of letting the therapist anywhere near him, but he affected a leer. "Is she pretty? Maybe I'll keep her around for a massage or two."

Jane sighed again. "You don't do lechery with any conviction, so that won't scare her away. Besides, I'm paying her enough so she'll stay no matter what you throw at her."

"We'll see about that," he muttered as Jane headed for the door.

Chapter 3

Allie shifted on the green velvet cushion of her chair and surveyed the sitting room where the housekeeper had told her to wait. Gavin Miller owned an entire house in the middle of Manhattan. His Julian Best books and movies must bring in a ton of money.

At the Havilland Rehabilitation Center, Allie had worked with rich—even famous—patients, but she'd never gone to their homes. If she could make it work as a freelancer, it could be really interesting to see where her patients lived. And really intimidating.

Boy, did she need to make it work, too. Between losing the job at Havilland Rehab and her recent divorce, her bank balance was plunging downward faster than a moonshiner running from a revenuer. Thank goodness her boss at Havilland had felt bad about her dismissal, so he'd recommended her to Gavin Miller's literary agent.

She took a deep breath to calm her nerves. An exotic floral scent tickled her nostrils. That giant bouquet on the leather-topped table was real, not fake. She was pretty sure the furniture in this room was genuinely antique, too, and way older than Victorian. The Oriental rug beneath her cross-trainers glowed in deep jewel tones. She couldn't resist reaching down to run her fingers over its silky surface.

As she straightened, she caught a glimpse of herself in the gilt-framed mirror with an eagle perched on the top, and tugged down the hem of her V-necked navy shirt. Her matching navy athletic pants were still clean, despite her slog along sidewalks edged with February slush. The only thing that ruined her neat, professional look was her flaming red hair. She'd yanked it back into a tight ponytail, but nothing could hide the too-bright color.

Footsteps sounded on the marble floor of the hallway, and Allie stood. Gavin's agent had warned her that the writer might be a little difficult but not to let him discourage her. He really needed her help.

The man who stalked through the door was tall, lean, and scowling and didn't appear to need anyone's assistance. His green eyes snapped with temper, and his thick, dark hair appeared to have been tossed by a high wind. Angry energy crackled around him. In his black jeans and sweater, he made her think of some kind of sorcerer.

She had always found that the author photos on book jackets made their subjects look better than the reality, but Gavin Miller's publicity shot didn't convey anywhere near the power and magnetism of the man.

When his gaze caught hers, he paused for a moment to turn his scowl into a tight, false smile, and held out his hand. That's when she caught the wince that said he was in pain. Seeing that he needed her services dispelled her nervousness about meeting the famous author.

"Ms. Nichols, I'm Gavin Miller, and I'm afraid your time has been wasted. My agent hired you without my knowledge. Your services won't be necessary." His smile turned sly. "However, I will make sure Jane pays you for a full five days."

Five days wasn't nearly enough. She needed him to hire her for months.

The fingers he wrapped around hers were long, elegant, and strong. Despite the dismay roiling through her, she gave him a firm grip in return and produced her warmest, most disarming smile. She also laid on her West Virginia accent a little thicker than usual. "It's a pleasure to meet you, Mr. Miller."

When Allie had mentioned her enthusiasm for the Julian Best series, Ms. Dreyer had hesitated, making Allie wish she'd kept quiet. After a tense pause, the agent had warned her not to mention the books, but now Allie was desperate to make some connection. "I'm a big fan of your Julian Best novels. Every time one of your books was published, my mama would set aside a whole day to read it from cover to cover. Then she would give it to me so I could discuss it with her. A day was about as long as I could wait to get my hands on it."

Surprise registered in his eyes as his smile turned genuine. "My thanks to you and your mother. I'm always honored to meet an enthusiastic reader. I hope to have another novel for both of you to share soon."

A jab of grief hit Allie, but she kept her smile in place. "Mama passed on two years ago, so I have to enjoy Julian on my own now."

"I'm so sorry." A shadow crossed his face.

"Thank you. I have good memories."

"You're fortunate." His voice held an edge. He thrust one hand through his hair, and she understood why it looked the way it did. "Let me get your coat."

Allie clenched her hands in a tight ball at her waist. "Mr. Miller, I would like to just talk with you. Maybe you could spare me half an hour."

"Talk?" He had started toward the door but now turned back to her, his movement hitching as a muscle grabbed somewhere. "Aren't you supposed to assign me boring, painful exercises involving multicolored elastic bands?"

"It's helpful to discuss what you think the problem is before I develop a plan," she said. Even more important, she had to gain her patient's trust. Gavin Miller was going to be a tough nut to crack on that front.

His jaw muscles tensed. "I know exactly what the problem is, and physical therapy cannot solve it."

She knew about his writer's block, but that was another topic his agent had warned her against discussing. "When your body isn't working right, it can cause all kinds of trouble for the rest of you."

His eyes went stormy again. "She told you, didn't she? I'm going to strangle Jane."

"Like your doctor, I work under strict confidentiality." Allie sat down. It was a reverse mirroring technique. If she sat, Gavin should feel a subconscious impulse to copy her action. She hoped.

He hesitated, his glance veering from the door to the chair opposite her. With a muted shrug, he took two strides and eased down onto the upholstered cushion. Then he interlaced his arms over his chest. "So, talk."

His redheaded inquisitor in her serious therapist costume took a breath. He was going to regret this, but it seemed marginally better than pacing around his office while he prayed for Julian to speak to him.

"Did you sleep well last night?" she asked.

He liked the soft twang in her voice. It wasn't Texas and it wasn't Deep South. He guessed Kentucky, maybe. He also liked the vibrant color of her hair. It had to be natural, because it wasn't a sophisticated auburn or an edgy burgundy. Judging by the way she had it pulled back in that strict ponytail, she probably didn't care for what Mother Nature had given her.

"Mr. Miller?"

"Sorry, what did you say?"

"I asked if you slept well last night."

"No, I didn't."

His examiner nodded, making the ponytail sway. What was her name? Allie.

"Did you dream?"

That seemed a strange question from a physical therapist. "Are you going to interpret my dreams now? How very Freudian."

"That's not my area of expertise, but the amount and quality of dreaming can indicate why you didn't sleep well." Her gray eyes were clear and earnest.

"Fine. I'll play." He cast his mind back to the night, trying to recall how many nightmares he'd had. "Last night was not particularly dream heavy. I remember maybe three scenes, none of them pleasant."

"Did the dreams wake you up?"

"No, I find it difficult to fall asleep. Once I do, even the worst nightmare can't rouse me." He'd given up on trying to sleep at about 3:00 a.m., reading for an hour before finally succumbing to exhaustion.

She nodded again. "What did you have for dinner last night?"

"You think indigestion gave me the nightmares? My stomach is made of sterner stuff than that." What had Ludmilla made him? She was an excellent cook, but no matter how she spiced the food, it tasted bland to him. "Salmon? Yes, salmon with grilled vegetables of some sort."

"Sounds healthy." Her drawl held approval. "Did you have wine with dinner? Or coffee?"

"I had water." He waited for the little nod of approbation before he added, "Flavored with bourbon."

He expected a frown, but she chuckled—a musical, throaty sound that pulled at something low in his body.

"My pa was partial to bourbon and branch water," she said.

"Are you from Kentucky?"

"No, sir, I'm from West-by-gosh Virginia." Her accent thickened. It was an answer he could tell she'd given often.

The "sir" should have made him feel old, but from her it sounded natural and charming. "So not quite southern, not quite midwestern. What brought you to New York?"

Discomfort flashed across her face. "A dream job. What brought you here?"

He applauded her technique. Answer the question so you put your inquisitor under obligation to do the same.

"Bright lights. Being at the center of the publishing industry." He watched her register each item before he threw her a curveball. "Escape from a small town in Illinois."

"You didn't like living in a small town?"

"I didn't like living with my stepmother." Now why had he told her that? He tightened his arms across his chest, which sent a ripple of pain along his shoulders.

"My best friend had that kind of stepmother," Allie said. "Just like the one in *Cinderella*."

That surprised a short laugh out of him. "Mine didn't quite make me scrub the floors."

"Lucky for you." Allie smiled at him, changing from earnest therapist to sympathetic friend in an instant.

He wasn't falling for it. "Don't you need to ask me more questions, or are we done with the inquisition?"

"I have a few more." She closed her eyes for a moment, as though consulting a mental list. "Is the pain worse in the morning or in the evening?"

"Aha, you're trying to catch me out. I never mentioned any pain."

She focused those limpid gray eyes on him and waited. He did his best to stare levelly back at her, but finally he broke and pushed out of the chair, his back complaining at the sudden movement. Stalking over to the bar hidden in an ornate English marquetry cabinet, he flicked open the doors. "Would you like some water?" he asked, rummaging in the minifridge.

"That would be nice, thanks."

He set two paper-thin crystal tumblers out and poured bottled spring water into them. Carrying them across the room, he handed her a glass before raising his to his lips. As she lifted hers for a sip, he noticed her hand. Short, neat nails with no polish. Slim fingers, but the back of her hand was square, giving the impression of strength.

"Are you more comfortable standing than sitting?" she asked.

"Depends on what you mean by comfortable." He gave her a slanted smile. "Physically or mentally?"

"I'll take an answer to either one."

He took another swallow, studying her over the edge of his glass. She sat straight with her knees and ankles together, her glass resting on one thigh. Her skin was creamy against the dark blue of her shirt, another clue that her hair color was real. Her gaze didn't flinch from his, but he caught the creeping pink of a blush rising in her cheeks. Her composure was not as firm as she tried to make it appear. "I was attempting to interrupt your interrogation by standing up, but you refuse to be distracted."

"I've heard that complaint before." She inspected the table next to her chair before she set her glass down on a silver ashtray. Leaning forward, she locked her gaze on his face. "May I try something? It won't take long."

"That's very open-ended. I'm not sure I can answer it."

"Will you trust me?"

"And that is an even more difficult question to answer." He looked at her supplicating posture. There was a taut edge of desperation in her face. He shrugged and sat down. "I'm not sure I can commit to trusting you, but go ahead and try whatever it is."

Relief softened the line of her jaw. "Thank you." She reached down to unzip her duffel bag, pulling a black plastic case out of it before she stood up. "I'd like to use a little electrical stimulation on your neck, if you'll allow me. It will help the muscles release."

"Why my neck?"

"I've been watching you move," she said, walking toward him, the case almost hidden behind her thigh. She looked as though she were approaching a skittish horse. "You're holding your neck and shoulders stiffly."

"So it isn't my animal magnetism that's been holding your attention."

She ignored his provocation and kept moving until she was behind his chair. "I'm going to touch your neck now, just to see where the worst tightness is. Is that all right?"

"Go ahead." Not being able to see her made the hairs on the back of his neck prickle.

He heard her rub her hands together and then felt a gentle pressure of warm fingertips walking along the knotted muscles down the back of his neck. Her touch sent a tingle dancing over his skin, and he nearly groaned out loud. It had been too long since he'd been touched with kindness. When she slid her fingers under the neckline of his cashmere sweater to follow the muscle along his shoulder, the sensation flowed straight down to his groin. It was an inappropriate response on his part, he knew, but he didn't want her to stop.

He swallowed a protest when she withdrew her fingers and smoothed his sweater into place.

"Have you ever had electrical stim before?" she asked.

He could hear the case being snapped open and then the crinkling of paper. "I've never had physical therapy of any kind."

There was a ripping sound before she walked around to stand in front of him. Her cheeks were tinged with pink again, and her ponytail had fallen forward over her shoulder. He had an almost ungovernable impulse to pick up the skein of glistening red waves to see if they felt as smoldering and silky as they appeared.

Allie held up a small, square white pad with a wire dangling from it. "I'm going to place four of these pads on your neck and attach them to this portable electro stim machine." She showed him a gray box that looked much like a clunky, old-fashioned cell phone. "I'll start the current very low and ease it up gradually. The moment you feel any discomfort, please tell me. It's completely safe."

He nodded without any thought of the stim. He just wanted to feel her fingers on his skin again.

Allie fixed her gaze on her patient and waited. Most people had concerns about what it would feel like. "Do you have any questions about the treatment?"

"No." He gave her a glinting look from under half-closed eyelids. There was an unsettling flame in his eyes. "You asked me to trust you."

"And you couldn't commit to it." She was sparring with him to delay touching him again. When she'd brushed aside the thick brown hair that curled low on his neck, she'd felt a shock of awareness. The shoulders under the luxuriously soft black sweater were broad and sculpted with muscle. The skin on his nape was satiny, and she wanted to stroke it in ways that had nothing to do with deciding where to position the electrode pads.

What was wrong with her? She'd never reacted to a patient this way before.

He angled his head down so his neck was exposed. "I'm putting my head on the proverbial chopping block. Work your magic before I change my mind."

She whisked behind the chair and placed the pad on one of the knots she'd felt. As she draped the wire down his neck, she could swear a shudder ran through him. "Are you comfortable?"

"Perfectly. Proceed." His voice was tight.

She positioned the other three pads and connected them to the stim unit. Checking the settings, she turned it on and watched him for any sign of distress. He sat utterly still, with his head tilted forward.

"Shall I increase the stimulation?" she asked.

"Push it. I can barely feel anything."

She dialed the current up to a moderate level.

"There's a slight sense of buzzing," he said. "Keep going."

She increased the current.

"More."

The setting was already in the high range, but she gave it a tiny bit more juice.

"Should it feel like there's a frenzied herd of ants stampeding around on my neck?"

She chuckled. "That's about the best description I've ever heard of what electrical stim feels like."

"I *am* a writer." His tone was dry. "How long will the stampede last?"

"Fifteen minutes." She figured that was as long as he would tolerate sitting still, but it was enough time to have some effect on his tight muscles. "You can lean back and relax. The pads will stay in place."

He lifted his head and slid back in the chair. "Must you hover behind me?"

"I'd like to monitor the stim unit, in case you become uncomfortable." She also wanted to avoid those penetrating eyes. That watchful gaze of his seemed to catch every flicker of feeling, every nuance of movement. It was nerve-racking.

"Well, monitor it from beside me." Irritated and demanding.

Allie rearranged the wires so she could place the stim unit on the table beside the writer. She carefully lifted a polished wooden chair with a needlepoint seat from its position by the wall and placed it by the table. As she settled in the chair, it creaked and she flinched. "I hope I didn't just break Louis the Fourteenth's favorite chair."

Instead of laughing, Gavin gave her a sharp look. "You know your antiques."

"All I know is that this chair looks old and fancy, so I named the oldest, fanciest person I could think of." Allie flicked her gaze to the stim unit's dials and back. "Was it really Louis the Fourteenth's chair? Because I'll get off it."

Now he barked out a quick laugh. "To the best of my knowledge, Louis never sat there, so you're safe."

"Is everything in this room old like the chair?" Allie wanted to distract him so he would allow the stim session to continue.

Miller's gaze skimmed around the parlor. "Most of it. This room was furnished during my collector period."

"You don't buy antique furniture anymore?"

"I discovered that old Louis's chairs aren't all that comfortable. We've made something called progress in the intervening centuries."

Allie shifted a fraction of an inch, and the chair groaned again, so she froze. "What period are you in now, if you're not collecting?"

He put his elbows on the chair arms and steepled his fingers, but she saw the way his jaw muscle tightened. "I am in a fallow period."

Bad question. "That's a good farming technique. Rest the soil so it gets fertile again."

"Metaphors are supposed to be my bailiwick."

"I didn't mean to use a metaphor. I grew up in the country. *Fallow* reminded me of that."

"So tell me about your roots, Ms. Nichols."

"Allie." He nodded. She breathed an inward sigh of relief. She had the country-girl patter down cold. "I'm from a little, tiny town in the mountains called Sanctuary. I grew up riding my pony like other kids ride their bicycles. My friends and I would pack some sandwiches, take our ponies down to the river, swim and have a picnic, and canter back home again before dark."

"A downright idyllic childhood." A hint of sarcasm undercut the pretty words. "Did you have a dog, too?"

"My family had five dogs and three cats. And sometimes an orphaned lamb that we'd raise and return to a local farmer."

"Where's the conflict?"

"Excuse me?"

The writer turned his body in his chair so he could look directly at her. "You left this vision of bucolic perfection and came to a rude, dirty, noisy city. What drove you away?"

"I told you . . . a great job. I mean, it didn't drive me away. It brought me to New York." Allie's story had never been challenged before. And she always left Troy out of the telling.

"Of course. In Sanctuary, no one would need physical therapy, because no one gets hurt in paradise."

She recognized the anger generated by pain. Since he couldn't write, which was the thing he was most successful at, he was in more than just physical distress. She kept her voice upbeat. "It's a really small town, so there are not a lot of job openings. I had to move, no matter what. New York offered many opportunities."

When they'd gotten engaged, Troy had given her the choice of New York or Los Angeles, so she'd chosen the city least distant from West Virginia.

"Do you handle only private clients like me?"

Right now, she handled only one patient, private or otherwise. Him.

"Until recently I worked in a rehab facility, but I decided to go out on my own." Not by choice, of course. Her ex-husband had gotten her fired. "I wanted to have the ability to develop longer-term care plans for my clients. Now I can help them not just to recover from a specific issue, but teach them how to prevent it from occurring again."

"So you can teach me how not to have writer's block?" His dark eyebrows were arched in sardonic inquiry.

He'd said it. She hadn't.

"I can teach you how to counteract the physical effects of writer's block."

He sighed. "And here I thought my agent had found a miracle worker."

"Is the stim level still comfortable for you?" She wished she could fix his writer's block as well as his muscle aches. She missed Julian Best.

"It's right on the border of discomfort. I like it." His smile rivaled a razor blade.

What could they talk about that wouldn't add to his stress? She'd googled Gavin Miller when Ms. Dreyer had called to tell her about the job, but most of the information pertained to either his writing career or his canceled engagement to the actress Irene Bartram, both of which were off-limits. However, there was that photo of him talking with the famous quarterback Luke Archer after a football game. "Are you a sports fan?"

"What would give you that idea?"

"You're a guy." Her smile invited him to share the joke.

"How gratifying that you noticed." He gave her a look that made little flickers of heat waltz through her. Then he tilted his head as though considering an important issue. "I like ice hockey and tennis."

"Not football?"

"Ah, you are referring to my association with the legendary Luke Archer." Anger sparked in his eyes. "I cheered him on in the Super Bowl, which was a mistake. He's become an arrogant ass. Pardon my language."

Surprise flicked at her.

"You're quite welcome to tell him I said so." Amusement slipped in alongside the anger in Miller's tone.

"I'm not likely to have the opportunity to speak with Luke Archer."

"Then I'm quite safe in saying anything I want to about him."

Her curiosity got the better of her. "Aren't you friends?"

"Former friends."

"I'm sorry."

He laughed, and this time it was real. "He pissed me off last night, so I'm venting. Mostly because it's impossible to get a rise out of the Iceman. I suppose I still consider him a friend."

"That's his nickname, right? The Iceman?"

"One he is not particularly fond of, although he certainly fostered it."

The stim unit emitted a soft beep, indicating that it had shut down.

"Have fifteen minutes passed already?" Miller sounded almost disappointed.

"I can set it for another fifteen minutes. It will be even more effective on the muscle knots." She rose carefully from the creaky chair.

He hesitated a long moment before shaking his head. "I'm just wasting your time. Go work your magic on someone more appreciative."

If she had someone else to work on, she wouldn't care if they were appreciative or not. "Ms. Dreyer has paid for my time, so you should take advantage of it."

"Ah, so tempting," he said with that unsettling gleam in his eye. "But I must decline. Remove the pads."

Once again he leaned forward so his neck was bared to her. As she bent to disconnect the electrical leads, she caught the scent of him, a slightly spicy, exotic fragrance from his hair that must be the shampoo he used, with an undercurrent of the body-warmed wool of his sweater. It was clean, masculine, and hazardous to her professional demeanor. She fumbled the wire, yanking on the pad that was attached to his neck. She stroked the pad in apology, hoping to soothe any hurt. "I'm so sorry."

He took a deep breath. "Barely felt anything." His voice held that strange tightness again.

She paused a moment and closed her eyes, forcing herself to focus on the job and not the man. Once she felt in control, she finished disconnecting the wires and began gently peeling the pads away from his skin. It shouldn't hurt, but she still found herself brushing her fingertips over the soft skin as a sort of healing massage.

It was impossible to gauge his reaction, because he remained motionless until she had the pads and stim unit back in their case. "You can move now," she said. "In fact, I'd like you to, so you can tell me how it feels."

He tilted his head to one side and then the other. "It bends more easily."

Pleasure glowed through her. "Think how much better it would be after a longer treatment."

He held up his hand to stop her. "Jane thinks if I can get my muscles to release, my muse will come dancing out of hiding. But she has the cart and the horse in the wrong order. All your good work will be undone by tomorrow morning, because you can't break through writer's block with a clever little machine." He stood and offered her a charmingly apologetic smile. "It's been a delight to meet you, Allie. I'm the worst sort of patient, so count yourself fortunate that you don't have to deal with me any further."

Disappointment and a touch of panic stifled the glow inside her. She placed the stim unit case back in her duffel bag and zipped it closed. She straightened to look Gavin Miller right in his ocean green eyes. "Mr. Miller, it's the worst patients who need help the most."

He went still again, his expression turning somber. "You are a wise and determined woman, but you are overmatched here. I am far more pigheaded than you could ever be." He picked up her duffel, hefting it with a pained look. "You're also strong. What do you have in here . . . gold bricks?"

She gasped and reached for the handles. "You should not be lifting anything heavy with your back problems. Please give it to me." Her fingers grazed his, so she felt their warmth as she tugged at the bag.

He resisted for a split second before relinquishing it to her and rubbing his shoulder. "My chivalrous impulses are few and far between for good reason."

"You shouldn't attempt any jousting or sword fighting, either," Allie said, following him into the entrance hall. His snort of laughter gratified her, but it didn't lift the sense of failure that made her feet feel like lead. The duffel was indeed heavy, and she didn't look forward to hauling it the many blocks back to the subway in abject defeat.

Miller swung open a door concealed in the dark wood paneling to retrieve her coat from the closet. As he held it for her to slip her arms into, his fingers brushed the bare skin of her neck under her ponytail, making her hiss in a breath at the intimate contact. It was the same spot where she had laid the pads on his neck, and she wondered if he had felt even a shadow of the same sensations that were zinging through her body, leaving a trail of heat behind them.

She stepped away from him and turned to zip up her coat. Before she pulled on her leather gloves, she held out her hand. "I wish you the best of luck, Mr. Miller. Your books are terrific, and I look forward to the next one. After your fallow period, I bet it will be the best yet."

Miller took her hand, his grip strong and warm. "From your lovely lips to God's unresponsive ear," he muttered. But then he smiled, and this time it reached his eyes, turning the stormy green to rich jade. "Perhaps your little shot of electricity has indeed penetrated my thick skull and reset my brain."

Allie nodded and withdrew her hand with a sense of loss. She marched out the door and down the steps with her head held high, as though she hadn't just lost her one and only client. She'd seen the security cameras on the front of Gavin Miller's brownstone, so she kept marching down the block until she could turn out of sight onto Madison Avenue.

Only then did she slump against a storefront and let the tears of desperation stream down her cheeks.

Chapter 4

In the narrow, dingy hallway of her apartment building, Allie yanked the mail out of the bent metal opening of her mailbox and flipped through it to find both credit card and phone bills. How the heck she was going to pay them she had no idea. Her divorce had cost more than she had budgeted for, she'd gotten fired from the rehab center, and now Gavin Miller didn't want her back. "Nothing like piling on an already bad day."

Grabbing her heavy duffel, she trudged up four flights of steps and unlocked the array of locks on her apartment's battered door.

No cat greeted her. "Pie?" she called, dropping the bag. Her gray rescue cat was elderly and had a myriad of health issues, so Allie worried about her. As she jogged down the hall to the living room, she heard voices and realized the television was on.

She came to an abrupt halt as an unsettling cocktail of fear and fury boiled through her. Pie had not met her at the door because the cat was curled up on Allie's ex-husband's lap.

"How did you get in here? You said you gave me all your keys."

Troy had the grace to look shamefaced as he hit the "Mute" button for the television. "I found another copy I'd made when I thought I'd lost the original."

"Do you understand what a restraining order is? You could go to jail for being here."

Troy set Pie on the couch and stood up, his expression beseeching. "We both know that was just because I was drunk. I'm cold sober now. And I never hit you or anything like that."

"No, but you came to my workplace *twice*, harassed the patients *twice*, and lost me my job. *And* you were drunk." Allie was torn between throwing something at the gorgeous, self-centered face that she'd adored since freshman year in high school or turning on her heel and fleeing. "Leave now. Or I'll call the police."

But she wouldn't call 9-1-1. She still couldn't do that to him. It was true that he had never been physically violent, just verbally abusive. Which, in some ways, was more insidious. If he'd struck her, she would have left him a lot sooner.

"Allie, sweetie, I just wanted to share my good news with you."

"Unless it involves winning the lottery and splitting the jackpot with me, I don't want to hear it." She folded her arms and jerked her head toward the door. She didn't want him to know that her throat had gone tight with nerves. He was an expert at exploiting any weakness in her.

Evidently, the news was too good for her to ruin his sunny mood, because he smiled and walked around the coffee table. "I sort of won the lottery. I got a gig on a soap opera. Just a minor character, but I've been promised three episodes. And maybe more, if viewers respond to me." His deep blue eyes lit up. "This is the break I've been waiting for."

"That's great." The flatness of her voice contradicted her words. She'd heard this song and dance before.

He took her by the shoulders and smiled down at her, a curl of his streaked blond hair falling onto his forehead. A little tug of memory reminded her that she used to love brushing that curl back. Now she wanted to grab a pair of scissors and chop it off. "This isn't an audition," he said. "I have a signed contract."

She shrugged out of his grip. "Congratulations. Best of luck." She hated to be this way, but she'd learned that she had to protect herself from trusting her ex.

"The show films in LA, so I'm moving there."

"Now that *is* good news." Hurt clouded his eyes, and guilt gave Allie an undeserved jab, even as relief loosened the tension in her throat. "You've always wanted to live on the West Coast."

"I'll miss you," he said, his voice ringing with sincerity and longing.

She believed him. He still didn't take responsibility for all the ways he'd hurt her, so he didn't understand that more than their marriage had ended. All the love she'd felt for him in the dozen years since he'd asked her out on their first date had been ripped out of her heart, leaving raw, painful wounds.

She moved a step away. "I wish I could say the same. But you have my blessing to go, if that's what you came for."

"I thought you'd be happy for me. We could celebrate together. I brought a bottle of champagne." Now he was starting to get annoyed. "It's in the refrigerator, chilling."

"Seriously?" Astonishment gave a weird, breathless edge to her voice. "I'm supposed to celebrate with you when I have a restraining order against you?"

It was a vivid reminder of how he used to manipulate her, denying the awful things he'd said to her, shifting the blame for his problems onto her. She'd loved him, so she had believed it was somehow her fault and her obligation. Until he'd pushed it too far, and she'd found the strength to stand up to him.

"But we were married. You wanted me to do good." When his grammar slipped, she knew he was upset.

She put a chair between them. "I don't wish you ill, Troy, but I'm not going to celebrate with you ever again. Go to LA. Have a great life."

"I . . . you . . ." He ran one hand through his tousled curls before he took a deep breath and pinned her with his gaze. "Is this really how you want me to remember you?"

His words took her back to the two naive kids they were when they got married and braved the callous streets of New York City. Troy was so beautiful and talented. He was going to be a star on Broadway. But his ambition was shared by thousands of other more beautiful, more talented actors. Audition after audition had passed without Troy landing a role.

Disappointment had given his beauty a ragged edge, which made it more interesting in some ways. But his ego had proven too fragile to survive the relentless rejections, and he'd taken it out on her, especially when he tried to blunt his failure with alcohol.

Those were the memories she wished she could erase.

"I don't want you to remember me at all," she said. "Start with a clean slate." Maybe if he was gone, she could do the same.

"I thought you loved me."

"I'm not going through this again." Upset to find herself shaking, she walked into the kitchen and wrenched open the refrigerator door. She stood there for a moment, hoping the cold air wafting out would cool her rioting emotions. Picking up the champagne, she noticed it was an expensive brand. So typical of Troy to spend money he didn't have.

Returning to the living room, she held out the bottle, her hand steady by sheer force of will. "Take it to LA. Celebrate your first television gig there."

He jerked the champagne out of her hand. "You used to be a nicer person."

No, she used to be a doormat, trying to soothe his mood by letting him hurl ugly words at her. She'd thought that's what a loving wife did, but Troy kept escalating the emotional abuse until she'd nearly lost all sense of herself as a person. Thank goodness, she'd found the gumption to file for divorce before she disappeared altogether.

Allie sucked in a deep breath. "Let's just say good-bye like civilized people." She held out her hand, but he stepped back, his face a mask of anger.

"Civilized people cheer each other's successes." He spun around and headed for the door.

"Troy! I want my key back." She turned her palm up. She couldn't afford to change the locks.

He rummaged in his pocket and pulled the key out, throwing it on the braided rug at her feet. "I'll never set foot in this place again." He stalked into the hallway.

"Nice exit line," she called out just before the door slammed.

She raced to the door to throw the dead bolt. Tottering back into the living room, she sank onto the couch, shivering with anger and regret. The regret was for the memory of the two foolhardy kids who had said "I do" before they knew each other—or themselves—well enough to handle the pressures of failure together.

As she stared at the cracked plaster ceiling, she felt the weight of soft cat paws on her lap. "Did you come to comfort me?" she asked, stroking Pie's satiny fur. The little cat's purr calmed her jangling nerves. "I wish I could have just hidden under the bed like you when Troy was in one of his moods."

Now she regretted giving her ex the champagne. Even though it was before noon, she could use a drink. After all, she had no place to go today.

Or tomorrow.

Damn Gavin Miller for refusing her help, especially when she could see that he needed it. And she needed the money.

"But he's really hot, Pie. Which would be kind of a problem."

She'd worked with actors, models, and athletes before without ever feeling a moment's attraction. Why would she feel this tingle of awareness around the writer?

"Maybe it's because I'm a divorced woman now. Gavin Miller is my rebound." The idea of the rich, powerful author as a short-term fling made her smile.

She gave the purring cat a few soft strokes before lifting her off her lap. "Okay, Miss Pie, it's time for me to send out more résumés."

Chapter 5

Morning sun seeped through the blinds to paint stripes of light and shadow on Gavin's blue comforter. He groaned and swung his legs over the edge of the bed. Another night of tossing and turning. He gingerly rolled his head from side to side. Then he did it again.

"Well, I'll be damned," he said, tilting his head to various different angles. "The stampeding ants worked." The decrease in pain sent relief flooding through him.

He needed to get Allie Nichols and her machine back to keep the magic going.

Swiping the cell phone off his bedside table, he hit speed dial for his agent. "Jane, this is a once-in-a-lifetime opportunity. You get to say, 'I told you so.'"

She snapped out a short laugh. "I'd gloat, but I'm not sure which piece of my excellent advice you've decided to take."

"The physical therapist. I attempted to throw her out, but she convinced me to try some electrical gizmo. This morning I can move my neck again."

Jane sighed. "So you're not going to buy out the contract."

"No." Gavin was definitive. "But I want the physical therapist to come back."

"I hired her for five sessions this week."

"Yeah, but I fired her." Gavin allowed himself to smirk as he said, "However, I told her you'd pay her anyway."

"So that was my punishment for presuming to know what's good for you when you don't."

"I need her phone number."

"I'll text it to you. And now here comes payback . . . *I told you so.*"

He knew Jane was putting every ounce of smug satisfaction she could into her last four words. "You enjoyed that entirely too much."

"I deserved to." Her tone turned serious. "I'm glad you're letting someone help you."

"My plan is to buy one of those machines and get her to show me how to do it myself."

"Now you're just jerking my chain."

"One of the many gold ones you own," Gavin said, but he felt surprisingly buoyant at the thought of another session with the red-haired PT.

Allie practically danced up the steps to Gavin Miller's front door, barely feeling the weight of her loaded duffel bag. She'd thrown in every therapy aid she thought might tempt the writer to sign on for more sessions.

She just had to keep her unprofessional reactions under control.

Ringing the bell, she waited for the housekeeper to open the door. The paneled mahogany swung inward to reveal Gavin Miller himself framed in the doorway, his dark hair neatly combed, his powerful shoulders outlined by charcoal wool, and his legs looking long and muscular in worn black denim. "Ms. Nichols, come into my parlor."

He reached for her bag, but she swung it behind her legs. "No chivalry yet," she said.

He raised an eyebrow but gestured her inside.

"Thank you for reconsidering," she said, following him into the spacious entrance hall, her rubber soles squeaking on the deep green marble floor. The lowering February clouds had spit needles of frigid rain as she walked from the subway, so her shoes were wet. But the nasty weather couldn't dampen her mood after she'd gotten Miller's phone call requesting her return.

"I can tell by the bulges in your bag that you're expecting to use all kinds of implements of torture on me." He held out his hand for the puffy blue coat she'd shrugged out of. "But I want you to use only your magical machine."

The teasing gleam in his eyes robbed his words of offense, but she heard the underlying truth of his intentions. However, she'd changed his mind about the stim. She could change his mind about her other methods, too.

"No torture, I promise," she said. "But we might want to combine some different elements to make the stim even more effective."

He gave her a wary look. "You remind me of my agent. And that's not a compliment."

"Ms. Dreyer has been nothing but courteous to me."

"Don't be fooled. Jane is an apex predator."

Miller started toward the parlor.

Allie stayed where she was, her grip tight on her duffel's handles. "Mr. Miller, I'd like to work where you could lie down and be more comfortable. Ms. Dreyer said you have a fully equipped gym with a massage table."

He halted. "There are probably giant cobwebs hanging from the treadmill. No, I shouldn't insult Ludmilla that way. I'm sure she's kept the gym spotless, despite its disuse. By all means, let's descend into the dungeon." He waved her down the hallway. "And since you're going to be sticking electrical wires to my bare skin, I think you should call me Gavin."

Bad idea. She needed the distance of formality.

As it was, she could feel his presence behind her, sending tingles up and down her back. His long stride brought him up beside her, so now a sideways glance caught the way the light picked out auburn glints in his dark hair. And threw shadows below his sharp cheekbones.

Allie turned her gaze resolutely forward just as Gavin swung open a door set in the paneling. Pewter wall sconces flashed on without human intervention, illuminating a set of gray-carpeted stairs leading downward.

"The torture chamber awaits," Gavin said, indicating that she should precede him.

As she hit the bottom step, Allie let out a gasp of delight. She spotted a high-end massage table in one corner. Mirrors covered two walls, while a third held a rack of polished stainless steel and black rubber free weights. Various exercise machines were arrayed around the spacious room. She stepped onto the gym floor and bounced to savor the elasticity of the thick rubber floor covering.

"There's a resistance pool through there." Gavin pointed to a brushed metal door.

"Is it heated?" He could exercise in the pool, using the heat to loosen up the muscles.

"I see you're getting ideas that go well beyond electric current." He seemed amused rather than annoyed. "The temperature is adjustable, so I can do a polar bear plunge or steam in a hot tub. Or use the sauna."

Allie took in the amount and quality of the equipment and shook her head. This gym cost more than she could make in twenty years.

"Let's get started. Come over to the massage table, and I'll set up the stim unit. I brought a bigger one this time so it can cover more muscles and run longer."

She'd bought the high-end stim unit with her first bonus check from Havilland. Troy had wanted to blow it on dinner at an ultra-posh restaurant, but she had reined him in. Instead, they went to a great Italian place in SoHo and got sloshed on red wine. Which left enough bonus to start stocking her duffel bag.

"How long can you use it?" He watched her lift the bag onto the table and unzip it.

"A couple of hours, but we'll start with thirty minutes and see how you feel." A flush climbed her cheeks as she said, "I thought we might try some massage, too."

She shouldn't be blushing over that. It was her job. She was a trained professional.

"I won't raise any objections to that." Gavin gave her a wicked smile, which fanned the heat in her face higher. "Maybe you could even walk on my back."

Allie snorted. "That would *not* help your problem."

She felt Gavin's attention as she set up the stim machine, plugging it into the outlet and laying out the wires and pads on a side table.

"Could a layman use one of those on himself?" he asked.

"Trying to get rid of me?" she countered.

"I'm just thinking ahead. I don't wish to monopolize your services."

She almost snorted again. She could work here twenty-four/seven and only her cat would feel deprived. "A layman could try. It would be difficult to attach the pads to your back without help."

"You could show Ludmilla how to do it."

She turned to face him full-on. "On my business card I have a bunch of initials after my name because it takes some expertise to safely administer electrical stimulation."

Surprise flashed across his face and she thought she'd gone too far. But one corner of his mouth curled up in a self-mocking smile. "Unlike writing a book, which anyone can do."

"Not me," she said, relaxing again. "I am firmly in the reader camp."

"Ah, but I bet you could tell some interesting stories about your clients."

Was he testing her? "Nope. It's all confidential." She fitted a cloth cover over the table's padded top. "Why don't you hop up here?"

He braced his hands on the edge and levered himself onto the cushion with fluid grace. "I imagine I need to remove my sweater," he said, crossing his arms and seizing the hem before he ripped it up over his head.

Her gaze skimmed over the bare chest dusted with dark hair. His muscles were so well defined that she could have used his torso to illustrate a lesson on male anatomy. He might be avoiding the gym now, but he must have been using it regularly not too long ago. She lifted her gaze to find his longish hair mussed as though he'd just gotten out of bed. She winced inwardly at the dangerous image.

"Lie down on your stomach, please, and put your face in the headrest. Let me know if the angle is good."

Kicking off his well-shined loafers, he spun on the table, settling himself facedown, his arms by his sides, with the ease of someone who'd done it before.

Now that he couldn't see her, she felt less self-conscious. However, being presented with the broad, muscular—and bare—expanse of his back sent the tentacles of desire snaking through her again. She closed her eyes for a moment to reset her brain.

When she opened them, she mentally overlaid his skin with an anatomy chart, reminding herself to view his body as just a combination of muscles, tendons, and bones. "I'm going to put some mild pressure on your neck and back now, just to see where the tightness is," she said, rubbing her hands together to warm them before she began to probe the knotted muscles with her fingertips. As she dug into his warm olive skin, she recited each muscle to keep her focus on the medical. *Levator scapulae. Trapezius. Rhomboideus. Posterior deltoid. Latissimus dorsi.*

Her mind went to work on the problem of how to position the stim pads for maximum effect, and she almost forgot whom she was working on. He flinched once when she hit a sore spot, but mostly he lay quiet and still as she explored his back.

"I'm going to attach the pads now. And then I'll put a light blanket over you to keep you warm."

He grunted his understanding. She placed the pads, attached the wires, and covered him with a soft white blanket she found on a shelf beside the massage table. It was ten times nicer than the one in her bag of tricks. Then she turned on the machine, slowly adjusting the current upward.

"That's good," he said. "Now there are several herds of ants racing around over my back."

"Let me know if it begins to bother you. Since the stim will last longer, you may find your reaction to it changes over time."

It was harder to gauge his body's response to the stim when the blanket was covering him, but she checked for any restlessness or subtle shifts in his position.

A few minutes passed in silence, and she allowed herself to look around a little more, although she brought her attention back to her patient frequently. *Her patient.* She sighed in relief as she realized that was how she was thinking of him now.

"So what does one do while the ants tramp around?" His deep voice was slightly muffled by the headrest.

"Some people sleep."

"Your electric insects are a little too obtrusive for that."

"Do you have a music system down here? I could turn it on." In a place like this, there had to be a state-of-the-art sound system. She was about to suggest an audiobook but decided that might hit too close to the source of his problem.

"What sort of music would you choose to listen to?" he asked.

"Me? This is your treatment, so you get to pick." Her taste ran to country and pop, neither of which a sophisticated writer would find appealing.

"I already know what I would listen to, so that's not interesting."

"The point is to listen to it, not talk about it," Allie said.

"I'd rather listen to you."

She felt a silly moment of pleasure. "I'm a hillbilly, so I like country."

"Johnny Cash or Blake Shelton?" he asked.

"Dolly Parton and Carrie Underwood."

His chuckle was a dark, rich rumble. "I like you. You've got attitude."

Another wash of ridiculous gratification flowed through her. "So what's your favorite kind of music?"

"I like a good Gregorian chant."

"You listen to monks singing in Latin? I was expecting you to say Beethoven." She wanted to bite her tongue when she realized that it was his character Julian Best who listened to classical music. She saw him shift under the blanket. "So what's the hot new group on the Gregorian chant charts?" she asked to cover her blunder.

"Why did you think I would choose Beethoven?" His tone left no doubt that he expected an honest answer.

She wasn't going to give him one. "You're an intellectual New Yorker. They tend to like classical music."

There was more movement under the blanket as he pushed himself up from the table, turning his head so she could see the anger stiffening his jaw. "You were thinking of Julian Best."

"Does he like Beethoven? I don't remember that. Please lie down."

Gavin turned onto his side, propping himself up on his elbow. The blanket hung over his shoulder but didn't cover his torso with its line of dark hair arrowing down to disappear under his jeans. Allie tried to meet his gaze, but that was worse than being attracted by his body. She moved to the stim unit and pretended to check the dials. "Should I turn the current down?"

"You are not a good liar, Ms. Nichols. You were confusing me with my fictional spy."

Allie admitted defeat and faced him again. "Don't writers put their own experiences in their books?"

"And their aspirations. Not to mention their nightmares." He seemed to be trying to hypnotize her with his eyes. "Julian's preference in music is only mentioned once."

She nodded. "In *Best Laid Plans*."

"Just how well do you know the Julian Best novels?"

"My mama and I talked about them a lot. They have much more depth than most thrillers." And she considered Julian her book boyfriend. "We even made up some stories of our own about Julian."

Gavin swung his legs over the edge of the table and sat upright, the blanket cascading onto the floor behind him. "What is Julian's favorite food?"

"I can only remember appetizers." She was trying to keep her mind on the conversation and not on the swell of his biceps. "When he's with Samantha Dubois, he orders caviar as a starter, but otherwise he always begins with steak tartare."

"What sport does he watch?"

"Ice hockey. He played when he was in college."

"What car does he drive?"

"Trick question. Anything with a big engine and good cornering. He doesn't care about cars." She smiled. "But when it comes to aircraft, he's picky. He likes a Citation Encore jet or an AW109 helicopter. You know, you should really lie down. The electrical stim doesn't work as well if you're using the muscles it's working on."

He didn't move. "Did Jane know you're a Julian Best fan before she hired you?"

Gavin's suspicions lessened as genuine bafflement clouded Allie's gray eyes.

"No," the physical therapist said. "How would she find that out?"

"By asking." He let a little smile twist his mouth. "Jane's a mastermind. She might have been trying two kinds of therapy."

Allie twined her hands together. "She told me not to bring up anything at all about writing."

"She's trying to protect my fragile muse."

"You're lucky to have someone who worries about you," Allie said.

He tried to read her face. It seemed so open, but he was beginning to wonder if she wore her country-girl persona as a mask. "You say that as though you don't."

"Could we please get back to your treatment? You need to lie down again."

He wanted to be able to see her reactions. "This *is* my treatment. I haven't thought about my aches and pains since we started talking."

She put her hands on her hips and cocked her head at him. "You won't *have* any aches or pains if you let me work with you."

Her stance pulled her therapist uniform tight, so he noticed the way her waist curved in before it met the generous swell of her hips. He traced the line of her body back upward to admire how the taut fabric of her shirt outlined the fullness of her breasts. She was a pretty little thing with her fiery hair and creamy skin. He wondered how many of her clients had tried to seduce her. The thought, coupled with her comment about his good luck in having Jane as a friend, made him frown. She had a feisty spirit, but she was evidently alone in a city that could devour the innocent.

He shouldn't care, but he had been a country boy in the big, dangerous city once long ago. He shook off his unsolicited concern. "I'll recline if you'll tell me what stories you and your mother made up about Julian Best." He started to lie down again but paused when he caught a flush of pink painting her cheeks. "Just what sort of tales were they?"

She shook her head, making that gleaming spill of red hair catch glints of light. "We thought Julian should find a good woman."

He propped himself on his elbow. "He has Samantha Dubois."

Allie gave a scornful snort. "She's a manipulative, conniving double agent."

"Julian knows that, but he chooses to be with her because she's the only kind of woman who can survive in his world."

"Well, she's not the right person for him." She dropped her hands to her sides, and he felt a pang of regret as the folds of navy fabric hid her curves again. "I'll tell you more if you'll lie down."

"You drive a hard bargain," he said, feeling the corners of his mouth twitch as he acknowledged the determined set of her jaw and shoulders. Feisty, indeed. He rolled onto his stomach and settled his head into the cushioned rest. "Staring at the floor isn't nearly as much fun as watching you."

He heard a little hitch in her breath and felt guilty. He shouldn't flirt with her, given that he was half-undressed and she had to put her hands on his bare skin. He just couldn't resist striking a few sparks off that redheaded temperament.

There was some rustling around before a tablet slid across the floor and into his line of sight. "Here's something to look at, since you're not sleeping." Her tone was accusatory.

A succession of beautiful color photographs glowed on the screen: a cheetah crouched in dry grass, its eyes burning with hunger; a silvery waterfall cascaded over mossy rocks in a blindingly green forest; a sperm whale hurled itself into a brilliant blue sky, trailing sprays of seawater from its fins. "Did you curate these?"

"I picked the ones I like, but they're all from *National Geographic*," Allie said. "They have the world's best photographers."

He let the photos scroll by for a few moments more. "I notice there are no people."

"People tend to feel less relaxed when another person is staring at them."

"Do they teach you psychology in physical therapy school?"

"Of course. The mind-body connection is important."

Her drawl lessened when she spoke about her occupation. He wondered which was more authentic: the accent or the lack of it.

The muffled thud of her footsteps sounded, and then he felt a waft of air and the featherlight brush of the blanket settling over his back again. He knew it was just part of her professional bag of tricks to keep her patient comfortable, but the gesture evoked nuances of caring that vibrated through him.

"Now tell me about Julian Best's love life as analyzed by the Nichols women."

Silence, and then the sound of a breath being drawn in. "Well, Mama and I decided that we wouldn't want to get involved with James Bond, because his lovers always ended up dead. For someone who was so good at his job, he really stank at protecting anyone he loved." Now her twang deepened, as did the conviction in her voice. She and her mama had clearly been spy-novel enthusiasts. "Plus, he was a sociopath. If someone got in his way, he killed them without any hesitation or regret."

There was another pause. "I hope you don't mind me comparing Julian Best to James Bond."

"Bond was one of my inspirations, so how can I complain? I even gave Julian the same initials."

"Do you think Robert Ludlum did the same thing with Jason Bourne? I've always wondered about that."

"I did, too, but Ludlum died before I could ask him." He let a smile sound in his voice.

"Inconsiderate of him," she said.

He loved her dry edge, and his smile widened.

"Anyway," she continued, "we always thought Julian was smarter than James Bond because he didn't just shoot everyone who got in his way. He killed people only when he really had to. So he needed to figure out really fast who would have to be killed and who wouldn't."

"A thinking man's James Bond," he quoted.

"Some reviewer said that, didn't they? It was on your book covers."

"The *New York Times* reviewer." He remembered the thrill of reading that praise. It had been his fourth Julian Best novel; the *Times* didn't take him seriously until he was successful enough to be published in hardcover. He missed the days when a good review was cause for celebration, and a bad review made him think about what he needed to improve. In fact, he no longer read any reviews. Too many conflicting voices in his head didn't help him write better books.

"So we figured he could find a way to protect a woman he truly loved. And we used to dream up stories of how he met her."

"Let's hear one." His brain began to play with situations in which his super spy met the love of his life.

"They were just for fun between me and Mama." He could hear embarrassment in her voice. "Nothing a real writer would find interesting."

"Let me be the judge of that."

The ants abruptly stopped racing around his back. Their absence seemed almost like silence.

"You're done," Allie said. He could hear the relief in her voice. He was about to warn her that he hadn't forgotten what they were talking about when she twitched the blanket back and began gently peeling away the stim pads. Every brush of her fingertips against his skin sent a streak of arousal down to his groin.

When she removed the last pad, she settled the blanket back over him. He was grateful when she said, "Relax for a few minutes so your muscles can release more fully."

He could hear the faint pop of wires being unplugged, the tiny ticks of equipment being stowed in plastic compartments, the rustle of her clothing, even the barely audible swish of her breathing. His eyelids drifted closed.

♥ ♥ ♥

Allie smiled to herself as she heard Gavin's breathing turn slow and even. She closed the stim unit's case but didn't latch it, not wanting the sharp noise to wake him. Perching on a nearby weight bench, she pulled out her cell phone and swiped into the Julian Best book she had started to reread after Ms. Dreyer hired her to work with Gavin. It would keep her eyes off the thick, dark hair and powerfully arched feet of her patient. Thank goodness he had a blanket covering the rest of him or even Julian Best would not be able to hold her attention.

Gavin was owed another half an hour of her time, so she would watch over him while he got some much-needed sleep.

Thirty minutes later the vibration of her phone alarm yanked her out of a tense scene between Julian and his nemesis, Sturgis Wolfe.

She stowed her phone and surveyed the still-sleeping writer, biting her lip as she debated whether to wake him or not.

Although she knew it was in her own best interest to talk with him now, while it was clear that the electrical stim had been effective, she couldn't bring herself to disturb his slumber.

She tiptoed around, gathering her equipment, and made her way upstairs. She finished closing up her stim unit in the hallway before she went in search of the housekeeper, finding her in a kitchen with sleekly modern cherry cabinets and pale gray granite countertops.

"Mr. Gavin is asleep in gym?" the housekeeper asked in surprise as she dried her hands on a white linen towel. "That is good. He does not sleep at night."

"Please tell him that's why I didn't wake him. I'll call him later about tomorrow."

"That is good," the older woman repeated in her Eastern European accent, ushering Allie back into the hallway. "You do a good thing for him."

As she lugged her duffel bag down the front steps, Allie hoped she hadn't been so "good" that she'd cheated herself out of the opportunity to work another day.

Chapter 6

Gavin swam up out of sleep at a leisurely pace until he realized he was lying with his face in a massage cradle. "What the hell . . . ?" He jerked up onto his elbows and saw he was in his own gym before memory surged back.

"You're awake. I have water."

Disappointment seeped through him. He had hoped for Allie's voice, not Ludmilla's. Grabbing the blanket with one hand to keep it over his shoulders, he sat up and tried to shake the fog from his brain. "What time is it?"

"Fifteen minutes past one. You sleep long time. Is good for you." Ludmilla stood with a tray holding a glass of ice water with lemon slices floating on top. "Miss Nichols say you should drink after treatment."

"Thanks." Gavin picked up the water and took a gulp. He considered pouring it over his head as a wake-up shock. "When did Ms. Nichols leave?"

"Two hours ago. She say not to wake you. She call you later."

He rolled his shoulders and then his neck. Damned if they didn't feel less tight. And he'd slept like a dead person.

"Now I go make lunch, Mr. Gavin. You come when you are ready."

Gavin sat on the table, sipping his water. He felt a strange reluctance to move, as though leaving the cushioned sanctuary would break the spell that had allowed him to sleep.

No, Allie Nichols had allowed him to sleep. With her herd of electric ants, her soft fingertips, and her West Virginia twang. And her passion for Julian Best.

He straightened as he remembered. Julian had been alive again in his mind. He'd started to imagine how Julian would meet a normal woman, how the spy could convince himself that he could protect her.

Gavin put down the water glass and slid to the floor. Pulling on his sweater and slipping his feet back into his loafers, he took the stairs two at a time up to the second floor.

He strode into his office and sat down in front of the computer screen, jiggling the mouse to wake it. When the blank page came up yet again, he typed, "Julian Best needs a good woman."

That was all he could manage, but the six words were more than he'd written about Julian in months.

He grimaced and scooped his phone off the desk to call Allie, cursing when it went to voice mail. His message was brief. "Schedule me for two hours tomorrow, whenever you can fit it in."

After lunch, he sat in front of the computer, hoping equally for Allie's phone call and more words. Instead, he got an e-mail from his stepsister Ruth.

She was the oldest of the three girls his father's remarriage had brought into their previously all-male household. She had been nine when Gavin was thirteen. The two younger daughters had followed their mother's lead, treating Gavin as a cross between a wild animal and a freak. Ruth had decided to adopt Gavin.

Today she was married to the man who had taken over Miller's Feed and Dry Goods, and was mother to two children. But for reasons he could never fathom, she remained his staunch ally in his battles with his stepmother.

Gavin, have you looked in the box I sent you? You'll want to see what's in there, I promise.

He didn't understand why she had to make such a big deal out of the shipping carton that had arrived a couple of weeks before. Irritated, he shot back, Why don't you just tell me what you think is so damned important about it?

Ruth's response came immediately. It's too complicated. Just open it. And don't be cranky. I'm the one who likes you.

Her last crack made him snort out a laugh. Liking is all relative with relatives, he wrote back, but I apologize for being a curmudgeon.

His stepsister retorted, We don't know what that means out here in the sticks of Illinois.

He snorted again.

The truth was that he *had* opened the damned box. It held the autographed first editions of his books that he'd sent to his father as they were published. Once Gavin saw the pristine books neatly wrapped in plastic, exactly as he'd sent them, he'd slammed the box shut again.

He hadn't expected his father to read them. Kenneth Miller read only the ledgers of the family feed store or biographies of Civil War generals. But Gavin had foolishly hoped for some acknowledgment that his ambition to be a writer had worked out after all.

He'd shoved the box into a corner at his beach house in Southampton, where he didn't have to be reminded of it or the wrench of disappointment it had delivered.

His cell phone buzzed as it scooted across the mahogany desktop. He seized it, hoping it was Allie saying she could come tomorrow. Instead, he saw Nathan Trainor's name on the screen.

He considered not answering, but he owed the man an apology. "Trainor, you know I'm a jerk, so I shouldn't have to say this, but I'm sorry."

The CEO's dry chuckle sounded over the phone. "Kudos for not beating around the bush, but it lacks a certain sincerity."

"Oh, it's sincere. I just don't handle pity well."

"You confuse pity with friendship," Trainor said, his tone serious. "There's an important distinction."

Gavin kneaded his forehead. "I don't handle friendship well, either. We writers are loners by nature. I'm still not sure why you and Archer put up with me."

"Now we get to the pity part." The humor was back in Trainor's voice, and Gavin relaxed. "And since you're so pitiful, Chloe and I would like you to have dinner at our place on Saturday. It's short notice, but some friends are visiting from out of town. We thought you'd like them, and vice versa."

Gavin's pity radar went on full alert. "I'm not planning to slit my wrists over the weekend."

Trainor's sigh was heavy. "For God's sake, it's a simple dinner invitation."

Why did he care about Trainor's motivation anyway? He had nothing planned for Saturday night, and Trainor's friends were always interesting. "Sorry. I forgot the pity/friendship distinction again. I'll attend with alacrity. Thank you."

"Come at seven."

"Are Archer and his new bride on the guest list as well?"

"If I say yes, will you refuse to join us?"

Gavin laughed. "No, I owe him an apology, too."

"With that to look forward to, I have no doubt that he will accept the invitation." Trainor hung up.

Gavin checked his phone for voice mail, just to make sure Allie hadn't called while he was talking with the CEO. Still nothing from the physical therapist.

He turned back to the computer, trying to conjure up the scenarios he'd been playing with as Allie discussed Julian's need for a different love interest. But no matter how hard he tried, he could not conceive of a different kind of woman for Julian.

It seemed that his muse didn't share Allie's conviction that Julian was capable of real love.

♥ ♥ ♥

Allie turned off the treadmill and braced her arms on it as she gasped for breath. She and Troy had rented a truck to haul home the exercise machine from Havilland Rehab when the center had updated their equipment. Although it took up most of the floor space in their bedroom, Troy had wanted it to keep fit for the leading-man roles he hoped to land.

Allie was grateful for it since she no longer had access to Havilland's gym. On grim winter days, it was a luxury to run indoors. Today she had needed to sprint off the anxiety tightening her throat because Gavin Miller hadn't called back about a session tomorrow. She scrubbed her face with a towel, took a gulp of water, and eyed the treadmill. The rehab center had to stay on the cutting edge of technology, but most people would still consider her machine state-of-the-art. She might get another month's rent out of selling it.

She pulled out her earbuds and peeled off her sweaty workout shirt. Maybe she should give up and leave New York. Now that her marriage and her job had ended, not much held her here.

But the thought of returning to Sanctuary was unappealing. There were so many memories of the happy times with Troy there. Even worse, they'd been a couple for so long that everyone thought of them together. Going back as the divorced half of that unit would be painful.

She draped her damp shirt over the rail of the treadmill. The truth was more complicated than that. New York had changed her. For all her nostalgia, Sanctuary felt like a place to visit, not live.

"I guess Troy rubbed off on me," she said, stooping to pet the cat who'd returned once the noise of the treadmill had ceased. "I got ambitious."

Pie jumped up on the bed, dislodging Allie's cell phone so it slid onto the floor. "Hey, be careful! I can't afford a broken screen right now." When she scooped up the phone to make sure it was intact, the icon for a voice message stared out at her.

"Well, shoot, why didn't I hear the ding?" She checked the volume to find it on mute. She must have forgotten to reset it after her session with Gavin. Hope bubbled up when she saw the message was from the writer.

His voice rolled out of the phone—deep, curt, and commanding. "Schedule me for two hours tomorrow, whenever you can fit it in."

She whooped, making Pie lift her head and blink at her reprovingly. Allie swept the cat up in her arms and danced around the bed. "He wants me back. Mama's going to be able to keep you in kitty litter another couple of weeks."

❤ ❤ ❤

The next morning, Allie felt a pinch of worry when it was Ludmilla who opened the door instead of Gavin. But the housekeeper waved her inside. "Come in, come in. Mr. Gavin ask me to take you to gym. He gets phone call."

Allie had already unpacked most of her equipment when Gavin came down the gym stairs. "My apologies for keeping you waiting," he said. "Business matters."

He smiled, and she found it hard to draw in a full breath. His eyes gleamed jade green. His white teeth flashed against his olive skin. He focused on her with an intensity that sent vibrations zinging around in her chest before they settled low in her belly.

"I brought you here under false pretenses," he said.

That killed all the delicious shivers. "I'm sorry?"

"I don't think I can let your ants stampede over me for two full hours."

She forced a cheery tone. "That would be too long to spend on just electrical stim. I have several treatments planned."

Those green eyes glinted with interest. "I see I have a very limited understanding of physical therapy. What other delights are in store for me?"

"In addition to the e-stim, I was going to suggest some heat, some massage, and some gentle stretching."

The interest turned into something more unsettling. "A massage? I'm on board with that program."

Relief made her knees a little shaky. She'd get the full two hours after all. And she'd be stroking the bare skin of that sculpted back. She pulled her thoughts up short, even as she licked her lips.

He pinned her with his gaze. "We also have to talk."

"Talk?"

"Isn't that part of the therapy?"

"Um, to a certain extent." Where was he going with this?

He gave a brief nod. "Good. What's first?"

"On a scale of one to ten, with ten being the worst, tell me how bad the pain is now."

He tilted his head to several different angles. She noted when his face tightened with distress. "Around a seven."

"How was it after the e-stim yesterday?"

"Maybe a five."

"That's a good sign," she said. "Now I'd like to look at your alignment."

He held his arms out from his sides. "At your service. I even dressed the part today."

She had already noticed he wasn't wearing one of his expensive sweaters. Instead, he was sporting a black athletic shirt and training pants, the thin, sweat-wicking fabric outlining the hard curves of his muscles. It made her all the more aware of his body in a way she shouldn't be.

"Good choice," she said. "Would you stand with your feet about hip distance apart? Let your arms hang naturally at your sides."

With a slightly mocking half smile, he took up the stance she requested. She walked behind him to give herself a moment to force her brain into therapist mode. Closing her eyes, she envisioned the way Gavin's body would look if it were in perfect balance, without injury or stressors. Then she opened her eyes to compare the reality.

His pain practically leaped out at her. It showed in the way his shoulders were canted, in the angle of his neck, in the unconscious flexing of his fingers, and in the twist of his torso.

All her attention centered on how to ease the soreness he was feeling as she walked around, scanning his body from every angle.

"That is one ferocious frown," he said. "Am I in worse shape than I think?"

Now she'd worried him, which wasn't conducive to the relaxed mood she hoped to create. "You're just off-kilter, and I know how unpleasant that can be."

His eyes raked down her body, sending the blood to her cheeks. "I'm guessing that you've never been out of alignment."

"I'm only human, but I know how to counteract physical stress better than the average person." As proven by the amount of time she'd spent on the treadmill working off the trauma of her divorce.

"Physician, heal thyself?" He pivoted toward the massage table, and Allie pressed her hands to her telltale cheeks. Thank goodness he would be facedown for most of the session so he couldn't see her.

Hoisting himself onto the table, Gavin shucked off his shirt and tossed it to catch on a nearby weight machine. Her cheeks notched up several more degrees of heat at the display of the rippling planes of his torso with its glaze of dark hair. "Why don't you lie down and get comfortable while I make the environment more soothing."

Miller glanced around the room and snorted. "*Soothing* is not an adjective I would apply to a gym."

"You'd be surprised at what miracles I can work," Allie said.

He swiveled his legs onto the table to sit with his arms loosely crossed on his knees. "You have surprised me often enough that you no longer surprise me."

"Is that an oxymoron of some kind?"

"It's the description of a woman who isn't quite what she seems."

Allie found the light switch and flipped off all but the wall sconces. "I've never thought of myself as mysterious. I kind of like it."

"I'm not sure *mysterious* is the right word. You have layers."

"Like an onion."

He looked as though he'd eaten roadkill. "Please don't quote that nauseating aphorism about peeling back the layers and sometimes crying."

"You did it, not me."

He gave her a sharp sideways look and rolled onto his stomach, fitting his face into the headrest.

Allie chalked up a point for herself before she set up her tablet to play both photos and music and placed it on the floor where he could see it.

As the sound of a waterfall twined with the strumming of a sitar, Gavin said, "I feel the urge to chant 'Om.'"

"If it relaxes you, feel free." She attached the stim pads to the bare skin of his neck and back, focusing on the trigger points of his tension rather than the powerful geometry of his muscles.

"Do you meditate?" he asked in a deep, half-muffled voice that evoked images of wrinkled sheets and pillows in Allie's wayward mind.

"I try to. It's not so easy."

"You have a lot on your mind, do you?"

He wasn't kidding when he said he wanted to talk. She decided to consider his last question rhetorical. "I'm going to put the blanket over you now. And then I'm going to microwave some rice heat pillows to add another element of relaxation before I turn on the e-stim. I'll be right back."

She'd spotted the microwave during her last visit. It was built into a sleek wooden unit that also held a minifridge and a water dispenser.

"There's a microwave in my gym?"

"You mean you don't nuke pizza down here?" It was probably meant for exactly what she was doing: warming up heat packs.

"Ludmilla would have my head."

"Which is why I thought you would do it."

A muted huff came from the massage table. "You and Archer. Always needling."

Allie felt a sense of satisfaction as she pulled the warm, wintergreen-scented pillows out of the microwave. Being mentioned along with his illustrious friend meant she was making progress. Maybe this job would pan out after all.

She laid the pillows over his blanket-covered shoulders. She heard him sniff as the minty aroma swirled in the air. "This seems more like spa day than physical therapy," he muttered.

"Just wait until we get to the massage," she said, turning on the stim unit. "Tell me when the current feels good to you." She took it up gradually again.

"More," he said as she hit one level higher than the last session.

"Pushing it too high won't make it work better, you know."

"My friends will tell you that I'm always pushing."

She edged the dial up until it hit the maximum. "That's as high as it goes."

"Wimpy machine."

"I'll bring a stun gun tomorrow."

That got a laugh out of him before he asked a question she'd hoped to avoid. "What sort of woman did you and your mother feel would suit Julian Best?"

She blew out a frustrated breath but kept her voice calm. "I don't think that discussing Julian will help you relax the way your muscles need you to."

"Discussing Julian is why I asked you back here."

So that's what his warning about false pretenses meant. She considered just doing what he wanted. It would guarantee her the job for a few more days, at the very least. But her professional pride and personal compassion wouldn't allow that. "How about a deal? We spend an hour and a half working on your physical issues and thirty minutes discussing Julian Best."

"An hour on each."

"I can tell you everything Mama and I made up about Julian in twenty minutes."

"We're going to do something called brainstorming."

"*You* want *me* to brainstorm with you? I don't know anything about writing books."

He lifted his head and rolled onto his side, making his dark hair wave wildly around the sharp planes of his face while the heat packs thudded onto the floor. "I feel at a disadvantage negotiating without being able to see my opponent's face."

"Hey, I'm on your side."

"That remains to be seen." He pinned her with his gaze. "An hour and a half on physical therapy and an hour on Julian. I'll pay you for the extra time."

Her heart leaped. Another half an hour of pay. "I feel like I'd be cheating you to take extra money for talking about a . . . a nonexistent person."

"While I may not be using your professional skills, I would not dream of asking for your time for free." He held out his open hand in a gesture of entreaty. "Humor me."

Okay, she'd tried to turn him down. "Agreed. Now please lie down and try to relax." Without thinking, she reached out to give his upper arm a little tug. When she touched him, he flinched and dropped his gaze to where her fingers were wrapped around the swelling ridges of his biceps. She jerked her hand away. "Did I hurt you?"

"No," he rasped. "Quite the contrary. I just wasn't prepared. Time for me to get back to relaxing."

He flipped onto his stomach with a slight hitch in his movement, dragging the blanket back over his shoulders. Allie walked around to replace the rice packs on his shoulders. She stared at the back of his head as though she could see into his mind to decipher his odd reaction.

While the e-stim did its work, Allie perched on the nearby weight bench and debated how much of her made-up Julian Best stories to share with the writer. They were wildly romantic fantasies that she was sure would make Gavin snicker. She sighed. If she had to talk for an hour, she couldn't afford to edit out any material.

The stim unit shut down, and Gavin began to stir. She rested her hand on his blanket-covered back. "Stay still. I'm going to detach the stim pads and start the massage. That way your muscles don't have time to tense up again."

"I'm beginning to like physical therapy."

Allie smirked. "That's because we haven't gotten to the hard part yet."

Chapter 7

As she removed the stim pads, every brush of the therapist's fingertips sent flickering sparks racing across Gavin's skin. How was he supposed to relax when the stampeding ants had nothing on Allie's electrical charge?

He was a mature adult. He could control his responses.

Or he could until she removed the last of the sticky pads and began to stroke his shoulders with long, firm sweeps of her oil-slicked hands. Her palms felt like warm satin gliding over his skin. He nearly moaned as she kneaded a tight spot on the back of his neck, the pressure of her fingertips balanced right on the edge between pleasure and pain. His body soaked up her touch like a plant drawing in water after a drought. He felt lighter and more expansive. And aroused.

The crisp scent of wintergreen swirled past his nostrils again. "Are you wearing eau de mint?" he asked.

Her chuckle sounded from above him. "It's the massage oil. I figured you'd prefer this to something floral."

"Don't you have something neutral? I'll smell like Vicks VapoRub."

"I'll bring unscented oil tomorrow."

He heard the stiffness in her voice and felt like an ass. Truth was, he liked the smell. It reminded him of hiking in the woods of New England. His testiness was an attempt to shake off some of the sensual cocoon she had woven around him.

He kept waiting for a pause in the assault on his self-control, but she never broke contact, always keeping a warm palm pressed against his bare skin as she shifted around him. He remembered from some distant piece of research that this was one mark of a skilled masseuse.

"Okay, the fun part is over," she said, although the slide of her soft, warm hands over his skin belied her words. "Now you need to tell me if anything I do causes you discomfort."

And then she showed her true colors as she dug her thumbs into a knot on the back of his neck, sending a bolt of agony through the muscle. He grunted.

"Too much?" she asked, easing the pressure.

"Yes, but don't stop. You seduced me with your ants and your massage, and now I must pay for the pleasure."

However, the pressure lessened as she worked over the worst spots in his neck and shoulders. He got fond of the little spurts of breath she let out when she pushed especially hard. It was just enough advance warning so the pain didn't surprise a groan out of him.

And then she was stroking his back again, petting him like a dog who had done well. "Aren't you going to say, 'Good boy'?"

"What?" The rhythm of her movements never faltered despite the puzzlement in her voice.

"Isn't this my reward for letting you pummel me?"

"Your reward will be the ability to move without wincing. Now I'd like you to roll over, keeping your head on the headrest."

Her professional persona was impressive but not as much fun as her country-girl one. He felt her lift the blanket so he could shift without getting tangled. As he turned, he felt a shock of desire. The skin of her face and neck held a light sheen of effort, while curling wisps of fiery red hair clung damply to it. Her gray eyes were smoky, with some emotion he couldn't interpret, and her thick ponytail trailed over her shoulder to rest on the curve of her breast, rising and falling with her audible breath.

She looked as though she'd just made love.

Her gaze skimmed over his chest, but he felt as though she had touched him lower. Luckily, she floated the blanket back over him and moved to the head of the table.

She slipped her warm hands between his head and the headrest, cupping his skull in her palms as she leaned over to meet his gaze, her ponytail swinging just above his nose. "Now I'm going to ask you to trust me again."

The upside-down angle of her face was disconcerting, but her scent of wintergreen and something lemony combined with pure warm woman sent another streak of lust down to his crotch. "You've dosed me with electric ants, jabbed your thumbs into my already tortured muscles, and refused to discuss Julian Best. Explain why I should trust you."

She smiled, the inversion still disorienting him. "Because you know this is all good for you. I'm going to remove the headrest and hold your head in my hands. I don't want you to support any of your weight with your neck muscles. Relax into my grasp. I promise not to drop you." She flicked her ponytail back with a toss of her head. "That's where the trust comes in."

"Ah, that's an easy one. Barely any trust required." He closed his eyes. He could feel her fingers threaded in his hair, their tips resting on the nape of his neck.

"You may not feel that way when the headrest drops out from under you. I'm going to shift so your head is resting on one of my hands, but don't worry, I'm strong enough to hold you."

He felt her words in a way that had nothing to do with his physical problems.

But she continued with her work, withdrawing one of her hands while she centered her other one under the back curve of his skull. A couple of clicks and creaks and the cushion of the headrest vanished. He tensed, but the level of his head didn't shift by even a single millimeter. Almost immediately her other hand was cradling him as well. He willed himself to believe in her and let all the weight of his head rest on her palms.

"That's good," she said. He felt a flare of pride at her approval.

"Now I'm going to carefully move your head in various directions. Again, try not to assist me. Let your head sink into my hands, so I control all the movement."

"Ha! Don't you know that writers are control freaks? We make our characters dance to our own weird tunes. That's half the fun."

She angled his head ever so slowly to the right. "What's the other half?"

Just as the position became uncomfortable, she reversed the motion. "Rewriting," he said. "You know how you think of a brilliant response to an insult six hours later when it's utterly useless? A writer has a time machine. I can go back to the moment the insult was hurled and parry it with my slow but rapier-sharp wit."

"Relax. I've got you," she said, rotating his head gently to the right. "I guess us nonwriters think you just sit down at your computer and the book comes out the way we read it."

"We foster that myth. It makes us seem more like creative geniuses and less like mere craftsmen." There was something very restful about allowing Allie to manipulate his head. Her grip was firm enough to instill confidence but soft enough to feel like a caress.

"I have more respect for craftsmen. They work hard at what they do." Her voice held a tart bite, but her movements were calm.

"So I should show you my marked-up manuscripts to impress you." It sounded as though his capable little therapist knew an artistic sort she didn't care for.

"Now I'd like you to sit up," she said. "I'll help you so you don't stress your muscles."

He gave her his entire trust, letting her guide him upright with her skillful hands. Before she stepped back, she adjusted the blanket so it remained draped over his shoulders.

She met his gaze straight on. "Now, on a scale of one to ten, where is your pain level? I want an honest answer, not a diplomatic one."

He raised his eyebrows. "Have I given you any reason to believe I would be diplomatic?"

A smile tugged at the corners of her lips. "Good point. Give me your usual brutal honesty."

He rolled his head in a half circle and saw her wince as though she was afraid he would undo all her hard work. Astonishment flashed through him as he rolled it again. The muscles still pulled in his shoulders, and he could feel soreness where she had pinpointed his severest problems. But the grinding sensation at the base of his skull was gone, and he could turn his chin fully from shoulder to shoulder without a grimace. "Three," he said. "You're a witch."

"Glinda or Bellatrix Lestrange?"

He lifted a hand to probe the miraculously mobile back of his neck. "You use Bellatrixian methods to achieve Glindian results."

"It didn't hurt that much, did it?" A line of worry creased her forehead.

"I would face a charging rhino with less terror than you strike in my heart."

The furrow vanished. "I've been called a lot of names, but this is the first for a charging rhino." She glanced at her watch. "I guess we won't have time for the swiss ball."

"You have another implement of torture in your bag?"

She pointed to the large vinyl ball tucked in a corner of the room. "You own your own implement. I saw it yesterday."

"It looks so harmless, but in your hands I'm sure it will become a thing of horror."

"Enough to give you nightmares." Her tone was as dry as the Sahara.

He eased off the table and grabbed his shirt from the weight machine, pulling it on over his head with delicious, nearly painless ease.

"And now it's story time."

More like humiliation time. He would be so disappointed in her ridiculous fantasies.

Allie handed him the bottle of designer spring water she'd found in the minifridge. "You need to hydrate after the massage."

Thank goodness he'd put his shirt back on. Once she stopped actively working on him, Gavin's bare chest became a distraction. If she were honest, his eyes, his mouth, and his hair were distractions, too. The man was so darned mouthwatering. Maybe he was just so different from Troy's blond all-American good looks that she found the contrast refreshing.

Or maybe she had fallen a little in love with him while staring at his book-jacket photos over the years, picturing Julian as looking like his creator.

"May I pack up my equipment first?" she asked, heading for the bench where her duffel bag sat.

"I want your full focus, so go ahead. We'll go upstairs to my office for our discussion."

She wiped her hands on her towel and began stowing the stim pads. He prowled over to stand beside her, so close that she could feel the heat emanating from his body.

"You have a considerable investment in that bag," he said.

"Good tools are important."

He reached out to close his long fingers around her wrist, stretching her arm up so her hand was level with his face. "I would say this is your most valuable tool." He rotated her wrist slightly. "Small but filled with power."

She could feel the pulse in her wrist beating too fast against his fingertips. He was examining her hand as though it were some sort of independent artifact, a position she found both awkward and thrilling. When he traced along the lifeline on her palm, a shiver of awareness radiated up her arm and into her breasts and belly. She sucked in her breath and stood utterly still.

He released her. "I interrupted your packing."

She flexed her fingers, still feeling the echo of his grip on her wrist and his touch on her palm. "I'm almost done." Gavin's face lit with anticipation, which made her nervous. "You're not going to be able to use my silly stories in a book, you know."

"I wouldn't dream of it. They're *your* stories. But when we were talking about Julian yesterday, my imagination went to work for the first time in months." He took a swig of his water and looked at her in a way that sent swirls of warmth spiraling deep inside her. "You might be my new muse."

She reached for the handles of the duffel, throwing Gavin a warning glance when he tried to grab them first.

"Does it pay well, being a muse?" she asked.

"I've never paid my old muse a penny. Maybe that's why she's gone on strike."

"Well, darn." Allie was very aware of his presence just behind her as they climbed the steps. She walked stiffly, wondering what part of her body he was looking at, but she kept her words light. "I thought I'd discovered a profitable side business. Muse for hire."

"I know many writers who would pay you almost any amount if it were that easy."

Allie halted in the hallway, not sure which way to go. Gavin led her to the foot of the main staircase, where she stowed her duffel in the coat closet.

Turning, she looked up to discover a cascading bronze-and-crystal chandelier hanging from a plaster rosette three floors up, framed by the graceful curves of the staircase's polished wooden banisters. All that wasted space in a city that charged thousands of dollars per square foot illustrated with great vividness just how wealthy Gavin Miller was. Which meant she needed to treat him as a valued client rather than lusting after his body.

"Come with me," he said, inviting her to walk beside him up the stairs. Their athletic attire looked out of place against the highly grained wood paneling and the jewel-toned Oriental runner. She should be wearing one of Kate Winslet's gowns from *Titanic*, while he should be decked out in white tie and tails. She gave a little gasp as she pictured him that way, holding out his arm for her gloved hand to rest on. Her heart flipped in her chest as she imagined the feel of his hard muscle under the fine wool.

As they reached the second floor, he gestured toward a paneled door. "If you'd like to freshen up, please feel free. I might splash some water on my face myself."

She practically bolted for the bathroom, but he still managed to get there first, twisting the knob and pushing the door inward for her.

She slipped into a powder room that was twice the size of her apartment's kitchen, closed the door and leaned against it. She needed to get her rioting imagination under control. And her overheated face.

Shoving away from the door, she walked to the embossed copper bowl that served as a sink. One look in the mirror made her grimace. Her hair was frizzing around her face, several spots of massage oil marred her shirt, and her cheeks were flushed as though she had a nasty fever.

She gave her face a good scrub with cold water and redid her ponytail, using the rice paper–wrapped throwaway comb thoughtfully provided for a guest's bad hair day. Her shirt was a lost cause because dabbing the spots with soapy water would just make them more noticeable.

Well, Gavin Miller would have to accept that she looked like what she was: a working physical therapist. No lolling about on a chaise longue wearing a flowing silk robe for this particular muse. Or maybe that was more what muses for artists did. Allie made a silly face at herself in the mirror and walked out the door.

Gavin stood in the hall, with comb marks in his damp hair, swiping away at his cell phone. He lifted his head and smiled, creating a wave of sizzling desire that obliterated all her excellent resolutions about not lusting after him.

"Shall we?" He stepped closer and lightly pressed his hand into the small of her back to start her moving toward the front of the mansion. His touch rippled across her skin like the highest setting of the e-stim unit, but she couldn't avoid it without seeming rude.

He guided her through a half-open double door and removed his hand from her back to sweep it around with mock drama. "My domain."

The room was filled with light slanting through the three tall windows on the front wall. Like the hallway, the walls were paneled, but here the wood was lighter. Low flames flickered in a fireplace framed with carved rose-colored marble. The rest of the decor was surprisingly modern, yet it harmonized with the Victorian bones of the house.

A look of aversion tightened his jaw as he glanced toward the windows. It took her a moment to realize he was reacting to the desk placed there. It was a beautiful modern piece: polished rosewood inset with rectangles of ribbed silver-gray leather, so it evoked the leather-topped desks of old without imitating them. On the desktop sat a sleek computer monitor and keyboard, their brushed aluminum-and-leather casings clearly custom-made. An ergonomic chair was swiveled away from the desk, as though he had left in a hurry.

Turning his back on the desk, Gavin walked to an armchair upholstered in steel blue fabric and gestured toward the leather sofa it faced. "Make yourself at home."

Allie slid onto the edge of the couch cushion and pressed her knees and feet together.

Gavin sprawled into the armchair. He rolled his head around backward with his eyes closed. "God, it feels good to move like this." When he lifted his head and opened his eyes, annoyance flitted across his face. "You look like a bird who's ready to fly off at the slightest provocation."

Pulling out his phone, he tapped a button. "Ludmilla, would you bring hot tea to my office with two mugs? And steep some of that herbal stuff labeled *Calm*. My therapist needs it."

Allie cocked an eyebrow at him. "So you fell for that Starbucks marketing ploy."

"No, but I was hoping you would." He rested his elbows on the chair's cushioned arms and let his hands dangle from the wrists. However, his relaxed pose couldn't counteract the focused desperation in his gaze. "Now, tell me who you chose for Julian Best's ideal woman."

Allie looked down at the spray of burgundy orchids artfully arranged in a glass bowl on the coffee table. She twisted her fingers together on her knees before she met Gavin's avid green eyes again. "Me, of course."

"You?" The surprise in his voice was harsh. He must be disappointed.

"I told you it was just a silly story Mama and I made up." She shrugged. "Julian needed someone normal, and I'm about as normal as they come."

"You." This time he sounded reflective rather than shocked. He let his head fall back and stared at the coffered ceiling. "A flame-haired physical therapist for Julian."

She snorted at the poetic description of her carroty hair before she looked down at her hands again. "What we had fun with was imagining how Julian and I would meet. Sometimes it was while I was on vacation in Venice or Rome, because I always wanted to travel to Italy. Or I'd take a trip to New York, and Julian would jump into my cab. Or at an airport when he was trying to get out of the country and needed a fake wife for cover." She lifted her head. "It was never in Sanctuary, because we couldn't think of any reason for Julian to come there."

He angled his head down to pin her with his gaze. "So I'm curious. Julian falls for a so-called normal woman who's modeled on you. Did this normal woman come to New York for the job or for the adventure?"

She stared into the flickering fireplace and lied. "For the job. I outgrew my need for adventure during PT school."

"I sense I'm not getting the whole—"

Raised female voices wafted in from the hallway.

Allie swiveled toward the sound as Gavin launched himself out of his chair and strode toward the door, muttering, "What the hell is *she* doing here?"

Ludmilla and a stunningly beautiful brunette burst into the room together. The Polish woman was waving her hands as she protested in her native language. The brunette kept walking as though Ludmilla didn't exist.

"Gavin, darling," she said in a British accent, "are you all right? You look as though you've been dragged through a shrubbery backward."

Allie rose slowly, her eyes riveted on the scene unfolding in front of her. The exquisite woman was Irene Bartram, the actress who played Samantha Dubois, Julian's manipulative love interest. It was disorienting to see her in person, looking exactly like the character in the movie.

Irene was also Gavin's ex-fiancée.

Gavin dodged the air kiss the actress aimed at him. "You look like you just came out of the hair-and-makeup trailer," he said with a snarl that indicated it wasn't a compliment. "Now get out."

Allie gasped, which swung both of their gazes around to her. The actress scanned Allie from head to foot and dismissed her without comment, turning back to Gavin and resting one graceful hand against his chest. "I know we had a little spat the last time we were together, so I came to apologize."

Gavin stepped around Irene to approach Allie. "We'll resume our discussion tomorrow under the same terms. And you'll receive payment for the hour I didn't use today." He rubbed at the back of his neck. "Let's hope Irene doesn't undo all your good work." He turned away. "Ludmilla, will you help Allie with her coat?"

Allie felt Irene's gaze on her as she walked to the office door. It made her acutely aware of her soiled shirt, her messy hair, and her lack of makeup. Honestly, though, even on her best day ever, Allie couldn't compete with the actress's glossy raven locks, huge brown eyes, and perfect porcelain skin. So what did it matter that Allie looked the worse for wear?

She lifted her chin and met Irene Bartram's gaze straight on, giving the actress a friendly smile. Irene's reaction was to narrow those doe eyes.

As she and Ludmilla stepped into the hallway, Allie heard Irene ask, "Who's the little nurse?"

Chapter 8

"She's none of your business," Gavin said as he spun away from the door to face Irene, triggering a spasm in his back. He gritted his teeth until it passed. "And you and I did not have a spat. We had a knock-down, drag-out fight, during which I told you to remove yourself from my life permanently."

He paced to the fireplace and picked up a poker, jabbing at the fire before he looked at her again. "You do understand the meaning of the word *permanently*."

Irene eyed the poker with a half smile. "Are you planning to thrust that through my heart?"

"No, it's an antique, and I don't want to break it on a flinty object." Gavin hung the tool back on its brass stand, growling as his shoulder twinged.

Irene made a fluid gesture acknowledging the insult without looking insulted, and he understood a little of why he'd fallen for her so hard and fast. She embodied all that was most fascinating about his character Samantha Dubois. Or maybe he had just projected those qualities onto her because Samantha was his creation, and, like Pygmalion, he was already halfway in love with her.

Allie felt that Julian deserved better than Samantha, but Gavin wasn't sure he agreed with her.

"Darling, I came to help you." Irene drifted down into a chair, tucking her endless legs to one side and crossing her slender ankles in a way that drew attention to them.

Gavin choked on a humorless laugh. "Well, that *is* unexpected."

She curved her painted lips into a pleased smile. "I thought we could try some role-playing. I'll take the part of Samantha, of course, and you'll play Julian. We can do a little improv to get your creative juices flowing again." She gave him the same smoldering look she used to tempt Julian on-screen.

"Too bad the cameras aren't rolling. That would have been a great close-up." Gavin shoved his hands in his pockets. "Was it your idea to come, or did someone send you?"

"I'm doing an interview with *Good Morning America*, so I thought I'd drop by." She floated to her feet and glided up to him, her eyes clouded with concern. "I'm worried about you."

"You're worried about your part in the movie." Gavin reached out and took a curl of her hair between his fingers, marveling at the near blackness. It was natural, as he knew from intimate experience. He wondered if Irene was born self-centered or if her extreme beauty had warped her character.

She mistook his aesthetic appreciation for something warmer and plastered her body against his from knee to chest. To his disgust, physical attraction flared inside him. However, his ardor was quickly doused by a bucket of cold memory. He gripped her shoulders and peeled her away from him. "I'm no longer interested."

"But we can still be friends, and friends help each other," she said, accepting his rejection without batting an eyelash. "So I'm here for you."

"Was this Greg's idea? Jane said he'd called last week."

"Greg is also concerned about you," Irene said. "It's not surprising, given that he's been the executive producer on every one of Julian's movies."

"I guess you didn't tell him about our last encounter or he might have ordered you *not* to come."

"Greg does not *order* me, ever." Irene shot him a look that would have left him dead had it been a dagger.

"Just deliver your message and go," Gavin said. He dropped into the armchair he'd been sitting in earlier and massaged his tense neck muscles. That brought forth the memory of Allie and how exhilarated he'd felt at the prospect of discussing Julian with her.

What a contrast to Irene, whose presence sent a shock of self-loathing spiraling through his soul. He was the idiot who'd proposed to her. And had gone to bed with her again after their breakup when she'd shown up for his father's funeral weekend. He had felt utterly alone, and she had offered the illusion of solace. Until he'd overheard her chatting up his stepsister Ruth about the possibility that his unfinished Julian Best manuscript might be somewhere at his father's house.

"Were you planning to steal the manuscript?" he asked. "Or persuade me to finish it?"

"Are we going to rehash that? I was just making conversation with Ruth." Her eyes shimmered with tears that didn't quite spill over. "I came to the funeral to support you, because I know how your stepmother is. I didn't want you to face her without someone by your side."

He reminded himself that she was a far better actress than she got credit for. "You left in a hurry."

"You made it clear you didn't want me there."

"I suppose I did." He had a hard time remembering the sequence of events, because he'd been gripped by a fury that had nearly blinded him. If he had been writing the scene, he would have unraveled the threads of pain, sorrow, regret, betrayal, and, yes, love that fed his anger, but he couldn't step back and observe it when it had him in its suffocating clutches. "Maybe I overreacted."

She started toward him, but he held up his hand, palm out. "That doesn't mean I've changed my mind."

"What can I do to change it?"

He looked at her, standing with her arms stretched toward him in a pose of entreaty, and felt the pull of her beauty even as he smelled the poison beneath it. He pushed himself out of the chair. "Nothing. Tell Greg his ploy didn't work."

She dropped her arms. "Just answer me one thing. Are you going to write another Julian Best book? Because I've been offered other spy film roles, and I've turned them down for you."

"For me? That's rich." He laughed with a bitter edge. "I can't answer your question."

"You can't write because you're still angry with me."

"Do you think I would screw up a multimillion-dollar movie deal because of you?"

She made a gesture of impatience. "What else could stop you from writing your book?"

"I ask myself that every day."

♥ ♥ ♥

Allie sat on the couch with Pie curled up beside her, googling Gavin Miller and Irene Bartram's names together. After seeing the snarling antagonism between them, she was looking for clues as to what might have caused it. She found dozens of photos of the two of them walking various red carpets, with Gavin looking magnificent in a custom-tailored tuxedo. Irene was gorgeous, too, of course, but Allie's eyes always went to the writer.

It made her sad to see the difference in how he looked at the actress in the photos and his expression today. In those happier times, Gavin had an arm curved possessively around Irene's waist, and his ardent gaze fixed on the stunning woman by his side. Allie sighed. If Gavin ever looked at her with that kind of adoration, she'd melt into a puddle at his feet.

By contrast, while Irene's body was always turned toward Gavin, she smiled directly at the camera. Allie was willing to give her the benefit of the doubt about the pose. Irene was an actress, and she was there to be photographed.

"So what happened to these two lovebirds, Pie?" she asked, scratching behind the cat's ears.

She switched from pictures to articles. The standard story went that the two had met on the set of a Julian Best movie and had fallen in love instantly. The photos that went with the gossip showed them walking in and out of restaurants in LA and New York City. Allie spared one glance for Irene's outfit and then went straight to Gavin in a perfectly fitting suit or khakis, and a white button-down shirt or worn jeans and a black leather jacket. "Yummy!"

His hair was shorter, and his smile seemed easy.

After their engagement became public, there were several posed photos of them, with Irene displaying a ruby-and-diamond engagement ring.

And then the breakup announcement. Irene gave multiple interviews after it happened. She said it was mutual and amicable. They were still friends. There was no problem with her continuing to star in the Julian Best movies.

Gavin had no comment. One gossip site had posted a photo of him looking grim and tight-lipped, but the photographer might have snapped it when Gavin was ticked off over a parking ticket or something.

However, Allie knew what he looked like now, and it wasn't happy. In fact, he had looked at Irene with downright revulsion.

She scrolled through more articles and stopped at a photo that showed Gavin and Irene standing by a mound of dirt beside an open grave. The actress looked elegantly mournful in a fitted black coatdress, her downward-angled head crowned with a wisp of netting. Gavin wore a black suit and a dark tie. His face was somber and his jaw tight as he stared into the distance.

They held hands with fingers intertwined.

She checked the date on the photo. It was last fall, nearly a year after their breakup. The caption read: *Actress Irene Bartram supports former fiancé and bestselling author Gavin Miller at his father's interment.*

Sympathy twisted her heart. The loss of her mother still sometimes blindsided her. But since Irene had been there for him when he needed her, why had Gavin been so rude to her today?

Although Irene hadn't exactly exuded affection, despite calling Gavin "darling."

Allie remembered two actors she and Troy had known when they were married, who would spend several weeks demonstrating their love so publicly it was awkward for those around them. Then they would have a screaming fight, also generally with an audience, breaking up and declaring they couldn't bear to be in the same room with each other. They'd end up at a party together at some point, have sex, and fall passionately in love again. Allie found it baffling and exhausting, but Troy said some people needed that kind of drama to feel alive.

Maybe Irene and Gavin were like that.

Allie couldn't picture Gavin enjoying an emotional roller coaster, but she barely knew him. With a shrug, she swiped away from her Gavin research and checked her e-mail.

No response to her résumés.

Anxiety wrapped its fingers around Allie's throat. She picked up the cat and cradled her against her chest, soaking up the comfort of her purring. She turned Pie to face her. "If I don't get another job soon, I may be dining on Chunky Tuna Feast along with you."

Chapter 9

Gavin's fitful sleep had been tormented by sordid, sweaty dreams featuring a slit-eyed, naked Irene beckoning him into a giant spiderweb, which annoyed him for being a terrible cliché. Even his subconscious lacked creativity these days. His waking hours had been unsettled by anticipation of the book signing he'd agreed to do that evening. He cursed as he pictured the endless line of fans stepping up to the table piled with two-year-old books and asking, "When's the next Julian Best story coming out?" He wasn't sure whether his nightmares were worse than his waking visions.

Allie's arrival had been like a fall of fresh snow, clean and bracing. But even Allie's magic fingers couldn't release all the tension that the night had speared into his muscles and his mind, so he decided to cancel the Julian Best discussion part of their session. He couldn't face the many troubles swirling around his super spy.

Yet he found himself reluctant to let Allie leave. Her cheerful presence was a powerful antidote to Irene's poison and his looming public appearance.

"You look like something out of a Currier and Ives print," he said as she pulled on a blue wool cap with a yellow pom-pom on top.

The little therapist smiled. "Better than a vision of hell by Hieronymus Bosch." Her smile faded into a look of concern. "I hope you'll try the water exercises I gave you. The warmth and buoyancy help relieve stress."

Not once had she mentioned yesterday's ugly scene with Irene, but she'd clearly noticed the increase in the tension in his back and shoulders. Even though he'd claimed that the pain level was no different, she'd prescribed additional treatments for him. He needed to remember that she was trained to judge discomfort in many ways, so she wouldn't rely on his verbal answer alone. He said, "I'll give it some thought."

Much to his delight, exasperation flitted across her face for a split second. He loved provoking her into an unedited reaction. However, she said nothing as she picked up the equipment-loaded duffel bag that she wouldn't let him carry because it was too heavy. When she started toward the door, he frowned. "How do you get to my house?"

"By subway."

"So you carry your satchel of gold bricks for twelve blocks from the subway stop. Remind me never to get in a wrestling match with you."

She turned to give him a full body scan that he felt almost as a touch. Heat streaked down to his groin before she shook her head. "You have more leverage, so I wouldn't challenge you to wrestle."

Now he couldn't shed the image of his body and Allie's interlocked on a floor mat, their skin glistening with sweat as they slipped and rubbed against each other. Pushing that stirring but misplaced picture away, he made a decision. "I want you to save your strength for my back, so I'm going to send a car to transport you to and from our sessions."

"Send a car?"

"Yes, one of those things with four wheels and a driver."

A look of temptation followed by regret flitted across her mobile face before she shook her head again. "I can make my own way, thanks."

Irritation flashed through him. "Oh, for God's sake, swallow your hillbilly pride or whatever it is. I have half a dozen cars at my beck and call. Might as well use them."

She thought for another long moment, but this time he couldn't read her expression. "Thank you. That would be pleasant."

"Starting now." He pulled out his phone and texted Jaros to bring the car to the front door.

She plunked her duffel bag down on the floor and huffed out a breath. "Are you being considerate or bossy?" Dismay made her eyes widen. "I'm sorry. That wasn't gracious."

Gavin grinned. He'd gotten her to sass him. "I'm being controlling. I told you that writers are like that."

Instead of giving it back to him, she looked away, her mouth pressed into a flat line. He'd ruined the thing he needed from her today: her sunny good cheer. He cast around for a way to bring it back. "I have to do a book signing tonight," he said. "I'd like you to come. You can stand behind me and dig your thumbs into my tense neck muscles every time someone asks when the next Julian Best book is coming out."

She gave him a polite smile and said nothing.

"Well, will you join me?" he asked.

"Are you serious?" Astonishment rang in her voice.

"About you coming, yes. Not about massaging my neck." The more he thought about it, the more he liked the idea of her presence. "It's at seven at Murder Unlimited in Tribeca. There will be decent wine, which makes it marginally bearable."

"Um, if I'm not going to massage your neck, why do you want me there?" She seemed baffled by his simple invitation.

"As a true fan, you deserve it. Wouldn't you like a signed hardcover copy of *Good, Better, Best*? It will be my gift to you." That should bring the Allie he knew back.

Pleasure lit her eyes for a moment. Still, she hesitated before saying, "Um, why would your publisher set this up if there's no new book? It seems sort of . . ."

"Like rubbing salt in a wound?" He could hear the edge in his voice, so he worked to soften it. "It's a joint signing with a first-time author my editor and agent are excited about. My presence is supposed to draw in more customers."

"Have you read the new author's book?"

"Yes, I gave it an enthusiastic cover blurb."

Her lips curved in a soft smile. "You're very generous."

"I was a debut author once." He remembered the nerves before his first book signing and the fear that no one would show up. That's why he'd agreed to help out. "Jaros will pick you up. I'd do it myself, but I have to be there an hour early, and I won't subject you to that boredom."

"I'd be honored to come." She gave him a pointed look. "But I'll take the subway."

"No subway."

She considered his command for a moment. "How about a compromise? You can send your car for me to come to work, but I'll get to the book signing on my own. It's not that far from where I live."

Other than muttering, "Stubborn little cuss," he stopped arguing. He was too shocked by the flood of gratitude and relief that flowed through him when she had agreed to come.

Allie checked the numbers on the nearest buildings as she came up out of the subway and turned left. She strode along the narrow sidewalk until she spotted the blood-spattered sign for Murder Unlimited.

The bookstore was in a turn-of-the-century building with a cast-iron facade. Tall windows painted rectangles of yellow light on the cracked sidewalk, and a crowd of people milled around inside. She took a deep breath and pulled open the door, the quiet hum of voices contrasting with the city street noise. A sign with Gavin's head shot and a photo of a studious-looking young woman announced a book signing tonight.

Excitement fizzed through her at the thought that Gavin wanted her here. She couldn't wait to see him in his element, surrounded by books and adoring readers.

As she hesitated on the threshold, a young man wearing black-rimmed glasses, skinny jeans, and electric blue wingtips greeted her. "Welcome! The coatrack is over there. The wine is in that corner. And the line for the signing begins by the bookshelf with the large yellow arrow on it. Get your books signed and then bring them to the register." He gave her a well-rehearsed smile. "We trust our readers to pay after they play." He leaned in. "So are you here for Gavin Miller or Kendra Leigh?"

"Both. Gavin told me how great Kendra's new book is."

The clerk raised his eyebrows. "You know Gavin Miller? Then let's take you to the head of the line." Without waiting for her response, he grabbed her elbow and began edging through the crowd with a tap on one shoulder and a nudge to another.

Allie tried to stop him, but her escort was on a mission, and soon they had cha-cha-ed to within sight of the signing tables. "Okay, I'm good here," Allie said when her guide paused for a second.

She ducked behind a bookcase and stripped off her unfashionable quilted winter jacket, stuffing it on top of a row of Agatha Christie paperbacks. She hadn't worn a hat so she wouldn't have hat head, but she ran her palms over her hair, just in case.

She hoped her attire was appropriate for a book signing. She'd chosen black pants and kitten-heeled leather ankle boots, topping them with a funky gray-and-black geometric-print tunic she'd bought from an artist friend. For once, her hair's gaudy color looked sophisticated, adding a splash of drama to her monochrome outfit.

Sidling around the bookcase, she watched Gavin scrawl his name in four books for one customer, chatting and smiling the whole time.

He looked the part of a thriller writer, with his longish dark hair combed back from the striking angles of his face and a leather jacket slung over the back of his chair. He wore a black silk shirt open at the collar. Her pulse did a little tango as she thought of what was under the silk.

At the table beside Gavin's, Kendra Leigh tugged nervously at her brown braid when a customer approached her. She pushed her glasses up on her nose and gave her new reader a hesitant smile before she carefully wrote in the paperback.

Gavin should give her some lessons on charming the clientele.

As the enthusiastic fan stepped away from his table, Gavin glanced around and caught sight of Allie. The smile that flashed across his face hit her like a medicine ball to the stomach. It wasn't the author smile he'd had on earlier. It was an I-am-over-the-moon-glad-to-see-you smile. She pressed her hand against her chest to slow the crazed flipping of her heart. His gaze flicked down to register her gesture while his smile took on a wolfish edge.

He beckoned her toward him before saying something to the customer standing in front of him. As Allie walked forward, he pushed back his chair and stepped away from the table. At the same time, a tiny blonde woman in a crimson sheath dress approached him and put her hand on his arm. Allie hesitated, but Gavin once again waved her nearer as he and the blonde moved away from the crowd into a private space between the bookshelves.

"You're here," he said. His green eyes skimmed over her and lit with something stronger than gratitude. "Your hair is glorious." Then as if he hadn't just said something personal, he glanced back at his table. "It's a bit of a madhouse right now, but don't leave. It will die down."

Allie considered the line snaking through several rows of bookcases. "In about three hours."

"You don't give me enough credit. I've done a few of these before." He turned her to face the blonde. "Jane, this is the brilliant physical therapist you sent me. Allie, Jane."

"Ms. Dreyer," Allie said, offering her hand and a smile of gratitude. "Thank you so much for giving me the opportunity to work with Mr. Miller."

The agent shook Allie's hand, her stack of gold bangles chiming softly. "Gavin says you've worked miracles, so I want to thank *you*. Since Gavin's tied up at the moment, let me get you some wine."

"Oh, gosh, I'm fine." Allie didn't want to bother Gavin's agent.

"I insist. I want to hear about how his treatment is progressing. We can talk in the VIP room in back."

Allie cast a questioning glance at Gavin. He nodded. "You have my permission to answer her questions about the therapy. She has a vested interest, after all." He touched the back of Allie's hand, sending a shiver of delight up her arm. "You'll stay until the bitter end?"

"Absolutely."

Another smile that eased the tension in his face and made her feel as though her presence meant something to him. He leaned down to whisper beside her ear. "I may need a massage by then."

"I brought my tools." She held up her hands. Was that really why he wanted her to stay? Her gratification fizzled out.

Gavin returned to his seat while Jane led Allie back through the bookcases to a cozy room where it appeared a private gathering was taking place. Two tall men stood talking by a table spread with sandwiches, wine bottles, and cupcakes, while two women chatted on a brocade-covered love seat. Allie nearly gasped as she recognized Luke Archer, the newly retired superstar quarterback of the New York Empire. If he'd come to Gavin's book signing, they must have gotten over their quarrel.

Jane proceeded to the buffet table. "Red or white?"

Allie was having a hard time not staring at the quarterback. The man's golden blond hair and ice blue eyes were even more striking in person. And he was so tall. "Wh-white, please."

Jane handed her a glass and turned to the two men. "Allie, meet Nathan Trainor and Luke Archer." Jane had a little twinkle of humor in her eyes as she introduced the legendary athlete. "Nathan, Luke, this is Allie Nichols, Gavin's physical therapist. She's doing great things for him."

Luke held out his huge hand. "I've worked with my fair share of PTs, so I know how hard your job is. I imagine Gavin isn't the easiest patient."

Allie nearly laughed as she remembered his attempt to throw her out the first day. "Once he got used to the idea, he was fine."

"A pleasure, Allie," Nathan said, giving her a firm handshake. "We're all friends of Gavin's, so we're glad he's found someone to help him."

The name Trainor was nagging at her brain, and then she remembered. This was the CEO of Trainor Electronics and the inventor of the battery used in virtually every laptop in the world.

The two women joined the group and were introduced as Miranda Archer and Chloe Russell. Allie smiled wistfully when the two men slid their arms around the women's waists with obvious affection.

They chatted for a few minutes, although Allie mostly just listened. Everyone was very pleasant, but she felt overawed. Then Jane said, "I'm going to steal Allie away for some private conversation."

Jane hooked her arm through Allie's and drew her aside to a quiet corner holding two mismatched upholstered Victorian chairs and a Moroccan-inlay occasional table. The agent surveyed it and said, "I think it's supposed to evoke Sherlock Holmes's study." They sat, and Jane leaned in, fixing her blue eyes on Allie. "Tell me how Gavin's therapy is going. He seems better."

"He's making good progress now that's he committed to the treatment. We're still working on relaxing the muscles, but soon he'll be able to start exercising them, too. That should prevent this from happening again."

"I'll be honest," Jane said. "I thought he would refuse to do it."

Allie made a wry face. "It was close."

"Dr. Benson said you were good with difficult patients." Jane leaned in a little more. "Gavin mentioned that he's talked to you about his writer's block."

"I didn't bring it up until he did," Allie was quick to say. "He found out that I'm a fan of the Julian Best books. That's why he invited me here." She decided not to tell Jane that she'd used that information as a last resort to keep him from firing her.

Jane shook her head. "Gavin wanted allies tonight. He considers you one."

Allie remembered Gavin's smile of greeting and dared to hope Jane might be right.

"Has he discussed Julian Best with you?" Jane asked.

"A little." Allie wasn't sure if Gavin wanted her to talk about this part of their sessions. "We've been focusing on his physical issues."

"His physical issues are just a symptom of his creative problem," Jane said. "If you can help him get the writing flowing again, that would fix everything else."

"I'm not really qualified for that."

"You're as qualified as anyone else," Jane said. "Gavin wouldn't let one of those creativity coaches anywhere near him, but he's talking to you." She laid her hand on Allie's arm. "He's a friend as well as a client to me, and it kills me to see him suffering like this. He's been putting an immense amount of pressure on himself because he's missed some deadlines. Not to mention that the movie is stalled without a script. I think the stress is blocking his creativity. Writers need to write, or they begin to have mental and emotional problems." She sat back. "Whatever you can do to help him, do it."

"I'll try my best." Allie began to understand why Gavin's muscles were clenched so rigidly. He was carrying a heavy load of responsibility.

"I have a feeling your best is impressive," Jane said, giving her a warm smile. "By the way, I might have another patient for you."

Allie forced herself not to hug the agent. "Thank you for the vote of confidence. Let me know who, when, and where."

There was a stir as an auburn-haired man strode into the room. "Doc, it's good to see you," Luke Archer said, shaking the new arrival's hand.

"Congratulations on your Super Bowl triumph and your retirement," the doctor said. "I'm glad you decided to stop punishing your body before it was too late."

"I could have played another four years easy," Luke said, "but I found better things to do with my time." He looked across at Miranda with a private message in his eyes.

Allie nearly sighed out loud.

Jane stood. "Now here's someone you should meet. Come with me."

The doctor greeted the rest of the group as Jane and Allie approached.

"Allie, I'd like you to meet Dr. Ben Cavill," Jane said. "Ben, allow me introduce you to this very talented physical therapist, Allie Nichols. She's working with Gavin quite successfully."

Ben raised his eyebrows in surprise as he shook Allie's hand. "Miller hired a PT? I'm shocked."

Everyone seemed to know about Gavin's prickly personality, yet they all cared about him. Gavin was a fortunate man.

"I hired her, but she did the heavy lifting of persuading him to accept treatment," Jane said.

Nathan swiveled to look at Allie. "I'd like to offer you a position on my contract-negotiation team."

The group laughed, and Allie felt color light her cheeks at the compliment. "Deep down, he knew he needed help, so it wasn't that difficult," she said.

"When Gavin most needs help, that's when he pushes you away," Miranda said, her brown eyes filled with understanding.

"I'm always looking for good specialists to recommend," the doctor said. "Let's go talk shop."

Once again Allie sat in the Sherlock Holmes corner, except this time she felt as though she was going through her PT final exams all over again. Ben Cavill knew his stuff and wanted to make sure she knew hers. She must have passed, because at the end of their conversation, he handed her his business card and asked for hers.

Allie nearly broke into a jig as she and the doctor headed back to the main seating area. Jane had disappeared, probably to stand watch over her authors. Allie slid into a chair that was slightly removed from the intimidating group of friends and let the conversation flow around her.

The only time she was tempted to join in was when Chloe and Nathan began discussing their wedding plans. Allie wanted to know why they were getting married at a Marine base in North Carolina when they could rent an entire cathedral, but didn't want to presume to ask. As if reading her mind, Chloe turned and said, "Nathan's father is a major general in the Marine Corps and is stationed at Camp Lejeune, so we're going to have the arch of swords in full regalia."

"That sounds magnificent," Allie said.

"Chloe and my father have forged a close alliance," Nathan said. "When those two master tacticians put their heads together, I stay out of their way."

The approach of new voices interrupted the conversation, and Gavin walked in, surrounded by a small entourage. He was carrying a cardboard carton and talking with Kendra Leigh, who looked like she would turn and flee when she saw everyone gazing in her direction.

Gavin stopped to survey the group. "Good evening, my friends. I'd like you to meet the new sensation of the mystery-writing world, Kendra Leigh. She has very kindly signed copies of her debut book for you, and I am presenting them as my gifts." He slid the carton onto the coffee table and pulled out two copies of the paperback. "There's one slight catch. Seth, the marketing manager, wants to take a photo of all of us with the books in our hands." He nodded to the young man who'd been Allie's guide.

Kendra looked panic-stricken, so Allie edged over to her as Gavin and Seth discussed the best way to fit everyone into the photo. "Is this your first book signing?"

The writer swallowed. "Yes."

"Gavin says your story is terrific. I can't wait to read it."

"He really said that? I thought he endorsed my book because we have the same editor."

Allie laughed. "Gavin is brutally frank, so he wouldn't praise your book if he didn't mean it."

"But he's been so nice to me tonight." Kendra looked confused. "He gave me some pointers on how to keep the line moving and even suggested a tagline for my autograph."

So Gavin could be kind and helpful. Maybe that explained why he still had friends, despite his crankiness.

"All right, we have a plan." Seth raised his voice to get their attention. He proceeded to arrange the group in a way that suggested they were carrying on an interesting conversation about Kendra's book. Allie gave him kudos for composition, even as she did her best to hide in a corner so no one felt obliged to include her in the publicity shot.

"Allie!" Gavin shifted out of his position to find her. "You need to be in here, too."

"No, I'm good," she said, moving a step farther away.

His affable host mask fell away, and he frowned, saying with a note of irritability, "Allie."

She almost laughed as she gave up and walked toward him. This was the Gavin she knew.

Seth positioned her between Gavin and Chloe, who had been selected to hold a copy of Kendra's book in a way that made the cover visible without looking like a deliberate display. "If you don't already have a marketing manager, I'd hire this guy," Allie murmured to Gavin as she watched Seth finish the arrangements and raise his cell phone to snap several shots.

"A thousand thanks from all of us at Murder Unlimited," Seth said. "This will be on the store's Facebook page and as many other outlets as I can persuade to use it."

As everyone relaxed and fell into more natural poses, Seth jogged up to Gavin. "Would you mind checking my caption and adding a couple of names?"

Gavin took the proffered phone and pointed to the photo. "That's Chloe Russell, Nathan's fiancée. And this is Allie Nichols, my, er, assistant." He lifted an eyebrow at Allie and gave her a half smile before he tilted the phone so she could see it. She winced at the sight of her hair looking like a splotch of orange paint, but everyone else appeared to be at a cozy cocktail party that just happened to include books.

"Will you e-mail me a copy?" Gavin asked as he handed the phone back to Seth. "I'll put it in my scrapbook." Another slanted smile at Allie.

Kendra bolted almost as soon as the photo was taken, but the rest of the group stayed around, chatting for another few minutes. Allie was flattered and touched that Gavin kept her by his side, making sure she was included in the conversations.

As people began to say farewell, Chloe leaned in to give Allie a quick hug. "We're having a little dinner party Saturday night—just a few friends, including Gavin. Why don't you come? We'd love to have you."

Astonishment robbed Allie of coherent thought. She caught an echo of the same feeling on Nathan's face as he glanced down at his fiancée. "Um, I, well, thank you." She had no idea whether to accept or decline. She had no plans for the weekend, so there was nothing holding her back except the fact that these people were ultra-rich, and she was nearly flat broke.

"Great," Chloe said, misunderstanding Allie's stammer and giving her a happy smile. "Gavin knows our address. Come at seven."

"Thank you." Panic banished astonishment. What did you wear to a billionaire's dinner party? What sort of hostess gift could you bring to people who could buy literally anything? Could she ask Gavin any of these questions?

As she debated, Gavin's friends departed, leaving the two of them alone in the VIP room.

"I'd better go home, too," Allie said, her head spinning. "I have a very tough patient to see tomorrow morning."

Gavin snorted. "I am putty in your powerful hands." He reached into the book carton and pulled out a hardcover wrapped in a plastic bag. The angles of his face softened, and she felt her breath flutter in response. "This is for you. With my thanks for coming. I signed it."

As Allie accepted it, their fingertips brushed, sending a flicker of pleasure over her skin. "I wish Mama could see this. Me getting an autographed Julian Best book from the author himself." A tiny burn of tears stung her eyes.

"Maybe the last Julian Best book."

She looked up to find Gavin's expression had turned desolate.

Allie shook her head. "You're going to write a boatload more if I have to pummel them out of you."

That chased away the bleakness. "And that's why I asked you to come here," he said, his sea green eyes changing from stormy to intent. He took a step closer so she could smell the rich leather of his jacket. "There's just one other thing I need to do." He stretched out his hand to stroke her hair before he picked up several strands to rub between his fingertips.

His movements sent a tingle dancing over her scalp that made her eyelids drift half-closed to savor the delicious sensation.

"It's as silky as it looks, but not as warm," he said, his voice a rasp. "It should singe my fingers like a flame."

"Then it would set my clothes on fire," she managed to say.

His eyes changed color again to something unsettling as he continued to toy with her hair. "H. Rider Haggard wrote a book called *She* in which the heroine bathes in magic flames to make herself immortal. That's what your hair makes me think of."

"Um, I'll see if they have a copy here." Between the low rumble of his voice, the hot light in his eyes, and his touch on her hair, Allie was having a hard time breathing.

"It's a love story, not a murder mystery," he said, holding her hair a moment longer before he stroked it back into place alongside her face, his fingers lingering on her cheek for a fraction of a second longer.

This was even more confusing than the dinner invitation. Maybe she wasn't cut out for working with rich people.

"I'll order it from Amazon." She needed to leave, but he seemed to have hypnotized her so she couldn't move.

He barked out a laugh. "Don't let them hear you say that in this store."

"I'll see you in the morning," Allie said, relieved and disappointed to be released from his strange magnetic spell. She forced herself to walk calmly to the bookcase where she'd stuffed her coat, seizing it and bolting out the door, just like Kendra Leigh.

Gavin seemed to have that effect on people.

Chapter 10

Gavin had been monosyllabic throughout his treatment, but Allie was used to his moods by now, so she just did her job. He had tensed up again, so she had to really probe the knots. It was the nature of her work: one step forward, two steps back. The human body didn't heal in a linear progression.

Besides, she had some idea of what his appearance at the book signing last night had cost him, given his lack of a new book to sign or even to promise for the future. She hoped Kendra Leigh appreciated the guts it had taken for Gavin to support the first-time author with his public presence.

As she walked over to get the swiss ball, Gavin snapped, "Can't we dispense with that today?"

"You know it will help."

"Not where I really need help. You owe me a discussion about Julian."

She didn't point out that he was the one who had canceled their two previous attempts to discuss his spy hero. "Why don't we talk about Julian and then revisit using the ball?" she said.

He skewered her with a look. "Are you sure you weren't a literary agent in a past life?"

"Physical therapy is not easy, so I've learned the art of negotiation," Allie said, stowing the ball back on its rack.

"You call it negotiation. I call it blackmail."

Gavin slid off the massage table and reached for his shirt, his torso twisting so his muscles stretched and flexed in ways that made liquid heat flow through her. He'd also just demonstrated that her work had relaxed him.

"You look like you're moving more easily," she said.

He yanked his shirt down over his head and scowled at her. "Damn it, I am. You just had to ruin my bad mood."

"I've been called obnoxiously cheerful." She grinned at him.

He couldn't hold on to the scowl. "As long as you don't sing 'The sun'll come out tomorrow,' I can tolerate you. Barely."

"Am I allowed to thank you for the book now?" He'd written an inscription about her mother that had made her cry. "What you said was beautiful."

"Don't get maudlin on me," he said. She could tell he was pleased, though. He came close enough to cup his hands over her shoulders. "Thank you for coming to the book signing. Every time someone asked when the next book was coming out, I reminded myself of our discussions about Julian. It kept me from bolting."

She had a hard time focusing on his words because she was savoring the warmth and strength of his hands on her. It was odd. She had touched him so often, but having him touch her was an entirely different sensation. She could feel it radiating down her arms and through her chest before it wound deep within her.

"I can't picture you running away from a book signing," she said, trying to counterbalance her yearning.

"Maybe not." He released her as one corner of his mouth quirked up. "I don't mind offending my friends, but I try never to upset a reader."

She wanted to close her eyes to hang on to the phantom heat still glowing inside her, but Gavin seized her elbow and towed her toward the stairs.

"Time for a chat."

He let her precede him up the steps and into his office, waving her into the chair she'd occupied when Irene had stormed in. Allie had wondered if the actress would show up at the book signing and had been relieved when she hadn't.

"What would you like for refreshment?" Gavin asked, after paging Ludmilla on the intercom.

"Water's good."

He cast an exasperated glance at the ceiling. "Ludmilla, bring water, coffee, tea, and a selection of sandwiches."

Allie decided now was the best time to broach her embarrassing topic. "Before we start on Julian, can I ask you a question?"

He raised his eyebrows. "Have you ever needed permission?"

"Um, I'm not sure if I should go to the dinner party at Chloe and Nathan's house. Nathan looked surprised when Chloe invited me, so it seems kind of . . . weird."

His eyebrows arched even more. "Weird?"

"You know." She made a vague gesture. "They're really rich and they just met me, and I don't understand why I got invited."

"Would you come to a dinner party here?"

"Here? That's weird for a different reason. I work for you."

"I'm trying to follow your logic. Not to be a braggart, but I'm quite rich as well. However, my wealth wouldn't stop you from dining here. Your employment would." He sat back in his chair. "Whereas Nathan and Chloe's wealth stops you from dining with them?"

Allie gave him one of her patented don't-mess-with-a-mountain-woman looks. "You know what I mean."

"I suppose I do. They're good people, Allie. Nathan made his money the old-fashioned way, by earning it. Neither he nor Chloe thinks that being rich makes them better than anyone else."

"Maybe it doesn't make them better, but it makes them different. And I have no idea what to wear!" Allie said in frustration.

Gavin laughed, a throaty, rich, fully committed sound of amusement. "Finally, we get to the crux of the matter."

His laughter fizzed in her blood like bubbles in champagne. It was the first time she'd heard him sound purely happy. "My wardrobe doesn't run to haute couture," she said.

"I don't remember Chloe or Miranda wearing anything particularly fancy at the book signing."

"Trust me, everything they had on was designer." The simpler the skirt or blouse, the easier it was to tell that it was perfectly cut for the wearer.

"I'm going to let you in on a little secret. Chloe worked for Nathan's company as a temp. And Miranda was the assistant concierge in Luke's apartment building. They both know what it's like not to own designer clothing."

Allie felt a small measure of relief. "Okay, but do I wear a cocktail dress, a regular dress, or nice pants?"

"Good God, I don't know. Call Chloe and ask her."

"What are *you* wearing?" she persisted.

"I haven't given it a moment's thought."

"Well, think about it now."

Gavin looked at the ceiling again. "A pair of gray trousers, a black silk shirt, and a tweed blazer. With black loafers. Satisfied?"

"That helps, but I'll take Chloe's phone number, please."

He texted it to her cell phone.

She decided it would be useless to ask him what she should bring as a hostess gift.

"You *are* still planning to come, aren't you?" Gavin shifted in his chair.

Allie knew she shouldn't, but it was too tempting to find out what a billionaire's dinner party was like. Even more intriguing was the prospect of watching Gavin interact with his friends. "I'll be there," she said.

"I'll pick you up. Now that you've become accustomed to riding in a car in New York."

It had been a luxury to walk out of her apartment this morning and have Jaros, the chauffeur, take her duffel bag out of her hand to stow it in the trunk while she settled on the soft leather of the Bentley's backseat. It turned out that Jaros was Ludmilla's husband, which somehow made it all seem sort of cozy and friendly.

Ludmilla rolled a cart in the door, ending the conversation. Allie accepted some hot tea and a plate of dainty finger sandwiches just to please the housekeeper.

As Allie bit into the most delicious combination of turkey and avocado she'd ever tasted, Gavin nodded and said, "Keep eating so I can work you mercilessly."

She'd been dreading this, knowing that she had nothing of value to offer the writer. She took another bite of the sandwich as a delaying tactic.

"Which is your favorite Julian Best novel?" Gavin asked.

She'd expected him to grill her on how Julian would meet the woman of his dreams, so the question relieved her. "That's easy. *Best of Times.*"

"Why?" Gavin toyed with a sandwich but kept his gaze on her.

"It's the book where he finds out that Samantha is a double agent. Then he has to make the decision about whether to continue their relationship or break it off. We get to see more of Julian's thoughts than usual as he struggles with the implications of his discovery. His emotions and his job clash, so it reveals depth in his character." She'd gone on too long. "Sorry. I really love that book."

Gavin smiled. "Don't feel you have to stop. There's no sweeter music to an author's ears than having a reader speak passionately about his book."

"Okay, I have another favorite for a completely different reason. *Best Laid Plans*, because we meet Julian's brother. Giving him family adds another dimension to his character. And the plot in that book is really meaty."

"Any other favorites?" Gavin took a bite of his sandwich.

"*Best of Both Worlds* has a really great setting. I liked all the details about space stations and resupplying them. That was exciting and different." Allie shrugged. "Mama and I used to try to list them in order of our preference, but we never could because there was always something we loved about each book."

"I guess that answers my question about which book you liked the least."

Allie buried her nose in her teacup.

"Allie?"

She put the tea down. "I didn't want to say this, but *Good, Better, Best* didn't work for me. But that's just my opinion."

"The dagger to the heart." His words were dramatic, but when she glanced up at him, he had a slight smile playing around his lips. "What was wrong with it?"

Allie debated how to phrase it. "You know all that character growth I talked about? It was like it was all erased. He went back to being the Julian of the early books. I felt frustrated when he seemed to regress."

Gavin leaned forward in his chair. "You are a perceptive reader. That book was an early manuscript, one that originally got rejected by the publisher. I revised it heavily, but the story didn't lend itself to emotional growth, so I let Julian cruise through it without being touched in any profound way." He shook his head. "I did my fans a disservice by releasing that book."

"It was still a really good story," Allie said, sorry that she had been so frank. "Not everyone wants their spies to have feelings."

"Don't backpedal," Gavin said. "Your honesty is valuable to me. At this stage of my career, I don't get a lot of that, except from Jane. So let's talk specifics."

They spent the next hour discussing the books. Gavin would choose a scene and ask Allie questions about how she responded to it. She forgot to be tactful as they ranged over what succeeded and what had fallen short. Her mind was racing, making connections she hadn't made before and digging deep to figure out why she liked or disliked something.

When Gavin called an end to the discussion, exhilaration was surging through her, as though she'd drunk from a cold, clear spring of pure thought. Talking with him made her feel like a real literary critic because he treated her opinions with such respect.

"I haven't had this much fun in a long time," she said, stacking her empty dishes and reaching for his.

"Ludmilla will get those," Gavin said.

"I don't mind. I need to move, because there's all this excitement zooming around inside me." She carried the dishes to the cart.

When she turned, Gavin was standing close to her, the air between them vibrating with his heat and breath and scent.

Very slowly, he stretched his hand out to trace along her cheek and jaw with his fingertips. His touch mesmerized her, so she stood motionless while he skimmed down the side of her neck to the place where her collarbone was bared by the V of her shirt. Wherever he touched, her skin lit up as though charged with electricity, making her breathing go shallow and her heart stutter.

He took one step closer so that she had to tilt her head back to meet his eyes, their green gone translucent. He brought his other hand up to thread into her ponytail, cradling her head. The aroma of the wintergreen massage oil wove around her, carried by the warmth of his body as the fabric of their shirts brushed together. If she breathed too deeply, the tight tips of her breasts would touch the wall of his chest.

For a moment, they both stood like that, the only movement the soft brush of his thumb across her collarbone.

"No." He pulled his hands away from her and stepped back. "You don't deserve that." He threw himself into his chair.

She sucked in a shaky breath as his sensual spell dissipated. "I don't deserve what?"

He shook his head. "You gave me a great gift, and I was about to express my gratitude in the worst possible way." He pulled out his phone and tapped at the screen. "Go home, Allie, before my self-control snaps. Jaros is waiting for you out front."

She had thought he was going to kiss her. Hoped for it because she had gone temporarily insane. It was against the professional code of ethics to have a sexual relationship with a patient. Maybe a kiss did not have to lead to sex, but it was still crossing the line.

And Gavin could tempt her into crossing all kinds of lines.

Gavin watched Allie skitter out of his office and hated himself.

It was all that energy vibrating between them. She was so excited about his books that she had transmitted it to him. Allie remembered details about his stories that he had forgotten. She made Julian come alive again. He had begun to feel a stirring of interest in where to take his character next.

Her gray eyes had snapped with intelligence, and her West Virginia twang faded away when she got engrossed in the conversation. Except when she mentioned her mother. Then her voice slowed to a deep, warm drawl.

Her creamy skin had taken on a rose flush as she debated with him, and her flaming ponytail flowed over her shoulder like a river of fire. Now that he knew what that silky hair felt like, he wanted to sink his fingers into it again.

When she had sparkled at him and told him what fun she'd had, something inside him had given way. He'd needed to touch her, to feel that sweet exhilaration under his hands, on his lips, against his body.

Thank God he'd stopped. His Allie was a woman of principle, so he knew damn well that if he kissed her, she would refuse to be his therapist any longer.

And he couldn't afford to lose her.

Chapter 11

Allie's cell phone pinged with a text saying Gavin had arrived in front of her building. She checked herself in the mirror even though she'd already changed her clothes half a dozen times.

Her final decision had come down to a conservative outfit of black trousers topped by a forest green silk blouse with long sleeves and a deep V neckline. She'd accessorized with high-heeled black pumps and a string of pearls that had belonged to her mother, hoping the real gems would offset her sale-rack clothes. Her hair was pulled up into a loose bun, leaving a few tendrils waving beside her face.

She'd decided to forgo a hostess gift since she figured billionaires didn't need anything she could afford. A handwritten thank-you note afterward would have to suffice.

Shoving her phone into the black patent-leather clutch, she ruined the outfit as usual by shrugging into her puffy blue winter coat. She gave the cat a stroke to calm herself.

As she walked out the battered front door, she saw Gavin leaning against the fender of a low, sleek car with black paint that glinted in the city lights. He was dressed exactly as he'd said he would be—all dark and perfectly tailored—which made him look as powerful and dangerous as the car.

Desire poured through her. She wanted to press herself against that gorgeous, hard body she'd become so familiar with and wind her fingers into his thick, dark hair. She wanted those perfectly curved lips on hers while his hands explored her skin. Gavin had stopped whatever was about to start between them, so he probably wouldn't initiate it again. But if he did, she had to stay in command of her rioting senses and call a halt herself.

"Good evening, Allie," he said, straightening before he swung open the passenger door. "I'd say you look lovely, but it's hard to tell under the quilt you're wearing."

She knew the coat wasn't exactly high fashion, but all her insecurities surged back. Then she laughed with a certain relief. Gavin's snarkiness had undercut her sudden flare of arousal. "The weather is too cold for elegance."

"My car is already warmed up, so you might want to remove your Arctic-level outerwear."

"Okay." She unzipped her puffy jacket and started to shrug out of it. Gavin's fingers brushed the nape of her neck as he did the gentlemanly thing and took her wrap. She closed her eyes while desire shimmered through her all over again.

He tossed her coat into the backseat and offered his hand to help her into the front. It would be rude to ignore his gesture, so she put her hand in his, feeling another shudder of longing when his warm, strong fingers closed over hers. Thank God he was driving so he would have his hands occupied.

As he slid into the driver's seat, she said, "You didn't want a chauffeur tonight?"

"Nathan has parking at his building, and I like to take the Maserati out for a spin myself." The city lights caught the flash of his smile.

"Julian Best doesn't care about cars, but I do. This beauty is my favorite. She does zero to sixty in under five seconds."

She couldn't take her eyes off his hands as they stroked the gleaming wood of the steering wheel. "Do you know how to fly a plane, like Julian?"

"Yes, but I'm more of a sailor."

"So you have a yacht?"

He gave her a sideways glance. "A sailboat."

"The only boat I know my way around is a canoe," she said.

"Isn't West Virginia famous for white-water rafting?"

"I've done that a few times, but always with a guide." She'd loved it, even when she got dumped out of the raft in the middle of the frothing rapids.

"Intrepid Allie. You'll have to come sailing with me sometime."

"Sure." That wasn't going to happen.

Jane had hired her to work with Gavin for only five days, and Gavin had not rehired her for next week. So, technically speaking, their patient-therapist relationship was over. But it left her in a kind of ethical limbo, because she hoped Gavin would ask her to continue treatment. He certainly needed more. "How's your neck feeling?"

"On a pain scale of one to ten"—she could hear the smile in his voice—"about a three, which is damned impressive for five days of therapy. But let's not talk about work tonight."

"So no Julian?"

He shook his head. "Tell me about your hometown of Sanctuary. The name alone is intriguing."

Allie had often used cozy stories about her hometown to help clients relax with her. But, of course, Gavin didn't allow her to skim the surface. He asked questions about what kinds of jobs people did there, how lively the cultural scene was, the ways people socialized. He rolled the names of people she knew around on his tongue. Even though he was blocked, she could tell his writer's brain was at work, gathering material.

Not that she minded. She liked talking about her roots. Until Troy had forced her to leave, she'd been happy there. She wished she could still find contentment at home.

"And here we are," Gavin said, spinning the wheel to turn into a driveway guarded by a bulky man in a dark uniform. The guard scanned Gavin's driver's license with a handheld gizmo before a massive metal gate swung inward to reveal a valet station. Two young men leaped forward to open their car doors. "Put it in Nathan Trainor's garage," he said, handing his key to the valet. He took Allie's elbow and led her toward a bronze door tucked into a corner. Another valet swiped a card to unlock the elevator, and the gleaming door slid open.

"Wow!" Allie breathed, taking in the polished wood paneling set in frames of bronze that matched the door. "It's like a fortress."

"The downside of wealth," Gavin said, setting the elevator in motion. "There are security cameras everywhere and a battalion of bodyguards in the building."

"Do you have bodyguards, too?" She hadn't noticed any at his house, although she had spotted the outside security cameras.

"Sometimes. People are less inclined to kidnap writers." His smile was grim. "Even bad guys feel sorry for us." He stepped away from her to skim his gaze down her body. "Now that I can see you, may I say that your attire is perfect for a dinner with billionaires? In fact, you look so lovely that I'm tempted to keep you all to myself."

"Say it as often as you want," Allie said, but her pulse throbbed at the seductive caress of his voice.

Fortunately, the elevator door slid open, offering a much-needed distraction. As she looked around, Allie nearly gasped out loud. They were in an entrance hall that rivaled any mansion's. The floor was an ornate marble mosaic while a curving staircase soared upward past a magnificent chandelier. A man in a navy blue suit with hair graying at the temples stepped forward.

"Evening, Ed," Gavin said, shaking hands with the other man. "Allie, this is Ed Roccuzzo, Nathan's majordomo and a former drill sergeant."

"Ms. Nichols," Ed said, taking her proffered hand. "A pleasure."

Allie wasn't sure what a majordomo did, but she knew to respect a drill sergeant. "Please call me Allie."

He nodded and turned. "Follow me, if you would."

They walked down a hallway past huge rooms furnished with perfectly chosen furniture and artwork. Allie couldn't believe she was inside a skyscraper. Ed stopped in front of a door and gestured them through. Six people were seated around a massive glass coffee table in front of a roaring fire. Beyond them a wall of windows displayed the sparkling lights of nighttime Manhattan.

"Allie, Gavin!" Chloe jumped up from the comfortable-looking modular couch, her brown hair catching gleams of firelight, and gave them each a quick hug. "Come and sit. What would you like to drink?"

Allie wanted water, but there wasn't a single water glass on the coffee table. "White wine, please?"

"Chardonnay, pinot grigio, or sauvignon blanc?" Ed's voice came from just behind her.

She pivoted and gave him an overwhelmed smile. "Whatever's open."

He winked at her, and she felt better.

Chloe drew them over to the table, where introductions were made. The other guests were the Archers, Ben Cavill, and Priscilla Duval, who had once worked at Trainor Electronics. Priscilla was tall, slender, and so elegant that Allie felt like a frump once again. As Chloe settled them all, Allie found herself beside the doctor, which suited her just fine. Medical matters were well within her wheelhouse, and she could watch Gavin out of the corner of her eye.

"Our guests of honor are stuck in traffic," Nathan said, "so we'll wait a little longer for dinner."

Allie checked out the clothes. The ladies wore pants and blouses just like she did, and the gentlemen were casual in trousers and open-necked shirts. Everyone else might be wearing couture, but at least her ensemble didn't stick out like a sore thumb. Her anxiety trickled away, leaving her relaxed enough to enjoy herself.

The conversation ranged over topics even Allie could contribute to occasionally, although mostly she watched. Chloe was a warm, attentive hostess. However, every now and then, her gaze would go to the gray-eyed, intense Nathan, and the two would exchange a look filled with love. Then there was the blond football legend, Luke Archer, who kept his beautiful, dark-haired wife tucked firmly against his side in a way that tugged at Allie's heart. So rich people could fall in love, too.

Voices came from the hallway, and everyone swiveled to see Ed usher in another couple. Allie couldn't believe her eyes when a dark-haired woman with the lovely, serene face of a Madonna glided into the room. Allie stood up abruptly. "Claire? Claire Parker?"

Claire halted and stared. "Wait! Is that Allie Nichols?" she asked.

"I can't believe it!" Allie said, rounding the sofa and hugging Claire. "I haven't seen you in, what, ten years?"

"I'm so sorry about your mother's passing," Claire said, taking both of Allie's hands. "She was a wonderful lady. Always ready to lend a helping hand to anyone in need."

"I miss her," Allie said, feeling the tears prickle. "How's your sister doing?"

Claire's eyes lit with joy. "So much better since she left Frank. In fact, I think we may have a wedding sometime soon. She and Robbie McGraw."

The giant of a man standing beside Claire cleared his throat.

"Oh, Tim. I'm so sorry. We got caught up in catching up." Claire smiled in apology. "Allie, this is my husband, Tim Arbuckle."

"You took over Doc Messer's veterinary practice," Allie said, putting her hand in Tim's enormous grasp.

"You must be from Sanctuary," Tim said, a twinkle in his eyes. He had a slow smile that made you trust him instantly.

Allie laughed. "How did you guess?"

"It seems to be old home week," Gavin said from beside Allie. She hadn't noticed his approach.

Claire threaded her arm through Allie's. "We all grew up in the same town. I'm a few years older than Allie, but it's a small place, so everyone knows everyone. Well, except for Tim, because he left when he was really young and returned just a couple of years ago."

Chloe joined the little group, her face glowing with delight. "I'm patting myself on the back for bringing you all together. Not that I knew I was doing it, but I'll take credit anyway."

They decided to go right in to dinner because Tim confessed that he was hungry. "It takes a lot of fuel to keep this body going," he said.

"I hear you," Luke Archer said.

As they walked down the hall to the dining room, Claire fell into step beside Allie. "How do you know the Trainors?" she asked in a low voice.

"I just met them. I'm Gavin's physical therapist," Allie said. "What about you?"

"I started as Nathan's art adviser, back when I was in New York. He walked into the gallery where I worked when he started collecting," Claire said. "But we've become friends. I just brought up a new Julia Castillo painting he bought and advised him on the best place to hang it."

"I heard you'd gotten famous in the art world," Allie said. "I love it when a fellow mountaineer hits it big."

Chloe was arranging her guests around the oblong table in the dining room. "I have to do a little regrouping based on our newly discovered connections," she said, putting Allie between Tim and Gavin.

"Let's find time to talk later," Claire said.

As Allie waited for everyone to settle, she glanced around the room. Two chandeliers that looked more like sculptures than light fixtures hung over the polished wooden table with its inlaid border. An enormous Oriental rug covered most of the floor. The walls appeared to be covered in a shimmering green fabric. Another wall of windows offered a view of the Hudson River.

The table itself was set with leather place mats and gleaming modern silver flatware, centered by a row of pillar candles alternating with bowls of orchids. It was simple but beautiful in a way that only lots and lots of money could create.

Yet she wasn't the only person from Sanctuary, West Virginia, at this table. She sat up straighter.

"You're not going to spend the entire dinner reminiscing about riding your ponies down to the old watering hole, are you?" Gavin's tone bordered on obnoxious.

"We might even throw in a yeehaw or two," Allie said, amused by his crankiness. He almost sounded jealous.

Luke Archer heard the exchange from across the table and nodded, his pale blue eyes picking up the flicker of the candle flames. "Don't let him get under your skin, Allie. It's best to ignore him when he's in one of his moods."

"I rescind my apology, Archer," Gavin said.

"I knew it was too good to be true," Luke responded.

Nathan laughed. "You should have gotten it in writing."

"You forget that I haven't written anything in months," Gavin said. But this time it was a joke, not a bitter statement of fact.

Allie was fascinated by the three men. They appeared to be so different, yet the bond between them was strong and clear. She didn't think it was based solely on their wealth, although that seemed like the only common denominator among a genius tech CEO, a newly retired sports legend, and a bestselling novelist.

A squadron of servers glided into the room and placed plates of trout pâté on crisply toasted bread rounds in front of each guest. She bit into one and nearly groaned at the subtle deliciousness.

"Is this Grandmillie's secret family recipe, Chloe?" Miranda asked. "You have to persuade her to share!"

"Grandmillie won't even share it with me," Chloe said. "Only our chef, Bernard, knows the ingredients, and he is very closemouthed. Something about honor among cooks."

The conversation went on to a wide array of subjects ranging from intense to humorous. Allie occasionally joined in, especially when the topic turned to Sanctuary. Mostly, though, she savored the fantastic food and tried not to shiver when Gavin's arm brushed against hers. Or when he threw her a sideways look that invited her to share some private amusement.

She'd been close to him during their treatment sessions, but mostly he'd been facedown. Now she could see the way his hair waved over his temples and notice the tiny scruff of his dark whiskers. Like Luke's, his eyes reflected the candle flames, making them seem to dance. When he smiled, she could see how the skin stretched over the sharp, masculine line of his jaw. At one point, he put his arm around her shoulders when he extolled her skill as a PT. The weight and warmth of it penetrated through the silk of her blouse and soaked into her skin.

By the time the dessert of chocolate soufflé with warm vanilla sauce was served, Allie's nervousness had dissipated. No one bragged about their private jets or their chauffeurs or their trips all over the world. Those things were simply part of their normal conversation, as though there was nothing extraordinary about them. It made the gulf between her and these people seem as wide and deep as the Grand Canyon, but it didn't bother her anymore. She could hold her own here.

Chloe rose from the table with her cheery smile. "Let's have after-dinner drinks in front of the fire. This is the kind of weather that demands some extra warmth."

Allie wondered if she could ask for hot chocolate as an after-dinner drink and smiled at herself.

"Share the joke?" Gavin murmured near her ear as they both stood.

"I'm just being a hillbilly," Allie said, shaking her head.

"You know, there are three West Virginians at this party, and I wouldn't call any of them hillbillies," he said. "Tim's medical research held Ben spellbound. Claire advises the most sophisticated collectors on what artwork to spend millions on. And you are a miracle worker."

"Hillbilly is a badge we wear proudly." But gratification sent a flush climbing her cheeks.

"I'm beginning to understand that."

As they started toward the door, Gavin put his hand on the small of her back to steer her in front of him. She felt the imprint of his palm and the splay of his fingers like a brand on her skin. The heat spread over her back and scorched deep inside her. It was tempting to stay close to him so he would leave it there, but she forced herself to take a step away. When his hand dropped, she nearly groaned in deprivation.

Back in the den—or whatever they called the big, comfortable room—Allie made sure there was another person between her and Gavin at all times. Yet she could often feel his gaze on her. She made a tactical error and sat down on an empty couch to talk with Miranda, who had also grown up in a small town. Allie felt the cushions shift as a weight settled beside her. A delicious tingle wafted over her skin, so she knew it was Gavin without having to turn in her seat.

"Did you know that Miranda can milk a cow in under nine minutes?" Gavin's deep voice seemed to stroke up and down her back. "Can a hillbilly do that?"

Allie sat back so the three of them could see one another. "One of my best friends from home can, but I'm not a farmer's daughter." He knew that, of course.

"Gavin's pretty handy on a farm himself," Miranda said, her brown eyes warming. "Last fall he came up to my family's place in upstate New

York with Luke and hauled hay and feed, not to mention loading the cheese van."

"If you dare to tell her what I wore to load the van, I will share a photo of your husband in the same attire on social media," Gavin said.

"I thought you'd already tweeted that," Miranda said, a teasing note in her soft voice.

"That was your husband's threat, not mine," Gavin responded. "He's the one with three-quarters of a million followers. I don't tweet."

"Okay, now I'm dying of curiosity," Allie said. "Do you really have photos?"

Miranda gave a low peal of laughter. "No, they blackmailed each other into not taking any."

Allie made the mistake of glancing at Gavin. He was smiling, a deeply amused, completely-at-ease kind of smile that made his eyes crinkle at the corners, his teeth flash white, and his striking face relax into softer angles.

Thank goodness Miranda took up the slack in the conversation, because Allie was dazed by the impact of that smile. She swiped up the port she had been sipping and took a large swallow. The sweet, strong wine burned down her throat, making her eyes water.

Miranda smiled, too. "I have something to share about Gavin. He helped bring Luke and me together."

Gavin waved dismissively. "It was inevitable."

"We're both pretty stubborn, so I'm not sure about that," Miranda said.

"As soon as he won that Super Bowl, he would have swept you off your feet," Gavin assured her.

"I might not have made it to the Super Bowl without Miranda." The quarterback strolled up behind his wife's chair and bent to drop a kiss on the side of her neck. "I wasn't in great shape when I met her."

"What did Gavin do?" Allie asked. "I can't picture him playing Cupid with a bow and arrow, wearing nothing but a diaper."

Luke lifted an eyebrow. "He told me I was an idiot."

"That sounds more like him," Allie said.

"And he told me to admit my feelings to Luke." Miranda tilted her head up toward her striking husband. "It didn't go well."

Luke's face grew serious. "You had more courage than I did."

"This is becoming nauseating," Gavin said, taking her hand and pulling her upright. "Time to get you home."

Luke put a hand on his wife's shoulder. "Miller hates for people to know that he's a romantic at heart."

"And Archer likes to kick a man when he's down. Comes of being a football player, I suppose."

"I never kicked a man," Luke said. "I had defensive players to do that."

Gavin snorted and put his hand on Allie's back again. She was pretty sure her skin was sizzling underneath his touch as he moved her toward their host and hostess.

They departed with a flurry of exchanged cell phone numbers so everyone could keep in touch. Allie imagined her phone felt like a gold ingot with the weight of all those billionaires' private contact information.

Gavin was silent as the elevator glided downward to the garage. Allie made a few attempts at small talk, but he had retreated into monosyllables again. That left her to consider the unexpected revelation that he had intervened in Miranda and Luke's romance in such a significant way. She cast a sideways glance at his brooding profile while something inside her softened at the kind of insight and caring his intercession showed. Not many people would risk involving themselves in someone else's love affair.

When they stepped out of the elevator, he wrapped his arm around her shoulders to guide her toward the Maserati, which stood waiting for them. Allie gaped in astonishment. "Are the valets psychic?"

"Ed called down as soon as he saw we were leaving." Gavin waved the valet aside and opened the door for Allie.

"What a way to live," she said, shaking her head as she slid into the leather seat.

"The rich aren't really different," Gavin said. "They're just insulated from the normal wear and tear of life."

As he folded himself into the driver's seat, she said, "Where do you park your cars?"

"In a garage down the block." He steered the car out onto the street. "I'm not going to apologize for having money, Allie, because I sweated for every penny of it. I shared a hellhole of an apartment with multiple roommates for two years before I sold my first book. I choose never to live with cockroaches again."

"I'm not criticizing you. I'm just—what's the right term?—overawed."

"Good word choice," he said with a flash of a smile.

"High praise from a writer."

Gavin wove through the late-night Manhattan traffic with the skill of a race-car driver. Too soon they arrived in front of her apartment. Amazingly, there was an empty parking place a few doors down, so Gavin could pull in.

"Thanks for the ride," Allie said before she remembered the question she desperately needed an answer to. "We haven't talked about what time I should come on Monday."

"And we're not going to."

Panic and despair felt like fists tightening around her throat. "You said that the treatment is working. Why wouldn't you want to continue?" She swiveled toward him in her seat.

His hands were still gripping the wheel, but he was staring at her with an intensity that made her skin prickle.

"I don't want to be your patient any longer," he said.

"I know you feel better, but you have a ways to go before you're back to normal."

He shook his head. "I don't want to be your patient," he repeated, "because I want to do this."

He released the wheel and leaned toward her, reaching behind her head to cup it in one hand as he slowly brought his lips to hers.

The kiss was a question, asking if she wanted this, giving her time to say no. But the moment she felt the firm heat of his mouth against hers, she knew she wasn't going to stop him. She might have to share Pie's cat food when she ran out of money, but she craved the kiss of this fascinating, pain-damaged man the way she craved chocolate. It was bad for her in so many ways, but the flavor was so darned delicious.

She softened into him, putting her hand on his chest so she could deepen the contact. The moment he felt her yielding, he buried his fingers in the coiled bun of her hair and angled her head so he could lay a line of kisses along her jaw and against her neck.

"Allie, you taste like innocence and sin all mixed together." His breath whispered against the sensitive skin behind her ear, and she purred like her cat.

"Don't mistake hillbilly for innocent," she said, turning her face so their mouths met again. She teased his lips with the tip of her tongue, loving the firmness of his skin, the mild rasp of his whiskers against her chin, the crisp, herbal scent of his shampoo. She slipped her fingers into his hair, remembering the thick, slightly coarse feel of it from their treatment sessions. It had a strong texture that suited a powerful man.

In return, he unraveled her bun so her hair cascaded down over her shoulders. "You should always wear your hair down," he said, stroking it. "No, you should wear it up so men can fantasize about tearing out the pins and watching it fall down like a curtain of fire. And picture it spread over the pillows on their beds."

He took her mouth again, his hands sinking into her hair on either side of her face. She moaned as the touch of his tongue stirred a deep, simmering longing. She clutched at his shoulders to press her aching breasts against him, the delicious contact sending sparks into her belly.

He lifted his head. "We need more space. Let's go inside."

"What?" She thought of the three cramped rooms of her apartment with the treadmill in the bedroom and the kitty-litter box in the bathroom. "No! My apartment will remind you too much of the days before you sold your book."

"Does it have a bed?"

"Only a double."

"Then we'll have to get very, very close together." He smiled in a way that made her insides turn molten with desire.

"Wait here." He pressed a quick kiss on her lips and sprang out of the car.

Was she really going to do this? She clenched her hands around the straps of her handbag.

He opened her door and held out his hand, his strength evident in the easy way he pulled her to her feet. She wanted to feel that strength over her and inside her. But she halted as he wrapped his arm around her waist and started toward her apartment building's battered front door. "If we do this," she said, "I can't be your physical therapist anymore."

He sighed. "I have an alternative in mind. We'll talk about it later." He propelled them both forward again, and Allie felt a strange sliding sensation of pleasure. He wanted her as badly as she wanted him.

When she sorted out the right key, he took it from her and fitted it into the lock, sweeping her through the open door. Starting up the stairs, he asked, "How many flights?"

"Four."

He laughed and climbed faster, almost carrying her along with him. "So this is how you stay in shape. An aerobic workout with every return home."

His hard thigh grazed her hip as they continued upward and jostled each other in ways that kept raising her temperature. By the time they reached the fifth floor, she felt as though one kiss from him would make her explode.

As her door swung open, he backed her up against the wall inside, kicking the door shut behind them. Then he gave her the full length of his muscular body, driving his thigh between hers so the friction made her moan, and letting her know the level of his arousal by the feel of his erection against her stomach.

"How's your breathing?" he asked as he twined his fingers with hers and raised her hands up over her head to pin them against the plaster.

The change in position dragged her breasts against him, and she gasped and rocked her hips without conscious thought. "Breathing? What's that?" she managed to say.

"You may need resuscitating." He explored her mouth slowly and thoroughly, making her twist and squirm as desire scorched through her, lighting exquisite fires wherever their bodies touched. The ache between her legs grew overpowering, but still he held her in place.

He released her mouth to whisper in her ear, "This is my revenge for having to lie still while you ran your hands over my skin."

"It wasn't easy for me, either." She deliberately ground her pelvis against him, the pressure lighting up her nerves like a skyrocket.

He groaned and pulled back from her. "Where's the bedroom?"

She almost laughed. There weren't many possibilities in her apartment. Then she had a moment of concern. "Are you allergic to cats?"

"No. How many do you have?"

"Only one. I'm not a crazy cat lady." *Yet.* She led him through the living room by their intertwined hands. "But she sleeps on the bed."

Sure enough, Pie was curled up on the pillows mounded under the patchwork quilt. The cat lifted her head and blinked at them as they dodged around the treadmill. Allie shook her hand free of Gavin's grip and deposited her pet outside the room. "I don't think we want to share this moment with Pie."

Seeing the tall, sophisticated writer in her poky little bedroom, filled as it was with just a bed, dresser, and treadmill, made her question the wisdom of this encounter. The radiator clanked and groaned, drawing her eye to the rust-stained, peeling paint on its surface. She grimaced.

"Stop," he said, covering the width of the bedroom in two strides and picking her up in his arms.

She let out a small shriek and grabbed at his shoulders. "Stop what?"

"Comparing my home to yours. It doesn't matter." He carried her to the bed and laid her down before stretching out half on, half off her. He spread her hair out over the quilt. The burn of his eyes as he handled the strands, and the gentle tugging on her scalp, sent little thrills of pleasure dancing through her.

She lifted her hand to trace over his lips and along his jaw. "It doesn't matter right now," she said, "but it will."

"Stop," he said again. He skimmed his hand over her shoulder until he reached the swell of her breast, his fingers spreading to explore the contours until he brought them in to roll her tight nipple through the silk and lace covering it.

It was like having an electric shock except the sensation was thrilling. She pushed into his hand. "Gavin, yes!"

He pinched harder this time, so her hips lifted as the electricity seared from her breasts to the hollow deep inside her.

She didn't want a slow seduction. Lifting her head, she kissed him with all the frustrated longing in her body as she ripped the buttons of his shirt out of their buttonholes.

He laughed. The husky sound sent more heat searing through her as he went to work on the buttons of her blouse, giving her a wolfish grin when he discovered the front clasp of her bra and flicked it open. Brushing aside the black lace, he cupped her bared breasts and circled the pads of his thumbs over them.

"Oh my God, yes," she murmured as his touch made her writhe. She pulled open his shirt to return the favor, running her palms over the springy dark hair she'd been hungering to touch for days, following the line of it over the rippled muscles of his abs down to his belt buckle.

"Ah, Allie."

She kept going down to run her fingers along the hard ridge of his erection. She stroked it twice, and then he rolled away to unbuckle his belt and yank down his zipper, pushing his trousers and briefs off. She reached for his cock again, but he brushed her hands away, unbuttoning her pants and working them over her hips. She hooked her fingers in her black lace panties and got them to her knees before he took over to drag everything off.

As he shifted back up, he trailed his fingers along her thigh to brush through the hair at the V of her legs, the featherlight touch so close to her yearning that it sent a shudder through her.

"Flame-haired here, too," he said, his eyes like green glass lit from within. He slid one finger down into the wet heat, finding her swollen clit and nearly making her explode right then.

She opened her thighs to him as he slipped his finger into her aching hollow while his thumb massaged her sensitive spot. Arousal coiled tighter and tighter at every stroke. Her hips bucked against his hand when he added a second finger inside her, stretching and filling her so the pressure built to an almost unbearable point. He flicked his thumb, and she clamped her thighs around his wrist as her internal muscles convulsed and released into a burst of red-hot climax. She dug her heels into the mattress as he drove his fingers deeper so her body clenched and exploded again and again.

As the aftershocks diminished, she relaxed back down onto the quilt and opened her eyes. Gavin slipped his hand from between her thighs and propped himself on his elbow to look down at her before he put his fingers in his mouth. As he sucked her taste from his skin, his eyes burned hotter. When he used his doubly wet fingertip to trace a spiral lower and lower on her belly, she whimpered with pleasure and exhaustion.

"No rush," he said, the circling gentle but relentless. "I just want to touch."

She felt her hips rock in rhythm with his caress and groaned. "How is that possible?"

"What?" He splayed his fingers over her abdomen, one just grazing her hair down there.

"That I can be aroused again so soon."

He smiled in a way that sent arrows of heat streaking through her, then slipped his hand around her hip to wedge it between her and the quilt, kneading the fleshy curve of her bottom. The motion of his fingers made her moan and roll into him, lifting her knee up over his thigh so his erection slid against her wet center.

"Allie," he rasped, the tendons of his neck standing out. "You can't be ready yet."

"Let me be the judge of that." She rocked her hips to stroke his cock.

"Condom," he ground out, reaching around her to grab the envelope he'd tossed on the bed as he stripped out of his clothes.

"Allow me." She took the foil packet out of his hand and tore it open, fitting the condom onto him and then stroking it slowly and sensually down over his erection.

"And that's where I was imagining your fingers the whole time you were massaging my back."

"So the therapist-patient relationship wasn't working for either of us." She danced her fingertips over his balls just to tease him.

"But this new relationship suits me just fine." He pulled her knee higher so it rested on his hip and then guided himself into her with a single, strong thrust. They both let out long, inarticulate sounds of satisfaction as he seated himself within her.

"I like this even better than your hand," she said with a gasp.

He angled his forearm along the underside of her thigh and gripped her bottom to hold her in place while he flexed his hips to go deeper. For a moment he remained still so she could feel his heart pounding against her, hear his breath rasping in his throat, and look into the green depths of his eyes. It was a strange, profound moment of connection.

His grip tightened and he began to move, his pace slow but building, ratcheting the tension in her body a turn tighter each time he drove in. As sensation piled on sensation, she could no longer hold his gaze, letting her eyelids flutter closed to savor the feel of him filling the yearning inside her. He whispered her name, telling her how good it felt for him, how beautiful she was. And then his breath came in pants as he lost control, bringing them both to the edge with fast, powerful strokes. He came with a shout, pulsing hard inside her, his grip like steel on her buttock.

She shifted to bring her clit against the wiry hair at the base of his cock and ignited her own orgasm, her pelvis pushing into his as she shuddered into glorious release.

He loosened his hold on her behind, smoothing his palm over her skin as though to erase the feel of his fingers digging into her. Then he slipped out of her, sending more tremors rippling through her and dragging a long sigh from her throat. She heard the swish of a tissue being pulled from the box and knew he was removing the condom before he pivoted back and gathered her against him. She snuggled into his neck, inhaling the scent of clean, sweaty, satisfied male as the heat of his body enveloped her.

"Gavin."

"Allie?" His voice was a rumble in her ear.

"Nothing. I just like your name."

"Your name is not the thing I like most about you at this moment." She could hear a smile in his voice, but when she felt the brush of his lips against her hair, tears prickled behind her eyelids.

To counteract her stupid reaction, she fished. "Which thing *do* you like most about me?"

"That would be hard to choose. I think it's your entire lovely naked body wrapped around me." He paused. "But *you* are focused on my name."

"It's the sum of all your parts."

He laughed, creating a veritable earthquake in his chest. "Cleverly done, Ms. Nichols. I must remember that line."

She smiled, gratified that a world-famous author would want to use something she said. "When you hang around a writer, you get inspired."

The muscles of his chest moved against her breasts as he pulled the edge of the quilt up to wrap it around them. "The inspiration goes both ways."

"Really? Have you started writing again?" Hope glowed in her chest as she tried to pull her head back to see his face. But he held her tucked into him.

"Not quite there yet, but ideas are beginning to flicker in the formerly blank void of my brain."

"That must be a relief."

His arms tightened around her. "Beyond measure." She felt his lips on her hair again. "And I credit you."

She liked that and she didn't. Had he made love to her because he was grateful? "Maybe you were just ready."

"You don't want to be my new muse?" He shifted as though her words bothered him.

"I've heard it doesn't pay well."

He didn't laugh as she'd hoped. "We'll talk about that later." He ran his hand down her back in a slow, sensual stroke that lit up her nerve endings. "Right now, a better idea has appeared in my brain."

Chapter 12

Gavin came awake with the feeling of being watched. He checked Allie's breathing as she nestled against his side, hearing the slow, even cadence of sleep. Then he saw the cat sitting on Allie's pillow, staring at him in the half-light of the Manhattan night. Allie had let Pie into the bedroom after they'd made love for the second time, when the creature had begun to yowl.

The cat blinked. Gavin's father had never allowed pets in the house, and Gavin had learned not to ask. However, when he was about nine, Gavin had made friends with the cats that lived in the parking lot of his father's store. They were permitted to stay solely to keep down the rodent population and had short, hard lives. When his father caught him feeding them the meat from his sandwich, he was punished. The cats needed to be hungry to encourage their hunting. Gavin had fed them anyway.

Then one of the female cats gave birth to kittens that looked like little furry jelly beans. His father gathered them up in a burlap bag to drown them.

The remembered pain smashed through him again. He had begged for the kittens' lives. His father had shaken Gavin's hold off his arm, telling him the kittens would just starve, and then hurled the bag into the frigid water of the river.

Gavin had avoided the cats after that.

Pie blinked again and then curled herself into a ball on the pillow with some of Allie's hair underneath her.

Gavin let his gaze travel around the room. Despite the drawn curtains, it was impossible to entirely shut out the city lights or the noise of sirens, growling delivery trucks, and taxi horns. The noise level was much different at his mansion, where his bedroom was in the back of the house, its thick walls stuffed with insulation.

Allie's place reminded him of his younger self, when he'd paid the bills by proofreading for a law firm and then stayed up far into the night, writing. Words had poured from his fingers onto the computer screen in a spate of white-hot creativity. He would write a scene three different ways, just for the fun of it. Of course, he'd had no deadlines, and no editor's voice whispering in his ear that the reader needed it from a certain character's point of view.

He'd papered the inside of the kitchen cabinet doors with printouts of all his rejection e-mails, the defiant gesture a way to stave off his fears that his father might be right.

Then the phone call had come from Jane. She'd read his Julian Best novel and saw potential. Was he willing to do significant revisions?

He'd hung up the phone and danced a mad jig in front of his desk before he sat down and started rewriting. Jane had been astounded when he e-mailed her the edited manuscript two days later. She'd expected it to take two weeks.

The afternoon Jane called to tell him they had an offer from a publisher, he'd opened a new credit card—the others were all maxed out—so he could treat his roommates to a celebratory dinner.

And then he'd moved, his apartments getting steadily larger and less cockroach infested with each book sale. When the movie franchise hit big, he'd bought the house in Southampton and then the mansion in Manhattan.

He looked around Allie's room again, noting the framed posters from the West Virginia tourism department, the plaid curtain hung across the closet in place of a door, and the chunky oak dresser that looked as though it might have belonged to someone's grandmother. The high-tech treadmill stuck out in the cozy room, and he began to wonder about it. As he scanned with more focus, he noticed a pull-up bar screwed into the doorjamb.

Allie wasn't really built for pull-ups, no matter how strong her massaging muscles were. A queasy feeling hit him in the gut. A man had lived here long enough to install his exercise equipment.

He wanted to leap out of the bed and rip aside the closet curtain to check for men's clothing.

His muscles must have tensed, because Allie stirred. "You awake?" she murmured, her voice sleep slurred.

"I don't think Pie approves of me."

Allie chuckled and slipped her hair from underneath the cat. "You're on her pillow."

"Hence the glare that woke me." He felt desire stirring in his groin as Allie's soft breasts moved against his chest. He traced down the line of her back and relished her shudder in response. But he didn't want to push her too hard. "Do you use that treadmill a lot?"

Now he sensed tension in *her* muscles. "Only when the weather's bad."

"How about the pull-up bar? Is that a physical therapist thing?"

"That's left over from a previous roommate," she said, her voice tight.

So she wasn't going to talk about the man. Gavin knew so little about this woman in his arms. It shocked him that he felt so comfortable with her.

"Would you like something to drink?" she asked, throwing the covers aside.

"Do you have any beer?" That might tell him how recently the roommate had left.

"I have some really lousy white wine." She padded to the closet and pulled out a large T-shirt, which she dropped over her head, ruining his view of her body. "Oh, wait. Do you like scotch? I have an excellent single malt."

He preferred bourbon, but the delight in her voice was too good to rain on. "That would hit the spot." He swung his legs off the bed and pulled on his trousers to follow her through the living room.

The cat dodged between his ankles as he walked through the kitchen door.

"No, Pie, I'm not feeding you," Allie said, opening a cabinet and rising on her tiptoes to reach for a bottle on the top shelf.

For a moment, Gavin let his gaze roam over her body at full stretch, the rose-colored cotton fabric outlining her graceful curves, both front and back. Then he remembered to pretend to be a gentleman.

"Let me get it," he said, coming up behind her and plucking the bottle of scotch from its high perch. The fact that her nicely rounded bottom pressed against his semihard cock was a bonus. He held the contact as long as he could before she slipped away to get two tumblers.

She turned to him with a glass in each hand, her red hair rioting wildly over her shoulders.

"You look like a maenad, ready to tempt a man to madness with drink," he said.

"Didn't they rip men apart?"

"Only when provoked." He filled both glasses.

"I can think of a few times when I was pretty close to being that provoked." She lifted her glass with a wry twist of her lips. "To self-control."

"To divine madness." He touched his glass to hers.

He watched her take a sip and swallow hard, her eyes watering. She wasn't a scotch drinker. Jealousy nipped at him again.

"A patient gave me this, but it's not really my favorite." Her voice had a husky edge from the alcohol.

All right, but the bottle was a quarter empty, so whom had she drunk the scotch with before? He tasted the amber liquor. "Your patient knew his single malts."

She smiled, her eyes glinting in the overhead light.

"Let's take our scotch back to the bedroom," he said. "I have an urge to lap it out of your navel."

❤ ❤ ❤

Allie woke up naked and alone, disappointment deflating her as she realized that Gavin was gone. What had she expected? He was a billionaire author, and she was his physical therapist. *Former* physical therapist. In the cold light of morning, he had undoubtedly bolted before things got awkward.

The smell of bread toasting and the sizzle of something on the stove top revised her imagined scenario in a way that had her scrambling out of bed. She rummaged through her lingerie drawer until she found the sea foam silk nightgown Troy had given her on their anniversary. It slithered down over her bare skin like a caress. As she walked toward the kitchen, the slit on the side flared open to show her bare leg. Problem was it had spaghetti straps, and the apartment was chilly in the morning, so she had goose bumps as well as visible nipples. Not that Gavin would mind the latter.

"Good morning." She smiled as she walked into the tiny kitchen, which seemed entirely filled by Gavin, wearing nothing but trousers so his sculpted torso was a visual feast.

He glanced up from whatever he was stirring in the skillet, and his eyes went hot as his gaze skimmed down to her ankles. "I was planning breakfast in bed."

She walked up behind him and wrapped her arms around his waist, letting her cheek rest against his bare back, his abs contracting under her touch. She loved the way the silk felt between her breasts and his skin.

She heard the click of a burner being turned off.

"Maybe we'll have brunch instead," he said, turning within her arms to run his hands down her back. He cupped her bottom, rubbing the slick silk against her with his palms, before lowering his head for a long kiss.

She could feel him harden, and she twined her fingers into his hair, wanting him even closer. His mouth tasted like coffee—heady, dark, and rich. Their bodies slipped against each other thanks to the slick silk of her gown. She felt moisture begin to pool low in her body.

He gathered the back skirt of her gown up in his hands until he found her bare skin. "Wrap your legs around my waist," he said, taking a step away from the stove and lifting her as he spoke. "There's not enough room in here."

She gave a little jump and landed on his hips. The front of her gown bunched between her legs, the fabric rubbing against her as he walked to the couch, his hands on her bare buttocks. He swiveled and sat on the edge of the cushion, letting her weight settle on his thighs.

His erection pressed right on her clit, and she moaned as the friction sent a surge of arousal through her.

He reached behind his back to unhook her ankles before he locked his hands around her waist and lifted her into a kneeling position. She seized his shoulders as he brought his mouth to her breast, sucking on it through the silk. She dug her fingers into the hard muscles and pressed into the heat and motion of his touch. Every draw of his lips hurled a shock of energy from her breast to the V between her thighs. "Gavin, yes!" She felt her hips rock in time to the suction.

Then his hand was between her legs, his fingers sliding into her. He pulled his head away to blow on the damp silk. "You are wet everywhere," he rumbled before he moved to her other breast.

His fingers worked inside her, matching the rhythm of his mouth. She became a mass of pure sensation, hanging on to his shoulders as her only anchor. The tension inside her wound tighter and tighter until she shook with the desire to climax.

And then his mouth and his hand were gone. She opened her eyes to find him digging in his back pocket. He came up with a condom, ripped open his fly, and rolled it on before she could move.

"I want to feel you come around me," he said, guiding the tip of his cock just barely inside her. He put his hands back on her waist and held her gaze. "Now." He pulled her down as he pushed up, so he entered her in one swift thrust.

Her orgasm ripped through her, making her grab his wrists and bow back, shouting his name to the ceiling. He rocked his hips slightly to push against her clit to ignite another wave of release. Her internal muscles clenched and throbbed around the hard length of him, squeezing so tight that she thought it must hurt him. He groaned but said, "I want to stay inside you forever."

As the convulsion of her muscles eased, he began to move, his grip firm on her waist to position her the way he wanted. She shifted her hands back to his shoulders so she could ride with him, the ripples of her orgasm still echoing through her as he drove in and out, his rhythm building. He wrenched his hips up off the couch as he seated himself deep before he came with a roar. She felt the pulse of his climax and basked in the satisfaction of knowing she had done that.

"Oh dear God, Allie!" He brought both of them down to the cushion again. She tilted forward to rest her forehead on his shoulder. His breath whistled past her ear in gasps as they eased down from the intensity of their climaxes. The grip of his fingers on her waist loosened, and he stroked her hip bones with his thumbs.

"I want you to stay inside me forever," she echoed. Her body felt saturated with pleasure.

He groaned out a half laugh. "Even Julian couldn't manage that."

"Julian can do anything."

"I need to move you off my lap." He started to shift her to the side.

"No-o-o," she complained. "You're all that's keeping me from collapsing in a heap. Everything inside me has melted."

"Including me." He chuckled and set her on the cushion beside him, where she sprawled on her back, one leg dangling off the sofa.

He disposed of the condom while she closed her eyes to savor the satisfied hum of her body.

"I wish I could paint," he said.

She opened her eyes to find him staring down at her. Brushing at her hair, she said, "I'm pretty sure my hair looks like Bozo the Clown."

He perched on the edge of the cushion, his hip beside hers. "Your hair looks as though it's been mussed by passionate lovemaking." He picked up a curl and dragged the end over her bare shoulder. The tickle sent delight tingling over her skin.

He dropped the curl and leaned over to kiss her softly. "Now that I've satisfied one appetite, it's time to satisfy the other."

"What were you cooking when I interrupted you?" she asked.

"An omelet. I fear it will have to go in the trash." He kissed her again. "Feel free to interrupt me at any time."

"I think you're safe for at least fifteen minutes," she said, stretching luxuriously. She heard Gavin's breath hitch and arched a little extra for his benefit.

"Enough, siren," he said, standing.

She recalled the story of Odysseus being lashed to the mast of his ship so he could listen to the Sirens sing their songs of temptation without him being lured to his death. "Shall I tie you to the stove?"

"I'd rather be tied to your bedpost," he said, tossing a wicked grin over his shoulder as he walked to the kitchen.

She pushed herself upright. Her nightgown was a mass of wrinkles and showed a few damp spots from their activities.

Allie went into her bedroom, rummaged through her lingerie drawer, and sighed. She could manage sexy vamp for only one outfit. She pulled out a pair of peach lace panties with a matching bra. At least she would look good *under* her jeans and top. She squirmed into her snuggest jeans and donned a dark purple top with a deeply scooped neckline. Brushing her rats' nest of hair into shining waves, she frowned at herself in the mirror. Not exactly competition for the likes of Irene Bartram.

The sound and scent of sizzling butter made her jog across the living room. "Mmm, that smells heavenly," she said, pulling plates, glasses, and silverware out of the cupboards. "Coffee, tea, or orange juice?"

He gave her a sly look. "You."

"That wasn't on the menu."

"It was a few minutes ago." He slid a perfectly folded omelet onto the platter he'd set on the counter. "Orange juice."

She set the small round table, which was tucked into a corner of the living room, thanking the impulse that had made her splurge on a bunch of yellow flowers from the Korean grocery down the street. She poured the orange juice as Gavin walked out of the kitchen carrying the omelet platter. He set it down with a flourish so she could see the grapes and buttered toast points garnishing the sides.

He served her half the omelet with deft movements before seating himself on one of the ladder-back chairs. It looked small in comparison with his shoulders, which were now covered by his rumpled shirt.

She inhaled again. "There's a whole lot of butter going on here." Picking up her fork, she took a mouthful, discovering the cheese he'd added as filling. "Perfect. It's absolutely perfect."

"And now you have sampled one of the three dishes I make with authority."

"I could happily eat this every morning for the rest of my life." She choked a little as she realized how that might sound.

"Speaking of life, I have a proposition to make to you."

"You already did that last night. And I accepted." She gave him her best come-hither look.

"I hope you will accept this proposition with equal enthusiasm." His attention fixed on the fork he was twirling back and forth between his fingers. "You know the Julian Best books inside and out. I need someone to bring my series bible up to date." He brought his gaze back to her. "A bible is a reference document that contains all the characters, places, and other pertinent information that need to remain consistent across all the books. I had an excellent assistant who set up the bible and kept it going for the first nine books. However, he moved to Australia, possibly to escape from Julian Best. Then a less-thorough assistant took over." His tone turned sardonic.

Allie's thoughts seesawed. Did he really want her help with the bible? Or was this a way to keep her around for his entertainment?

She tried to remember how much she'd revealed about her financial situation, although he might guess what it was from her apartment. Maybe he felt sorry for her.

"I would pay you the same amount as Jane did, since I'm taking up time you might be spending with another patient. And we would work around your therapy schedule." He gave her a wolfish smile. "Your nights are off the clock, however."

She stalled. "So, no daytime fooling around?"

His gaze scorched over her. "I can't guarantee that."

God knew she needed the money, but she couldn't work out the right and wrong of the situation. Everyone seemed to expect artists to sleep with their muses. Was it okay to work for a writer you were having sex with?

She understood the problems of having a romance with your boss, but this wasn't a corporate office, so the power dynamic was different. She could walk away at any time without repercussions to her career. It was clear that Gavin found her input helpful, so was there anything wrong with being paid for her time?

She shook her head, more in an attempt to clear it than in refusal. "I don't know."

He reached across the table and took her hand, his fingers closing around hers. "Allie, I *need* you. I don't know what the going rate for a muse is, so I came up with this scheme. I can't ask you to sit around my office and talk to me without paying you. The guilt would corrode the relationship." He looked away. "I know you can't be my therapist any longer. I screwed that up."

"That was a mutual screwing up. I'm the one who's bound by the PT code of ethics."

His gaze came back to her, his green eyes storm dark. "Tell me I haven't pushed it beyond the point of no return."

The heat and power of his grip seemed to seep through her, under-mining her ability to think through all the implications. *He needed her.* She was a healer and he required healing.

"Let me think about it," she said, rubbing her forehead with her free hand.

He groaned and let his head fall forward. "Goddamn it, why do you have to have principles?" Then he raised his hand like a stop signal. "No, I don't mean that. What you are is why I want you."

"Say that again so I can understand it," she said, but he had already made her heart dance with pleasure.

"Your principles are part of the person you are, and I want your person." His smile was strained, as though he was trying to force humor where he didn't feel it.

But she had heard him the first time, and it had made her decision for her.

"I'll take the job."

A look of relief banished the strain from his smile. He squeezed her hand. "Thank you." The simple words held surprising depths of emo-tion. "When can you come tomorrow?"

Allie took a deep breath. His honesty deserved the same from her. "Anytime. Here's the thing: I don't have any other clients right now. I was working at the Havilland Rehabilitation Center until very recently. I lost my position because my ex-husband showed up drunk and harassed the patients there. Twice. My boss felt bad about it, but he had no choice. I'm still looking for another job."

Gavin rocked back in his chair. "You were married?"

Chapter 13

That explained the treadmill and the pull-up bar, but it didn't explain the shock that vibrated through Gavin. He'd thought of Allie as a sweet, fresh, untouched country girl. A hard-drinking ex-husband knocked that image on its ear. He examined her face, looking for signs of bitterness or despair, the things he'd felt when he and Irene blew apart.

But the same Allie looked back at him, her gray eyes clear, her creamy skin unlined, her mouth soft and tempting.

"How do you do it?" he asked. "Do you have a portrait tucked away in basement storage?"

"A portrait?" Her eyebrows drew downward as she puzzled over his comment. "Oh, you're talking about *The Picture of Dorian Gray*." Her jaw tightened. "What terrible sins do you think would show on my portrait?"

"Not sins. Disappointment, disillusionment, despair."

"Mama always said I was a natural-born optimist. I see the good in everyone, even when it's not there." Now her mouth had a bitter twist.

"You were very fortunate in your mother." And he had not been. "Your ex-husband was an alcoholic?"

"Troy? No. He was an actor."

Gavin laughed. "You say that as though it's even worse."

She flattened her hands on the table. "The constant stream of rejections got to him, so he would sometimes drink too much. We came here with such high hopes." She met his eyes. "He has real talent. He just doesn't have a thick skin."

"I know all about rejection."

"You mean your first Julian Best novel didn't sell right away?"

Gavin snorted. "It took me a while to find Julian, and even then, it took Jane's ruthless editorial pen to whip him into shape."

"It's rough when an editor doesn't like your character, but it's got to be worse when a casting director doesn't like *you*."

"You must have loved him very much."

She looked startled.

"You're still making excuses for him." He had done that for Irene. For too long.

She twisted her fingers into a lock of her hair, making him want to do the same. "Troy and I were high school sweethearts." She shrugged. "He's in LA now with a short-term role on a soap opera. If they like him, it might become permanent. I wish him success."

The information about her ex being three thousand miles away loosened a tightness Gavin hadn't known he was feeling. "How long were you married?"

"Five years, give or take." She picked up her fork. "You should eat or your omelet will get cold."

Five years. His omelet was already cold, but he ate it so he had time to rearrange the pieces of Allie in his mind. She'd been part of a couple for a significant amount of time. That changed a person, especially when the couple broke apart.

If she were a character in one of his books, he'd have to go back and rewrite all the scenes she was in to drop in clues about her backstory. He'd made assumptions based on his own preconceived notions, not on her reality.

"Why do you keep looking at me that way?" she asked, her tone challenging.

"Because I can't wrap my mind around the fact that you were married for so long."

"Long? My grandparents were married for fifty-seven years." She began to stack the plates. "I was a failure in the longevity department."

"There must have been serious problems for you to give up on the marriage."

"At some point you have to admit you made a mistake." She shrugged and stood up. "The one positive feature this building has is plenty of hot water, so you can shower while I do the dishes if you'd like. And if you don't mind the cat's litter box." She gave him a rueful smile.

"I'll help you with the dishes," he said.

"You cooked. I clean up. That's the deal in this household." She headed for the kitchen.

So many divorced couples he knew hurled all the blame at the other partner. His Allie took it on herself.

Walking to the bedroom, he opened the door Allie had closed, and the cat bolted out like a gray streak.

"Yes, Miss Pie, I saved you some of my breakfast," he heard Allie say from the kitchen.

The warmth in her voice tempted him to go watch her interact with the cat, but he wanted a *New York Times*, so he retrieved his shoes and socks. As he tucked in his shirt, his cell phone vibrated.

"I'm alive and well, Ludmilla," he said.

"I know, Mr. Gavin. Security tell me if you aren't," his housekeeper said, deadpan. "You have important visitor."

He glanced at his watch. "On Sunday morning? I didn't schedule any meetings."

"Is friend on unexpected visit." A male voice sounded in the background. "One minute," Ludmilla said.

"Gavin, I didn't want Ludmilla to tell you who was here because I was afraid you'd refuse to come home."

A grin tugged at the corners of Gavin's mouth. "Hugh, you son of a gun. When did you get into town?"

Hugh Baker's acting career had been launched by his role as Julian Best, but he was now a superstar in his own right. He could have handed over the role of Julian to another actor, but his gratitude and friendship with Gavin kept him in the franchise.

"Late last night. I'm filming a PSA—sorry, public service announcement—for the next couple of days. I hoped I could beg a room from you."

Gavin mentally cursed Hugh's terrible timing. "No begging necessary." He heard the water stop running in the kitchen. "I'll be there in an hour."

"No, no, don't rearrange your day to suit me. I'll just take advantage of the amenities, like Ludmilla's superb cooking."

A faint sound of the housekeeper's voice came through the phone, and he knew she was pleased by the actor's compliment. In the right mood, Hugh could charm birds of prey out of the proverbial trees. What few people knew was that the actor had a dark side, which was why he stayed with friends whenever he could. It kept him on an even keel.

"I'll see you soon," Gavin said, disconnecting. Allie was standing in the doorway, watching him. He walked over to wrap his arms around her and bring her soft curves against him. "I have a surprise guest whom you'll appreciate. Hugh Baker."

Her face lit up. "The embodiment of Julian. So you're friends?"

"Since the first movie." Hugh had known it was the role of a lifetime, so he'd made a point of thanking the writer when Gavin visited the set. They'd recognized each other as kindred spirits and gone drinking together that night. He'd been amazed when he stumbled onto the set the next morning with a nasty hangover to find Hugh filming a strenuous action scene without visible aftereffects. That was the beginning of the actor's reputation for never letting anything get in the way of his job. Directors and producers loved him for that . . . and for his sheer, raw star power.

"You should get home, then," Allie said, putting her hands on his chest and pushing.

He frowned. "Don't you want to meet Hugh?"

"Old friends need time alone to catch up," she said.

He tightened his grip so that her hands were trapped between them and lowered his mouth to taste her. When she gave a little hum of pleasure, he slid his hands down to squeeze her bottom and pull her even harder against him so that she could feel the beginnings of his arousal. He raised his lips an inch above hers. "Let's take a shower together. I want to run my hands over your soap-slick skin. And then slide inside you where it's slick in a whole different way."

He felt the hitch in her breath. "You have company," she said, but her hands were fisted in the fabric of his shirt.

"Hugh would understand." He ran his hands up under her tee to feel her bare skin against his palms. He kissed the sweet, soft side of her neck. "Not that I intend to tell him."

"Have you seen my shower?" She tilted her head to give him more access. "It's so small we'll have to take turns standing in it."

"It will force us to get very intimate." He flicked open the clasp of her bra, and she sighed without him even touching her breasts.

"I used to have willpower," she said, rotating her hips against his now full-on erection.

And then they were stripping each other's clothes off and dropping them on the floor. Allie laced her fingers with his and led him to a door in the hallway.

The bathroom was filled with standard-issue white apartment-size fixtures as well as a large covered cat box. Allie was obviously a meticulous cat owner, because there was no unpleasant odor. The silver-gray of the towels and tiny rug matched the gray-and-red plaid of the shower curtain. Allie pulled it aside and turned to him with laughter in her eyes. "Maybe if we both inhale."

He eyed the small fiberglass shower cubicle, his vision filled with the image of Allie pressed against the wall with her legs wrapped around his waist while he pumped into her. His cock pulled even tighter. "It's exactly the right size for what I have in mind." He dropped the condom on the sink and backed her into the shower, laying his naked body against hers as she halted at the back wall. She reached around him and spun the water on, the first splash of cold droplets making him howl in surprise.

She laughed and threaded her hands into his hair. "I'll warm you up," she said, pulling his head down for a kiss that sent every drop of his blood to his groin. He had planned to take his time, to explore the curves and crevices of her body as he ran a bar of soap over her smooth skin. But his plan blew to bits when she dug her fingers into his flanks, gripping the muscles hard as she ground herself against him while the now hot water sluiced over them.

Allie was the one who slid the soap over him, running it downward to circle his cock, making him throw his head back with a long groan as pleasure rampaged through him. He grabbed her wrist to rub his hand over the soap before he slid his fingers between her legs, thrusting up inside her with two at once. She gasped and arched, and he felt her fingernails on his buttocks.

Keeping his fingers hooked inside her, he scrubbed his other hand on the soap she held and found her already tight nipple, rolling it between his slippery fingers. She bucked harder against him, the pressure against his cock arousing to the point of pain.

As he worked his fingers on her and in her, he watched her head fall back against the shower wall, her eyes closed, the eyelashes tipped with droplets, her red hair darkened and straightened by the water, her lips parted on her gasps. He felt a ripple of contraction inside her and stopped so he could grab the condom and roll it on.

And then he made his vision real. He lifted and pushed her against the shower wall, her breasts crushed against his chest, her knees riding his hips, the water cascading down on top of them. He thrust up into her, hard and deep, savoring the way his name tore from her throat and her grip tightened on his shoulders. She was as wet inside as out, and he started to move in a rhythm that was nearly brutal. She panted and then went utterly still before her inner muscles clenched his cock like a fist, setting him off as she shouted and writhed against him while he pumped into her, the release coming from the soles of his feet and the tips of his fingers to concentrate low in his gut.

He kept his weight against her until her muscles ceased to ripple around him. Her head fell forward onto his shoulder, and she murmured, "Oh, Gavin," on a long sigh. If he could have, he would have stayed there for hours as the water ran over them like a warm blanket. But he could feel the muscles in her legs trembling, so he slid out of her.

While he helped her unhook her legs and ease her feet onto the shower floor, her arms remained firmly around his neck. He turned her face upward between his hands. "The water should turn to steam when it hits your skin, because you are scorching hot." He licked a drop off her bottom lip.

"That would make it hard to get clean."

"Oh, I like you much better dirty," he said.

She stood on her toes to kiss him lightly. "I'll let you have the shower so you can get clean and go home to your famous friend."

Once again he rained silent curses down on Hugh.

Allie toweled off and pulled on workout clothes while the water ran in the bathroom. As the stretchy fabric brushed her in intimate places, she felt a slight tenderness as well as little sparks of sensation. Since Troy had left, she hadn't been touched by a man. She'd almost forgotten how it felt to glow with deep-down physical satisfaction.

She picked up Pie. "I'm going to regret this in the long run, but right now, I feel so good."

The sound of the shower stopped, and after a few moments, Gavin walked out with one of her towels wrapped around his hips so she could see the long, powerful muscles of his thighs flex as he moved. He scrubbed at his wet hair with another towel, making the rectus abdominis muscles slide under his skin.

When he pulled the towel from his head, his dark hair was a mass of damp, rumpled waves. A few drops of water dotted his chest, and Allie wanted to lap them off. He looked magnificent.

Allie hugged Pie too tightly, and the little cat mewed in protest. "Sorry, Miss Cat," she said, releasing Pie onto the bed.

Gavin watched with a faint smile as the cat sat down in the middle of his shirt, which Allie had retrieved from the floor and smoothed out on the quilt. "You have good taste, kitty," he said. "That's my favorite Armani."

When Allie reached for the cat, he waved her away and picked up his underwear and pants, pulling them on with fluid movements so that now she could admire the muscles in his back.

Allie cleared her throat. "What time should I come tomorrow?"

"Tomorrow?" His fingers stilled on his belt buckle. "You're coming tonight."

"I told you—"

"That I needed to catch up with my friend. We can do that before dinner, at which your presence is required."

Allie folded her arms across her chest. "And how do you plan to introduce me?"

"As Allie Nichols. How else?" He arched an eyebrow at her before he returned to dressing.

"You know what I mean."

He lifted the cat off his shirt before he turned to her. "I do not have to explain myself or you to anyone else."

"Maybe you don't, but I have to."

"Not to Hugh, and he's the only guest tonight other than you." He finished buttoning his shirt and took her by the elbows to pull her against him. "Come to dinner." He kissed her, his lips warm and firm and persuasive.

Somehow she resisted, knowing she needed some time and space to absorb Gavin's sudden and intimate presence in her life.

She angled her head back to break the kiss. "It's better if I don't."

"Better for whom?" He surprised her by doing nothing more than blowing out a long exhale and letting her go. He sat on the bed to put on his socks and loafers. The cat butted her head under his elbow, and he gave her a quick pat. "I'll be back after Hugh goes to bed."

"What?"

"You won't come to my place, so I'll come to yours."

"I wanted some time to think."

He gave her a smile with a sharp edge. "Exactly what I don't want you to do." He stood and ran his hands up and down her arms before interlacing his fingers with hers. "You believe people care about what you and I are doing. I assure you they don't."

"*I* care."

"Those pesky principles again." He brushed his lips against her forehead and then her lips. "I just want you to know that while I dine with Hugh, I'll be making plans for what I want to do to your lovely body."

Chapter 14

Gavin strode into the den to find Hugh seated on the sectional couch reading a script. He stifled the desire to tell his old friend to go find a hotel to stay in. Gavin knew his scrupulous little Allie would think up all kinds of reasons she shouldn't be with him, and he wouldn't be there to banish them before they took root. The thought of never touching her again sent a shudder of near panic through him.

The actor tossed the papers aside and rose to shake Gavin's hand with a strong grip. "It's good of you to take me in without any notice."

"I hardly think you'd be at a loss for housing if I tossed you out on the street," Gavin said.

"Your temperament hasn't improved, I see." Hugh stepped back to give Gavin a hard survey with those famous turquoise blue eyes. "You don't look like hell."

Gavin laughed. "A resounding compliment."

Hugh sat and crossed one denim-clad leg over the other with the same elegance that he brought to the Julian Best role. "A lot of people are worried about you."

Gavin sprawled in a chair opposite him, leaning forward to grab a bottle of beer from the tray on the coffee table. "Friends or enemies?"

"Both, but why should you care what your enemies think?"

"Irene came to visit a few days ago." Gavin took a long pull from the bottle.

A look of distaste crossed Hugh's saturnine features.

"How do you manage the love scenes when you feel that way about her?" Gavin asked.

"Superb acting." Hugh lifted his beer in a mock toast to himself. "What did she want?"

"I think Greg sent her to try and drag another Julian Best novel out of me."

"Even Greg wouldn't be that stupid. He heard what happened at the funeral."

"It's not stupidity . . . it's greed." Gavin took a swig of beer. "What's the gossip mill got to say?"

"That you're burned out on Julian. There are rumors about hiring a ghostwriter to produce a new script."

Gavin stood and paced over to the window, staring out at the winter-bare branches of the trees in his garden. "They can't. I own Julian—lock, stock, and barrel. Jane made sure of that."

"You, of all people, know how much money Julian generates. No one is going to give that up without a major battle."

Gavin spun to face Hugh. "Aren't you tired of playing the suave, indestructible super spy?"

"Not at all," Hugh said. "It's an iconic role."

Gavin went back to garden-gazing. "I didn't know what a responsibility it would be."

"Walk away. You've launched careers, generated box-office gold, and lined the pockets of many an agent and producer. You don't owe anyone anything."

Gavin shook his head. "Not like this. Not when the damned movie ended with a giant question mark." He was tempted to tell Hugh about the recent feeble stirrings of his creativity, but he was afraid to touch the fragile feeling in case he killed it.

"What is it? Irene?"

"I threw her out." Gavin remembered the astonished expression on her beautiful face and felt a flicker of satisfaction.

"More people should."

Gavin pivoted to lean his shoulder against the window frame. "You mentioned the PSA. Are you here for the kids, too?"

One thing Gavin and Hugh shared was a difficult childhood, although Gavin suspected Hugh's had been far worse than his. The actor spent a lot of time and money helping disadvantaged children. Hugh would undoubtedly visit several of the many shelters he funded, but no one would know about that except the kids and staff. He didn't do it for the photo ops.

Hugh gave Gavin a look that said he knew the subject was being changed deliberately. "A fund-raiser . . . which you are not donating a penny to. You gave far too generously at the last one."

"It's only money." Gavin believed in giving back. No one should keep as much money as he had.

Hugh swirled his beer in the bottle. "Too bad it doesn't buy happiness." He laughed without humor. "I don't know where the hell that came from."

"From the heart." Gavin came back to his chair. "Shall we talk about it?"

"I'm just in the doldrums because I'm between movies." He gestured toward the discarded script. "Which is why I'm considering this rom com. It's not bad. Clever dialogue, unusual setting, emotional without being sappy."

"You let me know if you want to discuss something of importance," Gavin said. "Shall I take a look at the script?"

Hugh slid it across the table. "Not really your genre, but I'd appreciate it."

"I might pick up some pointers," Gavin said, the corners of his mouth turning up. "I've been told that Julian needs the love of a good woman."

Hugh gave Gavin the kind of evil smile Julian Best reserved for his enemies. "That will piss Irene off royally. Do it."

❤ ❤ ❤

Allie skimmed the lint roller across the quilt on her bed while Pie complained outside the closed bedroom door. Gavin might not be allergic to cat hairs, but she'd winced at the number that had adhered to his wool trousers when he sat on her bed.

Excitement buzzed through her at the prospect of seeing Gavin again soon, overcoming the fatigue caused by a night of making love and an afternoon of wrestling with her conscience.

Technically, Gavin was no longer a patient of hers as of Friday, but she knew how she had thought about him all week. Did that make what she had done last night and this morning wrong?

She'd reread the physical therapy code of ethics. Not surprisingly, there was no mention of the correct amount of time to wait after therapy was completed before having sex with a patient.

Part of her guilt was that Gavin needed more therapy, and she could no longer provide it. She would have to find him a new therapist . . . and that would be awkward. Not to mention that, as of tomorrow, she would be sleeping with her employer.

She moaned, slamming the lint roller against a pillow before forcing herself to face the facts. She needed money and she wanted Gavin. He'd offered her both tied up in one gorgeous package with a great big bow, and she didn't have the strength of will to hand it back to him unopened.

Or maybe it's that she was beginning to believe she deserved to have something good happen for a change.

Pie let out another ear-piercing meow. Allie couldn't stand it any longer, so she opened the door. "Pick one spot and stay there," she said as the cat leaped onto the pristine quilt.

Now she faced the daunting task of deciding what to wear to greet her rich, famous, sexy-as-hell lover. Rummaging through her closet, she nearly despaired until she pulled out a hanger that had gotten wedged behind the rest. Okay, she had shoved it to the back of the closet.

It was the skimpy black bandage dress Troy had bought her to wear for a New Year's Eve party with his theatrical friends a few years ago. He had told her that her usual wardrobe was boring, and he wanted everyone to know he had a hot wife.

She'd worn the dress, even though she had felt uncomfortable the entire night because the tight, stretchy fabric emphasized every curve and hollow of her body. The skirt was so short that she couldn't bend in any direction for fear her panties would be on display. Her heart had hurt as Troy strutted around with his arm imprisoning her waist, sliding his hand down to squeeze her bottom when he saw someone watching. The whole performance had made her feel cheap and vulgar.

Now she would have the satisfaction of using the dress for her own pleasure.

She rooted around for high-heeled sandals with thin black straps that crisscrossed her arches and ankles.

Then she pulled open her lingerie drawer. She picked up black lace panties before she let a devilish grin curve her lips. She dropped the undies back in the drawer and closed it.

Allie was dressed, if you could call it that, and experimenting with hairstyles when her cell phone rang.

"Allie, I'm on my way now." Gavin's voice had a slight growl in it. "And I wanted to share my plans with you."

All the breath seemed to whoosh out of her body. "Your plans?" she squeaked.

"The ones I told you I'd be working on during dinner." He began to talk.

Allie had to sit down on the bed by the second sentence because her knees went weak. Her nipples were so hard, she could feel them pushing against the tight elastic of the dress. Inside, her desire liquefied and pooled in her belly.

"Stop," she finally said as she lay on the bed panting. "I don't think that's even possible."

He chuckled in a low, sexy rumble. "Maybe my writer's imagination ran away with me there."

"Why are you doing this?"

"You've never had phone sex before?"

"Not like this." Troy had occasionally whispered a few dirty words into the phone when he was headed home from an audition, but he hadn't painted a deliciously pornographic picture like Gavin's.

"Ah, we have arrived at your doorstep."

"We?"

"Jaros drove me."

He hung up, and Allie tottered to the window to see Gavin cross the sidewalk with the stride of a stalking panther as the long silver Bentley pulled away from the curb. Then her intercom was pinging, and she headed for her door to buzz Gavin in.

She pulled down the hem of her dress, hoping there were no dark patches on the back from the dampness between her thighs. Her hair flowed loose over her shoulders since Gavin had interrupted her attempts at something more sophisticated. She had already turned off most of the lights and lit a few candles to give the apartment a soft glow.

Footsteps sounded outside her door before Gavin gave it a sharp, demanding knock. She took a deep breath and turned the doorknob.

He stood in the ugly hospital-green hallway with his hands thrust into the pockets of his black jeans, a leather jacket open to expose a V-necked black T-shirt. The waves of his deep brown hair glistened in the fluorescent lighting. The moment he saw her, his face lit with pure lust, and his lips curled into a feral smile. A shiver of half excitement, half nerves ran through her.

He didn't move, just let his gaze travel up and down her body before raising it to her face. "You look ravishing. And ready to be ravished."

She stepped back so he could come in. "You look—"

He closed the door and snaked his arm around her waist, slamming her body against his before his mouth came down on hers. His tongue swept into her mouth while he stroked the length of her back with his hands. His erection was steel hard against her stomach.

All the pent-up arousal he'd built with the phone call exploded inside her. She pushed her hands under his jacket and ripped up the hem of his T-shirt so she could run her fingers over his bare skin, tracing the muscles she knew so well and making him moan so deeply it vibrated through both of them. He splayed his fingers over her lower back to grind her hips into his, sending the electric heat of pure desire searing through her. She gasped and wrapped one arm around his neck to crush her breasts against him, throwing her head back for leverage.

He skimmed his hand along her thigh and under her dress until his fingers encountered the bare curve of her bottom. He went still for a split second before he hissed in a breath. "Only very bad girls don't wear panties. And I love very bad girls." He slid his hand higher, bunching the material of her skirt on his wrist as he kneaded her buttock.

He lowered his head to speak beside her ear, his breath blowing hot against her skin. "You know what I want to do to you right now?"

She swallowed and shook her head in a tiny motion.

"I want to bend you over the arm of your sofa, shove this dress up to your waist, and come into you from behind, hard and fast." As he spoke he slipped his fingers between her thighs, sliding easily inside her. "And you're so wet that I think you want the same thing."

"Oh God, yes," she gasped.

Before she could turn, he had scooped her up in his arms and carried her the few yards into her living room, setting her on her high heels facing the rolled arm of the sofa. He stood close behind her to cup her breasts, his thumbs tweaking her tight nipples so lightning seemed to streak from there to the knot of longing between her legs.

"Gavin, I want you inside me." She leaned into his hands, bracing her arms on the couch as she angled forward.

He pulled his hands away as she bent farther over. She heard the whine of a zipper and the rip of foil. Then he made good on his desire to yank her dress to her waist, so she could feel the denim of his jeans against her thighs and the brush of cool air against her bare bottom. She felt the tip of his cock as he positioned himself, his hands gripping her hips, and then he thrust into her with one powerful, exquisite stroke, both sating and magnifying the wanting within her.

"Again!" She spread her thighs farther apart to let him come in deeper.

He withdrew nearly to the tip before driving in again. She tightened her inner muscles around him, ratcheting her own pleasure higher as he growled, "You will be punished for that."

He gave her bottom a light smack that made her squeal in surprise. And then he withdrew and slammed into her fast, hitting some perfect angle that made her insides begin to clench. She pressed back into him so her clit found more friction. He tilted his hips to help her as he increased the rhythm of his strokes, sending her over the edge into a mad convulsion of an orgasm. She buried her face in the cushion to muffle her scream of release.

Almost immediately, he seated himself fully in her, and she felt the pulse of his climax while he roared his own pleasure. He stayed inside her, his hands spanning her hips, as she panted and shuddered through the delicious aftermath of satisfaction. She let out a long, low hum of pleasure when he slowly slid out of her. She felt the touch of his palms skimming over the curves of her bottom, and then he eased the dress down to cover her.

She didn't expect that gesture. The courtesy of it made tears prick behind her eyelids. She started to straighten, pushing up with her elbows, and Gavin was there, helping her out of the now-awkward position.

He turned her into him and wrapped his arms around her. "That was far better than anything my imagination could conjure up," he said, his heart thundering against her ear.

All she could do was nod against his chest. Her brain hadn't yet regained full functionality after their wild, mind-blowing encounter.

He moved her to the couch and settled them both so she was on his lap. The soft denim that stretched over the hard muscles of his thighs rubbed against the sensitive spot between her legs, and she sucked in a breath as sparks shimmered through her.

He started to shift her, but she shook her head. "This is perfect."

"That's the word I was looking for."

Allie's eyes closed as the rhythm of his breathing slowed and steadied. And then she felt soft little paws on her bare thighs and started to giggle.

"What?" Gavin asked, his voice heavy with satiation.

"We have company." Allie opened her eyes as Pie tried to find a comfortable way to recline on the abbreviated skirt of her dress. The cat was small, but the dress was smaller, so the cat's back half was on Allie's bare skin. Something about the juxtaposition of sweet, cozy cat and tight, slutty spandex made Allie giggle harder.

"That's not the reaction I was looking for," Gavin said. But he stroked Pie's gray fur. The cat's contented purr vibrated against her thighs.

"I-it's h-hard to b-be a f-femme fatale with a cat c-curled up on my s-slut dress," Allie said, laughter interrupting her speech.

"You looked like a femme fatale just wearing your PT outfit," Gavin said.

That threw a bucket of cold water over Allie's giggles, and she stiffened. "I didn't do anything unprofessional."

"No, and it was damned frustrating."

"Seriously." She pulled away from him so she could see his face. "I didn't indicate in any way that I wanted to . . . to do . . . this." She gestured at her dress.

He muttered a curse that included Hugh's name. "I knew this was going to happen." He tilted his head to kiss the side of her neck. "No more thinking."

"I don't feel right about this," Allie said, trying to ignore the rippling pleasure his lips were creating on her skin.

He sighed against her, his warm breath sending the ripples wider. "And I haven't felt anything so right in a long time." He let her pull a few inches away before saying, "Scruples are very inconvenient."

"Will you let me find you a new PT?" Allie needed to do something to assuage her guilt.

"I'm not sure I follow."

"I see the way you hold yourself and wince when you think no one's looking. You still need physical therapy, but I can't be your therapist." She gave his chest a gentle thump with her palm.

"I don't see why. Who the hell would know if you're still doing therapy with me?" There was a growl of irritation in his voice.

"I would."

He rubbed the back of his neck as he looked at the ceiling. When he returned his gaze to her, his look and tone were pure seduction. "There are all different kinds of therapy, you know."

"My degree isn't in sex therapy, so you're out of luck with that," she said.

He put a big, warm hand on her bare thigh and gave her a hot, sexy smile. "Surely you can give me a massage. Lovers do that for each other without any training at all."

This was a man who was used to getting his way. "I'll give you a massage every day that you work with another PT."

Exasperation banished the seduction from his face. "You are relentless, woman."

"It's one of my best traits."

He scowled for a moment. Then the thunderclouds cleared from his eyes, and he squeezed her thigh. "Done. Now about that massage . . ."

He hadn't done any PT today, but when he slid his hand under her skirt, Allie decided to give him a pass on that.

A couple of hours later, they lay in bed together, Allie on her back, staring at the cracked plaster ceiling, and Gavin on his stomach, with one arm wrapped over her waist.

"That was a hell of a massage," Gavin said, his voice muffled by the pillow. "I think it cured every health problem I might have for the next ten years."

Allie traced the line of his brachioradialis muscle with her fingertip, a smile tugging at her lips. "You did as much . . . um . . . massaging as I did."

He snugged her closer to him. "Relax."

"If I got any more relaxed, I'd be a puddle." Her body hummed with satisfaction.

"I can smell thinking."

"Are you implying that my head is made of wood?" She put her thumb against a pressure point on his arm and pressed gently.

"Ow!" He tightened his arm around her. "You shouldn't use your anatomical training for evil."

"So what exactly will I be doing to earn my pay tomorrow?"

Gavin rolled onto his back. "I knew you were thinking." He turned his head to look at her, so close that she could see the separate rays of green and gray in his irises. "You'll be assisting me. That's what assistants do."

"Where will I be working? In your office? Along with you?" She shifted to her side and propped her head on her hand.

He reached out to wind a strand of her hair around his fingers. "In my writing office, not my business office."

"You have two separate offices?"

He released her hair and stacked the pillows so he could sit up against them. "I own the house next door. It has space for my business manager, my marketing manager, my bookkeeper, and my other assistants, as well as my security team."

Allie pushed herself upright beside him, grabbing at the sheet as it started to slip downward. Gavin was quicker, tugging it to her waist so he could drag his fingers along the swell of her breasts. She'd thought her nerves were fried, yet electricity zinged straight to her core, wringing a tiny gasp from her throat.

She pulled his wrist away and tucked the sheet under her arms. "How many people work there?"

"About ten, I guess."

"So you don't need me."

The wicked little smile hovering around his lips vanished. "It depends on how you define *need*." He flexed his neck to one side and then the other. "You're going to help me write again."

Allie's throat tightened with anxiety. "How?"

"I don't know." He frowned at the wall. "But since we started talking about Julian, I'm getting fragments of ideas. Nothing I can hold on to, but more than I've gotten in months."

"So I'm supposed to just talk to you about Julian."

He levered himself away from the pillows to give her a heavy-lidded look. "Between other activities."

"That's what I mean. We can't do *this* while you're paying me. You have to give me an actual job or I can't accept your money."

He sighed. "You'll be updating the series bible. We'll talk about Julian while you're doing it. I promise you that's real work." His voice deepened. "Once you're off the clock, though, I can't be responsible for what might happen."

She eased her grip on the wads of quilt she'd clenched while they talked about her job. This time when he tugged at the sheet, she threw it aside so his lean, gorgeous body was bared, too. That ended the discussion.

Chapter 15

The next morning, Allie sat in a high-tech ergonomic chair at a sleek modern desk that had been installed in Gavin's private office. She scrolled through the series bible, trying to figure out the best method for entering names, places, and events. She was determined to earn her pay by being the most thorough, meticulous assistant he'd ever had.

"Where's Gavin disappeared to?"

The voice was weirdly familiar, and Allie spun around to see Julian Best stroll into the room.

Her heart did a cartwheel in her chest. This was the man who'd starred in her adolescent dreams of dangerous, exotic romance.

"You must be Allie." Julian scanned her with his brilliant turquoise eyes.

"You know who I am?" She rose out of her chair.

"Gavin told me you're working as his assistant. I'm Hugh Baker." He walked forward with his hand extended.

Hugh Baker, not Julian Best. "I know," she said as she shook his hand. "I just had a moment of . . ." She wasn't sure what to call it.

He flashed that famous, sinful smile. "Of thinking I was Julian Best." He shrugged with an offhand grace. "It's one of the hazards of playing a cultural icon."

"I just wasn't prepared, although I knew you were visiting Gavin." She waved at her computer. "My excuse is that I was immersed in Julian's world." And Gavin had said the actor was starring in a public-service commercial, so she'd assumed he'd be filming by now.

"My apologies for interrupting you. Ludmilla said Gavin might be here."

"He went to his business office next door for a conference call."

A frown drew Hugh's brows downward. "I hope not with LA."

"I honestly don't know." It felt awkward to stand in front of her desk chair as she talked with a world-famous movie star. "Would you like to sit down to wait for him?" She gestured toward the sofa and chairs in front of the fireplace.

He thought about it before he nodded. "I don't have to be on set for another hour or so." Sauntering to a wing chair, he sat and crossed his legs.

Allie perched on the edge of the couch. Now that she had gotten past the shock of seeing Julian Best in the flesh, she had time to notice that he was wearing a blue button-down shirt and faded jeans. "Shall I ask Ludmilla for something to drink?" She wasn't sure if she was hostess or employee, but she felt like she had to do something.

"I just had breakfast, thank you." He surveyed her again from under his slashing black eyebrows, making her feel like a beetle under a magnifying glass. It was a look Julian used on his adversaries.

"Do you film in New York often?" Allie blurted out in desperation.

His smile banished the nerve-racking examination. "Not often enough. Gavin and I used to see each other more when the movies were being shot regularly." The smile evaporated. "He says you're helping with his writer's block."

"I'm not sure how."

"He's counting on you heavily, so I hope you won't let him down." He wasn't glowering at her any longer, but she heard the warning in his voice.

"He told you that?"

"When he speaks of you, there is hope in his voice. I haven't heard that in a long time."

Allie squared her shoulders. Gratification warred with nerves. "I'm just updating the series bible."

Hugh leaned forward. "I'm not naive. Clearly, your relationship with Gavin goes beyond the office."

Allie felt the heat of a blush singe her cheeks. "I . . . er . . . I . . ."

"That's none of my business." He held her gaze with his. "But do not betray his trust."

"How would I do that? *Why* would I do that?"

"In answer to your first question, there are so many ways I can't begin to count them. In answer to your second, I cannot imagine a single reason." Footsteps sounded from the hallway, and Hugh sat back. "But too many women have found one."

Gavin muttered a curse under his breath when he saw Allie sitting across from Hugh. He'd wanted to be beside her with his arm firmly around her waist when she met the embodiment of her youthful fantasies. Then he noticed the rigid set of her shoulders and the flash of anger in her eyes. What the hell had Hugh done to provoke that redheaded temper?

"Allie, I see you've met Julian . . . I mean, Hugh," Gavin said, sauntering over to drop onto the couch beside her.

"Bastard," Hugh said without anger. "We've already been through that."

Gavin slid his arm around Allie's waist. She stiffened and tried to draw away. He tightened his grip. "Hugh's very discreet."

"Thank goodness, because *you're* not," his flame-haired imp snapped at him.

Hugh smiled. "Give him what for, Allie."

Gavin watched as she wrestled with the problem of how to subtly remind him that they weren't supposed to be lovers during working hours. Finally, she just took hold of his wrist and pulled it away from her hip. He let her scoot sideways to put two feet of space between them, since he had laid his claim to her in a clear and decisive way.

He turned to Hugh, who was watching the byplay with an appreciative gleam in his eyes. "I thought you were filming today."

"They don't need me for another hour. Something about permits."

"So you decided to bother my hardworking assistant?"

He heard Allie's little huff of exasperation as she muttered, "You can't have it both ways."

"I came looking for you," Hugh said. "Who was your conference call with?"

"A couple of foreign publishers." Hugh looked relieved, while Gavin felt a spurt of irritation. "I can handle Greg and his cronies."

"But I'd be pissed off if they were pressuring you again," Hugh said. He turned his gaze on Allie. "Greg's the executive producer of the Julian Best movies."

Allie shifted on the sofa, and Gavin felt the weight of her concern. "I take back what I said about your discretion," Gavin said, tossing a glare at his friend.

"Allie understands your situation." Hugh stood and gave her a smile with an odd edge. "It was a pleasure meeting you. Make sure he pays you for overtime."

As soon as Hugh left the room, Allie launched herself off the couch and stood with her hands on her hips. "You can't do that when I'm working."

She looked delicious with her gray eyes sparking, her shoulders thrown back so the curves of her breasts were emphasized, and her fists highlighting the hourglass of her waist.

"Gavin!"

He pretended to be startled while he let the desire he was feeling show on his face. "What did you say? I was distracted. By you."

She made that huffing sound again and crossed her arms over her chest. "I'll resign right now."

This time there was steel in her voice, and he felt the clutch of panic. He raised his hands in surrender. "You're right. I might be observing the letter of my promise but not the spirit of it."

He kept underestimating her. She seemed so straightforward, with her slight twang and her no-nonsense sass. But the layers were there. He'd glimpsed them in her passionate, adventurous lovemaking and in the bread crumbs she'd dropped about her marriage.

She nodded, her silky ponytail swinging with the movement. "Good. I have some questions about how you'd like things done in the bible." She started toward her new desk.

"Allie, what did you and Hugh talk about?"

Color blossomed in her cheeks again, but he saw that it was from anger, not embarrassment. "You told him I was going to break your writer's block, so he wished me luck. He figured out we're personally involved, too." She shook her head. "I knew this was a bad idea."

"No!" Gavin sprang off the couch and nearly seized her by the shoulders before he remembered his promise. "I put you in an awkward position, but I"—was he willing to admit it?—"wanted to make sure Hugh knew you were off-limits."

Allie looked at him as though he'd told her he'd been abducted by aliens. "You thought Hugh Baker would be interested in me?"

"And that you would be interested in him," Gavin said through gritted teeth. "He *is* your romantic hero come to life. And although I don't see it, I've been told he's devastatingly handsome."

Her eyes flashed with delight. "He is, in a movie-star kind of way." She came close and put her hand on his chest so she could look up into his face. "This won't happen ever again, but I have to prove to you that when you walked into the room, I forgot Hugh Baker was here."

She rose on her toes and laid her soft lips against his as she slipped her arms around his neck. He couldn't stop himself. He splayed his hands over her back and bottom to pull her against him so her pelvis was locked against his hardening cock.

Her mouth opened under his as she gasped. He took advantage to find her tongue with his, stroking it slowly and with intent. He cupped the lush curve of her behind, flexing his fingers into the deliciously yielding flesh. His cock hardened more as he pictured her laid across his desk, her legs spread while he stood between them and plunged into the satiny heat between her thighs.

She gave a little sigh and rocked her hips into him before sliding her hands down his shoulders to his chest and wedging her elbows between them. She levered herself away from his kiss. "We have to stop."

"I need more convincing that Hugh means nothing to you," he said, bending in a last-ditch attempt to reclaim her lips.

She leaned back to avoid him. "Time to be professional."

"Have you ever had sex on a desk?" he asked, running his hand up and down her back in a slow, seductive rhythm. "It's the perfect height for me to push your thighs open and slide inside you with my tongue and then my cock. I'd start slow and stroke in and out until you begged me to go faster and harder. Then—"

She put her hand over his mouth. "No more." But her breathing was as ragged as his.

He traced a circle on her palm with the tip of his tongue and felt a shudder run through her. If he could slide his finger inside her, he knew she'd be wet and ready. The thought made his erection tighten.

"This isn't going to work, the two of us alone here," she rasped. "I'd better go to your business office."

He angled his head back to dislodge her hand. "You don't want me to kiss you in front of the whole staff, do you?" He eased his hold on her, letting his hands skim over her tempting curves one last time before he stepped back. "Here's my deal. I won't touch you unless you touch me first. After all, you started it."

She gave a shaky laugh. "So you think I have more willpower than you do?"

"I think you have more scruples than I do." He slanted a half smile at her. "Because I have none."

She lifted her chin. "Okay, *now* can we get some work done?"

"Let me bring my chair over."

"I'll do it. I don't want you carrying anything heavy." She took hold of his wrist to stop him.

"It rolls, sweetheart. And I've recently carried you a few times without causing serious damage." He savored her blush as he ran his free hand along her other arm, just to bother her. "By the way, you're touching me."

She released him. "Not in that way."

He laughed and wheeled his chair over to her desk. Allie clicked around the series bible database, peppering him with questions about how he used the cross-referencing, how much information he needed about a character, and more.

After forty-five minutes, he pushed his chair back and rolled his head around to stretch the tight muscles. He'd wanted to savor the warmth of her nearness, the faint floral shampoo scent of her red hair, the rustle of her cotton blouse as she moved her arm. Instead, he'd had to focus all his mental powers on her queries and suggestions.

"Leave me a few brain cells for writing," he said.

She fidgeted with the mouse. "Am I sucking out all your creativity?"

"No, no. You're just making all my assistants before you look bad." His cell phone buzzed from the desk. He glanced at the caller ID to see it was Ben Cavill. Frowning, he picked up the phone. "Excuse me," he said to Allie, standing and moving away so she could concentrate on the job she insisted on doing.

He'd met Ben through Nathan and had signed on with his concierge medical service. The doctor had given him his annual physical a few months ago, declaring Gavin healthier than he'd expected of a man who spent too many hours sitting in front of a computer.

"Did you mix up the test results and just discover I'm dying of a rare, incurable disease?" he asked the doctor in greeting.

"Lord, deliver me from writers," Ben said. "Too much imagination, which begets hypochondria."

"Well, you didn't cure the one thing I asked you to."

"There's no known medical remedy for writer's block. I take it you haven't made any progress on that front?"

"A glimmer." That was all he wanted to say about it. "If I'm not dying, what can I do for you?"

"Tell me about your physical therapist, Allie Nichols. I have a client who needs one, so I thought I'd get your feedback on how your treatment is going. If you recommend her, I'll put the two of them in touch."

A strange panic boiled up in Gavin's throat. He didn't want to share Allie with anyone else. He needed her to fan the faint embers of his creativity and warm the long, desolate hours of his sleepless nights. He stalled as he walked across the hall to the empty library. "When would your client want to start with her?"

"The sooner, the better."

Gavin knew Allie needed the job. If she performed well, Ben would recommend her to other patients. "She's knowledgeable and professional and has given me tremendous relief. There was noticeable progress in just a few days." The panic reared up and howled, wrenching a self-preserving lie from him. "However, I know she's booked solid for the next two weeks."

"Damn. That's the problem with good people. They're always in demand," Ben said. "I'll keep her in mind for the next time. Thanks."

Gavin rubbed at his chest as guilt tightened around it like an iron band. But at the same time, the shriek of his fear calmed to a mere whimper.

What kind of man had he become?

❤ ❤ ❤

Allie swiveled in her chair to find Gavin scowling as he walked back into the office. "Is there a problem?" she asked. "You look . . . unsettled." Actually, he looked both annoyed and guilty, but she didn't want to voice that.

"Because there's a very sexy woman sitting in my office, and I'm not allowed to touch her." He stood behind his chair and gave her a challenging look.

Although she felt the heat radiating from her cheeks, she refused to engage. "I have another question for you." She pointed to the computer screen. "I keep seeing references to the title *Holiday Best* with character names I don't recognize. Is that an unpublished book?"

He grimaced. "It was the draft of a novella, set at Christmastime. I don't know what came over me to thrust Julian into a schmaltzy setting like that."

An unread Julian Best story! Excitement fizzed in her chest. "May I read what you wrote?"

"It's a rough draft, and it's unfinished." But he rolled her chair sideways so he could get to her keyboard. "Here it is. Just don't ever tell anyone else about it."

"Was it Jane's idea?" It was hard to imagine Gavin's decision to write about a happy family holiday. But she was beginning to get glimpses of the humanity under the snark. It worried her, because he was already too enthralling.

"Good God, no. In fact, she was skeptical but willing to give it a look."

"It seems . . ."

When she didn't finish, he said, "Strange that I would propose a warm, fuzzy story? Believe me, Julian wasn't baking Christmas cookies."

"I'm sure he was on the outside looking in. You would make the reader feel how lonely his spy's life is, how alienated he has to be from normal people to protect our Christmases." She looked at his capable hands resting on the keyboard with such familiarity. "Why didn't you finish it?"

She waited through a lengthy silence before he said, "I guess I owe you an answer. It might even help with my, er, issue. I started the novella when I got stuck on a scene in the book I'm supposed to be writing. Sometimes a change of direction helps shake loose new ideas."

He lifted his hands and leaned back in his chair, making it creak on its wheeled base. "Then my father had a heart attack. I needed to deal with his medical situation because my stepmother isn't good in a crisis."

She couldn't stop herself from offering the comfort of touch, so she laid a hand on his forearm where it rested on the arm of his chair. "No wonder you didn't feel Christmassy."

He shifted his gaze to the window. "I'd spent all my life trying to prove something to my father, and all of a sudden he'd been struck down. I had no one to brace myself against."

"What about your stepmother?"

He gave a bitter bark of a laugh. "She tried to deny me access to my father in the hospital, but he overruled her. So I could make sure he was getting a high level of care. However, at the funeral service, she barred me from the family pew."

Fury made Allie tighten her grasp on his arm. "She really is evil."

He brought his other hand to cover hers, reminding her to ease her grip on him. "I never felt like I was part of the family after my father married Odelia anyway. But when she tried to exclude me from the burial ceremony, that . . . was a problem. One I dealt with more forcibly than was perhaps necessary."

Allie tried to imagine how it would feel to be kept from saying a final good-bye to her parents.

"I didn't do her bodily harm, although it was close," Gavin said. "However, I expressed my opinion of her at full volume in front of the priest and the entire assembly of mourners."

She could picture him marshaling all the linguistic skill at his disposal to give his evil stepmother what she deserved. "I bet you were brilliant."

He flinched at her last word as a shadow of guilt crossed his face. "Whether she loved my father or not, she had lost her husband of twenty-odd years. We were two animals in pain, tearing at each other."

"She was supposed to stand in as your mother. To protect you."

"That ship sailed almost the moment my father announced they were getting married."

"Why would he marry a woman who couldn't love you?"

Gavin interlaced his fingers with hers. "The housekeeper retired. He hired her after my mother . . . left. Mrs. Knox and I got along fine for three years while my father spent all his waking hours at the family store. But her husband wanted to move to Florida." He shrugged. "My father couldn't find another housekeeper, so he found a wife instead. Odelia was a widow with three young daughters, so I suppose Dad thought she would be maternal." His tone turned bitter. "There weren't a lot of prospects in Bluffwoods, Illinois, and my father wouldn't leave his precious store long enough to search farther afield."

Allie heard the reverberations of the aching loneliness that had enveloped a small boy. A mother who deserted him. A distant father. Even the housekeeper had abandoned him. She wanted to gather the grown man into her arms and rock him like that lost child. "Your mother just . . . left?"

He blew out a long breath and looked down at their entwined fingers. "I think that's a story for another day." He lifted their hands to kiss the back of hers. "You should have been a psychotherapist, not a physical therapist."

But he'd written some of it into Julian Best's past. "Now I know why you became a writer."

"To punish my father?"

"I imagine that was a bonus. No, to make things come out right in the end."

"You are far too clever, my dear." He disentangled their fingers. "Now I have papers to critique."

"You teach?" She couldn't imagine the impatient, snarky Gavin guiding a classroom of students.

"You sound surprised."

"Well, you're not the most tolerant of people."

He laughed. "I lead a creative-writing class in genre fiction at NYU. The students expect me to be bad tempered. Remarkably, I rarely am with them."

"I'd love to see you teach."

"Because you can't picture me doing it." He chucked her under the chin with a sly smile. "Just to surprise you further, it was my idea to offer the class. When I took creative-writing courses, I suffered from the intense snobbery of my fellow students who wrote only literary fiction. I offer validation to my fellow commercial hacks."

"Still making things come out right." Her heart went soft at the knowledge that this was a man who worked to prevent others from suffering as he had. She reached out to curve her hand along his cheek and jaw, and he turned his head to brush her palm with his tongue.

"Hey!" She pulled her hand away and gave him a light smack on his biceps.

"You can't stop yourself from touching me, so why not just give in?" His voice was honeyed with seduction.

"You have papers to grade." She put her foot on the base of his chair and gave it a shove so it rolled a few inches away.

Gavin smiled and rolled himself backward, using his long legs to propel the chair across the carpet until he reached his desk. The bout of playfulness lightened Allie's heart after the shattering revelations about his childhood.

How did a man who had grown up in such a loveless home understand how to be a mentor to students and debut authors, an adviser to struggling lovers, and a valued friend to billionaires and superstars? She sank deeper under the spell he had wrapped her in, but with the fear that his magic was affecting her heart.

❤ ❤ ❤

Gavin scrawled a final note on the last page of the short story. It was by one of the students he believed had the potential to make a living as a writer. She struggled with structure, but her writing voice was quirky and distinctive, a gift of pure talent.

An odd choking sound came from Allie's desk, and he pivoted in his chair to see her rummage in her purse. She pulled out a tissue and blew her nose. Producing a second one, she seemed to be dabbing at her face with it.

"What are you working on?" he asked.

She kept her back to him. "I'm reading your novella." Her tone was clipped and abrupt.

"It must be worse than I thought." Strange that he had to remind himself to breathe as he waited for her answer.

Slowly, she spun her chair around to face him. Her eyes were red rimmed, and she hadn't quite wiped all the tears from her cheeks. "It's heartbreaking. You have to finish it."

Chapter 16

Allie felt like an idiot, weeping over Gavin's book. But now that she knew its author, she suffered along with his character even more intensely. "This story reveals Julian's emotions in a way you've never done before."

The relief that had softened Gavin's posture was replaced by a frown. "That might not go over well with my hard-core male readers."

"You've still got plenty of twisty plot and action scenes. It's the contrast with the cheery Christmas atmosphere that makes Julian's isolation so vivid. Those hard-core readers might not even notice the emotional content because it's implied, not stated."

"Because I'm a damned good writer." He ran one hand through his hair, giving it that storm-tossed look she'd come to love. "I'll take a look at the novella later. Maybe it's salvageable."

Allie decided to go for broke. "Why not make it a whole novel? There's so much depth in it, I feel like it should be expanded to give it more scope."

"A . . . whole . . . novel." He gave his hair another rumple, but his posture had pulled taut, like a racehorse at the starting gate. "An entire book set at Christmastime."

She kept silent as he tilted back his chair to stare at the ceiling.

"It's risky," he said, but she could hear a vibration of interest in his voice. When he brought his chair back to level again, his gaze was inward, as though he was already playing with the possibilities. "Let's run the idea by Hugh at dinner."

"I'm going home for dinner," Allie said. "I have a cat."

Gavin's brows drew down. "Feed it after work and come back."

"She needs company." Allie had no desire to spend time with Hugh Baker after he'd practically accused her of being some sort of con woman. She'd had her fill of actors anyway.

"*I* need your company. Bring the damned cat here."

"What?"

"The cat can have all the company it wants here."

"Pie is a she, not an it." He was getting a little high-handed. "Trust me, you don't want Pie in any of your fancy cars. She gets motion sick."

"That's what plastic was invented for. Jaros will take care of cat proofing."

Boundaries. She needed to set boundaries. It was one lesson she'd learned the hard way with Troy. "I am going home after work and staying there until tomorrow morning."

He got up and stalked over to where she sat, looming over her with a hot gleam in his eye. "Then I'll join you there after dinner."

"Not again. You have a houseguest, and it's rude to leave him alone."

He took a step back, his expression baffled and frustrated. "What the hell is this about? Hugh couldn't care less where I spend the night."

It was about setting limits before she let him roll right over her. "But I care."

"I'll tell Hugh to find a hotel room."

"It's one night." Thank goodness he was being an arrogant jerk, or she might have a hard time holding on to her resolve. "Give it a rest."

He rubbed at the back of his neck as he tilted his head from side to side. She couldn't decide if it was an unconscious gesture or if he was doing it deliberately to make her feel guilty.

"Fine," he said. "But tomorrow . . ." His smile sent a promise and a warning, and she felt an unwilling fizz of response in her breasts and her belly.

Allie was reading in bed with Pie curled up beside her when the apartment intercom buzzed. She glanced at the clock on her bedside table—10:34. It must be a resident who'd forgotten a key and was randomly trying neighbors' intercoms. She decided someone else could help the person out. It buzzed again, but she ignored it.

Her cell phone began to dance on the bedside table. "He wouldn't," she muttered, scooping it up to find out that, indeed, he would. "Gavin, did you just buzz my intercom?"

"I came to apologize." He sounded tightly wound.

"For coming here when I told you not to?"

"For being an ass."

"If you were sorry, you wouldn't have come here, because that makes you, well, an ass all over again." It sounded ridiculously circular.

"You mean I'm digging myself an even deeper hole." He gave a ragged laugh. "Please, let me explain. In person."

She heard something in his voice that concerned her, so she sighed. "You see that coffee shop about halfway down the block? I'll meet you there in fifteen minutes."

"Why should we meet in a coffee shop when I'm standing in front of your apartment building?"

She knew what would happen no matter how good her intentions were. "Because if you come up here, it will just muddy the waters."

A pause and then he said, "I see," with a mixture of satisfaction and annoyance. "The coffee shop it is." He disconnected.

Allie sat staring at the phone in her hand. A strange exhilaration vibrated through her, half excitement, half trepidation. To have Gavin Miller trek down to her dingy neighborhood late at night because he felt the need to apologize in person was heady stuff.

Yet she knew she was playing with fire. He was dark, complicated, and powerful, in ways that were far out of her limited experience. She had the feeling that Gavin had depths in his soul that her ex-husband couldn't even comprehend, much less descend into.

Refusing to dress up for his intrusion, she threw on jeans, a T-shirt, and a hoodie, and left her hair in its neat nighttime braid. Grabbing her jacket and purse, she jogged down the stairs and out the front door, half expecting him to be right outside. But for once, he'd listened, which suggested he was truly repentant.

She hunched her shoulders against the cold February night and walked the half block to the Achilles Coffee Shop, a clean but no-frills place where you got coffee in small, medium, or large with milk, cream, or sugar.

The shop held five round tables on the vinyl tile floor. Gavin sat at the one in the window with three paper hot cups in front of him. He wore black from head to toe, and his dark hair was rumpled. While she watched, he rolled his head in a circle and winced, reminding her that she needed to find him another PT.

As she walked through the door into the overheated shop, Gavin stood, the grim expression on his face lifting.

"I thought I might be sitting here alone for the rest of the night," he said, holding the chair for her.

His uncertainty pulled at her heart, so she stood on tiptoe to give him a peck on the cheek. His eyes lost some of their wildness at her gesture. "Is that why you bought three cups of coffee?" she asked as she seated herself.

When he sat, the vinyl-and-aluminum chair creaked. "I bought you a coffee and a tea. I wasn't sure which you'd want at this hour."

"Tea's good, thanks." So he did know how to let her make her own choices.

He picked up one of the cups and set it closer to her. As he brought his arm back to his side, she caught a tiny flinch of pain. Guilt jabbed at her again.

Gavin rotated his cup with one hand. "I'm a desperate man," he said, "but that's no excuse. I overstepped when I pushed you about tonight."

"Desperate?" Allie wasn't sure what he meant.

He concentrated on the revolving cup. "The Christmas novella. You got me thinking about it. I had some ideas. Even thoughts about how to resolve the last movie's cliff-hanger. Then I got pulled away for those goddamned meetings, and when I came back, you were gone." He brought his gaze to meet hers, letting her see the bleakness in them. "I tried talking to Hugh about the story." He shook his head and winced again, making her want to massage away the pain. Leaning forward, he turned his hand palm up on the tabletop. "I need *you*."

The baldness of the statement socked her in the chest. The uncomfortable angle of his shoulders tugged at her desire to heal.

But she'd nearly lost herself the last time she put her own needs aside because someone else's seemed greater. She had to remember the lessons it had cost her a marriage to learn.

She forced a calm, rational tone. "We can work on the story all day tomorrow."

He curled his open fingers into a fist. "My class meets tomorrow afternoon."

"Gavin, I can't just move in with you."

"Why not? I've got room for a small army in my house. Pie can have the run of the place. A kitty-litter box in every room, if it . . . she wants."

He made it sound so reasonable. "I just got through a difficult divorce."

"Please, tell me all about it. I want to understand you." But what glittered in his eyes seemed as much curiosity as sympathy.

"I'm not a character in one of your books."

"I know. You'd be so much easier to deal with if you were." His lips curled in a rueful, lopsided smile.

She couldn't help it. She laughed. "I can just imagine you writing me into your bed, then into your shower, then back into your bed."

"I'd find much more creative locations than those." But the light in his eyes went dark. "I wasn't exaggerating when I said I was a desperate man. The writer's block . . . it's not just about missing the deadline or holding up the movie production. Everyone thinks those external pressures are what's giving me neck spasms." He went silent.

"It's prevented you from doing what you do best, hasn't it? It makes you feel like you have no purpose." She could relate to that.

His nostrils flared as he pulled in a breath. "What's the point of getting up in the morning? To go to meetings about foreign rights and marketing plans? Other people are experts on that. I'm just there as a courtesy."

"Do you feel like your creativity is all bottled up inside you and can't get out?"

He fiddled with a sugar packet. "It's worse. There's no pressure at all. Just a vast, blank void. No world where I am in total control." He looked up at her, his eyes pools of despair. "I wasn't joking about wishing you were one of my characters. I'm not all that good with living, breathing people."

The harsh fluorescent lights of the coffee shop accentuated the shadows of fatigue under his eyes and the unhappy lines bracketing the corners of his mouth.

"I'm sorry." She didn't know what words of comfort to use, so she reached across the table to fold her hand around his. It took him a long moment to drop the sugar packet and relax his fingers into her grasp.

"I've been told I confuse friendship with pity," he said, "but I don't want your pity."

"What I feel is empathy." And an almost overwhelming desire to help him, something she needed to be wary of. In battling his pain, he might unintentionally hurt her, lashing out with teeth and claws the way Pie had when Allie tried to give the little cat medicine that would save her life.

She must have made an unconscious movement of withdrawal, because he gripped her hand with a sudden urgency. "Tell me I haven't scared you away."

"My mama didn't raise a coward."

"That's my Allie." He traced her knuckles with his fingertip, sending tiny waves of delight dancing over her skin. "I know I'm cranky and overbearing, but I thought you could stand up to me."

"When I did, you didn't like it."

He looked toward the plate-glass window that framed the dark, quiet street. "I panicked."

"You know it's not me who gives you the ideas, right? They come from within you."

"You're the catalyst." He brought his gaze back to her.

She wanted to be his inspiration. Another dangerous desire.

"I said I'd be there tomorrow, and I will be."

"When I'm with you, I believe that."

Her resolve weakened. It would feel so right to take him up to her apartment and show him that she would be there for him. After all, she was used to healing with her touch.

He released her hand. "I'm going to take my needy presence away so you can get some sleep. Because tomorrow night I intend . . . no, hope to keep you awake for several hours." He gave her a long, hot look. "Allow me to escort you back to your front door, where I will place a chaste kiss on your forehead and depart into the night."

"You don't have to go to extremes," Allie said. "I'll take a down-and-dirty kiss on the lips."

And she got one that left her knees so weak she could barely climb the four flights to her apartment.

Chapter 17

When Allie walked into the office the next morning, Gavin was staring at his computer screen. "Thank God!" he said, swiveling his chair so he faced her. "What do you think of adding a subplot about Julian's handler, Virgil? Readers are always asking for more about him, and this seems like a good place to expand his character."

"Good morning to you, too," Allie said, walking over to her desk and setting down her purse and her to-go cup of coffee.

Gavin offered her a rueful smile that made him look almost boyish. "When I'm engrossed in a story, I forget about the social niceties. Top of the morning to you. You look exquisitely beautiful today. I hope you slept well."

"Such insincerity. You made sure that I tossed and turned all night."

He raised an eyebrow. "The tea kept you awake?"

So last night wasn't going to be discussed in the cold light of morning, even though she'd lost sleep over the despair she'd seen in him. She lifted the bag in her hand. "I brought fresh croissants from the best bakery in the city, which just happens to be two blocks from my apartment building. Be nice or I won't share them."

"Ah, that explains why I was suddenly thinking of the rue Yves Toudic." He stood and sauntered over to her, dipping his head to give her a quick kiss on the lips. His were warm and tasted of coffee. Their touch sent a ripple of desire through her. She put her hand on his chest to push him away, but the feel of his solid muscles under the black cashmere just made things worse.

"Rue what?" she managed to ask.

"It's the street where Du Pain et des Idées, the best bakery in Paris, is located."

"Wait! Julian eats there in *Best of Both Worlds*. The name is so cool that I thought you'd made it up."

Gavin snaked his arm around her waist and pulled her close again. "You are utterly delicious, my dear."

"And I'm your assistant," Allie said, as much to herself as to him. She was still reeling from his revelations of the night before, and it made her more vulnerable to him.

He slid his arm away with a sigh of resignation. "In that case, answer my question."

She pulled a still-warm croissant from the bag and wrapped it in a napkin before handing it to him. "Virgil is such a shadowy figure that I'd love to know more about him. What kind of subplot?"

"I was thinking he might be forced to go out in the field with Julian. Team them up so they learn more about each other in the process. After all, Julian doesn't know much about Virgil, either."

"How much do *you* know about Virgil?"

"Ah, that would be giving away trade secrets." Gavin bit into the croissant and groaned before taking another bite. "Your first duty every morning is to pick up a dozen of these to bring here." He polished off the rest of the croissant and licked his fingers, making her remember other ways he'd used his tongue. A shudder ran through her.

She pulled another croissant from the bag and held it out to him.

"Aren't you going to eat one?" he asked as he took the pastry.

"The smell broke down my willpower, and I ate it before I got back to my apartment. So the rest are for you."

He ate the second one more slowly, giving her time to admire the fluid movements of his fingers as he tore off pieces of the flaky pastry and brought them to his mouth. It took a few bites before she realized he was dragging out the process on purpose while he watched her from under hooded eyes.

"You are a bad person," she said, tossing the bag on her desk.

"An indisputable fact." He grinned and polished off the croissant in one swallow. "Let's discuss Julian and Virgil." He waved her toward the couch. A cheerful fire burned in the fireplace, and she was happy to sit near it. He settled himself in a chair, stretching out his legs in their dark gray wool trousers.

"First, tell me how your neck feels." She'd noticed he was holding one shoulder higher than the other one, as he had last night.

"Did you bring your marching ants?"

"I told you I can't treat you anymore, but I'm going to call someone who can."

"My neck is fine. My"—he stared at the fire—"actions yesterday just aggravated it temporarily."

"Look, I'll give you a massage later—as a friend—but I want you to get professional treatment. Your writer's block may have created the problem, but it's become a real physical issue now."

Gavin shifted in the chair. "This person you're going to call, is it someone Ben Cavill works with?"

"Not that I know of. Why?"

"You and Ben spent a lot of time talking medical business at dinner the other night."

"He wanted to know more about my qualifications because he might be able to recommend me to his patients." She had hoped to hear from him by now, since the doctor had seemed very interested in her background. "It would be great for my career."

"I imagine he just hasn't yet had a patient who needs PT." Gavin dropped his chin to his chest and looked up at her from under his dark eyebrows. "Can we get to work?"

For the next hour, they slung ideas back and forth. Gavin used her as a sounding board and also as a reference to the books. Allie was a little surprised he didn't remember every detail of every book.

Gavin gave a wry shrug along with a wince. "I don't reread them after they're published. After writing the book, revising it, copyediting it, and proofreading it, I believe the book has been made as good as I can make it. Then it gets sent out into the world to stand or fall on its own merits. I feel as though the books aren't mine anymore. They belong to my readers."

"So the books aren't your babies?"

"Only when one gets a bad review." He winked.

"I thought authors weren't supposed to read their reviews."

"I don't . . . anymore. But I used to because I had to know what readers were saying. As a result, I developed a thick skin—or maybe it was just arrogance—so bad reviews no longer bothered me. Much."

Gavin's cell phone vibrated on his desk. He sat forward as though he was going to stand and then stopped. "I've gotten into terrible habits. Like answering my phone during writing hours because anything seemed preferable to the frustration of not being able to write. That stops today."

This time he rose to approach Allie. He held out his hand and drew her to her feet. "Thank you, my dear." He placed a gentle, almost reverent kiss on first one cheek and then the other. "That's a gratitude kiss." Then he slanted his mouth over hers hard, his tongue beguiling her into parting her lips so they could taste each other.

All her good intentions vaporized in the blaze of arousal that he sent burning through her. Where their thighs grazed, where her breasts pushed against his chest, where his pecs bunched under her seeking hands, every touch sent a charge of desire down to the dark pool between her legs. He lifted his head to look down at her. "And that's a kiss that means I want to take you to bed."

"I got the gist," she said, tracing her fingers over his tense anterior deltoid.

"But you're my assistant."

"And we both have work to do," she said, her voice a breathy rasp. "Just wait until you feel the massage I'm going to give you later. It's going to hurt so good."

He groaned and rocked his hips into her. "You're not reinforcing my work ethic."

"Pot, meet kettle," she said, squirming out of his grasp.

"I may have to write a sex scene to satisfy my lust."

"Does that work for you? Because reading sex scenes just makes me feel . . . lustier," Allie said, laughing, then dodging around the couch as Gavin made a grab for her.

She marched to her chair and forced herself to sit down without looking at Gavin. As his footsteps receded across the room, she sneaked a quick glance over her shoulder. He stood at a tall wooden desk with a pen in his hand, frowning down at a yellow legal pad. He tapped the pen against his cheek a couple of times and started to write.

The focus etched in the angles of his face and the tautness of his posture conveyed the intensity of a mind in the throes of creating. A thrill of excitement ran through her. She felt as though she shouldn't be watching because he left himself so unprotected, so she turned back to her computer, straining to hear the scribbling sound of his pen on the paper.

She started when Gavin's phone chimed.

He swore, and she turned to see him throw down the pen and roll his shoulders. "Time for class." He grinned at her. "I haven't been this annoyed about having to teach class in months."

"You're happy to be annoyed?"

"Grumpiness is my default setting, as you should know." He pulled a black leather briefcase out from under his desk, his expression becoming sober. "It's like the cell phone. I wanted to be interrupted then. Now"—he flexed the fingers of his writing hand—"I want to keep working."

He walked over to her and set down the briefcase. "And I want you to remember me while I'm gone."

He twined his hand into her ponytail, moving it aside so he could put his lips against the back of her neck. He touched the exposed skin with the warm, moist tip of his tongue, sending shivers of pleasure racing through her body. He moved to just behind her earlobe and repeated his seduction.

"Gavin," she breathed, as the warmth of his touch seemed to froth through her veins.

He leaned down beside her ear. "I want to do the same thing between your legs, but I wouldn't be able to stop, and I'd hate to leave a whole roomful of budding writers without a leader."

She let her head loll over the chair's back. Now his mouth came down on hers, his tongue plunging in and out until her hips rocked in the same rhythm.

"That's right, sweetheart," he said against her lips. "We'll be dancing together just like that tonight."

And then he straightened away from her, leaving her a boiling mess of unsatisfied need. "You'll come for dinner?" He emphasized the word *come*.

"Or I might just use my vibrator at home."

He smiled. "That will make you nice and wet for me." Picking up the briefcase, he flicked her cheek with his finger. "Dinner is at seven."

And then he had the audacity to walk out on her while whistling a cheery tune.

Allie raced up the front steps of Gavin's house at 7:10. She'd refused a ride from Jaros, and the subway had been fouled up. Ludmilla answered the door without her usual cheerful smile. "Mr. Gavin not here," she said.

"Not here?" He'd been adamant about her returning for dinner.

"Something happen. You talk to Mr. Hugh." Ludmilla led her to a comfortable, masculine den where the actor stood by the window, drinking a beer.

He turned, and Allie again experienced that weird shock of seeing a fictional character in the flesh. Once she got past the Julianness of him, she saw that Hugh appeared even more worried than Ludmilla did.

"I'm afraid Gavin's gone," he said.

"So I heard." Allie sat in a wing chair. She was darned if she was going to stand just because Hugh was. "Where?"

"Probably to the Bellwether Club. That seems to be his bolt-hole these days. Although no one knows with certainty. He just walked out of the house without a word." Hugh swallowed the rest of his beer in one gulp. "It's my fault, I'm afraid. I brought him bad news."

"What kind of bad news?"

Hugh walked over to the chair opposite hers with the same coiled energy he projected as the super spy. Dropping into it, he swiped up another bottle of beer from the coffee table. "All the actors who were signed for the next Julian Best movie were released from their contracts today. That means the producers have decided there won't be another movie in the foreseeable future."

So they'd given up on Gavin just as his creativity seemed to be returning. He would feel that like a physical blow. "He'd just started to expand the Christmas novella into a full-length novel." Allie was furious on his behalf. "He must be devastated."

Hugh took another swallow of beer. "He's not alone in that."

Allie stood up and paced to the fireplace and back, unable to sit still when she was so concerned about Gavin. He would plunge back into that dark void again, back to the place where he had no control over his world. She couldn't let that happen. She turned to Hugh. "Where's the Bellwether Club?"

"You can't get in there. It's for billionaires only, and they guard their privacy fiercely."

"Can't Gavin let me in the club?"

"He's gone off to lick his wounds alone, so he might not be receptive to that."

"I have to try. Do you know where the club is?"

"No, but Jaros does."

Allie headed for the door. "I'll text Gavin when I get there."

"What if he refuses to see you?"

"I'll sit on the front steps of the Bellwether Club until he changes his mind."

"I owe you an apology," Hugh said from behind her. "You're a better friend to him than I."

Ludmilla thought the plan was a good one, so Allie was quickly ensconced in the back of the Bentley en route to Gavin's club.

Allie stared at her phone, trying to figure out what words would make him agree to see her. Finally, she typed, Are you at the Bellwether Club? Ludmilla is worried.

The Bentley slid smoothly between crazily veering taxis and buses spewing clouds of exhaust as she waited. Finally there was a ping from her phone.

I'm fine.

Not helpful. Allie texted back, You didn't wear a coat so she thinks you're freezing to death on the streets.

Yes, I'm at the club.

She could practically hear him growling as he typed. That's a relief. Glad you're warm and cozy.

There was another pause before he responded. Is Hugh being a polite host?

She decided not to tell him she was on her way there. Maybe she could talk her way in. The West Virginia accent sometimes helped with that. I came to see you, not Hugh.

I'm not good company right now.

I think I should be the judge of that.

"Miss Allie, we are here," Jaros said as he guided the car to the curb.

Allie peered out the car window to see a tall brownstone with a massive stone staircase leading up to a door painted a solid, forbidding black. Carved gargoyles jutted from the building's corners and cornices. The shadows cast by the dramatic up-lighting made them seem to sneer down at her. The only indication of what the mansion housed was a small plaque by the door, on which the initials *BC* were painted in gold curlicues.

"They don't roll out the welcome mat here, do they?"

"Is not a place for people like you and me," Jaros said.

"We'll see about that." She pushed open the car door just as Jaros got out to hold it for her.

She yanked down the hem of her quilted blue jacket. Marching up the steps, she looked for a doorbell. There was none. Nor did the heavy door sport a knocker. Glancing around, she saw a camera camouflaged by one of the gargoyles. She waved at it. Nothing happened.

So she pulled out her phone and typed: I'm standing on the steps of the Bellwether Club, and it's cold out here. Tell TPTB to let me in.

It took close to a full minute before Gavin's reply popped up on her screen. Go away.

"Well, that's rude." But at least he was reading her texts. No. If you find me frozen to death out here, it will be on your conscience.

Is Hugh with you?

Would Hugh's presence be positive or negative in Gavin's eyes? It didn't matter. She wasn't going to lie to him. No. I'm alone.

Then Jaros brought you. Get in the nice warm car and go home.

So his brain was still functioning. Too bad. She waved at the security camera again and gave it her friendliest smile.

Since there was still no response, she walked down two steps and took a seat right in the middle of the staircase. She checked to make sure the camera could see her.

It began to sleet. Jaros started up the steps with an umbrella, but she waved him back to his position by the car. She pulled the hood of her jacket up over her head and stuffed her hands in her pockets, hunching over so her jeans wouldn't get too soaked. She hoped whoever was watching her on the camera would feel sorry for her.

It took longer than she expected, but finally she heard the quiet click of a well-oiled latch and footsteps. "Ma'am, this is private property," a deep male voice said from behind her. "You'll have to move on."

She turned to look up at a large man dressed in a dark suit, his hair cut short, with an earbud wire running down the side of his neck.

"I'm here to see Gavin Miller. He's upstairs in the bar."

"Ma'am, you need to remove yourself from these steps."

Allie gestured toward Jaros. "You must recognize Mr. Miller's driver, Jaros. He'll vouch for me."

Jaros jogged up the steps. "Miss Allie is friend of Mr. Gavin's. He will like to see her."

The security guard hesitated, clearly unsettled by the presence of the Bentley and its driver.

The door swung open again, and a small, slender woman with silver hair wearing a navy pantsuit stepped onto the portico. "Are you Allie?" she asked in a voice that held a lilt of Irish in its husky tones.

Allie stood. "Yes, I am. Did Gavin send you?"

"Come in," she said, nodding as the security guard leaped to hold the door for both of them.

Allie gave Jaros a covert thumbs-up before she followed the woman through the well-secured portal into the hallowed entrance hall of the Bellwether Club. She couldn't help gawking at the gigantic flower arrangement on the marble-topped table. It must have taken half a greenhouse to fill up the monstrous bronze vase. She got a quick glimpse of Oriental rugs on polished floors and a grand staircase with a carved banister before the silver-haired woman led her into a small parlor much like the first room she'd visited in Gavin's mansion. She guessed all these rich folks had to have someplace to put the unwanted commoners who dared to come to their front door.

"I'm Frankie Hogan," the woman said, holding out her hand. "I own this club."

"Allie Nichols. Thank you for letting me in."

The woman's handshake was brief but firm. She scanned Allie from head to toe before saying, "Ordinarily, I would have allowed Vincent to escort you off my property. However, Gavin could use a friend right now."

"How do you know I'm his friend?"

"I was sitting with him when your texts came in." Frankie gave her a wry smile. "He said a few things that I won't repeat, but I caught your name among them."

"Is he drunk?"

"It's hard to tell. He often pretends to be drunker than he is."

"He was thinking pretty clearly during our text exchange," Allie said. "He would have been easier to persuade if he was further under the influence."

Frankie gave her another of those assessing stares. "How long were you going to sit on the steps?"

Allie met her gaze straight on. "As long as it took."

"Come with me." Frankie headed for the door where a woman in an old-fashioned butler's uniform met them. "Jasmine, please take Ms. Nichols's coat."

Allie shrugged out of her sodden jacket, and Jasmine whisked it away. Frankie started up the stairs. Once again, Allie had to keep her jaw from dropping. The walls were paneled with gleaming dark wood while a massive brass chandelier hung from the center of a stained-glass skylight four stories above them. Oil paintings of fox hunts, sailing ships, and seventeenth-century ladies and gentlemen dotted the walls, each lit by its own brass lamp. Her ankle boots sank into the thick blue-and-burgundy Oriental runner that covered the steps.

Frankie caught her staring and smiled slyly. "It's my little joke."

"Whatever it is, it's not little." Allie shook her head in wonder.

"My members appreciate the humor of a club so clubby that it's a caricature."

"Because?"

Frankie paused at the top of the steps. "Every member made his or her fortune from the ground up. Many of us were not welcomed at the more established clubs. So I started a place where initiative and drive are valued above accidents of birth."

Allie looked at her hostess—with her smooth pageboy, the tailored suit that fit her slender figure to perfection, the fierce intelligence shining in her eyes—and grinned. "I knew I liked you."

"I'll reserve judgment until Gavin sees you," Frankie said, but there was an amused note in her voice.

Allie walked beside her into another paneled room, this one containing a brass-topped bar that matched the brass-topped tables placed at wide intervals around the room. She scanned the scattered patrons and saw Gavin sprawled in one of the upholstered leather chairs, scowling at a waiter who offered a tray with a mug on it.

"Why the hell would I want coffee?" Gavin growled as Allie and Frankie approached. "I've worked hard to get this drunk."

"Ms. Hogan ordered it for you," the waiter said, nodding toward them.

Gavin followed the waiter's movement and transferred his gaze to Allie. As he half rose from his chair, an expression she couldn't quite read crossed his face, something vulnerable and maybe even relieved. The tension in her chest softened. "Allie!" Then he dropped back down into the chair, and a cynical smile twisted his lips. "Talked your way past the fire-breathing dragons at the gate, did you? I should have known you could do it."

Allie wanted to take him in her arms and smooth down his wildly rumpled hair, like her mother used to do when she was upset. Instead, she perched on the chair beside him. "Ms. Hogan was nice enough to save me from pneumonia."

"Frankie hasn't got a nice bone in her body," Gavin said. "She just doesn't want to deal with me herself."

"Or maybe I'm trying to help you win your bet," Frankie said.

For a moment, Gavin looked baffled. "Oh, the drunken idiocy from last fall." He surveyed Allie with a speculative gaze before he shook his head. "She's my muse."

"What bet?" Allie asked, glancing between Frankie and Gavin.

Frankie lifted one shoulder in a shrug. "Evidently, I was wrong." Then she walked away.

"Would you like some coffee to chase away the chill?" Gavin nodded to the mug the waiter had left on the table. "Although it would serve you right if you got sick. I told you to go home."

Allie wrapped her cold fingers around the steaming mug gratefully, even though she didn't want the coffee itself. "Hugh told me what happened." The slump of Gavin's shoulders made her heart twist. "Movie people have the attention span of gnats."

"They gave up on me, Allie." He sloshed more liquor into his tumbler. "Abandoned me like rats from a sinking ship. And it was their goddamn idea to end that last film on a cliff-hanger, not mine."

"Last I checked, you don't write your books for the movies. You write them for your readers." She moved the bottle out of his reach. "And your readers have not abandoned you. Look at the turnout last Thursday."

"My readers. I've failed them, too." The desolation in his eyes made Allie shiver despite the warm mug in her hands.

She put down the coffee and leaned forward to take his free hand between hers. He let her, which she considered a good sign, but his fingers lay inert. "Gavin, you have the Christmas book."

"Ah, yes. I am exuding Christmas spirit right now."

"That will make Julian's point of view all the more emotionally compelling. Because you understand how he's feeling."

"It's gone." He knocked back half his drink.

"What is?"

"The spark. The idea. It was barely there to begin with."

"Are you kidding? We discussed it for over an hour. You scribbled on your legal pad for another two hours."

He withdrew his hand from her grasp. "Sweetheart, I appreciate your attempt to cheer me up, but you're fighting a losing battle."

"So you were just wasting my time and energy today. I call that mighty inconsiderate."

"I'm paying you for it." His lips curled into a hard smile.

That hit a nerve, so she snapped at him, "You insisted on that, not me."

"You should leave."

"So you can wallow in self-pity?"

"Because I'm going to say something I'll regret."

Tamping down her annoyance, she laid her hand on his thigh, feeling the soft wool of his trousers over the hard warmth of his muscle. "Gavin, come home with me."

"Move your hand a little higher and maybe you can persuade me."

She lifted it to cup his cheek. "It's a better idea than giving yourself a whopping hangover."

Stubble scraped at her palm as he jerked his head back. "I can have you thrown out. That's one of the perks of being a member."

Allie knew he was attacking her to stave off his anguish, but her temper was fraying. "Frankie let me in because she thought you needed a friend."

"You are not my friend. You are my employee and my lover. The latter not nearly often enough." He toasted her mockingly.

His repudiation sliced through her, so she pulled in a deep breath to counteract the hurt. He was just like Pie, struggling against her rescuer. Except the blood Gavin drew couldn't be stanched with a Band-Aid.

Folding her arms over her chest, she narrowed her eyes at him. "You want to pick a fight in the super fancy Bellwether Club? It's no skin off my back, because I don't know a soul here. But these are your people. You have to face them in the morning." She leaned in and lowered her voice while she held his gaze. "I get it. You're trying to make me leave. And you're just about to succeed."

He shifted in his chair as something that might be guilt flickered in his eyes.

She leaned farther in and dropped her voice to a whisper. "But I want you to think about whether you really want me to go."

She was so close to his face that she could see the lines of pain etched around his mouth and the purplish shadows under his eyes. Her anger began to seep away.

He turned his head to stare down into his glass, swirling the amber liquid while a muscle twitched in his jaw. "I'm trying to do you a favor."

She sighed in exasperation. "I sat outside in the sleet until they opened the door, so I've already proved that I want to be here. Now it's your turn. If you say to stay, I will. If you insult me one more time, I will leave faster than a mule running from a swarm of pissed-off bees." Maybe an appeal to his sense of humor would break down his reluctance to accept her help.

Not even a shadow of laughter lurked in his eyes as he raised them to her. They had darkened to nearly gray, without any light in them. He just looked at her in silence for a long moment, giving nothing away.

She held her breath. Maybe he did want to be alone to lick his wounds in miserable solitude.

"I—" He stopped and took a swallow of his drink. "Stay." Then he added a plea she never expected to hear from him. "Please."

Gavin knew he'd revealed too much, but her words had brought light into one small corner of the gaping black hole inside him. He couldn't tell if she was simply too stubborn to admit defeat or if she really cared, but right now, it didn't make much of a difference. She'd told him she would stay.

And his Allie always kept her word.

He glanced up to find that she was no longer glaring at him. Instead, her face was gentle with understanding. He didn't want to contemplate what she thought she had discovered about him.

As he brooded on that, he realized that this was the second time he'd been pitied at the Bellwether Club. Maybe he would have to find a new place to hide. Or new friends to hide from.

Friends. All of a sudden he had more of them than he could handle. That thought brightened another corner of the void.

He started to reach for the bottle before he realized that Allie had moved it across the table again. He should finish it off just to prove he hadn't totally given in. As he leaned forward to seize it, he realized he had lost interest in getting drunk.

There were other, more interesting paths to forgetfulness.

"Let's go home," he said, leaving the bourbon where it sat.

Her face lit up. "Great idea."

"Don't humor me. I'm not doing it because you want me to."

"I didn't think that for even a split second." She stood and watched as he lurched to his feet.

Alcohol affected him in an unusual way. A surprisingly small amount knocked his sense of balance askew, so he staggered as though he were falling-down drunk. Yet inside his mind, everything was painfully clear. Which was a damned nuisance when he was trying to drown his troubles in drink.

It worked in his favor this time, because it gave him a reasonable, rational excuse to put his arm around Allie. "Would you mind giving me a hand, sweetheart? Bourbon affects my inner ear."

"Conveniently," she said, but she moved to his side and let him drape his arm over her shoulders while she wrapped her arm around his waist. He didn't even have to pull her close to him, because she got right up against his body, her grip surprisingly powerful. Then he remembered that her job included helping the injured and paralyzed learn to walk again.

How appropriate.

Chapter 18

Allie could tell when someone was faking it. Gavin wasn't. He leaned heavily on her as they wove across the thick carpeting of the bar. She was accustomed to holding up those who were unsteady on their feet, but Gavin was much larger than she was, and she usually had some equipment to help her. She had to wedge herself against his warm, hard body to keep him upright.

Which was the best kind of torture, as she felt the imprint of his fingers on her shoulder, the lean strength of his oblique muscle under her palm, the graze of his thigh against her hip, and the heat of him infusing his cashmere sweater. The scent of expensive bourbon wafted past her nostrils as he exhaled a huff of frustration when he veered off course.

Either he was much drunker than he wanted to admit or he wasn't lying about how he reacted to alcohol.

As they emerged from the bar, Frankie appeared at the top of the stairs. "I think you'd better use the elevator," she said, gesturing down the hallway. "I don't want a lawsuit for two broken necks. Jaros will meet you at the back entrance so you don't have to deal with the front steps, either."

"Frankie, you are an arch manipulator," Gavin said. "How did you guess that my little slip of an Allie could practically carry me out bodily?"

"I know a strong woman when I see one," Frankie said, giving Allie a wink.

"Considering the amount of money I pay to belong to this club, I would think you'd let me get drunk here in lonely majesty," Gavin said.

"You weren't meant to drink alone," Frankie said as the elevator door slid open.

Gavin stumbled forward into the elevator, taking Allie along with him.

Frankie leaned in and pushed the lowest button. "Vincent will meet you downstairs."

"Thank you for everything," Allie called out as the door glided closed.

She thought she caught a smile of satisfaction on Frankie's face, but her glimpse was too brief to be sure.

The club owner was more proof that Gavin could command loyal friendship.

Gavin braced himself against the wall, taking some of his weight off Allie's shoulders. "I knew you'd come," he said.

She wished she could see his face to find out if that was good or bad. "You didn't make it easy."

"It was the Bellwether Club or Southampton, so be grateful I chose the former."

The doors slid open on a stone-floored hallway with flickering wall sconces that were shaped like human arms holding torches. The security guard, Vincent, stood waiting.

As Gavin staggered out of the elevator, Vincent stepped forward to lift the writer's other arm onto his shoulders.

"Thank you," Allie said with sincerity as her load lightened.

"Yes, ma'am," Vincent said.

"I feel like a sack of coal," Gavin complained.

"Yes, you do," Allie said. "A very heavy one."

Gavin laughed, and she felt him shift more of his weight away from her.

Vincent steered them out a door made of massive wooden planks bound together by medieval-looking metalwork.

"It's a dungeon," Allie murmured, entertained by Frankie's whimsy.

"But Frankie won't tell me where the torture chamber is," Gavin said.

The Bentley gleamed in the light cast by a heavy iron lantern, and Jaros leaped forward to help guide Gavin into the backseat.

Allie settled in beside him, waving her appreciation to Vincent before Jaros closed the door with a solid thunk. The privacy screen was raised, and Jaros's voice came through the intercom. "Home, Mr. Gavin?"

"Where else?"

"Yes, sir."

The car purred into motion along the narrow alleyway.

"I just hope Hugh has gone to bed," Gavin muttered. "I can't stand any more pity today."

Annoyance pinched at Allie. "When your friends care, you think it's pity?"

Gavin shifted on the seat so she could see his face, which meant that he could see hers. "Aren't you here because you feel sorry for me?"

"I'm here because you just got a body blow right when you thought things were looking up. I expected you'd want someone to talk to, to lean on. Someone who could help you through the bad time. That's not pity. That's caring." Maybe more than she wanted to acknowledge to herself.

"Well, I certainly leaned on you, didn't I?" But in the filtered illumination of the New York City streetlights, she could see the tension in his jaw ease as something flickered to life in his eyes. He slid closer, slipping his hand under her hair to hold it away from her neck. "I must reek of bourbon, so I won't kiss you on the lips, but . . ." He found the skin pulled tight over her jawline and pressed his lips against it before he licked along the edge of the bone.

Enveloped in the cushioned leather of the big Bentley and the scent of Gavin's spicy soap mingled with expensive liquor, Allie felt a bolt of electricity streak down her neck to fork at her breasts, bringing each nipple to a hard, aching peak. Then it seared low into her belly to coil itself into a hot, yearning knot. She gasped, and he dragged his lips along the tendon of her neck until he reached her clavicle. Tracing it with his tongue, he brought one hand up to her breast, his palm putting just the right pressure against the tight point.

She understood that he was seeking a different kind of oblivion than the bourbon would bring. He could lose himself in the giving and receiving of physical pleasure and forget his despair for a time. As the vibrations of his touch echoed through her, she wanted to open herself to him, to ease his pain so she could bring him back to the brilliant, perceptive man she was coming to find irresistible.

She threaded her fingers into his hair and pulled up his head to find his mouth. "I like the aroma of bourbon," she said before angling her head so she could feel the firmness of his lips and tease him into opening them.

Gavin groaned against her, the vibration adding an extra dimension to their kiss. He pulled her closer, but their knees got in the way. "On my lap," he said, his hands on her shoulders, urging her toward him.

She did him one better, turning to kneel with one knee on either side of his thighs. The denim of her jeans slid on the leather seat as the car accelerated, so she skidded up against him with her legs practically wrapped around his waist.

"Good use of momentum." His voice had gone hoarse.

She could feel his erection pressing against her, harder as they hit a pothole, even with the Bentley's expensive suspension. "Ahh, Gavin."

He slid his hands under the hem of her silky top and found the catch of her bra, opening it so she felt the bra come loose. Then he was kneading her breasts under the fabric, his thumbs rubbing over the sensitive tips, the electric sensation zinging through her. She braced her hands on the top of the car's seat and threw back her head, letting him touch her any way he wanted to because he needed to be in control right now. He pushed up her shirt and bra so that he could suck on her breasts, pulling at the nipples with his lips, swirling around them with his tongue, grazing them with his teeth.

She tried to muffle her moans, but her skin grew more and more sensitive so that each touch reverberated deeper and lower inside her. Only the hard grip of his hands on her waist could keep her still enough for him to torment and tantalize. She reveled in the feel of his fingers pressed into her skin to hold her for his pleasure. She wanted to offer him this, to make him forget for a little while. It was an act of love. The thought startled her before it was swept away under his delicious assault.

He unbuttoned and unzipped her jeans, slipping one hand into the V of her thighs, gliding against the slickness he'd created there.

"Allie, you are so sweet and wet." He found her clit and massaged it, the contact sending waves of pure arousal crashing through her. She could feel the build of her orgasm tightening and tightening. Then he wedged his hand farther down so he could slide one finger inside her, flexing it to trigger tiny explosions in her center.

"Yes," she hissed, her fingernails digging into the leather cushion as she bowed backward.

His mouth was on one of the breasts she had unconsciously thrust forward, drawing hard on the nipple. She lifted partway off his lap so he could move his hand more easily in the confines of her jeans.

He took full advantage, working another finger inside her and thrusting in and out with short strokes while his palm dragged against her clit. She could feel herself grow even wetter as he pushed in while tonguing her nipple. For a long moment she teetered on the edge of climax, held suspended in the web of sensation he wove around her, and then her whole body clenched and exploded, clenched and exploded. Her mouth opened to shriek before she remembered Jaros was only a few feet away.

She swallowed her cry just before it broke from her, turning it into a long, ragged groan. She shook with the force of containing the power of her orgasm.

"Let go, Allie," Gavin said, flexing his fingers at a different angle. "Come for me."

Her body shuddered as it tightened around him again and released. "No more," she begged, collapsing with her head on his shoulder, his hand still in her jeans and her body. "I can't."

He went still, wrapping his free arm around her while echoes of her orgasm rippled through her. She could hear the rasp of his breathing and feel that his heart was pounding almost as hard as hers.

"Mr. Gavin, we are home." Allie would have jumped at the intrusion of Jaros's voice except that her body was too wrung out to move.

Gavin gave a strange little bark of a laugh. "Take us to the garage, and leave us with the keys in the car."

"Yes, sir." The intercom's low hum cut off.

Allie felt a flush of embarrassment. "He must know what we're going to do."

"You've already done it." His tone held a flicker of amusement.

"Oh God, I won't be able to look him in the eye," Allie said. "Or Ludmilla."

"Discretion is an important part of Jaros's job. He'll never acknowledge what happened in any way."

"But he still *knows*."

Gavin did something with his fingers that brought her nerve endings back to full alert, banishing the driver and his opinions from her mind. It was hard to feel shame when a man's mouth was on your bare breast and his fingers were moving in mind-blowing ways inside you.

The car rocked a couple of times as though it were bumping over something; then it slowed to a stop. Allie buried her face in Gavin's shoulder again as she felt the car door close. "Is he gone?"

"Yes. We have the Bentley and the garage all to ourselves," Gavin said. "It's my private garage, so you don't have to worry about further interruptions."

He gave one last flex of his fingers before he pulled his hand out of her jeans. He sat her back on his knees before lifting his hand to his mouth to suck on his fingers. "Vintage Allie," he said, meeting her eyes with a look of pure lust.

Then he shifted and flipped her onto her back on the seat beside him, yanking her jeans down over her hips. She helped him work them off and then dragged her top and bra over her head.

He knelt between her thighs, his arm braced on the seat back as he swayed slightly. "You glow against the black leather." He used one index finger to trace a line from her forehead down over her lips, her neck, between her breasts, her abdomen, to the yearning place between her legs. "I want another taste," he said before he scooped his hands under her buttocks and tilted her upward as he lowered his head to meet her.

He put his mouth there, swirling his tongue around her clit before dipping the tip inside her. He stopped to blow a warm breath against her. "You taste like the mountains and the sea together, earth and salt." Then he licked her again, sparking little shocks deep within her, making her go liquid, causing tiny mews of pleasure to climb out of her throat.

She buried her fingers in his thick, dark hair, not sure whether to hold him there or pull him away as he teased her in already sensitized places.

But he brought the delicious torment to a stop, lowering her to the seat and disentangling his hair from her grip. "The taste of you is too good," he said, pulling a condom out of his pocket and unzipping his trousers to roll it onto his erection. "I need to be inside you."

He pulled her knees up to his hips, seated the tip of his cock just barely inside her, and buried himself in her with one hard thrust. She cried out at the same time he did, their voices combining in a single animal shout.

The swell and glide of him deep within her made her earlier orgasm seem somehow less because he hadn't been fully there with her. Now she could feel the power and pulse of him in the most intimate places. He moved, his hands wrapped around her knees holding her up off the seat, so he could drive in and pull out at the angle he wanted. He started slowly, thrusting and withdrawing in a deliberate, sensual rhythm, his breath sounding in the same tempo.

She opened her eyes to find his gaze locked on the place where their bodies came together, watching himself invade and withdraw. It sent a thrill rippling through her, and she tightened her inner muscles around him as he slid fully into her.

He met her gaze. "Minx," he rasped. And then he let himself go, closing his eyes as he drove into her faster, harder, deeper, while he groaned out her name over and over again like an incantation.

She felt the tension coiling inside her, the motion of his cock and the friction of his trousers against her clit enough to stoke her arousal again. Even his dark, husky voice seemed like a caress.

And then his grip turned to iron as he plunged into her and stayed, shouting and pulsing, so that her orgasm went off just seconds later than his, the joint convulsion seeming as though it would blow out the windows of the car.

As the cataclysm inside her quieted, Allie unclenched her fingers from the edge of the seat she held in a crazed grip above her head. She hoped she hadn't left fingernail marks in the expensive leather. Gavin's grasp on her hips gentled, too, and he eased himself out of her so he could lower her hips to the seat.

She gave a little moan at the absence of him.

"Are you all right?" he asked, stroking down her thighs with a featherlight touch.

She opened her eyes to see concern darkening his eyes as he knelt with his shoulder wedged against the seat. "*All right* would be an understatement."

His smile was relieved. Flipping open a compartment in the big car, he disposed of the condom. Allie noticed the fog on the car windows and lifted her arm to flatten her palm against the steamy glass. "This is so *Titanic*."

"I certainly felt the earth move," Gavin said, rolling her onto her side so he could lie on the seat beside her.

"No, the movie *Titanic*. When they make love in the car and steam all the windows up."

"Oh God, no! Don't compare us to that treacly costume disaster."

The cashmere of his sweater and the wool of his trousers were soft and warm against her bare skin as she snuggled close. "You mean you've never stood on a railing, held your arms out, and yelled, 'I'm the king of the world'?"

He snorted before wrapping his arm tightly around her waist and tangling his legs with hers. "Right here and now, I feel like the king of the world. No doomed ocean liner necessary."

She liked that, even though it was strange to realize that he was still fully dressed, and she didn't have a stitch of clothing on. "You know that French painting of a picnic in the park where the men are in these starchy suits and the woman is naked?" she said. "That's how I feel."

"You're talking about Manet's *Le déjeuner sur l'herbe*." The deep rumble of his voice vibrated against her back. "Were you shocked by it, like all the prim art critics of the time?"

"Well, yes. It's meant to be shocking. But I liked her confidence. She just sat there, looking at whoever was painting her picture, as though there was nothing strange about being naked outdoors with a couple of overdressed men." Allie cast back to the art history course she had enjoyed more than she expected, trying to remember the painting more clearly. "It's sexy, too. Like she's undressed so they can look at her and touch her. I always wondered if the woman in the background was bathing before or after she had sex with the men. It's clearly a small orgy." She could feel Gavin shaking against her and tried to twist her head around to see why.

His shout of laughter ricocheted around the confines of the car.

She allowed a smile to curl the corners of her lips. She'd made him laugh when, a half an hour ago, he'd been at the bottom of an abyss of despair.

"A small orgy," he stuttered between chuckles. "Isn't that an oxymoron?"

"Not to my mind."

His lips brushed her bare shoulder. "You are so good for me, my flame-haired sprite."

"Your *what*?"

"Have I never said that out loud before? That's how I think of you."

She liked the flame-haired part, even though it was way too poetic for her carrot-top. "A sprite? What do you mean by that, exactly?"

"A small creature with magical powers. *Mighty* magical powers."

"Okay. I'll take it." Lulled by the heat of his body, the satiation of her own, and the coziness of the car, her eyelids drifted closed.

"Allie."

She came awake with a start, staring around in confusion for a second before she registered the solid wall of Gavin's body against her back.

"Could we go back to your house tonight?" he asked, his voice strained. "I don't want to face Hugh just yet."

"Pie would love to see you again," she said, trying to wriggle out of his grasp to reach for her bra. "There's nothing she likes to sleep on more than Armani."

His grip tightened. "You don't have to move yet. It felt good to have you go loose and relaxed in my arms."

"So you weren't insulted?" Allie snagged her shirt and the bra tangled with it.

"Sleep is something to be treasured when you can't have it."

"We can sleep at my house in a nice soft bed. Not that I don't love leather against my skin." She twisted to give him a teasing smile.

"You're giving me ideas."

"Isn't that what a muse is supposed to do?"

He kissed her shoulder again and let her sit up, tracing his finger down her spine before he shoved himself upright.

She quickly shimmied back into her clothing, even as she felt the weight of his gaze on her. As soon as she was decent, he swung the door open, offering her a hand as she scrambled out.

"Oh. My. God," she said, letting her mouth drop open while she looked around the garage.

The floor was red brick, the walls were white brick, and the ceiling was white brick formed into vaults like a medieval church, from which hung a huge stainless-steel-and-glass chandelier. Six cars in various sleek shapes were arrayed around the space, their highly polished metal skins gleaming in the light. In the wall facing her were two arches, one with a brushed-steel door large enough for a car to pass through, and the other with a human-size door of the same metal.

"Are all these cars yours?" she asked.

"Remember my antique-collecting phase? I went through a car-collecting phase, too." He leaned his hip against the Bentley. "Pick a car, any car."

She surveyed the selection and decided the Maserati looked the most like a normal vehicle. "The Maz."

"My personal favorite, but you've experienced that one. Why not the Ferrari or the Lamborghini?"

"Because I'm driving, and I don't want to mess with those."

"I'm perfectly capable of driving," he said. "I only stagger a bit."

"Which means that if the police stop you and tell you to walk the line, you'll be in big trouble."

He pushed away from the Bentley, positioned himself on a line of bricks that ran straight across the floor, and focused his gaze downward as he put one foot directly in front of the other. When he reached the far wall, he threw her a look of triumph. "Straight as an arrow with nary a wobble."

"I'm still driving." Although it made her nervous to think about the perils of crazy cab drivers coming near such an expensive vehicle.

"Can you handle a manual transmission?"

"I can handle a tractor pulling a chisel plow."

"If I ever need a field tilled, I'll make sure to call you." He tapped in a string of characters on a keypad, causing a panel to slide back and reveal a dozen sets of keys hung in neat rows. He unhooked a set, and the panel slid closed.

"What are the extra keys for?"

"The cars out at my Southampton house," he said, weaving slightly as he walked to the low-slung black Maserati. He held open the driver's door for her and offered her the keys.

Allie shook her head in amazement as she got in the car. Sometimes she just plain forgot how rich he was. Maybe that was a good thing.

Her nerves ratcheted up another notch as she surveyed the array of dials and digital readouts on the high-end control panel. Gavin dropped into the passenger seat and pointed out the basics for her. She took a deep breath and punched the ignition. The car's big engine purred to life. She shifted into low and eased forward as Gavin pushed a button that lifted the garage door. Once out on the street, she tested the feel of the steering and the gearshift, finding both to be responsive and silky. "I could get used to this," she said, doing a smooth shift.

"Borrow it anytime you like."

"Ha! I wouldn't even know where to get gas for it."

Gavin was quiet on the ride downtown to her apartment, and she let him be, since she needed to concentrate on keeping the Maserati's paint unmarred. Her body hummed with satisfaction, both from the sex and from knowing she had gotten him away from the bourbon bottle.

She'd never succeeded in doing that with Troy. Once her ex-husband started drinking to dull the sting of yet another rejection, nothing she did could stop him until he passed out. It reassured her to find out that Gavin didn't climb into a liquor bottle and drown there.

She sneaked a quick glance at the man sitting beside her. His profile was washed by the multicolored city lights, but she couldn't discern any emotion in it. He was a complicated man, and he generated a whole mix of feelings in her, some positive, some less so.

What was with her and creative types? Troy the actor. Gavin the writer. Why couldn't she be attracted to a nice, stable accountant every now and then?

Her earlier thought about love popped into her brain, but she brushed it away as an overreaction.

She maneuvered the car into a parking spot half a block from her building and turned off the engine with a sigh of relief.

"Thank you," he said.

"For?"

"Taking me in tonight."

With those words he had her in his power again. He could have stayed in the presidential suite in any hotel in the city, yet he felt grateful for her tiny apartment with its four-story climb and water-stained ceilings.

"I couldn't leave you to sleep in your car," she said. "Any of them."

His laugh sounded rusty, but it was another laugh. He came around to hold the door she had already pushed open. As she stood, he draped one arm around her shoulders and scanned the streetscape. "Sometimes I wish . . ." He turned them toward Allie's building.

"That you hadn't made gazillions of dollars so you still lived in a place like this?" Allie asked. "That you'd never gotten a Julian Best book published, much less sold millions of copies and made movies out of them?"

"When you put it like that—" He shook his head. "I don't know what I wish."

"You wish for what we all do. All the good and none of the bad." Allie pulled her keys out and shoved one into the scratched-up lock.

Gavin pushed open the door, and the reek of someone's dinner cooked hours earlier smacked her in the nose. "Seriously, would you really want to live here again?" she asked.

"It all depends on whom you're living with," he said. "It takes people to make a home."

The loneliness in his voice made Allie's heart twist. "People can just as easily mess up a home, too."

"That's my line, not yours." He stutter-stepped and banged into the wall.

She looked up the long, uneven staircase. "Are you going to be able to get up the stairs?"

He levered himself away from the wall, but she saw the muscle in his jaw clench. "I just wasn't paying attention." He gave her a wicked look. "All the physical activity has burned away the effects of the alcohol."

"I'll walk beside you to help you balance," she said, stepping close to him.

He waved her away with an irritated gesture. "If I fall, I don't want to have your broken neck on my conscience. Go ahead."

With reluctance, she started up the linoleum-covered stairs, listening for his footsteps behind her. They sounded steady and even, so she kept trudging upward. When they reached her landing, Allie opened the door and called the cat's name. Pie strolled up, blinking her golden eyes.

Gavin closed the door behind them. "I thought only dogs came when called."

Allie picked up the cat and rubbed her cheek against Pie's soft fur. "She's a very sociable little cat. That's why I don't like to leave her alone too long. Troy was usually at home during the day, and I was home in the evening, so Pie always had a lap to sit on."

"Troy." Gavin's tone had an edge to it. "I keep forgetting about him."

"I wish I could." Allie went into the kitchen and pulled two bottles of water out of the refrigerator. "No, I don't mean that. He got me here to the big city."

Gavin had followed her and took the bottle of water she offered, twisting off the cap and taking several long gulps. She enjoyed watching the muscles in his throat move under the skin as he swallowed.

He lowered the bottle. "So, no regrets?"

She took a sip of water. "Remember when you said that you want who I am? The way I see it, I wouldn't be this person if I hadn't gone through all the experiences I have. They've worked on the raw material of me and turned it into this particular Allie Nichols."

"What doesn't kill you makes you stronger?" Gavin stared over her head. "But sometimes it does kill you."

Allie set the water on the counter and put her hands on either side of his face to tilt it down to meet her gaze. "You aren't dead by a long shot."

"I suppose not. The dead feel no pain."

"What you need is to have Pie sit on your lap and purr. It always makes me feel better."

"I was thinking more along the lines of having *you* sit on my lap." He ran the back of his fingers down her cheek before lowering his mouth to hers. His lips were cold from the water, but the inside of his mouth was hot when he invited her tongue to enter. That sent a spiral of heat twisting down between her thighs.

He lifted his head to look down at her from under half-closed eye-lids. "When I'm inside you, I feel unquestionably alive."

Afterward Gavin tried to sleep, but when he closed his eyes, Hugh's face materialized, his blazing blue gaze clouded with worry as he told Gavin the bad news. Allie was right: he had felt it as a physical blow when Hugh told him.

Now he was pissed off.

He had never missed a deadline before in his entire writing career. He'd allowed the scriptwriters to change the ending of the last movie against his better judgment. He'd donned a tuxedo in both snow and sweltering heat to support every damned movie's premiere in whatever city they'd sent him to. He'd smiled through vapid three-minute inter-views on every mindless talk show the PR team had booked him on. And after all that, they had given up on him.

Anger coursed through him, making him practically vibrate. He would blow their tiny Hollywood minds with the next Julian Best book. It would be so far beyond their expectations, they wouldn't know how to handle it.

He decided to heighten the emotion beyond even what he and Allie had discussed. Maybe he would kill off Samantha Dubois. He could do it right at the beginning of the book to grab the readers by the throat.

He smiled an evil smile as he imagined Irene's reaction. He felt the smile turning into a chuckle, and it hit him.

The blackness was gone. The woman curled in his arms had ban-ished it.

He looked down at her profile, at the creamy shoulder peeking out from under the comforter, at the spill of red hair across his chest and pillow. Yes, she had given him comfort with her body, but that wasn't what had pulled him back from the abyss.

It was the caring that sent her out into the sleety February night when he was hurting. The determination that wouldn't let the dragons guarding the Bellwether Club stop her from reaching out to him. It was the loyalty that kept her from leaving him, no matter how many insults he flung at her.

For a long moment, he wrapped himself in the security of Allie's presence, letting her permeate every cell of his body, every dark corner of his mind and heart. It was like floating in the sun-warmed azure water of the Caribbean Sea, the gentle waves cradling him. He basked in the sense of buoyancy, of being held safe, a hand always there when he reached out.

Allie shifted, murmuring something unintelligible in her sleep before settling back against his side.

Fear sliced through him like a razor-edged knife. No other woman had ever stayed, so why did he think she would be different? What could he hold her with? Charm was not his long suit, so that wouldn't work.

He controlled Julian Best, her fictional hero. But without Allie, Julian was just a cardboard cutout that Gavin could no longer bring to life.

Maybe he could bowl her over with his money. Letting his gaze roam around her bedroom, which was almost entirely filled by the bed and the treadmill, he wondered how he could leverage his wealth. She'd been impressed by his garage and car collection, but her admiration had held a tinge of amusement, as though these were just overpriced toys.

How right she was about that.

But money bought influence. His Allie wanted to work, and he could use his connections to find that for her. He winced as he remembered his phone conversation with Ben Cavill. The overwhelming need to keep her all to himself was going to haunt him, but the thought of her hands on another man's skin made bile scald his throat.

He had to find a way to enchant her, to take her away from all the stresses and distractions of their real lives.

Southampton would be perfect. Only a few hardy year-round residents suffered through the steel-edged ocean wind of winter there. He could sweep Allie away there tomorrow, which would give them three days of solitude before his obligation at the Barefoot Ball. And that event would make her mouth drop open.

The decision made, he scooted down in the bed to see if the elusive oblivion of sleep would find him. His foot met a warm weight, provoking an annoyed meow. He lifted his head to see Pie give him an accusing look before the cat stalked up alongside Allie to settle on her pillow.

"And you're coming, too," Gavin muttered. "No matter how many times you throw up."

Chapter 19

"I can't go to Southampton," Allie said, her fork clattering onto her plate.

"Pie is invited, too," Gavin said. He'd left her sleeping while he went out and bought chocolate croissants at her favorite bakery, picked up a bouquet of peach-colored roses from a Korean grocery store, and made her an omelet. Only then had he brought up his plan to take her out of town for a few days.

"Oh." He could see her casting around in her mind for another reason she couldn't go.

"The change of scene will help with my writer's block. I don't want to be around Hugh right now." That was true, at least. He didn't want to see the pity—or caring or whatever Allie labeled it—in the actor's eyes. Her face softened, and he knew he'd found the right leverage. "You can continue to work on the series bible out there."

"How long would we be staying?"

"A few days. That's one of the conveniences of being a writer. My work is infinitely portable. Unlike Trainor, who has to haul himself into an office every day." He leaned forward. "Southampton is beautiful in the winter. The beach is empty and scoured clean by the wind, while the ocean is wild with spray lifting from its gray-green surface."

"Like your eyes," she said.

"My eyes?" He pulled back.

"I've always thought they looked like the winter ocean." The little minx smiled. She was enjoying his discomfiture. "Except at certain times when they warm up quite a bit."

"Any other of my body parts you'd care to comment on?"

"I adore your trapezius and your latissimus dorsi."

God, he loved her sass. "You know what I adore about you?" He whispered a few very improper words, making her cheeks flush bright pink.

"My mama would wash your mouth out with soap," she said, her eyes alight with laughter and a touch of sexual heat.

"I want to take you back to bed right now," he said, his desire fanned by his own words.

"Nope, we have to finish breakfast and go to work," she said, cutting off a piece of omelet.

"Not work. Pack."

She chewed and swallowed. "You know that Pie throws up in the car."

"That's what paper towels are for." He decided not to mention the helicopter just yet.

She gave him a dubious look. "It smells awful."

"I spent a couple of summers working on a pig farm, so cat vomit won't bother me." He'd taken the job to escape from working at his father's store . . . and nearly quit the first day when he had to clean out the pens. The stench had been almost unbearable. But he had gotten used to it and even came to like a couple of the pigs. After two summers there, his father had told the pig farmer he needed Gavin at the store full-time, and that had been the end of that small rebellion.

"You worked on a pig farm? Those places reek."

"It got me out from under my father's gimlet eye at Miller's Feed and Dry Goods."

She got that soft look again, as though she understood more than he had said.

He took a sip of coffee. "Bring warm clothes for Southampton. The sea wind can be bitter."

He decided not to mention the charity gala he planned to take her to on Saturday. She didn't need to bring anything for that because the dress was included with the price of admission, and it was a Barefoot Ball, so shoes were forbidden.

"I'll come to Southampton," she said. "But we work while we're there."

A wave of relief washed through him, easing muscles he hadn't realized were tensed. "We'll labor like proverbial dogs while Pie looks on with feline superiority."

♥ ♥ ♥

Allie dropped her sweater-stuffed duffel by the tote bag filled with cat supplies. Pulling the cat carrier out of her hall closet, she marched into the living room.

Gavin lounged on the sofa with Pie curled in his lap while he tapped out e-mails on his phone. He was in a surprisingly good mood, considering the crushing news from last night. Her theory was that getting her to agree to trek out to Southampton had soothed his bossy male ego.

She was not excited about the expedition. She winced every time she pictured Pie barfing on the Maserati's hand-stitched leather seat. But she couldn't afford to pay her neighbor to cat-sit.

She took a deep breath. "Okay, time to load up the cat."

Gavin looked down at the little creature dead asleep on his black wool trousers. "Is it difficult?"

"Not this part." Allie set the case down on the cushion beside him, unzipped the top, and stroked Pie to wake her up. The cat started, raising her head as Allie eased her off Gavin's lap and into the case.

"She's very cooperative," Gavin said, his tone admiring.

Pie yowled.

"But vocal," he added. "Shall I let Jaros know we're ready?"

"Jaros? What about the Maserati?"

"That's going in a different direction."

Allie shook her head. How amazing to have minions who smoothed every obstacle out of the way.

Jaros carried everything except Pie downstairs. Allie took care of the little cat. When they got to the car, Ludmilla popped out. "Let me see kitty," she said, reaching for the cat case. She peered through the mesh. "Pretty little Pie kitty."

Allie cast a questioning glance at Gavin. He shrugged. "Pie is going to have a nice ride out to Southampton in the Bentley with Jaros and Ludmilla. If you look inside the car, you'll see the handsome tent Ludmilla's own cat uses for travel."

"A cat tent." Allie stuck her head in the open door and saw a structure complete with a litter box, bed, and cat toys, strapped into the seat. "Are we taking the Maserati, then?"

"We're going by helicopter," Gavin said from behind her.

Allie nearly hit her head on the door frame as she straightened. "What?"

Ludmilla patted her on the arm. "I take good care of Pie kitty. She so beautiful. We be good friends."

"I know you will," Allie said, not wanting to insult Ludmilla's cat-sitting abilities.

Ludmilla patted her again and got in the car so Jaros could pass Pie's carrier in to his wife. He closed the door gently and turned.

"She love cats. She make Pie happy."

"I know. It's just . . ."

But Jaros had walked around the car and ducked into the driver's seat. Allie turned to Gavin. "Did you warn them that Pie barfs in cars?"

"I gave them full disclosure." His gaze roamed over her face. "Does it upset you too much to have Pie ride with strangers?"

The truth was that Pie liked almost every human she met. "I hate to have them clean up after her."

The Bentley slid away from the curb while Allie watched helplessly. Gavin took her by the shoulders so she had to look at him. "Tell me what will make you happy," he said.

His face was grave with concern. With an effort, she banished her guilt about Pie and the Bentley. After all, Gavin could buy another car if the smell was too bad. The thought sent a small bubble of hysterical laughter spinning in her throat. "I've never ridden in a helicopter before."

The smile that flashed across his face was worth the pretense. "That's my Allie." He slung his arm over her shoulder and escorted her to the Maserati.

She spent the brief drive to the heliport alternating between nervousness about the flight and wondering if Pie had barfed yet.

"You're very quiet," Gavin said as he drove the Maserati up to a chain-link gate. He flashed a card of some kind, and the guard waved him through.

"I've heard helicopters described as flying typewriters," she said, trying to lighten her own mood. "Which would explain why you like them."

Gavin smiled as he slotted the car into an empty spot between a Rolls-Royce and a Ferrari. "My helicopter is checked over three times before it flies, by my own personal mechanic, by my pilot, and by my copilot. And in case you're wondering, in an emergency, I can fly the chopper, although not smoothly."

"So you own the helicopter?" Allie had assumed it was a charter, which would have been expensive enough.

"And a jet. I think that's a requirement for membership in the Bellwether Club." He got out of the car and came around to hold Allie's door.

"Is that a joke?" she asked.

"Maybe."

He escorted her through another gate and into a permanent trailer with a door marked **VIP LOUNGE**. She surveyed the narrow space furnished with leather chairs, and snorted. "We have nicer trailers in Sanctuary, West Virginia. At least they're double-wides."

"No one actually lounges here," Gavin said, walking through the trailer to another door. As he opened it, the wind walloped her in the face. The only thing between them and the white-capped waves of the Hudson River was a stretch of asphalt holding several helicopters, their rotors drooping slightly.

A man walked up to Gavin, who handed over his car keys. "The bag's in the trunk."

"Yes, sir," the man said, taking off at a run.

"Do you mean *my* bag?" Allie asked. "I could have carried it."

"Since the trailer didn't impress you, I had to come up with another method," Gavin said, taking her hand and leading her toward a sleek black copter with blood red stripes.

She could barely hear the last of his words as the rotors on one of the other choppers began to rotate. The wind whipped her hair around her face like snakes while the noise rose to a deafening volume. When the rotors got up to speed, the aircraft lifted off as lightly as a dragonfly before turning to zoom out over the expanse of choppy water.

"I can't decide whether I'm excited or terrified," she said as Gavin helped her through the side door of the aircraft. Six cushioned armchairs faced one another across a polished wooden table. The interior reminded her of the Bentley, all leather and fancy-grained wood paneling, although the color palette here was deep red and silver. The opulence of it left her speechless.

Gavin climbed in after her, and the door was slammed shut. She heard the thud of latches closing and locking. "I assume you would prefer to face forward," he said, waving to a chair.

She nodded and sank into its pillowy embrace. "Can we talk while it's flying?"

He sat in the chair nearest her, stretching his legs out so his glossy loafers nearly touched her boots. "Of course." He cocked his head. "This isn't your average sightseeing chopper."

"No kidding." A vibration ran through the aircraft, and the pilot's voice sounded in the cabin.

"Please fasten your seat belts. We're ready to lift off."

Allie fumbled with the seat belt. It was configured just like an automobile's, but nerves made her clumsy. Gavin reached over, took the metal buckle out of her hand, and neatly clipped it into the latch.

She felt a slight sense of movement and peered out the window to discover that they were rising off the asphalt pad. Her fingers dug into the leather armrest as they climbed higher and executed the same maneuver the other chopper had, turning their nose to the river and skimming forward.

Gavin's hand closed over hers where she gripped the armrest, his fingers warm and strong. "Morley Safer claimed that helicopters induce a view of the world that only God and CEOs share on a regular basis."

"Which category do you put yourself in?" she asked.

He laughed and gave her hand a playful squeeze. "In my fictional world, I play God."

"I figured CEO was too boring for you," she said, tensing as the chopper dipped suddenly.

"It's just a touch of turbulence over the river. Think of the air as a road with a few potholes in it," Gavin said.

"Potholes, right. In New York, you can break an axle in one of those."

The laughter left Gavin's face. "I would never put you in danger."

That reassured her more than his pothole analogy. She nodded.

With that, Gavin switched into tour-guide mode, pointing out landmarks and tossing out intriguing facts or funny stories about them. "How do you know all this stuff?" Allie asked.

"Research. No one understands how much of it goes into a work of fiction. They think I can make it all up because my characters aren't real. But the settings are real, so the buildings and streets, the sounds and smells, even the quality of the light in any given season need to be accurate." He tapped his temple. "Of course, the weird, useless factoids are what stick in my brain."

As they flew over Queens and Long Island, Allie began to understand Morley Safer's quotation. They were close enough to see details, like the color of the cars in parking lots, but high enough to grasp the larger picture of the geography spread out around them like a relief map.

As they flew farther east, the expanse of the Atlantic Ocean began to dominate the view. A few ships crawled over its corrugated gray surface, but mostly it was empty as it stretched to the horizon.

"Make sure your seat belts are snug. It's windy, so we might hit a few bumps on the way down," the pilot's voice said.

Allie tightened her hold on the armrest again, but her nerves were only mildly frayed by the occasional jolting. Gavin's fingers were wrapped around hers as though he would never let go. She gave him a grateful smile and found him watching her.

"Mark flew combat choppers in the Middle East," he said. "He could land this craft in a hurricane under missile fire without breaking a sweat."

"As long as you're holding my hand, I'm fine." She turned her hand under his so she could return his grasp.

He looked startled, his gaze jerking down to their intertwined grip. He flexed his fingers as though he was testing the strength of their connection. "I'm not sure I'm worthy of such trust."

"Believe me, I trusted Ludmilla far more when I gave her Pie."

He sat back, his dark hair disheveled against the red leather of the seat. "Ruth would like you."

"Ruth?" Allie's grip on his hand turned convulsive as the helicopter jinked sideways.

"My oldest stepsister. She never lets me get away with anything, either."

Chapter 20

The helipad was just an asphalt-paved rectangle that faced Shinnecock Bay. As Gavin helped her out, Allie felt the chill of the sea air cutting through her clothes. It smelled of brine and foam and deep, rolling waves.

She started to look around, but her attention was drawn to the man beside her, his head thrown back as he faced into the wind, his black clothes plastered against his long, lean body, his hair combed away from his face by fingers of moving air, and his nostrils flaring as he inhaled. He looked as though he could wield the power of the elements with a gesture of his hand, and she remembered her impression of him as a dark wizard.

He turned to meet her gaze, his eyes lightened to almost silver by some emotion she couldn't name. "Thank you for coming here."

She surveyed the starkly beautiful salt marsh in front of them. "I'm glad I did."

Gavin steered her toward a chain-link fence that separated the landing pad from Meadow Lane, the two-lane road Gavin's house was located on. Gavin had given her all the local names as they flew in, but he hadn't shown her his house from the air.

Across the road was another asphalt rectangle surrounded by dunes, the parking lot for cars meeting incoming passengers. A single car stood in it, the driver leaning against the front bumper.

"You rich guys are really into reverse psychology," Allie said, pulling her jacket closer around her.

"What do you mean?"

"When you said we were landing at the Southampton heliport, I expected something more than two patches of asphalt. Can't one of you billionaires at least spring for a trailer here?"

"We didn't get to be billionaires by wasting money on a trailer when our drivers meet us right across the street." He guided her over the roadway to the waiting Bentley. "You should see this parking lot in the summer. It's wall-to-wall Bentleys, Maseratis, Ferraris, and Rolls-Royces."

"If you drive a Lexus, are you allowed to park here?"

"Only in the very back of the lot," Gavin said, before he nodded to his driver, who was holding the Bentley's door open. "Afternoon, Linda."

Allie had been eyeing the car, trying to decide if it was an exact twin of the one Pie was riding out in. When she heard the female name, her gaze went to the chauffeur, an attractive young woman with her hair tucked up under her cap. Allie smiled at Linda as she slid into the back of the car and gave Gavin a gold star for his lack of sexism.

As the car glided down Meadow Lane, Allie peered out the window, trying to catch glimpses of the beachfront mansions. Many were behind gates or dunes, but occasionally she got a sense of how large the houses were. "I guess you never pop over to the neighbors' to borrow a cup of sugar."

"Sugar? No, but I might beg a fifth of bourbon on a dreary Sunday."

"Seriously, do you know any of your neighbors?"

"Yes, but we all pay a great deal for privacy, so I wouldn't drop in for a visit unannounced."

"That's kind of sad. Anyone famous?"

"If you're looking for actors or singers, no. They gravitate toward East Hampton. Southampton is a staid crowd of financiers and businessmen."

"How'd you get in?" she teased.

"Money. The Hamptons are very democratic that way."

The car eased off the road and drove through two cast-iron gates that swung open as they approached. The driveway was surrounded by high, tangled bushes, so she could see nothing of the house or grounds. "I feel like Julian Best entering the lair of his archenemy, Sturgis Wolfe."

"Sometimes I get lazy and just look out my window when I need a description."

Suddenly the bushes fell away, and a winter-brown lawn spread out before them, leading up to a rambling mansion clad in gray shingles, the trim of its mullioned windows and graceful columns painted a crisp white. Allie loved the asymmetry of it, with oriel windows punctuating a gambrel roof here while a brick chimney poked up there. Somehow that made it seem less imposing and more inviting despite its massive size.

Linda drew the car up under the front portico with a flourish, jumping out to swing open Allie's door. The scent of the sea met her nostrils again, but the house sheltered them from the slam of the wind.

Gavin put his arm around her shoulders. "Welcome to my humble abode."

Allie snorted. "It's about as humble as you are, but I like it. It has charm."

"If I match it in humility, I hope I also match it in charm."

"That's not the first word that comes to mind."

He dropped his arm to her waist and bent so he could murmur in her ear. "Let's play word association. What adjective *does* come to mind first?"

She debated between honesty and humor but went for the first. "Fascinating." She could have added *dark*, *sad*, and *enigmatic*, but she didn't want to get that complicated before she'd even gotten inside the house. Other words—words about her feelings toward him—she was trying to banish from her own mind.

"I'll take it." His grip tightened. "Although I was hoping for *sexy as hell*."

"That's three words, so it's not acceptable."

He huffed out a laugh and started them up the brick steps to the wide planks of the front porch. He pulled open the bright red front door to usher her into a light-filled double-height entrance hall with a curving staircase climbing up on the left, and arched openings offering glimpses of elegant rooms on three sides.

"You leave it unlocked?"

"Linda opened it before she left. I didn't think you'd let me get away with being greeted by the butler."

"The butler. You have a butler here."

"It takes a substantial staff to keep this place running, even when I'm not here. And I don't really want to hire and fire them seasonally." His tone was slightly irritated.

"You're right. I'm just not used to . . . this." She waved her hand at the grand space around them.

"It's quite cozy when you get settled in."

Allie couldn't stifle her laughter as she took in the patterned marble floor, the long second-floor gallery, and the oversize brass chandelier above her head. "For a writer, your word choice is pretty inaccurate."

He held out his hand. "Let me show you why I bought this house."

His green eyes glinted with pleased anticipation as he closed his fingers around her hand. He towed her through a large, sunny room filled with casual furniture upholstered in soft greens and blues with touches of bright peach. It was, in fact, close to cozy. The wall opposite them was made entirely of french doors opening onto a porch paved with irregular stones in more vivid hues of the room's color scheme.

Gavin flung open a door and pulled her outside.

Before them was nothing but undulating sand dunes covered with waving sea grass and salt spray roses, bare except for their bulbous red hips. The dunes were bisected by a gray boardwalk that led straight to the wide, empty beach. The wind whipped sand up into a fine haze and tore foam off the tops of the breaking waves.

"Some people put swimming pools between the house and the beach," he said, raising his voice over the rush of wind and crash of surf, "but I didn't want a puddle of tame blue water between me and the raw power of the ocean."

Allie surveyed the sky filled with fast-scudding clouds, the beach stretching out to either side of them, and the restless sea that drew the flat line of the horizon, and understood. "It makes you feel insignificant," she said.

"Gloriously insignificant," Gavin said, his voice vibrating with something elemental. She glanced sideways to find him smiling with fierce excitement. She could imagine him at the helm of a pirate ship, dressed in black as he was now, shouting commands to the sailors climbing the rigging like monkeys as they bore down on their prey.

"Do you sail in the winter?"

He tore his gaze away from the view to look at her. "My boat goes to Florida at this time of year, I'm afraid. Would you like to fly down and take a cruise?"

She laughed at the same time as a shiver ran through her. Gavin wrapped his arm around her shoulders and pulled her against his hard, warm body.

"Let's go inside and I'll warm you up," he said.

"With some hot chocolate?"

"As long as you're willing to drink it in bed."

"So you brought me out into the freezing cold as a ploy to get me under the covers with you." But she was flattered and a little turned on by his unabashed desire for her.

"And I thought I was being so subtle."

They went back through the french door and took a different path through the big living room, ending up in a huge kitchen with restaurant-grade appliances. A brown-haired woman in a white chef's jacket, jeans, and clogs sat at a butcher-block table, scrolling through screens on a laptop. She rose as they walked in.

"Germaine, meet Allie Nichols. She has a yen for some hot chocolate."

Allie nodded hello, and Germaine smiled. "And for you, Gavin?"

"The same. We'll be in the office. Working." Gavin cast a sardonic glance at Allie as they exited through a different doorway.

"That was very master-of-all-you-survey," Allie said. "I'm surprised you didn't have her deliver the hot chocolate to your bedroom."

"If I thought you'd allow it, I would have." He headed for the curving staircase and made a wry face. "Today I walk up the stairs without assistance."

She heard a note of self-disgust in his voice. "You had good reason to be upset."

"That's no excuse for indulging in a drinking binge. The last time I did that, I made some bad decisions."

"The bet?"

He stopped midstaircase and directed a piercing look at her. "How do you know about that?"

"I don't. Frankie referred to it." She kept walking. "But I'm curious. What did you bet on?"

He remained where he was, his head tilted back to watch her. "Love."

Allie made a face at him. "If you don't want to tell me the truth, just say so."

"Do you think I'm so blackhearted that I wouldn't hope for true love?"

She stood at the top of the stairs, looking down into his face with its sharp angles framed by wind-tousled hair. He looked . . . vulnerable, as though he'd dropped the facade of wicked cynic for a moment. She found these glimpses of the sensitive man behind the pain dangerously compelling. "I think your heart is well defended, which is a natural reaction to being hurt by those who should care about you."

His expression shifted to self-mockery as he finished ascending. "Moats and battlements with archers on the ramparts. Or perhaps Julian with his sniper rifle."

"So you bet with Frankie?" Allie couldn't picture the self-contained club owner doing something that fanciful.

"Frankie doesn't believe in true love. I bet with Trainor and Archer, who were also drunk. No, maybe Archer wasn't at that point. The evening is somewhat blurred in my memory." He gestured toward a door. "The office."

But Allie stopped on the gallery, stunned. "Wait, how long ago did you make the bet?"

"Last fall. We gave ourselves one year. The clock is ticking." He made a pendulum motion with his hand.

"So Nathan hadn't met Chloe, and Luke hadn't met Miranda? Those two couples seem so . . . so . . ."

"In love?" Gavin's voice sliced like a knife.

"Even more than in love. So . . . bonded." Allie didn't know how to explain it. Chloe and Miranda were quite comfortable with their powerful partners. She didn't think she could feel that level of ease as quickly.

Then she remembered what Frankie had said about the bet: that by letting Allie into the club, she was trying to help Gavin win it. That meant the worldly, sophisticated Frankie thought Allie might be Gavin's true love.

She reached blindly for the gallery railing, clinging to it, as the world seemed to tilt off its axis. She'd considered him out of reach, their relationship something that would come and go swiftly like the flare of a match. But maybe . . .

Then the truth hit her. Gavin would have kept the bet a secret if he had the slightest thought that she might be the woman who would win it for him. Instead, he'd revealed its details without any hesitation.

"Allie? Are you all right?" Gavin put his finger under her chin to angle her face upward. "You've gone pale. Let's get you to a couch so you can lie down."

He took her elbow and hustled her into the office before she could protest. Just the feel of his fingers supporting her arm took on a new resonance. She couldn't dismiss it as simply sexual. Now that she had stopped denying there was more, her heart cartwheeled with joy before it sagged with despair.

Had she been crazy enough to fall in love with this cranky, sarcastic, cynical man? Yes, but she'd also fallen in love with the generous, courageous, sensitive man who hid behind the cynicism.

She shook her head in disbelief.

"Sit," he commanded, lowering her onto the taupe-colored cushions of a plush sofa. He stooped to take her ankles and swing them up so she rotated sideways. "Lie down."

"I'm not a dog," she said, pushing his hands away from her shoulders as he tried to ease her backward.

She needed to get away from him to figure out what the heck to do about these feelings. Her phone pinged from her back pocket, and she seized on that as an excuse. "I'd better check this text. It might be a prospective client," she said, putting her feet back on the floor and jogging out of the room.

She was afraid he would follow her, so she dodged through another doorway, finding herself in some sort of library–cum–game room. Bookcases lined the walls, and a polished wooden pool table dominated the middle. She braced her hands on the lip of the pool table and rocked forward, sucking in slow breaths to counterbalance the acceleration of her heartbeat.

Clearly, she suffered from some sort of self-destructive urge, going from an abusive actor to a blocked writer. A blocked writer whose mother had left him, whose stepmother hated him, whose father had recently died, who loathed his ex-fiancée, and who drowned himself in alcohol when he was upset.

But he had stopped drinking when she arrived at the Bellwether Club. He was beginning to create again. He was a passionate, generous lover. He helped out debut authors despite considerable emotional trauma to himself. And he was becoming attached to Pie. So he wasn't beyond redemption.

However, he wasn't in love with her.

She picked up the cue ball and rolled it across the table so it caromed off the bumper and back to her hand.

"Maybe that's better," she said. "I can't repeat my mistakes."

Her heart didn't agree with her brain, though. A slash of anguish hit her right in the chest at the idea of Gavin walking away without a backward glance. Well, maybe he'd toss a sarcastic quip over his shoulder as he went.

Unclenching her fingers from the cue ball, she placed it back in the center of the table. To distract herself, she pulled out her phone, hoping the ping meant a possible job. But the text was from Troy and said, Call me. You'll want to hear this.

She swallowed against the anxiety clamping a fist around her throat, typing, Are you in LA?

Yeah, so you don't have to call the cops, he typed back.

His dig sent anger prickling through her, even as the tightness in her throat eased at the knowledge that he was three thousand miles away. It was so typical of him to jab at her when he was the one who had initiated the communication.

She'd learned that it was better to respond promptly or Troy would escalate his attempts to reach her. He refused to believe she really meant that he should not have any contact with her. And since she didn't have the heart to notify the police when he called, it was partly her fault.

But she didn't want Gavin walking in on a conversation with her ex. She made her way back to the office to find him standing at the window, staring out at the sea again. As soon as he heard her, he pivoted, raking her with an inquisitor's gaze. "You look like it was bad news. Can I help?"

She shook her head. "Everyday life intrudes, even in the Hamptons. I just wanted to let you know that I need to make a phone call. I'll go to another room so you can get to work."

"Of course." He paused as though he wanted to say something more but then walked to his desk.

She felt weirdly disloyal, lying to him about calling Troy, but she didn't want to go down that twisty road.

She left Gavin in the office and returned to the pool room.

"What is it, Troy?" she said as he answered.

"It's sunny in LA, and they love me in my role, and I'm staying at Finn Bolger's apartment right on the water. Thank you for asking." His tone reached for irony but came off as boastful.

"Sorry, but I'm crunched for time, and your message sounded urgent." She forced herself to loosen her grip on the phone before the pressure cracked the screen.

"You're never going to believe who I'm acting in four scenes with." He paused for effect. "Irene Bartram!"

"She's in a *soap opera*?" Shock made Allie tactless, and she could practically feel the chill across all three thousand miles.

"Many stars got their start in *soap operas*." He mimicked her scornful tone perfectly.

"I didn't mean it that way. I thought she only did movies."

"She's lowering herself to do a guest appearance on *Saints and Sinners*." The frost melted into whining. "You love the Julian Best movies, so I thought you'd be excited. Irene and I have been talking about what it's like to work with Hugh Baker and Edwin Shaw."

She decided not to tell him that she'd met Irene Bartram and Hugh Baker and hadn't been impressed.

"I have to give you credit," he said. "All the times you made me watch the Julian Best movies paid off. Irene was bowled over by how much I knew. She says I have a profound understanding of the dynamic, and I should consider auditioning for a role."

"Glad I could help, Troy, but I have to go."

"Wait! I have some not-so-good news for you." She braced herself as Troy continued. "I know you love the Julian Best books, but Irene says that the author, Gavin Miller, has a bad case of writer's block. Can't write a word. He's way past his deadline for the next book. And she'd know because she was engaged to him." He lowered his voice. "It's so bad that they're hiring a ghostwriter to do the screenplay for the next movie."

"What? That can't be right!" Allie cast a nervous glance at the door to make sure Gavin wasn't racing in to see what she was yelling about.

"I think Irene would be correct, since she's starring in the movie. And she's going to get me an audition for a speaking role. She says I'd be perfect for Sturgis Wolfe's right-hand man." His excitement came through the telephone line.

Allie made sure to keep her voice calm this time. Troy didn't know about her connection with Gavin, and she wanted to keep it that way. "Does Irene have any idea when the movie will be released?"

"Late next year. I know you'd rather have a book," Troy said, although he'd never understood her preference, "but a movie is better than no Julian Best at all."

She might have agreed with that before she'd met Gavin, but not now. "I'm still hoping for another book."

"Did I tell you that they love me?"

"Yes, but I have to go to work."

"Okay." His tone was sulky, but he disconnected.

She lowered the phone. It didn't make sense. Hugh said he'd been released from his movie contract, and he wouldn't be mistaken about that. So why would they hire a ghostwriter to create a script? She didn't know anything about how contracts worked for books that got turned into movies, but Gavin must have some control over the character he had imagined into fictional existence. However, the fact that Irene had promised Troy an audition made the movie sound like a reality.

Now she had to decide if she should share this information with Gavin. If it were true and Gavin didn't know about it, he would be even more devastated than he'd been by Hugh's contract news. If it were not true, she would be upsetting him for no reason.

Wait, he had Jane, who was a really great agent, according to Gavin. She would know what was going on with the ghostwriter, and she would certainly tell Gavin if there was anything to worry about.

Allie blew out a breath of relief. She didn't have to upset Gavin unnecessarily. Damn Troy anyway.

She marched back to Gavin's office and said breezily, "All settled. Sorry it took so long. Now we can get to work."

He swiveled around in his desk chair and nodded to the coffee table. "Don't you want your hot chocolate?"

A tray with two steaming mugs and a plate of what looked like homemade miniature doughnuts sat on the table. She inhaled and caught the rich scent of chocolate, making her mouth water. "Do I ever. Got any tequila to add to it?"

"Hair of the dog?" He walked to a built-in cabinet and swung open the door to reveal a well-stocked bar. "Here we are . . . Gran Patrón Piedra. Probably a crime to mix it with chocolate, but it's all I've got."

"I was kidding," Allie said.

"But I wasn't." He carried it to the tray and poured a generous helping in each mug before he picked them up and offered one to her.

"This isn't going to improve your work ethic," she said, taking the drink.

"I hope it will completely destroy yours." He touched his mug to hers and took a sip.

She did the same and moaned at the deliciousness of the dark, slightly bitter chocolate, the creamy milk, and the kick of tequila. "Germaine is a genius."

"And you haven't even tasted her doughnuts." He took a pastry from the plate and held it in front of her mouth, his eyes glinting.

Allie knew she was being seduced, but she played along, taking a bite of the doughnut, chewing the light, cakey treat and licking the sugar off her lips. Gavin watched her mouth the entire time, his face tight with focus.

"You seemed to enjoy that," he said, offering her the doughnut again.

She took another bite, chewed, and swallowed, but before she could lick her lips, Gavin leaned in close. "Let me," he murmured before he flicked his tongue against her skin, lapping up the sugar crystals.

The touch of his tongue sent tremors of pleasure dancing over her skin. How was she supposed to subtly find out whether he knew about a ghostwriter when he was brushing the doughnut against her lips, making the sugar cling to them so he could lick it off?

"Your kisses are always sweet," he murmured before he sucked on her lower lip. Her body reacted as though his mouth was between her legs, making heat and arousal bloom inside her.

She put her hand on his chest and pushed at the hard, warm surface. "You promised we would work like dogs."

He put the half-eaten doughnut in his own mouth and chewed slowly before swallowing, his strong throat muscles working. "Drink up your hot chocolate, and then we'll see how interested you are in keeping our noses to the grindstone."

His gaze went to the windows again. Allie took one more sip before putting down the mug. "Let's go outside," she said. "Fresh air will inspire you."

"A walk on the beach?" He grinned suddenly. "I have a better idea, but you'll need to bundle up."

"Will we be back in time for Pie's arrival?"

"We're not leaving the grounds," he said.

After a quick trip to his bedroom to collect warm clothing, he escorted her through another wing of the house and out a side door, where they followed a winding path through fallow winter gardens. Gavin swung open a gate set into a high, arching hedge and waved her through. His eagerness vibrated in the air between them.

"Are you kidding me?" Allie said, as she took in the huge sheet of perfectly groomed ice spread before them, a hockey goal at each end. "You have your own skating rink?"

"And skates." He strode toward a small shingled building that sat at the side of the rink. It was stocked with skates in all sizes, hockey sticks, blankets, and a hot-chocolate machine. Sliding glass doors provided a view of the rink as well as the stone patio furnished with lounge chairs and a fire pit. Allie gaped at it all while Gavin rummaged around for skates.

"Does anyone use this except you?" she asked as he handed her a pair of figure skates.

"My guests." He sat down and looked up at her as he pulled on hockey skates. "The local high school hockey team practices on it when the weather allows, if that makes you feel better."

She plunked down on the bench beside him. It was weird that his owning a helicopter didn't shock her, but having a private skating rink seemed like the height of extravagance.

"I played on the hockey team in high school," he said, lacing his skates with swift efficiency. "It was one of the few frivolities my father allowed. Hockey practice meant I didn't have to work in his store."

So he had built this to remind himself of the happy times when he had escaped his father's grim control.

He secured the laces with a couple of abrupt movements before he straightened. "Skating means freedom to me. Now let's get your laces tightened."

Her heart twisted at her imagined picture of a younger Gavin shedding the misery of his loveless home life as he skimmed across the ice, tossing wisecracks at his teammates. Maybe that's where he'd begun to hone his cutting wit.

She felt his strength when he snugged her skates around her feet and ankles and tied the laces tight. As he leaned forward, she rested her hand on his broad back, savoring the flex of muscles under his jacket and offering comfort to the boy curled inside the man.

He kept a firm grip on her hand as they waddled along the rubber-surfaced walkway to the rink. Once they stepped on the ice, Gavin put his arm around her waist and swept her along beside him over the glassy surface, the powerful strokes of his legs propelling them faster and faster as they circled, their skate blades hissing beneath them. The cold rush of air whipped through her hair while the length of Gavin's lean, muscled body against her side kept her secure.

It reminded her of the Bellwether Club, where she had been the one supporting him. Here, though, he was letting her lean on his strength.

"Hold on!" he said, speeding around a corner, his thighs pumping as he fought the centrifugal force.

As they hit the straightaway, she threw back her head and laughed, letting all her barriers down.

"You love it, too!" he said.

The boyishness of his excitement made her heart contract before it flooded with warmth. This was the sweetness, the joy, she sensed in him beneath the sarcasm and pain.

As they sped around the next corner, he said, "You move with me perfectly."

She turned a sly smile up at him. "I've had some practice moving with you."

"You're playing with fire, my sweet." He slowed them to a stop and sandwiched her between his body and the side of the rink.

"Two-minute penalty for boarding," she said just before his mouth came down on hers.

He cradled her head in his hands while he used his weight to keep her body pressed against his. The kiss began as a tease of his lips against hers, a flicker of a touch, but the exhilaration of the skating turned to desire sizzling through her veins, and she pushed into him to feel the heat of his mouth.

"Minor penalty for unsportsmanlike conduct," he murmured against her lips before driving his tongue in to meet hers.

Liquid flame licked through her, so she grabbed his arms to bring him even closer. He groaned into her mouth and pushed his thigh between hers, lifting her onto her toe picks, the solid bulge of his rectus femoris muscle hitting exactly where she yearned for it.

"We can't make love on an ice rink," she said, even as she panted with the longing to do just that. She wanted to give him everything she was feeling.

"It's *my* rink, so we can do anything we want to." He wedged his thigh farther between her legs, making her gasp outright when the added friction sent a shock of electric delight surging through her.

She giggled. "It's a medical fact that cold makes it more difficult for certain parts of the male anatomy to function effectively."

"When you're around, my anatomy is quite capable of functioning at subzero temperatures," he said. "However, I'd prefer not to suffer from frostbite, so we're going where the water is in a softer state."

Chapter 21

"I'm not going in the ocean!" Allie protested. "Those Polar Bear Club people are crazy."

"Ah, but I'll be doing things to keep you warm."

"Not even what you do could keep me warm at this time of year."

Gavin laughed and steered her back to the skate house, where they stripped off their skates, leaving them lying willy-nilly on the floor.

Retracing their steps through the garden, Gavin took them around a different corner of his mansion. A wing constructed of glass and white columns jutted out in front of her. "Is that an indoor pool?" she asked.

"No self-respecting billionaire would be without one," he said, pressing his thumb against a panel beside one of the glass doors. It slid open, and she stepped into a light-filled space that smelled of water and warm soil. The soil scent came from the pots of huge ficus trees dotted around the stone patio that edged the pool.

"And now . . ." He reached for her jacket's zipper.

"But . . ." She looked at the transparent walls.

"The moment we walked through the door, the glass turned opaque to viewers from the outside."

"Is there anything you billionaires don't think of?" Allie dragged his zipper open and pushed his jacket down his arms.

They left a trail of clothes right up to the lip of the pool and dived in side by side as though they'd planned it. When Allie surfaced, Gavin came up behind her, snaking his arms around to cup her breasts and pull her back against him. His erection nestled hard between her buttocks as he tweaked her nipples with his thumbs. The water was just deep enough so her feet didn't touch the bottom, while Gavin could stand. It made him her anchor.

"Have you ever made love in a pool?" he murmured as he nipped at her earlobe.

"That's a very personal question." The pinch of his teeth zinged through her like lightning.

"You're right. I don't want to know." He skimmed one hand over her stomach to slide it between her thighs while the heel of his hand pressed against her. "I can't tell if you're wet for me."

"One drawback to sex underwater." She let her legs float apart in a shameless invitation and was rewarded when he slipped two fingers inside her, pushing them deep as he rubbed his thumb against her clitoris. There was pressure but no friction, making his invasion feel sensual and languorous.

"Ahh," she sighed out, tilting her head back to rest on his shoulder. With her pelvis locked in place by his hand and his cock, she could do nothing but drift in the sensations his questing fingers evoked.

He rolled her nipple between his fingers, making it tighten and peak. "I love that the water makes you slippery so I can go harder," he said. She felt as though he played her body like a violin with the strings stretched from her breasts to low in her belly.

The wet skin of his chest slid against her back as he began to thrust his fingers in and out of her, making her buoyant body shift in the water. He flexed his hips in the same rhythm so his cock slid against her bottom. The motion created wavelets that stroked her skin, adding another sensation. His breath rasped past her ear as he moaned out her name.

He crossed his arm over her breasts like a band. The strokes of his fingers drove her sensitive skin against the flat of his powerful forearm so the pressure eased and strengthened, eased and strengthened. Flares of pleasure added to the coil of arousal his skillful fingers were winding ever tighter.

As she felt herself beginning to crest, she seized his wrist. "Not yet. I want you inside me."

"I don't know if I can hold on long enough for that," he said in a guttural voice she'd never heard before. She felt the heave of his lungs, but then he withdrew his fingers, the motion nearly sending her over the edge. She arched and gasped but clung to her control.

He towed her with him to where their clothes lay and pulled a condom out of his trouser pocket. When she tried to take it from him, he moved it out of reach. "If you touch me, I'll be gone."

As he rolled it on, she could see the tendons in his neck standing out in his battle to keep himself from coming. She relished knowing she had brought him to that point.

"The shallow end," he said, once again pulling her against him and plowing through the water.

When the water was at his hips, he stopped. Allie liked what he was thinking and faced him, running her hands up his chest, just to feel the planes of his muscles. She smiled into the blazing green of his eyes as she slowly lay back in the water, letting it support her while she opened her thighs on either side of his.

"My mermaid," he murmured before she felt his hands curl around the outside of her thighs, pulling them wide as he positioned his cock between her legs. For a long moment, he stood there, gazing down at her, the tip of him brushing gently against her as the water lapped around them. The anticipation was exquisite as she waited to see whether he would take her fast or slowly.

Gavin tightened his grip on Allie's thighs as he fought the desire to drive himself into her with one hard thrust. He wanted to feel the connection she'd asked for. To be inside her. Her simple request had taken on more than the physical meaning.

When he had regained enough control, he eased the tip of his cock into her slick heat, feeling the slide and clasp of her around him. As he pushed deeper, soft little gasps came from her throat, and he felt tremors run through her body, echoing the shudders shaking his own. He sank his fingers into the flesh of her thighs and opened them more so he could go in farther. When his balls were pressed against her, he stopped, feasting on the sight of her impaled on him, her thighs creamy against his darker skin, her red hair waving around her head like silk ribbons in a breeze, her breasts glistening like rain-wet peaches.

She opened her eyes a slit and caught him staring. Her lips curved into a siren's smile, and he felt her internal muscles tighten around his cock like a fist in a velvet glove. Every molecule in his body screamed for him to move.

But he wasn't ready to let go yet. He wanted to stay joined with her, part of her.

She closed her eyes again. "I like having you there," she said, almost as though she had read his mind. "You fill the longing."

"Tell me how it feels."

"It's like a hollow ache, an emptiness that needs something inside it. Yet even when you're there in me, it hungers for more." She used the leverage of his hands on her and rocked against him. "It wants the motion, the release."

Her movement sparked a searing flare of desire. "And I want the same," he said, pulling out of her and then thrusting back in so fast and hard he felt the resistance of the water between them.

"Yes!" Her cry echoed off the glass walls. "Again!"

He was nearly crazed with the effort of withholding his climax, but he flexed his hips back and forward again, making her breasts bob and her hair ripple.

He rotated his hips so he hit her clit, and he felt her go still as she balanced on the edge of orgasm. Then she convulsed around him and triggered his release so fast that he barely had time to brace himself. He threw back his head and shouted as her clenching muscles seemed to pull his climax from every corner of his being.

She gasped his name over and over, her body seizing and letting go, seizing and letting go, magnifying his pleasure.

Finally, all he could feel were tiny shivers running through her, so he gently eased out. Even that movement made her moan.

"Don't let go of me," she said, her West Virginia accent strong. "Or I'll sink like a stone."

The ordinary request struck deep. He wanted to tell her that he would never let go. He was becoming a maudlin idiot.

"There's a lounge for two that has our name on it," he said, shifting his grasp to her waist and tipping her upright.

She draped her arms over his shoulders and buried her face against his chest. "You exploded my insides."

"That sounds gory and not at all pleasurable. And yet you seemed to enjoy it."

Her breath tickled his skin as she chuckled. "I'm a glutton for punishment."

"If you thought that was punishment, I guess handcuffs would be out of the question."

"As long as there are no whips in the room. I see enough real pain to find inflicting it the opposite of sexy."

He had a vision of her arms stretched up over her head with handcuffs gleaming on her wrists, her naked body stretched taut over a black velvet bedspread, and felt his cock begin to stir again.

"I've always wanted to play bad cop." He slipped his hands under her bottom and lifted her so he could walk up the steps of the pool. The feel of her most private parts against his abdomen added to his cock's interest.

"Does that make me the good cop?" Her head lay on his shoulder, and her wet hair streamed down her back like wet satin.

"That makes you my prisoner to do with as I will." He made it to the wide chaise longue and laid her on the striped canvas cushion. She curled up on her side. He stared down at the soft curves of her bottom and thighs. "And I will do many, many wicked things to you."

"Promise?" Her voice was sated and sleepy.

"I considered it more of a threat." He stretched out beside her and dragged the terry-cloth throw up from the foot of the chair to cover them. Sliding one knee between hers, he wrapped his arm around her waist to spoon against her back.

She snuggled in close to him with a happy little hum, her skin still damp and slightly cool in contrast to the heat between her legs.

As he lay there, Gavin felt as though the water had drained from his moat, the archers had wandered off the ramparts in search of some ale, and Julian had disassembled and packed up his sniper rifle. One small red-haired sprite had rendered his defenses useless.

Chapter 22

Allie came slowly awake in an unfamiliar bed in an unfamiliar room, but with a familiar purring sound in her ears. She also recognized the feel of the male body she was cradled against. Then she remembered that they were in Southampton, in Gavin's gigantic bedroom that faced the Atlantic Ocean. Which was why the morning sun was spearing brilliant rays of light through the french doors.

She rolled within the circle of Gavin's arm to discover that he was lying on his back with Pie ensconced on his chest, where the cat was enjoying the strokes of his clever fingers.

"Morning," he said, his voice rumbling under Pie's purr. "I told Pie to keep it down or she would wake you."

"It's your magic touch," Allie said, fascinated by the sensuous way he caressed the little cat. "We can't stop purring when you pet us."

He crooked a smug smile at her. "Your vocalizations last night were significantly louder than a purr, even Pie's."

"You weren't exactly Silent Sam yourself."

"I'm a writer. I feel the need to communicate."

"Most of your communication didn't have any intelligible words in it."

After their romp in the pool, they'd made love on the chaise longue before returning to the house to greet Pie. The cat had made the trip with only one "incident," which Ludmilla dismissed as nothing, but Allie still felt guilty.

Despite Gavin's assurances that they would work like dogs, they'd frittered away the rest of the day on a tour of the spectacular mansion, a walk on the wind-smoothed beach, and a candlelit gourmet dinner for two. It was like a deliciously romantic movie with Gavin cast as the hero, his mockery turned to charm, his snark turned to laughter, and his pain banished to a mere shadow lurking in the depths of his eyes. She felt herself falling deeper and deeper under his dark wizard's spell.

Through it all he'd never stopped touching her, which had led to uninhibited lovemaking in his huge bed for half the night. Allie stretched, feeling a few sore spots, but mostly utter, bone-deep satisfaction. As the emotional barriers came down between them, the physical connection became more profound and intense.

She must have made a noise of some sort, because Pie reached out and patted her cheek with one soft paw. "I can see that she's having a tough time settling in here."

"Wherever you are is her home."

"Me and some tuna."

"Don't undersell yourself," Gavin said in a surprisingly serious tone.

"You notice who she's lying on top of."

"I'm simply a large flat surface generating heat . . . and petting." He picked the cat up with one hand and gently set her down beside him before dragging Allie halfway on top of him to kiss her. His hands drifted up and down her back, each stroke going lower until he was caressing the curve of her bottom. "But I'd much rather pet you."

She had enough sense left to pull her mouth away from the temptation of his firm, warm lips. "Nope. Today we have work to do."

Ignoring her protest, he slid one finger between her legs from behind, sending a tendril of arousal spiraling through her. "Stop," she gasped as he grazed his fingertip over her most sensitive spot. There was nothing she could do to prevent him from feeling the liquid heat of her reaction.

"You're saying no, but I'm getting another message here," he said, slipping his finger partway inside her.

Her body betrayed her utterly as her nipples hardened against the solid planes of his chest.

He whispered against the whorls of her ear, "Let me give you just one little orgasm. Think of it as a prebreakfast treat."

His finger was doing wicked things against and inside her, and she felt the tightening deep within. She nodded against his chest, her cheek rasping against the dapple of hair there. "One . . . little . . . orgasm."

He shifted her farther up his body and spread her legs open so they lay on either side of his. Then he used his hand to drive her to the crest and over the edge of release as he told her how much he loved to make her come.

As she lay gasping, her body draped over his like a blanket, he sucked her liquid off his fingers. "More delicious than the finest brandy," he said, licking his lips.

"This time of day it should be orange juice," she said.

His fingers found her buttock with a light squeeze. "I'm trying to be seductive, and you talk about Tropicana."

"Hey, no bruising the fruit." She rolled off him to sprawl on her back. "You keep turning my bones to jelly, so I can't move."

"That's my nefarious plan. If you can't move, then I can do this." He rolled over and sucked her nipple into his mouth.

She'd thought her body was entirely wrung out, but the heat of Gavin's mouth made her arch up into him as electric sparks showered through her.

He lifted his head to grin down at her. "You moved."

"Pure involuntary reflex."

"What would happen if I kissed you down—"

As he began to scoot lower, Allie twined her fingers in his hair and tugged upward. "Have mercy."

He kissed her belly button. "Begging now. That's what I like to hear."

"Go take a shower and leave me alone to recover."

He lay propped on his elbow, looking down at her. "The shower is plenty big enough for both of us. In fact, we could invite several friends and still fit in it."

"A shower orgy?" Allie shook her head. "Nope, solo showers only today. I remember what happened the last time we got wet together."

"Ah, you're always wet when we're together." His eyes gleamed with a wicked light, but he gently pulled the sheet over her and rolled out of bed.

She wasn't so wiped out that she couldn't enjoy every stride he took across the room, the muscles in his tight butt flexing, his long thighs thick with sinew, and the back she knew so well rippling as he turned his head to catch her watching him. He grinned and kept walking.

Pie climbed onto her stomach and sat down to blink at her. Allie had a moment of disorientation at the sight of her gray rescue cat in the midst of the luxurious furnishings of Gavin's bedroom, with its multimillion-dollar view. Neither she nor the cat belonged here, yet they were both making themselves at home. "We shouldn't get too comfortable," Allie warned Pie. "Fairy tales never last."

After breakfast in another sun-drenched room that overlooked the beach, Allie dragged Gavin into the office. As had happened in the city, a second desk had been set up for her, and she settled into the chair with a sigh of relief. When she had a desk to sit at, she knew where she fit into Gavin's world.

He prowled around the room, picking up and setting down various objects. She swiveled her chair around. "Either sit down or find another room to pace in," she said. "You're making me twitchy."

He looked up from the small glass display case he was holding. "I was considering writing in longhand again today."

"Does that actually help?"

He showed her the case, which held a single black pen. "Stephen King wrote an entire book with this Waterman fountain pen. He says it's the world's finest word processor."

The case had a small handwritten card displayed in it. Allie peered at the writing.

To Gavin. In the event of emergency, break glass. Best, Steve

"Stephen King gave his special pen to you?"

"We were at an awards ceremony together and got to talking about writer's block. Back then, I couldn't even imagine it. He warned me that it gets us all eventually." Gavin's lips twisted. "Afterward, he sent me this as a talisman to ward it off."

Allie ran her finger along the case. "I'm surprised you haven't used it already."

"I was afraid it wouldn't work, and then I would have exhausted my last resort." He returned the pen to the shelf beside his desk and sat down, eyeing his computer as though it were a coiled rattlesnake.

Allie stood up. "How about I give you a nice shoulder rub? But it's not physical therapy, just to be clear."

His smile mixed gratitude with seduction. "I prefer to think of it as a sensuous massage from one lover to another."

"Whatever works for you." But his words stroked over her skin as she put her hands on his shoulders. He was wearing one of his seemingly endless supply of black cashmere sweaters over a pair of jeans, a look she particularly liked on him. Not to mention that the feel of his powerful muscles under the soft, expensive fabric was a treat all by itself.

As she kneaded his neck, she gave herself permission to evaluate his condition from a PT point of view. It was significantly improved from her first encounter with him. His body was coming back into balance, and the knots in his muscles were easier to work out. He should have come to Southampton sooner, since it was clearly good for him.

He moaned appreciatively as she worked, flinching only once when she hit an especially tender spot. After ten minutes, she switched to stroking him softly and bent to plant a kiss on his nape. "Now you should be relaxed enough to face the computer."

He reached back to catch one of her hands in his, bringing it around to press his lips into her palm. "Thank you," he said. There was such a freight of emotions in those two words. Gratitude, fear, resignation, and maybe, she thought, an acknowledgment that her presence helped him.

She blinked several times at the tears burning behind her eyelids and slid her hand from his grasp. "Glad it felt good."

"Anytime you touch me it feels good."

The tears stung her eyes again. She returned to her own desk, swallowing against the clot of longing in her throat. She wanted him to feel more than just pleasure at her touch.

She opened the files and began to work, although every now and then she slid a surreptitious glance over her shoulder to see what Gavin was doing. First, he clicked through what she assumed were e-mails, tapping out a short burst before scrolling onward. Then he sat scowling at the screen. Either it was an annoying e-mail or he was trying to work on Julian.

She pulled her attention back to her computer and got engrossed in reconciling some timeline discrepancies. As she finished correcting the various days and times, she realized she was hearing steady typing emanating from Gavin's direction. She sneaked a look and discovered he was gazing at the screen with fierce concentration but no frown.

Angling her chair, she pretended to be searching through some paper notes while in reality, she watched him.

His fingers flew across the keyboard. She could tell he was hitting the backspace key a fair amount, but it didn't slow his pace. There was no tension in his neck and shoulders, just alertness and focus. He leaned forward slightly in the ergonomic chair, with his legs bent and his feet flat on the ground. If she'd wanted to give a lesson in how to sit properly at a desk, she could use Gavin.

She was dying to ask him if he was working on the Christmas story, but she didn't want to interrupt his spurt of productivity. So she returned to her own work. Soon the sound of Gavin's rapid typing became soothing white noise just like the muted roar of the ocean. Out of the corner of her eye, Allie could see Pie curled up in a swath of sunlight that fell across the deep cushion of an armchair. Contentment wrapped around her like a warm down comforter, and she had to remind herself of the warning she'd given the cat earlier that morning.

The typing halted. She swiveled to see Gavin stretching luxuriously in his chair before he ran his fingers through his hair, mussing it, as he scanned the screen in front of him.

"You're a speed demon on the keyboard," she said.

He didn't respond, and she realized he was reading whatever was on the screen. He reached for the mouse and began scrolling. It must have been a full minute later when he swiveled toward her. "Did you say something?"

"Nope. Carry on." She smiled.

"I know you spoke. I was just so engrossed in—" He stopped and slowly turned back to the screen to stare at it. "Jesus H. Christ, that's eleven pages." He stood up, his gaze still on the computer screen. "That's eleven *new* pages. Of Julian."

Allie wanted to cheer, but she decided to keep it low-key, as though his output was perfectly normal. "Are they good pages?"

When he turned, he looked as though he'd shed ten years. "Who the hell cares? I wrote them." In three strides he was beside her, taking her shoulders and pulling her up to kiss her with more gratitude and relief than passion. He lifted his head, and his eyes were the green of the sea with sunlight filtering through it. "You! You did this."

"I was just lucky enough to be here when it happened." She didn't want to be held responsible for his creativity. Nor did she want his over-riding feeling toward her to be gratitude.

His grip did not ease. "You loosened something, so the knots came unraveled."

"That's what any good physical therapist would do." She smiled and kissed him lightly.

Gavin scanned her face, his gaze so intent that she felt it like a touch, as though his fingers were skimming over her skin, drawing her thoughts to the surface for him to read. "Whether you want to admit it or not, you're involved in this."

Allie had a sudden thought. "Should you let Jane know that you've broken through your block?" That would stop any plans for ghostwrit-ers and put her mind at rest about relaying Troy's news.

"No. I want to keep the pressure off for a while."

So he didn't quite trust his muse yet. "You could ask her to keep it confidential."

He paced back to his desk. "I would still feel the weight of her expectations." He swiveled the chair back and forth a few times before he sat down and positioned his hands on the keyboard. "Back to the grindstone." But he said it with a buoyancy that belied the words.

Now Allie had a new reason to worry about the potential ghostwriter. It would crush Gavin's joy and might stop his writing if he found out about the prospect. She couldn't bear to see him plunge back into his dark pit again. She needed to talk to Troy, to find out how definite the idea was.

"Mr. Gavin, Ms. Allie, is lunchtime."

Allie jumped at the sound of Ludmilla's voice coming from the doorway. She had gotten absorbed in one of her favorite Julian Best stories to distract herself from worrying about her dilemma.

Gavin continued to type, so Allie smiled at the housekeeper. "Thank you. Do we eat lunch in the dining room?"

"Wherever Mr. Gavin want to eat." Ludmilla walked over and tapped him on the shoulder, as though she had done it many times. "You try to starve Ms. Allie?"

He nodded and kept typing. Ludmilla winked at Allie and stood waiting. Finally, Gavin reached for his mouse, clicked a couple of times, and leaned back in his chair. He grinned at Ludmilla. "What's for lunch? I could eat a horse."

"No horse meat, that's for sure," the housekeeper said. "Germaine make delicious soup with clams and crabs and mussels. And I bake delicious bread."

They ate in the casual dining area off the kitchen at a small white-washed table. Pie sat in one of the two empty chairs, her gaze fixed on the tureen of seafood chowder steaming in the center of the table. Gavin fished out a chunk of crabmeat and offered it to the cat.

"Leave me some fingers," he said as the cat seized the crab and wolfed it down. He looked at Allie. "I thought she'd eat more delicately."

"Don't let her dainty looks fool you. She has a hearty appetite." Pie put one paw on the table before Allie removed it. "No. You stay on the chair or you get shut out of the room."

"You're very stern." Gavin fed Pie another piece of crab.

"She'll dive right into the soup if you give her half a chance. And no more crab for her. I don't want Ludmilla to deal with any more cat upchuck."

Gavin shrugged at the cat, who was giving him her best hungry-kitty look. "Sorry, but I'm not arguing with your mistress. I owe her."

Allie snorted, and they dug into the meal, which was as delicious as Ludmilla had promised. When Allie laid down her fork after eating much too large a slice of chocolate-pecan pie with freshly whipped cream, she said, "Back to work?"

Gavin swallowed the last of his cappuccino. "No, we have an errand to run."

"We?"

"It requires your participation." He stood up.

"If you think I'm going to meekly go with you, you've got another think coming. What sort of errand?"

He sighed and sat down again. "You'll enjoy it."

"How do you know?"

"Because it involves shopping."

"Since you're dancing around it, you must believe I'm going to object."

Gavin looked skyward before meeting her gaze again. "There's a charity ball here in Southampton on Saturday night to which I would like you to accompany me. It requires a dress, which I don't believe you brought with you. In fact, a dress is included with the very expensive tickets I purchased. But I look better in a tux, so the dress option was going to waste before I decided to persuade you to come with me."

"A ball? Out here in the middle of winter? I thought this was a summer place." Allie was torn between the thrill of going to a fancy party and the knowledge that she had no business doing so, especially since she was pretty sure that whole dress-with-the-tickets line was a lie.

"That's the gimmick. It's called the Barefoot Ball. Unless there's a nor'easter coming, it's held on the beach under giant tents with even larger heaters. Shoes are not allowed, but guests must wear black tie and ball gowns."

"And you just remembered it?"

"No. I just worked up the nerve to invite you."

That made Allie laugh, but she shook her head. "I'd be as out of place as . . . as Pie."

Gavin looked at the cat, who had given up on getting any more seafood and gone to sleep on the chair seat. "Pie has no difficulty making herself at home in any environment. And you are equally adaptable."

Allie hesitated, her conscience battling with her yearning.

Gavin put his hand over hers. "It would make me happy to treat you to this."

"Well, as long as I'd be doing you a favor, I guess I can go along with the plan." He looked happy, and he believed it was because of her. Emotions tangled in her chest, tightening around her heart.

She knew it was only going to make the stroke of midnight more painful, but she wanted to be Cinderella for one night. Although at this ball, there would be no glass slippers.

Chapter 23

When Gavin said they were going to a yacht club, Allie expected it to be elegant and clubby. Instead, the place looked like a bargain-basement sale, with rolling racks stuffed full of dresses scattered around the large entrance hall.

An immaculately groomed older woman rose from the desk set just inside the door. "Ah, Gavin, dear, so nice to see you." She glided up to Gavin to give him an air-kiss before turning to Allie. "I'm Petra Willoughby, the vice chairman of the Barefoot Ball. How lovely to have you as our guest, Allie."

Petra waved a hand at the racks. The huge diamond on her ring finger sparked in the sunlight. "We have a marvelous selection of dresses this year, donated by all the top designers. Letitia, darling, will you help Allie, please?"

Letitia was young, tall, stick thin, and dressed in black. Her smile, however, was sweet, and made endearing by one slightly crooked canine tooth. "Let's go find the perfect gown for you to wear."

"I'll be in the bar," Gavin said.

Allie felt a flutter of panic. She knew nothing about what to wear to a fancy Hamptons shindig. "Don't you want to help choose the dress?"

He looked surprised and dismayed, then pleased. "Why don't you show me the one you think is best, and I will exercise my power of approval . . . or veto."

Letitia nodded and walked with Allie into a large room that looked like the beach had been moved indoors. Green-and-white-striped cabana tents were lined up on the wooden floor in rows, some with their flaps tied up, some with them rolled down. Women of all ages, shapes, and sizes carried ball gowns, inspected ball gowns, and paraded around in ball gowns. Allie had to close her eyes for a moment against the sensory overload of colors, fabrics, and glittering sequins and beads. The symphony of female voices was low and well modulated, but the overpowering scent of competing perfumes made her cough. She opened her eyes, blinked a couple of times, and followed Letitia to an empty cabana. Inside stood a three-paneled full-length mirror, an empty clothes rack, and a cushioned stool.

"Did you have a particular designer in mind?" Letitia asked.

Allie tried to recall who designed the dresses she had admired at the Oscars but came up blank. "Um, not really. Nothing too revealing, though."

Letitia's face took on a calculating edge as she scanned Allie up and down. "I'll bring a few selections in to get an idea of what appeals to you. If you're thirsty, there's a bar set up at the far end of the room. Feel free to have some champagne."

Allie sank onto the stool and watched two women come out of the cabanas across from her to assess each other's dresses. One was dressed in a silver sequined number that highlighted her gilt blonde hair. The other wore a deep fuchsia chiffon that made Allie's eyeballs hurt.

She pulled out her phone to check her e-mails. Still no job offers. She'd thought for sure that Dr. Cavill would have one by now. There wasn't much more to do on Gavin's series bible, so she would be out of work and out of income soon. Now that he was writing once more, there would be no compelling reason for him to keep her around.

Maybe she'd swig some of that champagne after all.

"Let's see what you think of these," Letitia said, bustling in with plastic-bagged dresses draped over her arm. "There's only one of each style, so you don't have to worry about seeing your twin at the party."

Letitia hung six dresses face out on the rack and closed the cabana flap for privacy. "You can't tell much from seeing them on the hangers, so unless you hate one on sight, you should try them all on."

Allie made a concerted effort to shove aside her fit of the dismals and enjoy this last gasp of her fairy tale. Trying on beautiful designer dresses was an experience to be savored, not suffered through. So she stripped down to her panties because her bra straps didn't work with evening attire. Not surprisingly, Letitia had conjured up a strapless bra for her.

The first dress had pale blue lace appliquéd over an illusion-net bodice and a full lace skirt. It was exquisite, but Allie felt as though way too much skin showed through the netting, so she was relieved when Letitia shook her head. "Too fragile and indoorsy for a beach party."

The second was a sheath of green sequins that made Allie feel like a Las Vegas version of a mermaid. Letitia rejected that one as well.

As she was peeling it off, someone scratched on the canvas. "Allie, are you decent? It's Miranda Archer."

"Two seconds." Allie pulled on the robe provided in the dressing room and hauled open the flap.

Miranda stood outside in jeans and a T-shirt, her dark hair pulled back in a ponytail. She gestured toward the activity around her and said, "Can you believe this? It's like a giant slumber party."

Allie's nervousness melted away. "I could use a girlfriend right now."

Miranda's warm smile lit up her face. "Shall we share a tent?"

"Come on in!" Allie stood aside to let Miranda enter, introducing her to Letitia. "Can you handle dressing two of us?"

"It will be a pleasure," Letitia said, giving Miranda the same scan she'd done on Allie.

"I can help you get into one of your dresses while Letitia goes in search of mine," Miranda offered.

As soon as their assistant left, Allie lowered her voice. "Tell me the truth. Are the dresses really included in the cost of the tickets?"

Miranda nodded. "Hard to believe, isn't it? But Gavin is a huge donor to the gala since he lives out here, so I'm pretty sure he gets the best of everything."

"What does huge mean?"

Miranda quoted a number that made Allie's jaw drop. "I don't really understand how rich he is," she said.

"It's hard to comprehend. You'd think I'd be used to this since I've been a concierge for the very wealthy for several years." Miranda unzipped the plastic bag over the next dress on the rack. "But it's different when you're the one making the donations and riding in the helicopters and wearing the designer clothes. Speaking of which, this Valentino is gorgeous."

She slipped the dress over Allie's head and tugged the gossamer layers of fabric down into place, running the zipper up the back.

When Allie turned toward the mirror, she sucked in a breath. The dress had an underlayer of pale pink chiffon and an overlayer of translucent ivory silk organza embroidered with glittering golden starfish of varying sizes. The puff sleeves were unlined, so her arms were visible through the sheer silk, and the full skirt swirled around her legs. She tugged at the plunging V of the neckline, which revealed a large swath of her bra.

"You'll have to wear stick-ons with that," Miranda said, unzipping the dress again. "So let's ditch the bra for now."

Allie unhooked the bra and pulled it off. She swallowed hard. "That's a lot of cleavage."

Miranda fastened the matching fabric belt around Allie's waist and grinned. "When you've got it, flaunt it. You look stunning."

She felt stunning, even though she had the urge to cross her arms over her exposed chest. The pale pink lining picked up her skin tone and made it look almost as though she wasn't wearing anything under the sheer organza. The fabric drifted and swirled with her every movement.

"You'll need a necklace," Miranda said.

Allie put her hand to her bare neck with a sigh. "I don't have any jewelry with me. Gavin said it was just a casual weekend at the beach."

"He didn't tell you about the ball?"

"He was afraid I wouldn't come to Southampton at all, I think."

Miranda raised her eyebrows. "Then he'll just have to provide the accessories to go with it."

"Here we are." Letitia carried another armful of dresses in before she turned to inspect Allie's latest gown. "That's a winner, in my book. How do you feel in it?"

"Like I'll catch pneumonia from the draft across my chest."

"You'll feel better with the proper undergarments," Letitia said. "I'll get those before you model the dress for Mr. Miller."

The thought of Gavin seeing her in the dress made Allie cross her arms over her chest again.

"Trust me." Miranda's voice had a dry note in it. "He'll love it."

❤ ❤ ❤

"I figured I'd find you here." Luke Archer slid onto a bar stool beside Gavin.

"Which here?" Gavin casually turned over the pad of paper he'd been scribbling on. "Southampton, yacht club, or bar?"

Luke ordered a beer. "Bar."

"You have a low opinion of my character."

"Nope. I just couldn't think of any place farther away from the dress craziness than here." He held up the frosted glass the bartender set in front of him. "To swift decisions by our women."

Gavin lifted his glass of water to tap it against Luke's beer. "Off the training regimen already, I see."

"I forgot how good it is to have a beer whenever you feel like it." Luke licked his lips in appreciation.

"Is Nathan showing up here, too?"

"Later," Luke said. "He had some business calls to make."

"How's the studying going?"

Luke unleashed the grin that had made a thousand camera flashes go off. "Miranda's a good teacher."

"I know damn well that you don't need any tutoring. You just use it as an excuse to have your lovely new wife bend over your shoulder."

"So it works on all levels." Luke gestured to the pad of paper Gavin had hoped he wouldn't mention. "You writing something?"

The casualness of Luke's tone didn't fool Gavin. The other man's eyes were focused like lasers. Strangely, he found himself telling the truth. "Yes. Julian's back in action."

"That's good news, man. I've been missing his adventures."

"Not nearly as much as I have." Gavin set down his water. "Don't spread the word around, though. My muse has been a cranky bitch for the last several months, so I don't trust her."

Luke nodded before he looked past Gavin's shoulder, and his face seemed to lose all its angles while his blue eyes went from glacial ice to tropical sea. "Looks like some decisions have been made," he said.

Gavin swiveled on the stool to see Allie and Miranda walking across the bar with arms linked.

"We came to get the official seal of approval," Miranda said, her gaze on her new husband.

"Or veto," Allie said with a nervous smile in Gavin's direction.

All he could see was how Allie's upswept hair showed off the creamy skin of her shoulders above the deep plunge of the gown's neckline. He wanted to bury his face in the shadow cast by the curve of her breasts. Until he realized that other men would want to do the same thing.

Then he noticed that the fabric of the dress was nearly transparent, her arms clearly visible through the short puffed sleeves, and her skin glowing pink through the sheer ivory silk. He was sure that if she stood in front of a bright light, everyone would see the sinuous outline of her waist and hips and the ripe arc of her bottom.

He frowned.

"That's not a good sign," Allie said, her smile wavering.

Miranda finished her modeling spin and looked at Gavin. "I'm sure he's just trying to find the right words to express how beautiful you are."

He caught the slight note of warning in Miranda's perfectly modulated voice and realized he was being a jealous ass, but that didn't stop him. "She looks *too* beautiful."

Allie's smile firmed up as she turned to Miranda. "I knew he wouldn't like the cleavage."

"Cleavage! The whole damned dress just needs a strong light to turn it into Saran wrap."

"That shows what you know about haute couture," Allie said, floating up to him in the swirling dress. She bent to pick up the hem of the long skirt and show him that the layer of translucent organza was underlain by a layer of opaque pale pink. "It's an illusion. You can't really see my skin at all, except through the sleeves."

"Fiction can be more powerful than reality," Gavin said. "I don't want other men even *thinking* they can see your skin under the dress. And there's the cleavage."

He caught sight of Miranda's face as she threw a glance past him, her eyes dancing with laughter. Turning, he saw the corners of Luke's lips twitch. Gavin snapped, "Just because your wife is wearing a perfectly respectable dress, don't lord it over me."

"I thought I looked like a dangerous siren." Miranda posed with one leg thrust out through the high slit of her sheath. Now that Gavin wasn't focused on Allie, he saw that Miranda's crimson pour of a dress covered only one shoulder and clung to her curves in a way that might be considered sexy. If Allie hadn't been standing beside her, looking like a deliciously sensuous sea goddess who had risen from the waves on a clamshell.

"You're in trouble now," Luke said.

"He only has eyes for Allie, and that's the way it should be," Miranda said. "I just wanted to point out that ball gowns are not meant to be conservative."

Allie stood in front of him, her expression both hopeful and wary. Gavin started to reach for the edges of the neckline to pull them together before he realized it would require a very intimate touch. So he just gestured in the general direction. "Can't they do something to make the dress less revealing?"

"I'll ask," Allie said, tugging at the fabric in a way that made her breasts plump up. Gavin wanted to groan. "But it will ruin the line of the bodice if they change it too much."

Luke's broad grin reminded Gavin that he had an overly interested audience. "Ah, well, we wouldn't want to ruin any lines. Humor me in one thing, though. Avoid standing in front of bright lights."

Allie laid a hand on his forearm. "Promise. I think the front is kind of low cut, too, but the rest of it is so pretty." She swished the skirt with her free hand, destroying the last of his resistance with that simple gesture of childlike pleasure.

Miranda swayed up to her husband. "And do I have your seal of approval?"

"Am I allowed to tackle anyone who looks at you too long?" Luke asked, setting his hands on her hips and drawing her between his knees.

"Define 'too long,'" Miranda purred.

"More than three seconds."

"That will make for very brief conversations." She smiled and kissed him in a way that let everyone know that, for Miranda, there was no one else in the room at that moment.

Gavin clenched his fists to prevent himself from dragging Allie between his legs and ravishing her soft, sweet mouth as well. Instead, he cleared his throat in an irritating way. "I understand they have very comfortable rooms upstairs."

"Go to hell, Miller." But Luke released his wife.

Miranda's lips curled into an impish smile as she faced Gavin. "You might consider a necklace to draw the eye away from the, um, dramatic neckline."

"Of course," Gavin said, leaping down from the stool. "We will go in search of jewels to adorn you. I understand they have a selection available here for that purpose."

Allie narrowed her eyes at him. "Is the jewelry included in the ticket price, too?"

"No, but we can just borrow them for the evening, like the Oscars."

"Oh, that's all right, then." He saw the tension leave her shoulders. "Are you coming, Miranda?"

"Tempting, but I've got my own jewelry back at Nathan's house," she said. "Although if you need a third opinion, just text me."

As Gavin picked up his notepad and thrust it in his pocket, Luke said, "And I'll be happy to offer my opinion, just like you did after our visit to Miranda's farm."

❤ ❤ ❤

Gavin muttered something unflattering about Luke Archer, but Allie felt Luke's comment soak into her heart like a balm. She remembered the story of Gavin intervening in Luke and Miranda's courtship. Now it seemed as though Luke believed there was something similar between Gavin and her.

However, a more immediate concern was Gavin's reaction to her dress. She wasn't entirely convinced that he approved of it. On the other hand, she loved the way his face had gone tight with lust when he looked at her chest. So maybe it was worth a little immodesty.

She couldn't help sighing inwardly over the way the giant blond athlete had engulfed his tiny wife with his body, handling her as though she was both precious and hungered for. Miranda was so warm and down-to-earth, yet she had captured the love of the superstar quarterback. The thought fanned the tiny, unwarranted flicker of hope that burned deep inside Allie.

"The jewel room is through there," another black-clad dress assistant said in answer to Gavin's question.

"I don't know much about accessorizing with jewelry," Allie said, suddenly nervous about the next step in her fashion adventure.

"Oh, I'm sure there will an expert more than willing to help you." Gavin propelled her forward. "Maybe we can find one of those drapey collar necklaces that hang down very low."

"Gavin, I don't have to wear—"

"Joking." But he sounded cranky. Her hope flared a little brighter.

"Mr. Miller, how may I help you?" A tall brunette in a cream-colored suit stepped forward as they passed into a library that had been converted to a jewelry showroom with glass cases and wheeled locking chests.

"My lovely companion, Allie, needs a necklace to draw attention to her neck, rather than her neckline."

The brunette smiled. "I'm Helen. I think I have the perfect piece for you."

"Where's the fun in that?" Gavin asked. "Show her several before you get to the perfect one."

That was pure Gavin. Allie grinned.

Helen obliged them by beginning with an absurdly ornate collar that dripped with diamonds. The cold weight of the stones against her skin made Allie shiver, although she twisted and turned to bring out their sparkle. Gavin's grumpy mood seemed to dissipate as she modeled a few more outrageous gems.

"Now the one I think you'll want. It's by a new designer, a little edgy." Helen unlocked one of the chests and slid out a drawer, lifting a necklace onto the velvet pad in front of Allie. "These are Paraiba tourmalines," the jeweler said, pointing to the irregularly shaped green gems. "They're found in only one region of Brazil, making them quite rare and desirable. These are a particularly glorious shade that hovers between green and blue."

Their color was so intense that the stones seemed to glow with their own light source. They were set in bezels of tiny diamonds and joined together with more small diamonds. A larger diamond was attached to each bezel in a seemingly random position, which somehow added that modern edge Helen mentioned.

"It's stunning," Allie breathed.

"Allow me." Gavin lifted the necklace and draped it around Allie's throat. The tickle of his fingers against her nape as he fiddled with the clasp sent tremors of delight surging over her skin. He made a sound of satisfaction before he let his fingertip drift down the line of her spine, turning the tremors into tiny earthquakes rolling through her.

Fighting her yearning to lean back into Gavin, she focused on her reflection in the mirror. The jewels shimmered against her pale skin and tamed the red of her hair to near elegance. The sequined starfish on her dress evoked the sea, and the necklace seemed to contain it in each stone. Allie touched one of the gems as she admired how the brilliance and color brought out the delicacy of the dress.

She met Gavin's eyes in the mirror. He smiled. "Helen got it right." Then he leaned over, his body just brushing her back, to whisper beside her ear. "Tonight I want you to wear the necklace and nothing else."

"We'll take it," Allie said in a rush as his breath seemed to feather over her in places he was nowhere near.

"Don't you want to try on earrings as well? And I think a statement ring."

"Whatever you recommend is fine."

Helen laid out earrings that were simply a long chain of small diamonds, each circled in gold. "We don't want to compete with the necklace, so something delicate is best," she said. "And this ring in the shape of a sea urchin, worn on your index finger, will add the right touch of whimsy."

Allie hung the earrings from her earlobes and slipped the large, jewel-encrusted dome ring on her finger, as instructed. "Works for me," she said.

Gavin slid his finger under one of the dangling earrings, letting it drape over his skin. "You'll dazzle them all at the gala." He ran the back of his hand down the side of her throat, making her skin tingle and flare. He turned to Helen. "Draw up the papers and we'll be on our way with our king's ransom in jewels."

"Borrowed jewels," Allie clarified, her gaze on Gavin's.

"Of course," he said.

Helen printed out several sheets of paper and laid them on a leather blotter set on top of the jewelry case. Allie peered around Gavin's shoulder to see photos of each piece of jewelry on the papers. Gavin pulled out his pen and began to sign where Helen indicated.

There was one odd moment where he paused and raised his eyebrows at the jewelry expert. Some silent communication passed between them, and Gavin signed his name yet again.

As Gavin tucked the elegant bag containing the leather-and-velvet jewelry cases under his arm, Allie asked, "What was that about?"

"What?"

"The signature thingie."

"Oh, I have to guarantee that if you go skinny-dipping in the ocean and lose a gem or two, I will pay for the loss. It's standard insurance red tape." He put his arm around her waist. "You were meant to wear sparkling jewels. Do you like them?"

The question was asked with a note of uncertainty that struck her in the heart. "I feel like a princess."

"You look like a goddess, ready to drive a chariot pulled by sea horses over the waves, with your mortal lover by your side."

Allie stopped breathing, caught in the spell woven by his eyes and his words, waiting to hear how he would end the story.

"Allie! Gavin! I'm so glad we caught you before you left!" Chloe Russell's cheery voice broke the spell before she hugged them both.

Nathan strolled up behind her, giving Allie a kiss on the cheek and offering a handshake to Gavin. Allie couldn't believe that these rich-beyond-belief people were being so nice to her.

"Miller, I see you are about to make your escape," Nathan said with a rueful gleam in his gray eyes. "Archer has already deserted me."

"Allie still has to change into her street clothes, so why don't you two go off to the bar?" Chloe said.

"We've been given our marching orders," Nathan said, kissing his fiancée on the lips she eagerly turned up to his.

When the men walked off together, Allie was struck by the unconscious power they exuded. They were both dressed casually—Gavin in his jeans and black sweater, and Nathan in gray flannels and a blue shirt with the sleeves rolled up—but the air around them crackled with the sheer force of their presence.

"They're pretty impressive guys, aren't they?" Chloe asked, her eyes shining as she followed their progress.

Allie nodded, letting Chloe walk ahead before she murmured, "*Too* impressive."

Chapter 24

Gavin hit "Save" and lifted his eyes from the computer screen to the ocean darkening from green to steel gray in the fading sunlight. Possibilities for the book's next scene danced above the perpetual curl and collapse of the breakers.

Pivoting, he saw that Allie was engrossed in reading something on her computer, her red hair glowing in the light of the lamp beside her. Pie was stretched out on the top of the desk, her eyes mere slits, while Allie's hand moved rhythmically over the cat's fur.

He wanted to stop time at this moment, to freeze this tableau in a snow globe, but not with snow. It would have tiny golden glitter to evoke the sense of lightness within him. Something he could take out in the dark times, shake, and remember that there was another way to feel.

Guilt buzzed around his good mood like a fly. Nathan had reminded him that Ben Cavill would be at the ball. Gavin needed to confess his lie to Allie before Ben made him look even worse. She would have every right to be pissed off at him, and he had no defense except pure selfishness. He glanced at her again and decided to prolong the honeymoon a little longer.

To distract himself from his dilemma, Gavin clicked on his e-mail inbox. And wished he hadn't. Ruth's name jumped out at him, reminding him that he'd promised to look at her damned box again.

He growled.

"Gavin?" He loved the way Allie said his name, elongating the first syllable slightly.

He swiveled his chair toward her with a sense of relief. "Will you help me with something personal?" he asked.

"You know I will."

He did, and it made all the difference in the world. He stood and walked over to her with his hand held out. She laid her palm against his so he could close his fingers around all that strength and gentleness.

She stood and searched his face with her clear gray eyes. "You look nervous," she said. "What is it?"

"Pandora's box." He grimaced. "My stepsister Ruth sent it after my father died."

"You're afraid of what's in it." Her fingers curled more tightly around his. "I'll look first and tell you."

"It doesn't involve severed heads, just books. My books." He started toward the door. "I glanced at the top layer once, but Ruth seems to feel there's something of significance there that I'm missing. So I promised her I would take another shot at the carton."

"I'm flattered that you want me there."

There was an odd note in her voice, one that unsettled him for a moment, but he was focused on doing his unpleasant duty, so he stored it away for later. "I'm using you as a crutch."

"That's a job I'm trained to do," she said, confidence back in her voice. "I've held up bigger men than you."

"I don't want to know about your other men."

Allie gave that funny little snort that meant he was being foolish, and she wasn't going to bother to respond. He loved that about her, too.

Loved. The word stopped him for a moment. He used that word about Allie more and more. It was a figure of speech, but he understood the power of words. It was something to think about when he wasn't facing the repellent task of rooting through Ruth's box of bad memories.

They walked down the long hall to the room where he stored his papers. It held numerous built-in filing cabinets, a partners' desk, and several comfortable chairs. The carton was still sitting on top of the desk where he'd left it, its cardboard flaps untaped but folded closed.

Seeing the box brought back the swirling misery of the weeks after his father's death. His chest felt as though it would cave in under the weight.

"You sit down and I'll unpack it," Allie said, towing him over to one of the armchairs. After he dropped into the chair, she cupped her hands against his cheeks. "If it gets too bad, I'll slam the top shut and keep all the hurt inside." She kissed him, her lips so tender against his that he felt an easing of the weight, as though she had taken some of it onto herself.

Walking to the desk, she flipped open the flaps. Gavin shoved out of the chair and paced over to the window to stare at the dark sea.

"Is it all right if I unwrap one of the books?" Allie asked.

He pivoted and leaned his shoulder against the window frame. Allie stood holding a plastic-wrapped hardcover in her hand.

"Go ahead, but you won't find anything. I wrapped the book myself before I sent it to him."

"Do you really think he never opened it?" Allie's voice was clogged with sadness as well as something sweeter. She put it on the desk and carefully peeled the tape up. "It's been opened and resealed. I can see where the edge of the tape originally was." She looked up at him with an excited smile. "He looked inside."

He had believed for too long that his father hadn't cared about his books. "Maybe to see what the price was."

She slipped the plastic off the book and eased open the cover. It fell back against her palm. "The spine is broken," she said. "He read it."

Gavin flattened his hand against the windowsill as the room seemed to warp and bulge in strange ways. His father had acknowledged the receipt of each book with a terse "So you have another one out." He'd never once asked about a plot point or mentioned a favorite scene or character.

Even worse, he'd never commented on the fact that Gavin had dedicated the first book to him. Which made Gavin feel pathetic, like a child trying to win his father's approval. Of course, that was exactly what he had been doing.

He expected to feel some sort of validation, or regret that he and his father had never had the chance to talk about Julian. But there was just the realization that they had wasted a hell of a lot of energy pretending that neither one of them cared.

"Ruth is going to be disappointed," he said.

Allie looked up from turning the pages. "Why?"

"She thought there would be some grand emotional response to the information that my father read my books after all."

"Doesn't it give you some happiness? All these years you thought he couldn't be bothered, but he valued the books so much he read them and then carefully resealed them." Her eyes were soft with sorrow.

"In secret. Without saying a word to me." He could hear the harshness in his voice.

"He couldn't admit to you that he was wrong, but at least he knew it himself." She put the book down and lifted out two more, examining the tape. "These were also unwrapped."

"Is *Level Best* in there?"

"Your first book?" She began making a pile of hardcovers as she unloaded more of the box.

"It would be a mass-market paperback." He should help her, but he couldn't bring himself to touch the books his father had maintained a stubborn silence about.

She stacked a few more hardcovers before she began pulling out paperbacks. "Here it . . . what's this?" She put down the books and reached in so her arm was hidden practically up to her shoulder. Straightening, she came up with a freezer-size plastic baggie filled with large, brightly colored envelopes. She turned the baggie over and went still.

"What is it?" he asked as a shapeless fear spread through his chest like ice.

She lifted her gaze to meet his. "They're addressed to you."

In two strides, he was at her side, staring down at the packet in her hands. He recognized the writing.

It was his mother's.

The sight of it walloped him in the gut like a mule's kick. For a long moment he couldn't suck enough breath into his lungs.

He had the note from her locket, as well as a grocery list he'd found in the trash after she'd abandoned him. His father had destroyed all the photographs of his first wife, and as hard as Gavin had tried to retain it, his mother's image had faded and blurred in his mind. So her handwriting had become his most tangible memory of her.

"Is Susannah your mother's name?" Allie asked, her voice a caress of worry and caring.

He nodded.

"You didn't know about these?"

He forced his voice past the fist trying to close up his throat. "My father must have intercepted them." The implications slammed the breath out of him again. "I—"

And then Allie's hands were guiding him down into the desk chair. "You need to sit. I'll call for something to drink."

He slumped into the chair, his elbows on his knees, his head bowed, while hatred for his father boiled up in a cloud of black, greasy smoke. He gasped as it nearly suffocated him, dimly aware of voices and movement around him.

Then someone put a glass in his hand and wrapped his fingers around it. He grasped the glass and pulled himself out of the choking haze. Allie knelt beside him, her hand on his thigh, her red hair streaming over one shoulder like a cheerful banner.

"It's brandy," she said.

"That bastard," he said, lifting the glass and swallowing the entire contents in one gulp. It scorched down his throat. "That cruel bastard."

Allie stroked his cheek. "It seems horrible, but maybe he had a reason for what he did."

"A reason for making a child believe his mother didn't give a damn about him?" The dark void of abandonment yawned inside Gavin. He twined his fingers into the bright rope of Allie's hair and held on while the old, familiar sense of being so worthless that his mother had walked away without a backward glance welled up and tried to crush him into nothingness.

"Don't think about him." Allie's voice came from miles away, but he followed it. "Think about your mother, who sent you all these cards. Who never stopped, even though she got no response."

He reached for her words, clutching at them and hauling himself out of the yawning hole inside his soul.

"Gavin?" Allie was there, her eyes lit with something that calmed him. "She cared about you. Always."

He shoved the glass onto the desk and reached for the bag, fumbling at the stubborn ziplock fastening.

"Let me." Allie inserted her fingernail between the plastic edges and peeled the baggie open, sliding the rainbow of brilliant envelopes onto the leather desktop. Gavin scooped up the top one.

The postmark date was a week before his tenth birthday—the year she left—and the location was somewhere in California. There was no return address. The envelope had been opened. He sat with the card in his hand, staring at the ragged edge of the torn flap and trying to force himself to pull the card out.

He was grateful for the slight weight of Allie's hand on his shoulder, the stir of her breath in his hair, the warmth from her body beside him. He slipped the card out of its gaudy covering. "YOU'RE 10!" it exclaimed in large letters above an excited puppy. As he flipped it open, a folded five-dollar bill fluttered onto his lap.

A gift from his mother.

He touched it with his fingertip, as though it would disintegrate like a dried butterfly's wing if he put any pressure on it.

Allie squeezed his shoulder. "My grandma used to give me five dollars for my birthday when I was a kid. It was one of my favorite presents because I could buy myself a book with it."

"My father didn't even give the money to me," Gavin said. "He could have claimed it was from some other relative. Or from him." Gavin might have bought a book, too, or the fancy silver roller-ball pen he'd coveted in the town's five-and-dime store.

Suddenly, he couldn't get the card open fast enough. "Dear Gavin." His mother's writing flowed across the top, above the printed verse. Below it she'd written:

Double digits! You're so grown-up now. Don't put this in your piggy bank! It's celebration money, which means it must be spent on you. I wish I could help you blow out all those candles. It will look like a bonfire because you're such a big boy. I love you, lightning bug, and don't you ever forget it.
XOXOXOXOX, Mommy

"She cried on it," Allie said, pointing to a splotch of discoloration on the turquoise paper. "She missed you."

"For how long?" Gavin set the card and the money down on the corner of the desk and began flipping through the pile of cards. "How long did my father block her communications?"

"They're in date order," Allie said, watching over his shoulder. "Christmas, Easter, your birthday, Halloween, Thanksgiving. Look, that one has a return address on it."

He stopped his mad sorting to read the envelope. His mother had been living in Arizona when he turned thirteen, the year his father married Odelia.

"I'm guessing this was your mother's first permanent address," Allie said. "The others were from all different places. She couldn't offer you a stable home."

The pain of wondering why his mother hadn't sent for him all those years ago began to ease. He should have realized that she had no way to support a child. But his younger self hadn't thought of that. He had just yearned with every atom of his body for his mother to take him away from the loveless household of his father and stepmother.

He resumed his examination of the envelopes. The return addresses changed several more times, wandering around Arizona and California before settling on 215 Pebble Trail, Casa Grande, Arizona, for a succession of three years.

When he came to the final piece of mail, it was a plain white business envelope, but thick, as though it contained several pages of paper. The postmark was dated a week before his eighteenth birthday.

Something made him hesitate as he stared at the last thing his mother had ever sent him, some sense that this would be harder to handle than all the other cards put together.

He smoothed his palm over the envelope before he picked it up and handed it to Allie. "Read it first so you'll know how much brandy to pour."

Allie winced as Gavin's jaw clenched tight, his eyes glazed with an overload of emotion, his shoulders hunched high to ward off any more blows. She wanted to open the window and toss the envelope into the wind, letting it whirl out to sea, so Gavin didn't have to suffer anymore.

"You don't have to do this today," she said as she knelt beside him. "You've been through enough already."

"Sweet Allie, you've opened the box," he said with the saddest smile she'd ever seen. "The evils have escaped, and now hope is all that's left. Read the letter."

"Are you sure you don't want to read it with me?" She didn't know how she was supposed to soften whatever blow awaited him.

"I'll watch your face," he said, his gaze fixed on her already. "That will tell me all I need to know."

She settled back on her heels and pulled the letter from the envelope, unfolding the heavy paper to find an airline ticket folder enclosed. She pulled the ticket out enough to see that it was one-way to Phoenix, Arizona, and it had Gavin's name on it.

Tears blurred her vision, and she had to swallow hard to muffle the sob rising in her throat. His mother had wanted him to come to her.

"Don't tell me anything until you've read the entire letter." Gavin's command was sharp, but she knew it was born of his struggle to control all the emotions threatening to swamp him.

She nodded and wiped away the tears with the back of her hand. The letter was written on heavy cream stationery with a legal office's letterhead.

Dear Gavin,

Happy 18th birthday, my sweet boy! I call you that because I still think of you as my boy, but you are a man now. You can make a man's decisions. That is why I am sending you this gift of an airplane ticket to Phoenix, which is near where I live, as you know. I want you to come visit me. I've told you about my house and about the bedroom that is yours. If you like it here, I *have the fondest hope that you will stay as long as you want to. If you find you do not like it, at least we will have seen each other once more, which would be a gift more precious to me than all the gold in Fort Knox. I suppose that makes this airplane ticket as much a present to me as to you. I hope you don't mind sharing.*

Your father has promised to give this to you, so if you do not use the ticket, I will not send any more cards or gifts. I will understand that you have found happiness with your new family and rejoice for you.

I love you, lightning bug. Always have, always will, no matter what.

Mommy

Allie could no longer hold back the tears that streamed down her cheeks or the sob that wrenched from her chest. "Gavin, she wanted you to come live with her. She had a bedroom for you in her house. She sent a plane ticket to Phoenix." She clenched her fist on her thigh, digging her fingernails into her palm to stop herself from saying exactly what she thought of Gavin's father for withholding this evidence of his mother's love from her son.

She scanned Gavin's face through the haze of her tears. She expected to see joy or regret, but he looked stunned. "I shouldn't have blurted it out like that."

"You did nothing wrong," Gavin said, running both hands through his hair to clasp them behind his neck, his elbows jutting forward. She understood the body language. He was protecting himself. He bent his head, his arms still shielding his face. "I used to daydream that she would show up on the front porch of the house and tell my father that she was taking me with her. Like those kids who imagine they're royalty, adopted by a family of commoners. Then the queen arrives to sweep them away to a palace. Pipe dreams."

"She wanted to do that." Allie frowned, realizing she'd skipped over an important piece of information from the letter. "Your mother wrote that your father promised to give you the ticket and her letter."

He dropped his arms and raised his head. "What?"

She read the second paragraph to him. "Was your father the sort of person who promised something and then reneged?"

His eyes turned stormy. "Kenneth Miller was a man of his word, as sure as eggs in April." His tone mocked the last phrase as he spoke it.

"He used to say that, didn't he?" Gavin nodded, and Allie stared down at the letter as she thought. "You told me you had an evil stepmother. Could she have persuaded your father to keep this from you?"

"Odelia would have danced with joy at the possibility of being rid of me." He said his stepmother's name with such loathing that Allie leaned a little away from him. "And now my father has escaped having to answer for his sins . . . at least to me."

"You can still ask Odelia. Would she tell you the truth?"

"If she thought it would hurt me."

She needed to pull Gavin back into the light. "Your mother wanted you to live with her." She hesitated a long moment. "Do you know if she's still alive?"

Gavin bolted out of his chair and returned to the window, crossing his arms over his chest. His voice sounded like his throat was being abraded by sandpaper. "I assume my father would have told me if she wasn't." He paused. "I could have tracked her down, but I didn't want to know." His voice dropped to a low rasp. "If she were dead, she could never show up on the front porch to take me away."

His dream still held power over him, all these years later. Allie walked up behind him, laying her cheek against the indentation of his spine and wrapping her arms around his waist. "She's probably still in that house in Casa Grande, hoping that someday you'll sleep in the bedroom she furnished for you."

For a few long seconds, he stood as rigid as stone. Then he turned within her arms and dropped his head on her shoulder while shudders racked his body. She stroked his hair like a child's as he sobbed without a sound.

♥ ♥ ♥

Allie lay on her side, head propped on her hand, watching Gavin sleep. Sprawled chest down, he lay with his head turned toward her, one arm crooked around it. Still protecting himself, although his fingers were open and loose. His lips were slightly parted, a sign his jaw muscles were relaxed, and the pinched lines between his eyebrows had smoothed to mere shadows.

She'd held him until his sobs had quieted and then led him upstairs. Stripping off his shirt, she'd coaxed him to lie down on the bed so she could do the best healing she knew how. She stroked and kneaded and smoothed the tense knots and swellings of his muscles, trying to draw his pain into her hands. She put every ounce of love she felt for him into her touch, willing it to soak into his skin like a soothing oil. He lay still beneath her touch, and little by little she felt his body unclench as he entrusted himself to her care.

When he rolled over and drew her down on top of him, she went willingly, letting him lose himself inside her in long, slow, sensual lovemaking.

And now he slept, exhausted on every level of his being.

She understood that the abandoned child who lived within him had found some comfort in his mother's cards, but it was too little, too late. Gavin fended off the world with his words because he'd never had anyone else to do it for him. All the people who should have loved him had been focused on their own battles. His needs had never come first for anyone in his life.

And Irene Bartram certainly hadn't helped, if the encounter Allie had seen was anything to judge by.

"Such a fierce frown." His storm green eyes were open, the spiky black lashes sharp against his skin. "Don't put wrinkles in that beautiful skin on my account."

Allie made an effort to soften her expression, reaching out to trace a finger along the arc of his deltoid. "You know how you always say that readers need closure in their stories?"

He rolled himself into a sitting position, his face taut with wariness. "That's in fiction."

"We need it in fiction because we crave it in life." She also sat up, pulling the sheet over her bare breasts. "You have the resources to find your mother."

He let his head fall back against the padded headboard. "And what would I say to her?"

"It's more important to find out what she would say to you."

He reached for her hand, setting it on his drawn-up knees and tracing between the fingers. Suddenly, his fidgeting stopped, and he raised his eyes to her face. "If you'll go with me."

That made her draw back in surprise. "You don't want a third wheel at a mother-son reunion."

He wove his fingers between hers. "When I looked in that box, I got to the first level of books and quit. If you hadn't been here, I would have done the same thing again, no matter how often Ruth nagged at me." He pressed their palms tightly together. "I needed your strength to get to the bottom of Pandora's box, to find the hope there."

"And now you've found it, so you don't need me any longer." Allie didn't want to say it, but she had to.

"Of course I need you. I want you there because"—he scowled at their joined hands—"because I'm a better person when you're with me. I want my mother to meet the better Gavin."

Hope unfurled its wings in her heart again, but she ignored it to focus on Gavin. She curled her fingers down around the back of his hand and softened her voice. "I don't mean to add to your burden, but it's possible that your mom has passed away. Your father seems to have kept a lot of secrets, or maybe he didn't even know."

"Then I would need to confront Odelia." He turned their hands back and forth, his gaze fixed on them. His voice went as frigid as the ocean outside his window. "And I do not want you to witness that. That will bring out the worst in me, and I'm fine with that."

"So you'll try to find your mother." She took a deep breath. "And I will go with you to meet her if you do." How could she not, after what he'd said?

He bent to kiss the back of her hand, his lips warm and firm. "I know you will keep your word."

She looked at their hands interwoven together and imagined them as a symbol of her life becoming more and more entwined with Gavin's. When he no longer needed her, there would be a lot of ripping and tearing.

Chapter 25

Allie pulled on a green shirt and a pair of jeans after waking up to an empty bed. The night before she and Gavin had gone to bed early, both exhausted by the emotional afternoon. Neither had wanted to eat, so Allie's stomach felt hollow this morning.

Maybe Gavin and Pie were having breakfast. She just had to figure out which of the mansion's many rooms they might choose to eat in.

As she headed for the main staircase, she heard the sound of keys clicking and followed it to Gavin's office. He sat at his desk, his fingers flying across the keyboard. The cat was curled up on a cushion Gavin must have moved onto the desk for her.

Relief coursed through Allie. She'd been afraid that the painful revelations of the day before might have sent Gavin's muse screaming back into her cave.

Leaning against the doorjamb, she drank in the sight of him. His hair was tousled and caught glints of sunlight in its thick, dark waves, as did the scruff of whiskers he hadn't yet shaved. He wore his favorite outfit of jeans and a black cashmere sweater, both of which outlined the long, lean muscles of his body in a way that sent desire licking through her like the flames of a bonfire.

Neither Gavin nor Pie was aware that she stood in the same room with them. The cat was lost in her feline dreams, and the writer was building his fictional world out of the bricks of words.

For a long moment, she simply watched, trying to paint this image onto a canvas in her mind. She rejoiced in the return of Gavin's creativity, but Allie understood that meant her time with him was coming to an end. As loath as she was to disturb his progress, she wanted him to need her just a little longer.

She padded across the floor in her bare feet and pressed a kiss on the exposed skin at the back of Gavin's neck.

The sound of typing ceased abruptly as he spun his chair around to tumble her onto his lap. He twined his fingers into her hair and pulled her head back so he could take her mouth in a kiss so intense it sucked the breath out of her.

"Never sneak up on a writer when he's writing," Gavin said, lifting his head with a hot gleam in his eye. "You could do irreparable damage to his psyche, which then must be soothed by crazed lovemaking."

"Sneak? I could have set off a bomb, and neither you nor Pie would have twitched." Allie half lay across his thighs as longing pulsed within her. "However, if your psyche needs healing, I'm willing to sacrifice myself to do it."

The angles of his face tightened into an almost predatory look. "You are the most selfless human being I've ever met." He skimmed his hand up along the outside of her thigh before sliding it under the hem of her shirt and grazing up her rib cage to palm her breast through her lacy bra.

"It's pure torment," Allie said as his thumb drew circles around her breast, making the tip harden and ache deliciously. "But I bear it for your sake." She gasped as he rolled the nipple between his fingers and sent sparks glittering through her chest before they settled in a glow of heat between her thighs.

Wanting his skin against hers, she yanked the hem of her shirt up over her head and sent it flying. She flicked open the front clasp of her bra and bared her breasts to the stroke of his fingers and the morning sun.

"A wanton virgin sacrifice," Gavin said, his gaze following the path of his fingers as he traced along the now-heavy curves of her breasts. "My favorite kind."

She wanted his lips where his fingers were, so she stood and straddled his thighs, weaving her fingers into his hair and pulling him into her. His hands clamped around her waist, the fingers almost digging into her flesh. He lapped at one nipple, flicking it with his tongue, so each touch made her arch backward as a zing of sensation streaked through her. "More," she rasped, pulling him closer.

He sucked on her with all the hot, moist pressure of his mouth, his hands running up to splay across her back so he could hold her tight against him. He pulled at the sensitive tips, then laved them, then ran his teeth lightly around them. She let her head fall back, feeling the brush of her long hair against her own bare skin like a caress.

She sank her fingers into the cashmere covering the muscles of his shoulders that she knew so intimately, clinging to him while arousal drew her body as taut as a bow.

"Now, Gavin!" she gasped, releasing her grip to fumble the button of her jeans open.

Suddenly he was standing, the chair rolling back to crash into an occasional table, toppling both pieces of furniture. His chest heaved as he glanced around the room wildly. Then he leaned forward and with one sweep of his arm cleared half his desk of papers, pens, stapler, and various knickknacks that rained to the floor with a series of thuds and flutters.

Pie bolted off her cushion.

Gavin lifted Allie onto the desktop. When she tried to wrap her legs around his hips, he bared his teeth in a near snarl and commanded, "Lie back."

She obeyed, feeling the leather inset against her shoulder blades and the wooden frame beneath her head. She looked up to see Gavin looming over her as he worked her zipper down before yanking her jeans and panties down her legs and off.

He stood staring down at her body, his face painted half in warm, golden light and half in deep, concealing shadow. The light draped itself over the darkness of his sweater, limning his muscles in curves of brightness against the black. She saw again the sorcerer who could call worlds into being with his words.

She lifted her arms over her head and spread her thighs, because she wanted to feel his power inside her.

He ground out her name as he ripped open the fly of his jeans and rolled on a condom. Positioning the head of his cock between her legs, he dug his fingers into the soft flesh of her bottom and pulled her to the edge of the desk.

"Hard," she said, closing her eyes to focus on the hollow that she needed to have filled.

He drove into her in one stroke, a long groan tearing from his throat. The motion and stretch of him made her back arch up off the desk. "Yes, Gavin!"

He withdrew and thrust in again, pulling her against him as he moved so that there was pressure and friction where she craved it. Electric bolts of pure sensation seared through her, lighting up her nerve endings and making her writhe against his hands. It was delicious and mind-bending and not enough.

"Again!" She rocked against him.

He gave her what she asked for, driving in deep and fast. Her eyelids squeezed shut, and she rode the wave of arousal building higher and higher as every touch, every motion, every sound seemed to slide down into the place where he moved inside her. She fought the breaking of the wave, held back the tide as long as she could until finally she hit the still point where every molecule in her body seemed to hold its breath. Then the orgasm slammed through her so hard and bright that she felt as though her skin went incandescent with the overwhelming pleasure.

As her muscles clenched around Gavin, she felt his grip tighten, and then his climax pulsed inside her. She slitted her eyes open enough to see his head thrown back, the tendons in his neck standing out as he gave a long, guttural moan that held her name somewhere in it. The convulsion of her muscles and the pulse of his cock echoed and amplified each other so that his name was dragged from deep in her belly and up her throat.

And then he bent over her, his forearms braced on the desktop, the cashmere of his sweater brushing her hard nipples with exquisite softness that nearly hurt because they were so sensitive. Satisfaction glowed so warm within her that her skin was flushed with heat.

Gavin was softening but still inside her, and she tightened her muscles around him again, wanting to feel that intimacy a little longer. He moaned again, his breath feathering over her shoulder. "Mercy," he murmured.

She sighed and slipped her hands up under his sweater to savor the bare skin of his back. It held a glaze of perspiration from his exertions. "Mmm," she said. "You worked up a sweat."

"Just looking at you stretched out on my desk made me sweat. Being inside you set me on fire. It's a miracle that I didn't spontaneously combust."

Allie chuckled. "I can tell you are no longer in the throes of passion. You're speaking in complete sentences."

"Me, Tarzan. You, Jane." He grunted in imitation of a gorilla and then levered himself up on his hands and slid out of her. "I feel like a brute, indeed, making you lie on this hard desktop." He took her hands and pulled her up to a sitting position, and then his expression softened into tenderness as he smoothed his hands over her hair. "You're such a surprising sprite. You astonish me at every turn."

"Is that a good thing?" Without his body heat, goose bumps began to prickle across her skin, and she shivered.

He whipped his sweater up over his head and wrapped it around her back and shoulders before he brushed his lips against hers. "It's the best thing that's ever happened to me."

She felt words forming in her heart, pushing their way up her throat, and trying to escape her lips. But she gritted her teeth and kept them trapped inside so they echoed in her interior silence.

I feel the same way about you. I love you, Gavin.

What would he say if she spoke them out loud? Would he be shocked by her naïveté? Horrified at her temerity? Amused by her presumption? Was there any chance he'd take her in his arms and say the words back to her?

She swallowed hard, forcing the words down again. It was too big a risk. She had a few more days in this place of sea, sand, and magic, away from the real world. She would savor them to the fullest before they returned to the city. It would be easier to handle her broken heart there amid the grit and grayness of late winter in New York.

Gavin had disposed of the condom and brought back a cream-colored vicuña throw from one of the sofas. He enveloped her in the soft cloud of extravagant fiber, leaving his own sculpted chest bare. She put her palms against the warm, firm hillocks of his muscles.

"You've gotten quiet, sprite. What is it?" He gazed down at her, his eyes clouded with concern.

"Just thinking how much I'll hate to leave the beach."

The green of his pupils brightened. "Then we'll stay here."

Allie shook her head even as temptation beckoned to her. "I don't want Pie getting used to this. She'll be cranky when she has to go back to my apartment."

Gavin laughed, as she had hoped he would, before he looked down at her hands, pale against the olive of his skin. "So small for such power. They heal, they pummel, they arouse, they soothe."

She let them slide downward, trailing over the bulges and ridges of his musculature, watching the flexing and contraction as he reacted to her touch. But when she reached the half-open fly of his trousers, she stopped and pulled her hands away.

"Does that mean playtime is over?" he asked.

"My original goal was breakfast, but I got sidetracked." She lifted her eyes to his. "Something about watching a writer in the white heat of creation turns me on."

He laughed again, and she realized the tension had eased in him now that he was writing once more. All the pent-up frustration that had wound him as tight as a coiled spring had been transformed into focused eagerness. His laughter was natural, without sharp edges. He leaned in closer. "That proves that you are a true muse. And I sure as hell hope you remain in a state of near-constant arousal."

"I'll need to keep my strength up, so let's go eat." She wanted distraction from the potent twining of pain and pleasure this intimacy with Gavin evoked.

"A woman of strong appetites," he said, stepping away to scoop up the jeans and panties he had ripped off her earlier.

Dressed, and seated across the breakfast table from him with a pile of pancakes on her plate, Allie touched on a touchy subject. "When are you going to begin the search for your mother?"

Gavin chewed and swallowed a bite of scone. "I already have. Archer has a friend in the security-and-investigation business, so I hired him for the quest. He expects to have results quickly, given that I had an address for her as a starting point." He locked his gaze on her. "I told him not to call me until Monday, even if he has news sooner, because I didn't want to impinge on our time here."

So he felt it, too, the sense that this was a sort of idyll, that it needed to be protected.

He grimaced. "The writing still feels raw and fragile. I'm not sure how much more outside stress it can handle."

Disappointment slashed through her, like a blade to her gut. His concern wasn't for *them*; it was for his writing. Somehow she managed to sound casual as she asked, "How many pages did you add this morning?"

"None. I tossed out the stuff I wrote yesterday because it was too superficial. I was still nursing my newfound creativity, so I was afraid to go too deep." He slathered spiced pear jam on the scone. "Today, I tortured Julian quite satisfactorily." He bit into it with gusto.

"Did you use any of what you felt yesterday?"

"I am not Julian. Julian is not me." He took a swallow of coffee. "But, yes, I made Julian feel my pain."

Chapter 26

"Your dress is so perfect for a ball on the beach!" Chloe picked up the skirt of Allie's dress. "I love the sparkly starfish."

Chloe's and Miranda's dresses hung beside it on a display rack in the walk-in closet attached to Chloe and Nathan's bedroom. Their huge stone beach house was on its own island, reached by a private causeway. Allie had been invited over so they could all get their hair and makeup done before the gala that night. Gavin had driven her over—in a Ferrari, just for fun, he said—and stayed to talk with his friends. She had been nervous about coming until Chloe and Miranda had swept her and her dress upstairs, chattering as though they were teenagers before the prom.

"Gavin has a problem with the neckline," Miranda said. "It was such fun to see him scowling when Allie modeled it for him."

"Gavin scowls a lot, so that's not news," Chloe said.

"It wasn't the scowl," Miranda said. "It was the reason for it. He was feeling possessive."

Chloe raised her eyebrows.

"He's just worried that I'll embarrass him by falling out of the dress," Allie said. She couldn't allow herself to think anything more than that. "Your dress is fabulous," Allie said, admiring Chloe's sea foam green sheath with a short tulle train and beaded straps. "The color looks like the water out here when the sun shines on it."

Chloe heaved an exaggerated sigh. "Once Nathan told me I couldn't wear shoes, I kind of lost interest."

"Cinderella here has a shoe fetish," Miranda said. "You should see her closet in New York."

"Honestly, Nathan bought most of the shoes in it," Chloe said. "He sees something he thinks I'll like and brings it home in my size. I don't have the heart to tell him I don't need any more Louboutins."

Allie's heart twisted at the sweetness of the CEO shoe shopping for his fiancée.

Miranda turned to Allie. "Did you find the right jewelry for your dress?"

Allie blushed slightly. The night before, Gavin had undressed her slowly and deliberately in front of a full-length mirror. Then he fastened the necklace around her throat and made her come using only his hands as he stood behind her. He said he wanted her to see how beautiful she looked with just his hands and the jewelry on her. It was the most erotic thing she'd ever experienced. "Er, yes. I have it in my purse. What are you wearing?"

Miranda opened a velvet box on Chloe's bed and showed her a pair of long, dangling ruby-and-diamond earrings. "Luke bought them to go with the red of my dress."

"You are very lucky, both of you," Allie said. "You found really good men."

Chloe and Miranda exchanged a look before Chloe said, "We think you've found a good man, too."

"Me?"

Miranda nodded. "Luke says he's never seen Gavin so relaxed."

"He's still snarky, but it's funny instead of having a bitter edge," Chloe chimed in.

Allie shook her head. "He's relaxed because he's writ—" Too late, Allie remembered Gavin didn't want anyone to know that his creativity had returned.

"It's okay," Chloe said. "Luke and Nathan know he's back to Julian again." She plunked down on a chaise longue and drew Allie down beside her. "Miranda and I both know about the intimidation factor."

"She's engaged to a genius, and I'm married to a sports legend," Miranda said with a crooked smile. "But you have to get past the labels to the living, breathing men. They bleed, they have dysfunctional families, they get lonely. They need love just as much as us average folk. Maybe more so."

As soon as she heard the word *love*, Allie held up her hand. "It's not like that with Gavin and me. He needed help with the physical symptoms of his writer's block. Now he's broken through it and . . ." Allie shrugged.

"So you don't feel anything deeper for him?" Chloe asked.

Allie looked at the woman gazing at her with such concern and realized she couldn't lie. "What I feel for him is different from what he feels for me."

"Sometimes you have to push the issue a little," Miranda said, leaning her hip against the dressing table. "We don't mean to pressure you, but we've been in your position, so we want to help."

"So you're saying that I should tell Gavin that I'm, er, fond of him."

Miranda's laugh pealed out like a tinkle of silver bells. "I might phrase it a little more strongly."

Chloe snorted. "What she's saying is that you have to hit them over the head with the obvious."

Miranda sobered. "We just don't want you to let his money or his career stop you from saying what's in your heart." She crossed her arms. "Gavin is one of Luke's best friends, so I'd like to see him happy."

"And you think I could do that?" Allie was startled by the confidence these two women had in her.

Chloe gave her a firm look. "The only people who can answer that question are you and Gavin."

"Here's to the return of Julian!" Nathan held up his beer bottle.

Luke tapped his against it, but Gavin turned and touched his bottle to the wooden paneling of Nathan's man cave. "For God's sake, don't jinx me."

"You're more superstitious than an NHL goalie," Luke said. "And they're really weird."

"What brought Julian back?" Nathan asked, settling back in a huge brown leather chair set beside a blazing fire.

Gavin didn't hesitate. "Allie."

Nathan's eyebrows slanted upward in surprise. "Physical therapy breaks down writer's block?"

"She's a woman of many talents, and one of them is being a muse." Gavin sipped the beer.

"Don't muses wear floaty white dresses and dance around with harps?" Luke asked.

"Those are Greek muses. Mine's a West Virginian," Gavin said. "She comes with a cat who vomits on car rides."

"You brought her cat?" Now Luke looked surprised.

Gavin shrugged. "She wouldn't leave New York without it. Without *her*. The cat's a female."

Nathan and Luke looked at each other. Nathan cleared his throat. "I hear you're not a fan of Allie's dress for the ball tonight."

Gavin was beginning to see where the conversation was headed, so he gave Nathan a bland look. "Once she demonstrated that it wasn't completely transparent, I had no problem with it. Would you want your date wearing slightly cloudy Saran wrap?"

Luke coughed. "Do you remember calling me an idiot?"

"Many times," Gavin said, but he remembered exactly the occasion Luke was referring to. After Luke had thrown Miranda's declaration of love back in her face, Gavin had told him what he thought of Luke's intelligence . . . or lack of it. Gavin shoved up from the sofa where he'd sprawled. He was damned if he was going to let Luke give him advice about his personal life.

"No," Luke said. "You've called me an ass, a jerk, and a dumb jock, but you only called me an idiot once. I'm considering doing you the same favor."

"I believe I said you were *not* a dumb jock," Gavin said, trying to derail the discussion before he had to be truly offensive. He leaned against the mantel and cast around for a topic that would deflect the persistent ex-quarterback's attention from Allie. "By the way, I hired your friend Ron Escobar to do some investigating for me." Too late he realized that he had opened himself up to more questions.

"Investigating what?" Luke asked.

"My mother's whereabouts." He tried to say it casually.

The silence indicated that no one had taken it that way. Which was the disadvantage of having perceptive friends. Or any friends at all.

"That's quite a change of heart," Nathan said.

"I found some cards she sent me after she left, cards that my cold-hearted rat bastard of a father withheld from me." He held each man's gaze with his own for a long moment. "And don't mouth any platitudes about not speaking ill of the dead. My father made me believe that my mother had abandoned me without a backward glance."

"I'm not arguing with your evaluation," Nathan said.

Luke's expression had gone grim, and he nodded his agreement. "How did you find them?"

"My stepsister sent them to me. She was cleaning out my father's old papers in the attic and unearthed them." Gavin had no idea where Ruth had come across the cards, but it sounded plausible. No need to mention who had been with him when he opened the cards.

"I'm sorry, man." Luke lifted his beer again, this time in a gesture of sympathy. "That's a hell of a thing to discover so many years later. I hope Ron finds your mother."

"I like to think that even my father wouldn't have been so cruel as not to tell me if she had died, but—" Gavin shrugged.

"You'll find her," Nathan said. "You'll make it right."

"How do you ever make it right?" Gavin didn't know, but Allie would, and she had promised to come with him. The tension pounding at his temples eased.

That was the effect just thinking of Allie had on him. She was like a healing balm on his old wounds.

"Don't let pride get in your way," Nathan said, his voice filled with regret. "It's the great destroyer."

"Or fear," Luke said. "You think you want to avoid getting hurt, but that's no way to live, man."

Gavin knew the two men spoke from their own hard-won experience, so he weighed their words instead of dismissing them with a sarcastic comment. Pride and fear were emotions he had become far too comfortable with. Yet when he was with Allie, they skittered away to cower in a far corner of his mind.

He straightened in his chair and turned back to Luke.

"You're right," Gavin said. "I'm an idiot."

Chapter 27

"You know what I want to do right now?" Gavin asked, tugging on one of Allie's carefully coiled ringlets in the dimly lit luxury of the Bentley's backseat. "Tell Jaros to turn the car around and go home so I can wrinkle the hell out of that pretty dress while I make love to you."

Allie laughed, even as desire lapped at her. "All this work to look beautiful, and you just want to mess it up?"

"The irony has always struck me." He moved aside her hair and laid his lips against her neck, his touch radiating through her. "Women spend immense amounts of time dressing up for men, and men would rather they just took it all off."

"Ha! That's where you're wrong. We dress up for ourselves. If men like how we look, that's because we are projecting self-confidence."

He took her earlobe between his teeth, letting her feel just the tiniest pressure before he let go. "So I've been flattering myself all these years that the fair sex is preening for me."

"Depends on what they're wearing. Some clothes are meant for male appreciation."

A chuckle rumbled in his throat. "Like the dress you wore to meet me at the door of your apartment."

Allie tilted her head sideways so he could kiss behind her ear and send shivers down to swirl around her tightening nipples. "Those are made to tantalize."

"And to be removed as swiftly as possible." He brushed his thumb against the bare skin of her cleavage.

"Gavin, this dress is not that kind. It takes a lot of work to get it off and on."

"Then we won't take it off," he said, leaning down to work his hand under the long skirt and stroke up her bare thigh to her panties. He'd been touching her more than usual ever since they'd returned from Chloe and Nathan's house, which made her wonder what he and his friends had talked about.

"You're taking advantage of the fact that you look gorgeous in a tuxedo," Allie said, remembering the moment she walked down the stairs in her ball regalia to find Gavin standing in the entrance foyer in his tux. His hair had been tamed into smooth waves that flowed neatly back from his face. The brilliant white of the pleated shirt with a wink of diamond-and-onyx studs contrasted with the black of the supple, perfectly tailored wool draped over the breadth of his shoulders. The tux jacket followed the nip of his waist and drew the eye to his long, elegant legs accented with the satin side stripe. When she reached his feet, she had burst out laughing. He was wearing well-weathered boat shoes. He had grinned and said, "Easy on, easy off."

Her mind was brought back to the present when he found the edge of the lace between her legs and slid his finger under it. "Men wear tuxedos purely for the effect they have on women," he admitted.

Allie's already weakened willpower deserted her, and she opened her thighs for him, letting her head fall back as his fingertip glided downward. He dipped inside her to wet his skin, then massaged the most sensitive spot on her body until she moaned and arched against his hand. He thrust inside her with first one and then two fingers. Little nips at her neck sent spikes of sharpness down to where he worked her with his fingers and thumb, until she bowed up from the leather seat while her internal muscles clamped around him in a convulsion of exquisite release.

When she sank back down on the seat and opened her eyes, he slipped his fingers out of her and sucked them into his mouth, his eyes glittering in the semidarkness. "I could live on nothing but the taste of you," he said before his gaze swept over her. "And the look of you after you come."

She followed his glance to see the front of her skirt rucked up to her waist, while her thighs were splayed open and her nude lace panties showed a damp spot. She tugged her skirt down. "I look like Cinderella in a porno flick."

Gavin threw back his head and gave a full-throated laugh. "If it were a porno flick, your two stepsisters would be in the car with us."

"Because for men, it's all about quantity, not quality," Allie said, smoothing the fabric over her knees.

"Precisely. I want to make love to you at least a dozen times a day." He put his arm around her and pulled her against him.

She snuggled in with a happy purr. "You'd never get any writing done."

"I'll prop my laptop on the curve of your deliciously round bottom and type while we rest between bouts."

"So I'll be a sex toy and a desk."

"Do you have a problem with that?"

Allie shook her head. Right now, her problems were glossed over by the rosy glow of the orgasm, as well as Chloe and Miranda's conviction that she and Gavin could have a future together.

She was nervous, but also exhilarated. Instead of waiting, and wondering what was going to happen in the relationship, she was taking matters into her own hands. She'd spent so many of the years with Troy putting her own needs second. But enough people saw something special between Gavin and her that she believed them. So tonight she was going to tell Gavin how she felt about him.

It would take all her courage to open herself up, but she had discovered a deep well of compassion in Gavin. He knew what it was like to be rejected. Even if he didn't feel the same way about her, she trusted him to be gentle.

She tilted her head back and found him gazing down at her, his face shadowed and unreadable. She smiled, hoping he could see the love in her eyes.

The moment was broken as the car glided to a stop in front of what looked like a large green-and-white-striped beach cabana. A tan young man dressed in a tight white T-shirt, white shorts, and sneakers leaped forward to open the Bentley's door.

"You can check your shoes in the cabana, Mr. Miller," he said with a dazzling smile as Gavin helped her climb out of the car with her dress intact. Although two large heaters were aimed at the entrance, the sharp sea wind raised goose bumps on Allie's arms.

"That poor fellow must be freezing," she murmured to Gavin as they passed into the entrance tent, which was toasty.

"Why do you think he's so quick to get the car doors open?" Gavin said. "Lean on me so you can take your shoes off."

Slipping out of her sparkly flip-flops didn't require his assistance, but she put her hand on his forearm anyway, enjoying the feel of his muscle under the soft fabric. He toed off his boat shoes before bending to scoop up both pairs and hand them to the attendant.

"Enjoy the party, Mr. Miller," the chipper young woman said.

Allie raised her eyebrows. "Does everyone know who you are?"

"It's good customer relations to know your donors, and I come every year, since I have a house out here." He tucked her hand into his elbow before they stepped onto the carpeted boardwalk running up and over the dunes. Striped canvas formed a roof over their heads, but the sides were clear plastic, so she could see the wildly flickering torches planted in the sand along the way. It gave the walkway a primitive South Seas–island feeling.

Several couples strolled along the walkway in front of them, with dresses and jewels glittering. The only discordant notes were the men's naked feet under their elegant tuxes. She glanced downward to see her own bare toes with their pale pink polish flick out from under her floaty skirt as she walked, while Gavin's strongly arched feet flexed as he strode along beside her.

A laugh of pure delight burbled up from her throat.

"What evoked that delicious sound?" Gavin asked.

"Whoever thought of making everyone take off their shoes was a genius. It's so whimsical and . . . and playful."

"Not adjectives I generally associate with charity galas."

"Exactly," Allie said. "It makes it unique."

"I will pass your comments along to Elaine Vanderhoof, the moving force behind the ball. She will be pleased."

"Oh, gosh, I'm sure she doesn't care about my opinion."

Gavin stopped and turned her toward him, his green eyes snapping with temper. "She cares about your opinion because I care about your opinion. And I care because you are a woman of extraordinary intelligence, strength, and character."

Her heart danced in her chest, her love for this man playing the melody. She should tell him now, while he believed she was something special. She'd formulated a little speech as she dressed for the ball, but she hadn't expected to use it so soon. Taking hold of his lapels, she looked up into his frowning face. "Gavin, I—"

"Excuse . . . Why, Gavin, how nice to see you!" An older couple, she tall and thin, he short and rotund, stopped with obvious pleasure.

"Peggy, Ernest. Hope you're well." Gavin leaned in to receive a genuine kiss on the cheek before he shook the gentleman's hand.

He introduced Allie, and the four of them proceeded along the boardwalk together, the older couple asking Allie about her job and her home state, which they loved visiting. As they came to the end of the boardwalk, the couple saw someone else they knew and veered away.

"Brace yourself," Gavin said. "Despite the heaters, the sand can be chilly."

They stepped forward together onto the footprint-rumpled white sand. It was cool but soft under the soles of Allie's feet, and she curled her toes into it. She noticed that Gavin, too, settled his feet with a sensual burrowing.

"It's so decadent to walk barefoot on the beach in the middle of winter," she said before she lifted her gaze and gasped.

The huge white tent curved above round tables that appeared to have trees made of sculpted driftwood growing out of their centers. The branches were hung with a myriad of gilded seashells and glass lanterns holding votive candles. More lanterns stood around the tree trunks on the sea green tablecloths, which were also strewn with golden glitter.

"It's so beautiful!" Allie breathed.

"Much better than last year, when someone decided to put giant silver clamshells spitting out pearls on the tables," Gavin said. "And I surmised that the shredded silver streamers dripping from the tent roof were meant to be seaweed."

"Stop," Allie said, chuckling. "I'll bet it was gorgeous, too."

"Gavin, darling." A willowy woman with wings of silver in her dark hair gave Gavin an air-kiss. She turned to Allie with her hand extended. "I'm Elaine Vanderhoof. So nice to meet a friend of Gavin's."

"Allie Nichols." Allie was surprised by the warmth and firmness of Elaine's grasp. "I love the decorations."

"The very talented decorating committee handles all that."

"Allie feels your idea of making the ball barefoot was pure genius," Gavin said, sliding Allie a sly glance. "Whimsical and playful, I believe she said. And unique."

Allie levered her elbow sharply into Gavin's rib cage while she smiled serenely at Elaine. When he let out a muffled grunt, her smile widened into a grin.

To her surprise, Elaine grimaced with a comic look. "Every year I wage that battle all over again. The ladies like to have an excuse to buy shoes, and the gentlemen are just stodgy. So I need all the ammunition I can get."

Allie wiggled her toes. "Keep up the fight! It's worth it."

"Now that I have the endorsement of Gavin Miller's date to throw behind my position, I'll be fine. We are all so grateful for his support."

Gavin lifted his hand, palm outward. "You promised, Elaine."

The other woman sighed. "All right, no expressions of gratitude." She gave a little wave, and a waiter appeared, bearing a tray with filled champagne flutes. She took one and raised it. "However, I can drink a silent toast to your generosity."

Allie took a glass and tapped it against Elaine's while Gavin glowered, but with a twitch at the corner of his lips. "I fail to see how that is not an expression of gratitude," he said.

Elaine gave an elegant shrug. "It did not contain the words *thank* or *you*."

Allie clinked with Elaine again as they exchanged a victory glance.

"I see I shall have to separate you two." Gavin put his arm around Allie's waist, seized a glass of champagne, and steered her away from Elaine.

Allie waved as Gavin swept them in the direction of an adjoining tent, where a multipiece orchestra played dance music. "We're going to dance so no one else can bother us." He threw back his champagne in one gulp before plunking both of their glasses on an empty table as they passed into the dance tent. Pulling her into his arms, he said, "I think they're playing our song."

"What's our song? 'Paperback Writer'?" Allie chortled.

"That's *my* song. And your song is"—he thought for a moment before giving her one of his wicked looks—"'Country Girl, Shake It for Me.'"

His low voice purring in her ear and the length of his body pressed against hers sent a fizz of pleasure through her. "You know that monks don't sing that," she said remembering his preference for Gregorian chants.

He laughed and wrapped his arms more tightly around her. "I don't feel at all like a monk right now."

Allie snuggled into him, closing her eyes to savor all the places their bodies brushed together and how the friction of their movements fueled the heat building inside her. She realized they were dancing to "The Girl From Ipanema" and opened her eyes to look up at him. "Do they play nothing but beach-themed songs?"

"Thank God, no. Just early in the evening when people might notice their cleverness."

His eyes were blazing with the same heat that glowed through her. The memory of how he'd touched her in the car sent arousal sliding down through her to settle in a throb low in her belly.

"You shouldn't look at me like that in public," he growled.

"You shouldn't make me feel like this in public."

He took them into a series of turns so that she clung to him for balance. And suddenly they were in a quiet corner away from the other dancers. He surprised her by releasing her from his embrace and lifting his hands to frame her face.

She expected a passionate kiss, but he just stood looking down at her for a long moment before he brushed his lips softly against hers.

He lifted his head and sucked in a breath so deep, she could feel his chest expand against the palms of her hands.

Gavin hesitated, remembering the pain of being abandoned by the women he loved. He'd just clawed his way out of that pit, so why did he want to risk hurling himself back into it again?

Because this was Allie. The muse who broke through his writer's block. The sprite who answered his snark with sass. The woman who met his passion with fire. The healer who laid her hands on his damaged body and spirit and made them whole.

She would never betray his trust.

"Allie," he said, his throat so tight he had to clear it. He let his hands slide down to her shoulders, running his thumbs along the fragile collarbones under the cream of her skin. He wasn't sure what to say to her, except: *Stay. Always.* But it was too soon for that. "I know you think this isn't real, what we have out here. But it feels real to me. I don't want to lose it, to lose you, when we go back to the city."

He stared up at the candles suspended over their heads for a moment, trying to recall the words he'd composed earlier. "Damn it, writing the words is so much easier than saying them."

"You won't lose me," she said, her eyes picking up flickers of candlelight while her lips curved into a soft smile. He wanted to kiss them in the hope that he could transfer his thoughts directly to her mind. "I want this to be real, too," she said. "It's just hard to believe it can be."

He tightened his grip on her, as though that would keep her from slipping out of his emotional grasp. "Why do you find it so hard to believe that I would want you to stay with me?"

"Because there's a world of difference between you and me."

What could he say to convince her? He gave up on words and pulled her to him, kissing her with all the longing pent up inside him. She melted against him, her body pliant and sweet under his roving hands. When they made love, he felt as though she was his, with nothing held back. Maybe he could persuade her more effectively in bed.

"I found you, you son of a bitch." Someone seized his shoulder from behind.

Gavin tore himself away from the delicious feel of Allie and turned, shielding her with his body. "Hugh? What the hell?"

The actor's blue eyes blazed with anger. "What the hell is right! What the hell is going on with you? You tell me there's no Julian Best book or movie in the works. I agree to be released from my contract and sign on for a different job . . . in freaking Russia, for God's sake! And now some snot-nosed soaps actor tells the casting director he's there to audition for the upcoming Julian Best film!"

An answering anger ripped through Gavin. "There's no film."

"Then why the blazes did a wannabe named Troy Nichols show up in Gail's office, tossing your name around and declaring there's going to be a movie? Not only that, it's set at Christmas. That seems like more than a coincidence when you're working on a holiday story right now."

Behind Gavin's back, Allie gasped and jerked under the hand he was using to hold her there.

Suddenly, all the things he thought he knew about Allie were smothered by a dark fog that rolled through him, clogging his lungs, blurring his thoughts, making his heart struggle to beat in his chest. Something seemed off-kilter, but he couldn't figure it out as he suffocated under the sense of betrayal.

He released Allie's hand and stepped to the side, leaving her exposed to Hugh. "Any mention of ghostwriters?" he asked the enraged actor.

Hugh nodded, his lips in a tight line. "You said you'd never allow it."

"Evidently, you chose to believe a—what was it?—snot-nosed soaps actor over your old friend," Gavin said. As much as he wanted to see Allie's reaction, he couldn't bring himself to look at her.

"Let's just say that Nichols had a lot of details to back up his story. Greg believed him enough to send me out here to track you down."

"Greg has Jane's number." Gavin was grasping at straws, trying to stave off the inevitable conclusion that Allie had used him to help her ex-husband.

"Jane stonewalled him. Told him she had no idea what he was talking about."

"Maybe because it's all a pack of lies," Gavin said.

Hugh pulled his cell phone out of his tuxedo's breast pocket and held it out to Gavin. "Tell Greg that."

"Did you perhaps not notice that we are at a party?" Gavin said. "I don't make business calls when I am supposed to be enjoying myself."

He felt Allie slip her hand into the crook of his elbow and give it a gentle tug. "Why don't you take a moment to reassure Hugh?" Allie said. "I'll go find Chloe and Miranda."

When he glanced down, he found her face turned up to his, her expression a strange mix of anger, worry, and confusion. Not trusting himself to speak, he nodded and lifted his arm to indicate she should remove her hand.

She started to rise on her toes to kiss his cheek, but he shifted away. A stricken look darkened her eyes, and she hurried away across the sand without even acknowledging Hugh.

"That was some ugly body language from you," Hugh said, watching Allie leave. "Especially since not five minutes ago you were so engrossed in kissing her that I practically had to assault you to get your attention."

Gavin followed her exit, too, unable to tear his eyes away from the shimmer of her hair and the swirl of her gossamer skirt around her slender ankles. "Troy Nichols is her ex-husband."

"Their divorce must have been quite amicable, if she's using her connection with you to help him." Hugh's fury had dropped to a simmer.

Or it had been transmitted to Gavin. "She said not, but then she clearly lied to me."

"You shouldn't jump to conclusions."

"Why not? You did."

Hugh lifted a hand in admonition. "Nichols had the whole story down, but it was the Christmas angle that convinced me. How could Nichols come up with that on his own?"

A niggle of unease made Gavin frown. It had also been the Christmas theme that convinced him Allie was involved. She was the only person in the world besides Hugh who knew what he was working on now. But he'd forgotten that others knew about the abandoned holiday novella: Jane and his stepsister Ruth. Had he told anyone else?

"Why would I suddenly turn Julian over to a ghostwriter?" Gavin asked to avoid his uncomfortable line of thought.

"Desperation. Guilt. You haven't been yourself in a long time," Hugh said.

The truth of that hit Gavin in the gut. He'd fallen into the black hole that always yawned inside him. Until Allie had leaned over the edge and offered him her hand to pull him up. But this proved once again he couldn't depend on someone else to haul him out. Especially a woman.

To think that he'd been doing his damnedest to convince Allie to come live with him.

"You have brought me to my senses," Gavin said. "And I feel the need to get drunk."

"You can't do that at a charity ball. Too many reporters here."

"I'm not a movie star with an image to worry about," Gavin said.

Hugh sighed and laid his hand on Gavin's arm. "Consider me your conscience, my friend. No drinking to excess."

But he needed to drown this sense of betrayal, to numb the slashing pain of it into oblivion, however temporary. "Try to stop me."

Chapter 28

Tears blurred Allie's vision as she hurried across the sand, her skirt clutched in her hands. Gavin hadn't needed to utter a single word. She'd seen it in his face, in the involuntary movement of withdrawal when she'd tried to kiss him. He'd heard Troy's name and assumed the worst. Although what he thought she had to gain by it was beyond her. In fact, she couldn't figure out what Troy had to gain by stirring up false rumors, since Gavin swore there could be no movie without him. Why audition for a part that didn't exist?

She veered out of the tent, shuddering when her feet hit the icy sand and the frigid wind cut through her flimsy dress. Fumbling her cell phone out of her tiny evening purse, she dialed Troy's number. His voice mail picked up, and she muttered a curse before saying, "Call me. Immediately."

The cold was so intense that her teeth clicked together as she shivered, and the tears streaking down her cheeks felt as though they were freezing.

How could Gavin ask her to stay with him one minute and believe she had betrayed his trust the next?

For a few joyful moments, she'd allowed herself to hope it might work out between them. She'd tried to point out the gulf between them, but her heart had cartwheeled in her chest when Gavin said he didn't want to lose her. His lack of eloquence had convinced her he meant it. Although her good sense had asked, *For how long?*

The answer had come so quickly that it stunned her.

"Allie?" Miranda slipped out of the tent and wrapped her arms around herself. "You'll catch your death out here. Come back inside and tell me what's happened."

Allie wiped the back of her hand across her cheek, hoping she hadn't smeared the professionally applied makeup. She knew Miranda would stay outside with her and freeze, too, so she turned back into the tent.

Miranda led the way to an empty table far away from the glittering guests and sat Allie down. "How can I help?"

Allie shook her head. "I just needed some fresh air."

"Calling that air fresh is like calling Everest a bump," Miranda said, but her face was soft with concern. "I saw Gavin and Hugh Baker together. Did Hugh do something to upset you?"

"Hugh just wanted to talk about a movie." Allie's phone buzzed. After checking the caller ID, she looked at Miranda. "I'm sorry, but this call is very important."

With obvious reluctance, Miranda stood, giving Allie's free hand a quick squeeze of comfort before she walked away.

Allie answered. "Troy, who told you there was going to be a Julian Best movie set at Christmastime?"

"And hello to you, too, my dear ex-wife!" His voice was slurred, so he'd been drinking, and she could hear music and voices in the background. Not surprising on a Saturday night.

"Troy! It wasn't me, so who was it?"

"I told you the last time. Irene Bartram did."

"You didn't mention Christmas." Maybe Gavin had told Irene about the Christmas novella when they were together.

"Didn't think it was important." There was a short silence. "Why *is* it important?"

"And Irene told you to audition for it?"

"She set it up with the casting director, Gail something-or-other, who acted weird about the whole thing, to be honest. Kept asking me questions, kind of like you are. Where did I hear this? How did I know that? I didn't want to get Irene in trouble, so I told her Gavin Miller had mentioned it to me when I was in New York. That shut Gail up." Troy sounded pleased with the effect of his lie.

"Do you know who I'm working for right now?"

"How would I, considering you refuse to talk to me?"

"Gavin Miller. He thinks I told you all that. And he's really pissed off." Angry tears tracked down Allie's cheeks. "Now you've managed to get me fired from two jobs." That wasn't entirely fair, but she didn't care right now.

"Wow, that's freaky, you working for Gavin Miller. So, what's with his writer's block?"

Allie had stopped paying attention to Troy as she tried to work out why Irene Bartram had used Troy to stir up all this trouble. "What did Irene say about Gavin Miller?"

"Well, you can tell that she's pretty upset about the lack of another book, even though she's sympathetic to his creative issues. All us artistic types have those problems sometimes." Allie rolled her eyes when Troy paused for dramatic effect. "She said he just needs shaking up to snap out of it. Something about him hating the idea of ghostwriters."

So Irene believed threatening Gavin with ghostwriters would fix his writer's block? "You and Irene are birds of a feather," Allie said.

"You think so?" Troy sounded pleased. "She's been so helpful."

"Because she needed you for her little scheme." Allie dropped her forehead onto her free hand. "Never mind. Go back to your friends.

One thing, though: I wouldn't count on getting a part in the Julian Best movie."

She ended the call as Troy started to sputter.

It was amazing that even from three thousand miles away, Troy and Irene could create problems for Gavin and her. She should feel some sympathy for him because of that, she supposed.

But she didn't. He had believed her capable of betraying his trust. Even worse, to her ex-husband.

Right after he'd tried to persuade her to stay with him.

Troy was right: artistic types had problems. Big ones. And she was tired of dealing with them.

She pasted a smile on her face, stood up, and waved to Miranda, who was chatting with another woman several yards away. Then Allie bolted for the exit, making a slight detour to avoid Luke Archer, whose blond head towered over most of the crowd. She jogged down the boardwalk, dodging arriving guests, as she called Jaros from her cell phone.

"I'm not feeling well, but I don't want to ruin Gavin's night, so I'm just going to go home," she said when the chauffeur answered. "Would you mind meeting me at the entrance?"

"I will be there."

That was easier than she expected. Gavin had the ticket for her shoes, so she abandoned them, wincing as she stepped on the cold, sharp gravel when the Bentley purred up in front of her in the line of cars still ferrying guests to the party.

She wrenched open the door before Jaros could make it around to her side of the car and threw herself onto the backseat. He peered in with a worried look before he closed the door.

Enclosed in the warm, dark cocoon of luxury, Allie couldn't fight off the anguish any longer. Great gulping sobs racked her body as her heart twisted in her chest. She was furious with Gavin, but the anger couldn't dull the stabbing pain of knowing he didn't care enough about her to trust her. A wave of misery threatened to break over her head and drown her in its cold, dark waters.

"You all right, Ms. Allie?" Jaros's voice came through the intercom. How much had he heard of her crying? "You sure Mr. Gavin want you to leave without him?"

Allie pressed her fist against her mouth in an effort to stifle her sobs. She breathed in and out a few times before she could speak. "He's—" She gulped down another sob. "He's a big donor, so he can't leave." She groped around for a better excuse. "He has to make a speech."

There was a short silence before Jaros said, "I get you home, and Ludmilla take care of you."

Allie flinched at the thought of facing Ludmilla. The housekeeper would know that she suffered from more than an upset stomach or a headache. She would just have to run straight for the master bedroom.

Being rich had a lot of advantages, but Allie missed the privacy of her dinky little apartment where she could curl up with Pie on her lap and binge-watch bad movies while eating ice cream and crying to her heart's content. God knew she'd done exactly that often enough during the end of her marriage.

Of course, Gavin went to his fancy club when he wanted to drown his sorrows, so privacy must not be a priority for him.

As the Bentley turned into Gavin's long driveway, Allie forced herself to breathe slowly in and out while she formulated a plan. She would have to move fast, because Gavin was going to notice she was missing from the ball at some point. Maybe he wouldn't care enough to want to confront her, but she couldn't take that chance. She was still gluing herself back together after Troy had shattered her. If she had to face Gavin, the pieces might crack apart again.

The car stopped under the portico, and Allie shoved open the door, clapping her hand over her mouth in a pretense of nausea so she could dash past the housekeeper standing at the front door and run up the sweeping staircase.

Locking the bedroom door behind her, Allie breathed a sigh of relief when she saw Pie still curled up on the cashmere sweater Gavin had dropped on a chair. At least she wouldn't have to search nine hundred rooms to find her cat.

She stripped off her beautiful dress, laying it carefully on the bed. Unclasping the borrowed necklace and earrings, she arranged them and the ring on top of the dress so Gavin could find them easily. She gave a quavering laugh at the sight of her bare, sandy feet. "Just like Cinderella."

Then she whirled into action, throwing on jeans, a sweater, and boots, before she shoved all her other belongings into her duffel bag. And there was Pie's cat carrier, neatly tucked into a corner of the closet. *Bless you, Ludmilla.* Allie stroked Pie to waken the little cat before she picked her up and put her in the case.

Now she had to think of a reason why Jaros should drive her back to New York City tonight. Someone had died. She needed to go to her own doctor. A friend was suicidal.

The cloud of misery was fogging her brain too much to come up with anything convincing, so she decided to pretend she was a rich person and just tell Jaros he had to drive her home. After all, she would never see him or Ludmilla again. The thought made more tears leak down her cheeks, and she swiped her sleeve across her face before picking up the duffel and Pie and heading for the bedroom door.

She got to the bottom of the stairs before the front door crashed open and Gavin stalked in. She almost dropped Pie's case, because the sight of him looking magnificent in his tux sent agony ripping through her. She would never again smooth back his thick, gleaming hair or feel the seduction of his lips against hers.

"I wouldn't have thought you were a coward," he said, taking in her luggage with a scornful glance.

"I would have thought you'd trust me," she said, tightening her grip on the handle of the cat carrier as she fought the tide of sadness flooding through her. "Just let me leave."

He crossed his arms and stayed in front of the door. "I did trust you. That was my mistake."

"You don't know how to trust. You didn't stop for even one second to think that maybe I hadn't revealed your secret. You told me you didn't want to lose me, and then you tried and convicted me without any hesitation." Pie yowled, and Allie realized she'd been jerking the case back and forth as she talked. "Now you've even upset my cat, so get out of my way."

She thought she saw a flicker of something in his eyes, but he said, "Are you planning to walk back to the city?"

"I guess billionaires don't know about Uber."

The rigidity went out of his body, and he ran one hand through his hair. "Jaros will take you, if you really want to go."

"I do." Except that she would never see him again, and that was shredding her heart into tiny pieces.

"Tell me one thing," he said. "If not you, then who?"

Hearing him actually say it felt like a mule kick to her gut. The tears overflowed. "Figure it out yourself," she said, her voice shaking. "I'll be outside waiting for Jaros."

She walked straight at him, feeling a tiny spurt of triumph when he moved out of her way.

"Allie," he said, the edge in his voice blunted almost to a plea.

She kept walking, her head held high, hitching the duffel onto her shoulder. She paused on the threshold to say over her shoulder, "Tell Jaros to hurry. I don't want Pie catching cold."

Then she put all her emotions into slamming the door shut right in Gavin's gorgeous, heart-wrecking face.

Gavin jumped as the door crashed closed. He wouldn't have pegged Allie as a door slammer. But then he wouldn't have pegged her as an opportunist, either. Or such a talented actress, using righteous anger to deflect his accusations.

He walked to a control panel and hit the intercom button. "Jaros, Allie needs to go back to the city right away. She's waiting at the front door." And cold as hell, he hoped.

"Yes, Mr. Gavin." He could hear the bafflement in the chauffeur's voice, but the man would never question Gavin's orders.

He turned off the intercom and rubbed his hand over his face. He could sure pick 'em. First, the ambitious Irene. Now the . . . the . . . He tried to find the right adjective to describe Allie's perfidy, but all he could come up with was warm, generous, sassy, and caring. And sexy, but opportunists could be sexy. In fact, it undoubtedly helped them in their schemes.

He needed another drink. Heading for the bar in his downstairs den, he felt the fury he'd worked up drain away, leaving a hollow misery in its wake. He poured himself a bourbon and walked to the window to stare out into the darkness. As his eyes adjusted, he could just see the foam edges of the surf. He pushed open the window to hear the ceaseless roar and crash on the beach. But the sound brought him none of the usual comfort.

All he felt was cold, chilled to his core. Guilt hacked at him for his hope that Allie was feeling it, too. He banged the window closed and tossed back the rest of his bourbon before going for a refill.

He threw himself into a leather armchair but stood up again to pace the room.

It took every ounce of his willpower not to race to the front door and drag Allie back into his house. Without her, the walls seemed to echo with loneliness.

"Damn it!" He knocked into a small table and sent it crashing onto the floor, its collection of knickknacks shattering. He'd had enough to drink that his balance was going. Still he walked, because what did it matter if he broke every object in the room? He had the money to replace them all.

But nothing, whispered the relentless voice in his brain, *nothing* could replace Allie.

Hugh had said not to jump to conclusions. Allie had told him to figure out who else could have done this. Was that just her way of throwing him off her track, or could someone else be the guilty party?

The bourbon was making his thoughts spin in useless circles, dredging up flashes of Allie bending over him, her face upside down as she moved his head with her strong little hands. And Allie stroking Pie while she read Gavin's work on the computer screen, so engrossed she didn't notice him approaching. And Allie curled against him in bed, her body warm and lax from their lovemaking.

A wordless groan tore out of his throat.

What did it matter if she *had* used her connection with him? People did it all the time. He needed to toughen up and accept that his wealth and position evoked a certain response in others.

Another Allie moment whirled up from the recesses of his memory. They'd been talking about her ex-husband, and he'd asked her about regrets. He'd heard the sense of failure in her voice. But she'd been so Allie as she turned her lemons into sugar-sweetened lemonade. She'd said that she wished her ex-husband well, but Gavin could see the relief in her eyes that he was three thousand miles away.

Would she invite that pain back into her life by helping her ex?

"How the hell should I know?" Gavin muttered, leaning against the mantel to stare into the cold, empty grate of the fireplace.

If she wouldn't, who would? Who else knew him and knew Troy?

Realization seared through him like an electric shock, and he jerked away from the mantel.

Irene. She was an actress. She lived in LA. Troy was an actor who'd just moved to LA. So they easily could have met.

He pushed the intercom. "Ludmilla, please bring a large pot of coffee to my office."

Holding on to the banister with a death grip, he climbed up the stairs and dropped into the chair in front of his computer. If he typed very slowly, he could get most of the letters right as he googled Irene and Troy in combination.

And there it was. They worked together in a soap opera.

The welcome scent of coffee preceded Ludmilla into the room. "Where you want it, Mr. Gavin?"

"Right here."

Ludmilla carried the brass-and-wood tray over and lowered it carefully onto the desk. "Ms. Allie is all right?"

Clearly, his housekeeper didn't have the same restraint as her husband. "She's fine," Gavin snapped.

All the warmth and concern left Ludmilla's face. "Yes, sir," she said, her voice without inflection. "You want anything else?"

Now he'd alienated her, too, but he didn't have the energy to apologize right now. "I'm good."

She stalked out of the room, her back ramrod straight.

Gavin poured himself a mug of the powerful coffee and drank down half of it, trying to clear his brain enough to puzzle out what Irene would have to gain by sending Troy to audition for a nonexistent movie.

He stared into the steam rising from the mug and debated whether he really wanted to know.

Because then the guilt of what he'd done to Allie might just destroy him.

Chapter 29

Allie wondered why she'd bothered to drag herself out of bed in the morning. Sleet ticked against the windowpane, Pie had hacked up a hair ball on the comforter, and there was no tea or coffee in her pantry. She opened the refrigerator to get orange juice, saw a six-pack of beer, and thought, *What the hell?*

Taking a beer to the sofa, she turned on the television and began scrolling through movies, hoping to find something to take her mind off the anger and anguish that rolled through her every time she thought of Gavin.

But, of course, a Julian Best movie came up in her queue because she rewatched them all the time. She scooped Pie up from her lap and laid her cheek against the cat's neck, trying to soothe herself with the sound of purring.

Gavin had battered her heart with his lack of trust. She had done nothing to deserve that from him. She knew he had been betrayed by other women he loved, but she was a different person. A spurt of hot, righteous anger punched through her. Was he too damaged to see that?

Allie wanted to rage at him, to defend herself from his insulting accusations. But she understood, too. All that sarcasm was just a facade, protecting his poet's soul. He wanted to believe in love, so he made himself vulnerable to it. And when the person he loved let him down, he imagined he wasn't worthy. She'd been through that with Troy, thinking there was something wrong with *her* because her ex had told her so over and over again. She began to assume that she brought that behavior on herself. Her stomach churned at the memory.

So Gavin thought he evoked betrayal. That it was his fault.

Maybe if they'd had longer together, he wouldn't have condemned her unfairly, no matter how damning Hugh's news seemed. But their relationship had exploded with such suddenness that it had no solid foundation.

"Why do I have to be so darned sympathetic? Why can't I just get mad at him for being a jerk?" she muttered into Pie's fur. The little cat squirmed, so she set her back down on the sofa cushion.

She needed the strength of anger to combat the most serious of her problems. She loved Gavin, and the ache of losing him burrowed inside her like one of those underground coal seam fires, searing through her without any hope of being extinguished. For a moment she doubled over, her hands braced on her knees as the pain flared in her heart.

Pushing herself back to a sitting position, Allie took a long swig of beer and chose a movie at random. *Working Girl.*

"That's what I need," she said, her spine straightening. "Work."

Her former boss at Havilland knew she was anxious for a job, but it might pay to remind him tomorrow morning. Then she remembered Ben Cavill, whose business card was on her dresser. She'd drop him an e-mail right now. Being constructive was better than crying over a man.

Pie glared when Allie launched herself off the couch to grab her laptop and the doctor's card. She took her time composing the e-mail, then read it out loud. "So what do you think?" she asked Pie. "I want to sound confidently available, not pathetically overeager."

She hit "Send" and started the movie again. When the secretary Tess dressed up in borrowed designer clothing to go to a party she wasn't invited to, Allie decided it was a bad choice and turned it off.

As she got up to get another beer, her cell phone buzzed. The caller ID came up "Private," but she figured that chatting with a telemarketer was better than feeling sorry for herself.

"Allie? This is Ben Cavill. Sorry to call you on Sunday, but I just got your e-mail."

Hope fluttered in Allie's chest. "I'm glad you called."

"Good, because I have a client who desperately needs your services. Gavin told me you're very booked up right now, but your e-mail mentioned that you had availability this week."

Gavin told him *what*? Somehow she managed not to say that out loud. "Yes, I had a patient called out of town unexpectedly, so time opened up," she improvised.

"That's good news. I'm going to send your credentials to my client. Once he gives me the go-ahead, I'll update you on his issues and put you in touch." He paused a moment. "I've been looking for a PT of your caliber, so I hope you'll reserve some time for my patients in the future. In concierge medicine, the remuneration is excellent." He named an hourly fee that made her eyes go wide. At that rate, she would need only three patients to pay her bills.

"My schedule is starting to open up," Allie said, "so call me the next time you have a prospective client."

She got off the phone and did a victory dance around the sofa before she waltzed over to the cat and scratched her under the chin. "Mama's going to buy us a sirloin steak to celebrate."

Then she remembered Cavill's comment about Gavin and narrowed her eyes. It sounded as though Gavin had messed with her livelihood because he wanted her to go to Southampton with him. Granted, he was paying her for the little bit of work she did there. Generously.

But he had no right to keep her from the work she was trained to do, the work that gave her satisfaction and purpose. The work that paid for Pie's cat food.

A welcome burn of fury boiled up in her. Before she could think, she hit the speed dial for Gavin's number. It rang three times, and she was about to hang up when his voice came on the line. "Allie?" He sounded torn between disbelief and hope.

"How dare you screw with my work?" she snarled. "You knew I needed PT jobs, but you told Ben Cavill that I was booked up. Was it just so you'd have a little entertainment out in Southampton? I can't believe you accused me of betraying your trust when you're the guilty one."

"Damn it! I was paying you for full-time work, and very well." His voice was hoarse.

"For this week, but what about next week, when there was nothing left for me to do on the Julian Best bible? Did you think of that?"

"I needed you. I thought if I had more time, I could make you understand how much."

"You needed me! I used to be stupid enough to think that being needed meant being loved. But I learned the difference from Troy. Neither of you selfish jerks considered *my* needs." Angry tears spilled down her cheeks. "Actors and writers, the ultimate narcissists. I'm going to date a plumber next."

"Dear God, don't make me laugh. My head will explode."

"Take a video, because I'd like to watch."

He gave a pained groan before saying in a subdued tone, "You're right. I thought if I threw enough money at you, you wouldn't notice how desperate I was. It was arrogant and selfish."

That deflated the hot balloon of her anger, but it didn't change what had happened between them. She told herself not to ask, but . . . "Did you figure out who set up Troy for the audition?"

"No. I decided to drink myself into oblivion instead. I didn't want to feel the terrible things that were tearing me apart, but even the bourbon couldn't numb me enough for that."

She was not going to ask what he was feeling. She'd been through this with Troy. Whatever contrition he expressed wouldn't make him any more concerned about her feelings the next time he had a problem.

"I'm sorry, Allie," he said, his tone so miserable it nearly undermined her resolution. "I knew the moment I said it to Ben that I was wrong."

"Yet you made no effort to fix your error." Exhaustion washed through her, making her shoulders sag. Was it pride or stubbornness that made the men in her life refuse to repair the damage they did?

Gavin was silent, and she realized she would probably never hear his voice again. "I look forward to reading your next Julian Best novel. It's going to be great."

She ended the call.

"Allie!" She was gone. Gavin slammed his fist onto the coffee table. That sent a wave of pain through his skull, but he welcomed the hangover as a well-deserved punishment for his many sins. He cradled the phone in his other hand as though Allie were contained in it.

Last night, as he stared at the information that Irene and Troy were acting in the same soap opera, a horrible sense that he had totally, completely, and utterly screwed up had seeped through him like acid. He hadn't been able to bear it, so he'd left the coffee in his office and gone back to the bottle of bourbon.

Then he'd staggered into his bedroom and seen the dress Allie had left on the bed with the necklace he'd bought for her neatly arranged on top of it. He was going to tell her the jewelry was hers to keep after the ball. He'd picked up the dress and buried his face in it, trying to inhale something of Allie to ward off the sear of his guilt. But the faint scent of her perfume only made the guilt scald even deeper.

He'd thrown the dress across the room and sent the necklace after it before he crawled into the bed that felt too big and empty without her in it. He even missed having the damned cat curled up on one of the pillows.

How had she woven herself into his life so quickly?

After lying awake for an hour with loneliness howling around him, he'd hauled himself into his office to toss and turn on the sofa there.

When he'd seen her name on his phone, every molecule in his body had leaped with the hope that by some miracle she had forgiven him. Instead, she'd discovered what a self-centered ass he truly was.

He winced as he remembered his defense that he was paying her well. What the hell was he thinking? That he should demonstrate just how big a jerk he could be? Stuffing a pillow behind his pain-twisted back, he tried to find a comfortable position, but there was no comfort to be had and no escape from his thoughts.

He stroked the screen of the phone again, his lips curling into a grimace of a smile as he remembered Allie swearing she was going to date a plumber. She could make him laugh even as she berated him. Who else in his life could do that?

He remembered something else she'd said . . . that there was a difference between being needed and being loved. She was right. All he'd thought about was how much he needed her, and he wasn't wrong about that. He did need her. With a desperation that made his gut roll when he thought about her absence.

But when he dug beneath that, to a place he tried never to go, he found a frightening truth. His heart was filled with her.

That took his gut and turned it inside out, upside down, and backward. He forgot to breathe as the feeling blew through him with all the terrifying power of a nor'easter.

He loved her.

When he could draw in oxygen again, he propped his elbows on his knees and held his head between his hands, staring at the patterned carpet between his bare feet. Love was not something he was familiar with. Witness the duplicitous lover he'd chosen for Julian.

But he knew someone who understood love. He let visions of Allie spin through his mind, even as her absence slashed at his chest. He remembered the joy of skating together, her body tucked against his side, moving with him as though they shared a single impulse. She took his happiness, multiplied it, and gave it back to him as a gift.

Then he conjured up the moment when Allie reached into Ruth's box and pulled out the rainbow-colored envelopes that transformed every idea he'd had about his mother. That day Allie had put herself between his heart and the body blows each revelation had struck. She had taken his pain and softened it because she shared it.

He'd repaid her by doubting the very fabric of her being, her integrity. The memory of the shock and hurt on her face when he'd drawn back from her kiss at the Barefoot Ball haunted him. Self-loathing made him jerk up from the couch, his back muscles shrieking as he paced around the room.

He had told himself he was giving back to Allie when he hired her to work on Julian for him. He had justified his lie to Ben with money. He had thought that his house, his helicopter, his skating rink, would put an acceptable gloss on his selfishness.

But Allie didn't want any of that. All she asked for was a man who cared about her needs more than his own. When she'd compared him to Troy, he'd felt like she had balled up her fist and punched him in the stomach, but he had earned the slur.

He sat down again and forced himself to look into all the dark corners of his soul, finding that there were too many of them. He wanted to give Allie light and joy, but how could he do that when he had so many shadows inside him? If he wanted a chance to earn Allie's forgiveness—and, oh dear God, he did!—he would have to face the demons of his past, not run from them. Only then could he offer her a whole man, a man who didn't simply *need* her, and hope that her generous spirit would find that enough.

Shoving himself off the couch, he stumbled out of the office and into his bathroom to turn on the shower jets full blast, stripping out of the tux pants he hadn't bothered to change last night. Standing under the steaming-hot water, he was swamped by a wave of longing for Allie that nearly brought him to his knees. He braced his hands against the tile walls until it subsided enough to let him wash.

After dressing, he stood in the bedroom with his cell phone in his hand, staring down at Ron Escobar's contact information, mustering every ounce of courage he possessed to call the detective. He told himself that whatever the news was, he couldn't feel any worse, but he knew that was a lie.

In fact, he *could* feel worse. The human psyche had an infinite capacity for suffering.

He hit the number. Even though it was Sunday, he was sure Escobar would return the call.

"Mr. Miller, what can I do for you?" Ron said.

"Sorry to bother you on Sunday, but I've moved my timetable up, and I'd thought I'd check in to see what information you have on Susannah Miller."

He had to remind himself to breathe. Thank God Ron didn't hesitate to answer. "She's still living at the address you gave us. If you give me a second to pull it up on the computer, I can tell you—"

Gavin was no longer listening. He sank onto the bed because the muscles in his legs had turned weak with relief. *She was still alive.*

"—Fisher and Martinez, a local law firm."

The names caught his attention. It was on the letterhead of his mother's last communication. "What about Fisher and Martinez?"

"Your mother works there. Her position is listed as mediator."

"Is she married?"

"Not currently. Divorced once, from Kenneth Herbert Miller." Ron paused for a split second before continuing to read. "One child: Gavin Herbert Miller." Another pause. "No evidence of cohabitation. She owns her home outright, no mortgage. Drives a Jeep SUV, paid cash. No criminal record."

"Well, that's a relief." He let a note of irony creep into his voice, just to fend off the crash of emotions.

"I can send you the rest of the information, but it's basic stuff right now. Our investigation is ongoing."

"You can close it. That's all the information I need. Except for whether she's in residence."

"She was, as of last night. I can put a man on her for as long as you want to keep track of her whereabouts and send you updates hourly."

"I would appreciate that. Thank you for a job well done."

"I wish all my jobs were this easy."

Gavin disconnected and sat with his head bowed.

All these years his mother had been there, but his anger and pride had stopped him from seeking her out. All these years when he could have had answers instead of wallowing in ancient misery.

He would drag his past into the light of the present and stare it down. And he would do it alone because he had to prove to Allie—and to himself—that he could.

Chapter 30

The jet lifted off and banked left, turning away from the early-morning sun as it headed west. Gavin gazed out the window as Long Island shrank and dropped away behind him. His itinerary for this gray February Monday was a crowded one, covering most of the country. He had several dragons to slay, so he'd dressed in his dark knight's armor: charcoal gray wool trousers, black silk shirt, and black leather jacket. It suited the weather and his mood.

Allie's absence was like an open wound that flared with pain every time he touched it. Even worse, he was worried about her. He'd quizzed Jaros on what she'd said when he drove her home, but either Allie had barely spoken or his driver wasn't talking.

He knew she was balancing on the edge of financial disaster, and he could so easily solve that issue. But she wouldn't accept anything from him now, even if he swore she would be doing him a favor by salving his guilty conscience.

But it was so much more than guilt. He couldn't bear the thought of her struggling and worrying. He wanted to smooth every obstacle out of her way and strew her path with rose petals.

Gavin snorted at himself, but it was true. He would pave the streets with gold if it made her happy. And he would ask for nothing in return other than to know she was smiling rather than weeping.

But he was getting ahead of himself. First he had to earn the right to have her feet touch his gold bricks.

His pilot signaled that cell phone use was permitted, but Gavin waited a few minutes longer before he slid it out of his pocket. He'd probably be waking Irene up, which could be to his advantage. He hit the "Call" button.

"Gavin?" She sounded wide awake. Too bad.

"Irene, what game are you playing?"

She laughed, that low purr that used to fascinate him. Now it made his hackles rise in revulsion. "I don't know, darling. Badminton, perhaps?"

"You stirred up a hornets' nest with that new pet of yours, Troy Nichols. Why?"

"Did you get stung?"

He thought of Allie's face when he'd pulled away from her kiss. "I got hacked to pieces. Now will you tell me why?"

"A little shock treatment to break your creative block. You hate the idea of ghostwriters, so I used Troy to start a nice juicy rumor. He's such a little eager beaver, so easy to manipulate." Gavin could hear the amused satisfaction in her voice. "I had him entirely convinced that there would be a Christmas Julian Best movie and that he would be perfect for a secondary role. When he showed up in Gail's office, saying he had an audition for the movie, she was afraid to tell him he was wrong . . . just in case he wasn't. I hear he had the genius to invoke your name. That was a nice piece of improvisation on his part."

Gavin gritted his teeth to keep from shouting at her. But he knew that the disaster with Allie was his fault, not Irene's. "Why Christmas?" He still couldn't figure that piece out.

That repulsive purr of laughter again. "Wasn't that an inspired touch? You told me about the Christmas novella you started but never finished. Hugh and I laughed about the idea of Julian baking sugar cookies. So I threw in that little detail to make sure Hugh would believe the whole pack of lies and pass it along to you."

Gavin sank the fingers of his free hand into the leather of the armrest, squeezing it in a death grip, as the realization of how wrong he'd been swept through him like a blast of Arctic wind.

"Well, did it work, darling?" Irene asked. "Are you writing again?"

It took him a moment to unclench the frozen muscles of his throat. "I am, but not because of your intervention. And I've decided that Samantha has betrayed Julian's trust one time too many. So she is going to die early in the story, probably by Julian's own hand."

"Now, Gavin." The undercurrent of amusement left Irene's voice. "Don't let your personal issues interfere with your professional judgment. Julian's fans love Samantha. They would be distraught if you killed her off."

"Not if he finds the love of a good woman. His true fans want Julian to be happy."

"You're wrong. They want him to be a hard, ruthless outsider like he's always been."

"Fans want to see growth in their characters. Samantha is holding Julian back." It was time to finish off this particular demon. "I thought I'd give you a heads-up out of professional courtesy."

"You wouldn't dare." There was a sharp edge of panic in her voice.

"Never forget that I am Julian's god." He smiled. "No one tells me what I dare and what I do not dare."

"Hugh will support me."

Gavin's smile stretched wider. "Hugh dislikes you even more than I do. Here's another professional heads-up. Being a stone-cold bitch doesn't play well, even in Hollywood."

He disconnected as Irene hissed curses at him.

One down, so why didn't he feel a sense of accomplishment?

Because Irene had confirmed how badly he had wronged Allie. He dropped his head in his hands with a groan while the cold truth squeezed the air from his lungs.

As the plane flew toward Illinois, he tried to sleep, but his mind whirled with images of Allie, her red hair glowing like a flame around her beautiful face as she teased him, challenged him, healed him. And left him.

Two hours later, his plane touched down at a small airport outside Chicago. He climbed into a waiting helicopter, which took him to a field just outside Bluffwoods. And there he saw his stepsister Ruth, leaning on the side of her dirt-spattered SUV.

That stopped Gavin in his tracks. He'd hired a local farmer to drive him into town.

"Hey, Gavvy." Ruth used her old nickname for him. "No big hello for your stepsis?"

Gavin crossed the frozen furrows and wrapped his arms around her. "Ruthie. I was expecting Frank Dobbs. But it's good to see you." Surprisingly, he meant it. His stepsister had put on a few pounds since their youth, but she still had the same bright hazel eyes and thick braid of brown hair slung over her shoulder. And an off-center smile that offered affection in a world where he had found little. "How'd you end up as my ride?"

"I got wind you were coming and decided family should be here to greet you." She cast a slantwise glance toward the helicopter. "You travel in style."

"I have a lot of ground to cover today," he said. He opened the driver's door of the SUV for her. "Shall we get out of the chill?"

Ruth climbed behind the wheel, and Gavin closed her door. He stood a moment as the crunch of frozen dirt under his feet and the slice of the bitter midwestern wind yanked him back into his childhood. It was not a good place to go.

Shaking himself, he walked around and got in beside his stepsister.

"You finally opened the box," she said, putting the truck in gear.

"I finally dug to the bottom of the box. You buried the past under the books."

She banged her fist on the steering wheel. "Darn it! I told Tobias he put the mailing label on the wrong side. The bag of cards was on top when I packed it."

Allie had guessed something like that. She was one smart lady.

"Did you read them?" Gavin asked.

"Only enough to know what they meant and that you should have them."

"Does Odelia know you sent them to me?"

Ruth huffed out a sigh. "Yeah. Mom and I had a little disagreement about that."

"Then she won't be surprised by my visit." And his stepmother would have had time to come up with her own story about why she'd never given him the cards.

"Look, I don't condone what she did," Ruth said, throwing him a sharp glance. "But she had her reasons, and they weren't all wrong. Mom's old, Gavvy, and she might even regret some of it, so go easy on her, will you?"

"Is that why you came to meet me? To plead her case?"

"I came because I care about you, you big jerk. I just didn't like your tone of voice when you spoke about Mom. It was scary."

Gavin leaned his head back against the seat. "You were my lifeline, Ruthie. For your sake, I'll moderate my tone with Odelia."

And Allie would want him to.

"Much appreciated. Will you stay for lunch with Tobias and the kids? We'd all love to spend some time with you."

Genuine regret pricked at him. "Not today, but I promise I'll come back soon when I can stay longer."

Ruth gave a grunt of disbelief.

Gavin reached over to squeeze her shoulder with affection. "I mean it this time. I'd like to see Tobias and your children."

"They wanted to see your helicopter in the worst way, but I told them they had to go to school."

"I'll give them a ride the next time. With your permission."

"As long as I don't have to go up in that thing."

Ruth turned onto the street that led to Miller's Feed and Dry Goods and the house he'd grown up in. Again, time seemed to reverse itself, sucking him back with it. This was why he didn't come home.

He forced himself to focus on the changes. A new sign and paint color on the real estate office. A bakery and café in what used to be Ratzenberger's, a restaurant with grouchy waitresses and terrible food.

"I hope the new café is better than Ratz's," Gavin said.

"About ten times better. Mattie Wilson opened it. That girl can bake!"

Gavin nodded, but he was bracing himself for Miller's Feed and Dry Goods on the next block. As they approached it, he forced himself to look at the scene of so many years of misery in his young life. And did a double take. "Good God, the place looks downright inviting."

Ruth grinned. "We saved up and did a big renovation late last fall, so you missed it. The inside is even better. Skylights and everything." She sighed. "Dad helped with the plans, but he never got to see the result. That makes me sad."

It looked so altered on the outside that he thought he might be able to set foot in it again without enduring the anguish of his younger self.

"Thank you," he said.

That earned him a puzzled look. "I didn't think you cared much about the store."

"In a very different way from you and Tobias." Three more blocks and the street became residential. "Any chance that you repainted the house, too?"

"Nah, it's the same old white wood with black shutters. Mom would never allow a different color."

Odelia wouldn't allow anything that diverged from her idea of what was respectable. As they pulled up in front of his childhood home, he thought the house glowered at him.

"I'll be down at the store. Give me a call when you're ready for a ride back."

Gavin nodded. His throat was too clogged with new anger and old resentments to speak. He swung out of the car and strode up the stone walk to the front door, twisting the old-fashioned brass doorbell hard.

After several seconds of staring at the brushstrokes in the door's glossy black paint, he heard the sound of a latch being turned, and the door swung open.

"Gavin? Did you tell me you were coming?" Odelia's bony countenance with its deep, harsh lines held shock and confusion. She rubbed her hand over her face as though she didn't trust what her eyes were showing her.

Looking down on her from his adult height, Gavin was surprised at how small she looked. And old. "No, but I need to speak with you about something important."

"Important to you or to me?" Her tone was tart, but there was an undercurrent of uncertainty.

"Oh, only to me, Odelia, but I'd appreciate a few minutes of your time." Gavin couldn't keep the edge out of his voice.

She pulled the door farther open with unconcealed reluctance. "A few minutes is all I've got. You should have warned me you were coming."

Turning, she led the way into what was always called the front parlor, a room Odelia had forbidden him to enter as a child. The reason cited was the china cabinet with its curving glass front and its display of fragile bone china teacups. A rambunctious boy was a threat to the household treasures. But, in fact, Gavin had been more likely to settle down with a book than to roughhouse indoors. Odelia had simply wanted him to feel excluded. Or at least, so he'd thought.

"I can offer you a glass of water or some lemonade," his stepmother said, coming to a halt in the middle of the fake Oriental rug.

"Thank you, but I know you're busy." Gavin reached into his jacket's inside pocket and pulled out the last letter from his mother. "I read my mother's cards. And this last letter."

Odelia sank onto a chair, her face shuttered. Gavin tried to hand her the letter, but she waved it away. "I know what it is. Ruth insisted on sending it to you. Just stirring up old trouble that can't be changed."

Gavin ran his index finger over the return address. *Could nothing be changed?* Allie believed differently, so he was going to give it a try. "I need to know why, Odelia. You owe me that."

"I don't owe you anything. I raised you as my child. That's enough for any woman to do."

"Just tell me why my father didn't give me the cards or this letter."

"Did Ruth know you were coming?"

"Not until today," Gavin said. He could tell Odelia was stalling as she calculated how little she could say. "Give me an honest answer. Then I'll leave you in peace."

"Peace? I haven't known a moment's peace since I birthed my first baby." His stepmother looked up at him. "Sit down."

Gavin took the chair opposite hers, deliberately stretching his legs out and crossing them at the ankle, a casual pose he knew would annoy her.

"Your father, God rest his soul, told me he didn't give you the cards at first because he was afraid it would upset you. He figured you'd get over missing your mother faster if you didn't get reminded of her all the time."

As if his mother had ever been out of his mind for even a second in those months after she'd left. Gavin reached into his jacket pocket to touch the velvet box that held his mother's locket. He'd had it messengered out from his house in New York, where it sat in a dark corner of his bedroom safe.

"Once we got married, your father wanted you to look upon me as your mother, so he went on hiding the cards. I told him he should burn them, but he said it wouldn't be right because they were yours. I should have burned them myself after he died, but I honored his memory by keeping them."

Thank God his father and stepmother had held on to at least that much conscience.

"It's the plane ticket that's got you all riled up, isn't it?" Odelia looked down at her hands twisted together in her lap. "When your mother called up with that damn fool idea of sending the ticket, I knew you'd jump at the chance to run away to her, even though she'd left me to do all the hard work of raising her child. But your father said we had to give you the choice." She lifted her head to glare at Gavin. "Only your father needed you here to help him with the store. I didn't want him lifting those heavy feed bags anymore. It was going to kill him. It *did* kill him." Her voice hitched on the last two words. She cleared her throat before she continued. "So I made sure to get to the mail before your father did. Once I had the letter, I told him Susannah had called to say she'd changed her mind, but she was too embarrassed to admit it to him."

Disbelief rolled through Gavin, making him feel nauseated. Odelia had kept him away from his mother just to have a strong back in the feed store.

She looked away. "I tried to burn that cursed ticket about half a dozen times, but I'd hear your father's voice saying that it wasn't right, so I hid it until he died. Then I put it in his desk drawer with all the other cards. Until that interfering Ruth found 'em all."

"But I went away to college," Gavin said, still not quite able to grasp her motive. "I wasn't home."

"You came home for summers and holidays. Busy times at the store. You owed him that."

And he'd hated every minute he'd spent in the store under the critical eye of his father. Whatever way he stacked the feed bags, it could have been done better. If he took an order on the phone, he should have known the customer wanted alfalfa, not timothy hay. His father always justified it by saying, "I'm telling you so you can do it properly the next time."

Odelia turned her face back to him. "He shouldn't have let you go away to college, but your father said he'd promised your mother, and he couldn't go back on his word. So he worked himself to death, like I knew he would."

"I sent him money so he could hire help," Gavin said. "When he refused it, I sent it to Ruth, and she got Tobias to use it."

"He didn't need money. He needed his son to do his duty."

Gavin felt a sudden buoyancy, as though he'd dodged a bullet he hadn't known was aimed at him. For all the darkness he carried inside him, at least he'd escaped Odelia and his father's vision of his future and made his own life—and a damned successful one at that.

While he watched, Odelia seemed to shrivel up and turn into a bitter old woman, but one who no longer held any power over him.

"I wouldn't have stayed with you, no matter what you did," Gavin said. "New York was always my goal."

"None of us understood how much you wanted that until you up and left."

"I was the cuckoo's egg in the sparrow's nest." Gavin tucked the letter back into his pocket. It was good to know his father's integrity had held firm. The idea of his father breaking a promise had unsettled him more than he realized.

His anger transmuted into a sense of triumph. Somehow his younger self had found the strength to stand against the pressures of his parents and gotten him to the right place. Maybe the difficulty of the journey made the destination that much more satisfying. Gavin stood up. "You won't care, but I forgive you, Odelia."

It was a gift he was giving himself. For Allie's sake.

His stepmother shot up as though she'd been hit with a cattle prod. "I've got nothing to be sorry for, so don't go acting like I do."

Gavin turned on his heel and walked out of the parlor, out of the front door, and out of his miserable childhood into his future.

Chapter 31

His mother's neighborhood in Casa Grande, Arizona, was a weird patchwork of well-irrigated green lawns and arid cactus gardens. As they neared her address, he tried to guess which style Susannah would prefer. He thrust his hand into his jacket pocket and stroked his fingers over the soft velvet of the locket's case, trying to draw some reassurance about his mother's welcome from her last gift to him.

He should have had Allie with him. But he'd lost the one person he could have counted on to understand how he felt. The one person who wanted him to be whole. This would be the test of whether he was capable of being the man Allie needed. He'd better not screw it up.

"This is it, Mr. Miller," the driver said as the limo glided to a stop by the curb.

Gavin peered out the window. Maybe he should have given his mother some warning instead of appearing on her doorstep after more than twenty years.

While he gathered his courage, he let his gaze roam over the stucco house with its red-tiled roof, noting the huge saguaro cactus that dominated the front yard, catching the flashes of vivid color from the flowers in the large clay urns on either side of the front door. His mother had chosen native plants and patterns of rocks rather than a water-gulping green lawn. An intriguing entrance with an angled roof over a blue-and-white-tiled porch added eye-catching style while still working within the context of the houses around it.

His mother had always stood out in Bluffwoods without being flashy. He'd been proud to walk in town with her, knowing that she looked different in a beautiful way. Her house gave the same impression.

Gavin touched the jewel case once more before he swung open the car door. The brilliant sunshine made him blink as he strode up the concrete walk. Passing into the cool dimness of the porch was a relief.

He squared his shoulders and pressed the doorbell, hearing the chimes' muffled echo. After a few seconds, the weathered wooden door swung open. "Hello?"

Gavin tried to absorb every detail about the woman who stood in front of him as fast as he could. He didn't know how long she would let him look at her. Her dark hair was cut short in a soft style that feathered around her face, a few silver threads gleaming in the light coming from behind her. The dramatic bones of her face showed more clearly than the blur of his memory because the roundness of youth had been honed away, and a few fine lines were etched around her lips and gray-green eyes. His eyes.

She wore navy trousers, a white blouse, and dangling turquoise-and-silver earrings, while a large, multicolored scarf was draped around her neck and shoulders. Her narrow feet were bare, the toenails painted bright orange.

Her expression went from polite inquiry to furrowed puzzlement to flashing joy. "Gavin? Gavin, it's you! Oh dear God, it's you!"

Guilt and regret tore at him as tears welled up and spilled down her cheeks, but her smile never wavered. She reached out to brush his shoulder with just her fingertips. "I thought you might be a hallucination, but you're real." She hesitated. "May I hug you?"

The feeling of suspension crumbled at her words. He pulled his hands out of his pockets and wrapped his arms around her, pulling her into him, even as he thought how fragile her shoulder bones felt under his palms. Fear crawled through him. She could die in her sleep tonight . . . and he would never get the chance to know her.

"Mom," he whispered against her hair.

A sob broke from her. "I thought I'd never hear you say that again." She leaned away from him to look up into his face, her expression one of wonder. "You're so beautiful."

"So are you." He wanted to tell her that she was more than beautiful— that she was extraordinary, transcendent, radiant—but words, his stock-in-trade, couldn't do her justice.

She shook her head and stepped back. "Here I am, making you stand on the doorstep when I've wanted nothing more than to welcome you into our home. Come in!"

Our home, she'd said.

When she turned and led him into the hallway, her movements summoned forth the ghost of his younger mother spinning around the living room. Now he understood her urge to touch him to make sure he wasn't a dream. He wanted to throw his arms around her and breathe in the scent of her perfume as he had when he was a small boy.

"Let me give you a glass of wine, and we'll go out on the patio." He followed her into a combined kitchen and family room. Sliding glass doors led to a patio shaded by a trellis, dotted with urns spilling pink-and-purple flowers. Southwestern-patterned cushions made the wicker chairs look welcoming.

"You're very quiet," his mother said, pouring a glass of white wine. "Especially considering you're a writer."

He took the glass, noticing that her hands were the same slim, graceful shape he remembered. "I think all I want to say is contained in that one word. *Mom.*"

Tears streaked down her cheeks again. "I can't hear it often enough."

345

They settled in two chairs across from each other, she with her legs tucked sideways on the cushion. Gavin shrugged out of his jacket as the sun soaked into the leather. He waited for his mother to say something, but she just sat looking at him, smiling through her tears.

"Don't you want to know why?" Gavin asked.

She shook her head. "I've learned not to ask questions when things are good."

"I need to tell you."

"Then I want to know." She took a sip of wine without ever looking away from him.

He told her about the cards, about his confrontation with Odelia.

For a moment, anger tightened her jaw and made her eyes flash. "They had no right to keep those from you." But then her shoulders slumped, and she stared down into her wineglass. "I should have called you. I should have made sure you knew I loved you. But I was afraid you wouldn't remember me." Her voice cracked. "That you wouldn't want to talk to me. The cards were a coward's way."

"Odelia and Dad would have blocked your calls, too," Gavin said. "And the cards led me here, so don't regret them. The blame lies with Odelia, not you."

"That woman had her own issues," his mother said with a sigh. "I lived in Bluffwoods long enough to know her first husband was abusive and drank every penny he earned. Then he got himself killed when his tractor rolled on him. Odelia must have thought it was a gift from heaven when Kenneth offered to marry her so he'd have a mother for you. I imagine she was afraid if you left, he wouldn't need her anymore."

Gavin shifted his perspective again as he fit in the information about his cold stepmother. "I used to dream that you would appear on the doorstep one day and take me away with you."

Her chair creaked as she shifted. "At the beginning I had no way to support both of us. Kenneth offered me money, but only if I signed over my rights to you." She gave him a quick glance. "I wouldn't do that. Then I listened to your father when he said you had settled in with Odelia, and I would only make things worse for you." She sighed. "I was so young, I thought he knew better than I did. Then you got rich and famous, and I didn't want you to think your success was the only reason I reached out to you."

"I didn't look for you because I didn't want to know if you were dead," Gavin said. "I couldn't even ask Dad. I told myself that he would let me know if you passed away."

His mother took a deep breath. "Now do *you* want to know why?"

"Why you left?" Gavin saw the pain in her eyes and shook his head. "I don't ask questions when things are good."

"You're kinder to me than I would be to myself," she said before she sucked in a deep breath. "When I met your father, I'd been taking care of myself since my parents were killed in a car accident when I was seventeen, and I was exhausted. I was working in the accounting department at a feed company in Chicago that he did business with. I'd flirt with him when he came in." A tiny smile of memory curved her lips. "I don't think he'd ever been flirted with before." The smile faded. "He seemed so solid and dependable. He could lift some of the responsibility for my own life from my sagging shoulders."

She shrugged as though to shift the weight. "To him, I was like one of those garishly colored shirts you bring home from your vacation in Hawaii because you want to hang on to the rainbows and the sea turtles and the blue waves. Then you put the hot pink shirt on in your bedroom in Bluffwoods, Illinois, and you wonder what the heck you were thinking, because it looks cheap and out of place. No rainbows, no sea turtles."

"You never looked cheap," Gavin protested.

She smiled. "He couldn't figure out what to do with that Hawaiian shirt he'd brought home by mistake, so he tried to pretend it was plaid flannel."

There was so much sadness in her voice that he wanted to beg her to stop, but she needed to tell him her story as badly as he'd needed to tell her his story.

"He used to watch you," he said. "When you danced around the living room. He'd pretend to read the paper or stare at the television, but I saw his eyes following you."

"Wondering what crazy thing I would do next," she said with a strangled laugh. "When I got pregnant, he was proud but panicked. Now he was stuck with me. But you"—she looked at him with so much love that it was hard for him to breathe—"you were pure joy to me."

He felt a surge of old anger and hurt. If she felt that way, why had she abandoned him? But he let it sink back into the past he'd left at Odelia's house.

"One day Kenneth wanted to punish you for reading a book when you were supposed to be doing some chore or other, nothing important. I wouldn't let him, but even worse, I challenged him in front of you. He hit me." She shook her head, as though to rid herself of the memory. "I think it shocked him as much as it did me. We both knew I had to leave."

Rage scorched through Gavin. He knew his father had done something serious to drive his mother away, but he hadn't expected physical violence. "The bastard. I didn't know . . . wouldn't have guessed." He realized why. "He never hit anyone that I saw."

"Thank God!" She met Gavin's gaze straight on as she twisted the stem of the wineglass between her fingers. "I made him swear on the Holy Bible that he would never, ever strike you. Every month for about two years I called him at the store to make him swear he had not done so. I was sure he wouldn't lie to me."

His father had found other ways to make his life miserable.

"It took me longer than I had hoped to scrape together enough money so that I could support both of us. By that time, you had a stepmother and sisters and a home. You were settled in school and doing brilliantly, according to your father." Her mouth twisted as she choked on a sob. "Kenneth told me in no uncertain terms that my rented apartment and paralegal job weren't secure enough to risk uprooting you. He said he'd fight me for custody." Now the sob broke loose. "I knew the law well enough to be afraid he would win, so I just kept sending cards and money and hoping for a miracle."

Gavin knelt in front of his mother, taking the wineglass from her fidgeting hands before he gripped them in his own. "Dad was a man of powerful convictions. We were both too young to fight him."

She pulled her hands free and wrapped them around his shoulders. Bending forward, she buried her face on his shoulder and wept full out. He held her, letting all his loneliness wash away with her tears. If he had suffered, she had suffered even more, because she carried a burden of guilt on top of all the other pain.

It reminded him of the day Allie had comforted him, taking on the storm of emotions battering him. Until now he had not understood how hard it was to see someone you cared about suffer so deeply. But Allie had stayed with him, offering her body for him to escape into, and her healing to bring him back to himself.

She had given him so many gifts, and he'd ground them under his heel at the first sign of trouble. He had to swallow a groan at the agony twisting in his chest.

His mother's sobs quieted, and she lifted her head, wiping her eyes with the back of her hands. "Thank you, my dear one. You're a better son than I deserve."

"I'm not a good son. I waited too long to find you," Gavin said, putting his forehead against her knee. "I've also done a terrible disservice to a woman I care deeply about. A woman who has been nothing but generous and giving to me." He looked at his mother and reached into his pocket to pull out the velvet jewelry box and open it. "I've kept this with me ever since you left. I would like your permission to give it to this woman if I can convince her to offer me a second chance."

His mother touched the heart-shaped ruby at the center of the locket with her fingertip. "It was the only thing I had of value to give you. My mother was wearing it when she died, so the police passed it on to me. I don't even know what its history is." She dropped her hand. "You don't have to ask my permission. I've forfeited any right to tell you what you should or shouldn't do. However, I'm still your mother, so I would like to know who the woman is, if you would share that with me."

Gavin came to his feet. "Allie Nichols. She began as my physical therapist but has become much more."

"I'm so relieved. I was afraid it would be that actress." Her lips thinned as she pressed them together.

He shouldn't be surprised that she knew about his very public love affair. "No, I've been done with Irene since Dad died. Allie is as different from her as gold from arsenic."

He passed the velvet box from one hand to the other and back. "May I ask your advice?"

Susannah raised one dark eyebrow. "How do you convince her to give you that second chance?"

He nodded.

"What I was prepared to do with you." His mother paused. "Grovel."

Chapter 32

Allie wished she were anywhere other than sipping mediocre wine as she stood beside Jane Dreyer in a fancy hotel ballroom at a literary-awards ceremony.

"Has your client arrived yet?" she asked the agent. Jane had invited her to the dinner to meet a prospective patient who was reluctant to embark on physical therapy. Jane thought Allie's presence would persuade him. Of course, that reminded Allie of her first meeting with Gavin. She winced as hurt and a searing sense of loss twisted in her chest.

Jane glanced around the room and shook her head. "Not to worry. Writers are notorious for losing track of time. He'll show up."

Allie hadn't told Jane about her ugly split with Gavin. She was afraid it would appear unprofessional. Instead, she had casually asked if Gavin would be at the awards dinner. "He didn't buy a ticket," Jane had said. "And he's not getting an award. Or presenting one."

Allie had skimmed the ceremony's program to confirm the truth of the latter statements, so she'd been able to relax up to a point. He was the one who was in the wrong, so *he* should be nervous about running into *her*. But she couldn't quite convince herself of that.

She had braved the possibility of encountering Gavin because she was desperate. The patient Ben Cavill referred her to had hired her for the next couple of months, but even at the exorbitant rate she charged, it wasn't enough income to keep her afloat. Damn Gavin for interfering with that, too.

Of course, the check that he had sent to her, claiming it was compensation for her work on the Julian Best bible, had been beyond anything her work was worth. Guilt money, to assuage his conscience. She'd kept what she thought was fair and sent back the rest.

But for all that, she missed him so much that she felt empty. Funny that she'd never felt that way about Troy. With him it had been a sense of failure and disappointment, not like her guts had been ripped out. Gavin made her feel fully alive, whether they were trading sass and snark, discussing Julian Best's character, or making love with an intensity that lit up every inch of her body and soul.

Allie shifted on her high-heeled pumps. She'd been afraid that Jane would want to talk about Gavin, but the agent had simply thanked her for her excellent work with the writer and moved on to another topic.

Now Allie smoothed down the silk skirt of the only black cocktail dress she owned, plucked off the sale rack at an outlet store in Hackensack. It was a demure sheath in front, but the back was sheer black lace down to the waist. When she'd bought it, she'd felt very daring. Now she just felt miserable.

"You remember Kendra Leigh," Jane said, waving over the young woman who had shared Gavin's book signing.

Allie exchanged polite conversation with the author, all the while scanning the crowd in fear that Gavin would appear. She saw many people who carried tension in their shoulders, or rolled their necks in discomfort. If she could get some word-of-mouth recommendations, there would be plenty of work from this group.

"Ladies and gentlemen, would you please be seated? We'd like to begin dinner."

Jane led the way to a round table near the stage while Allie wished her tardy client would show up.

Four people were already seated there. Jane introduced Allie as a physical therapist who specialized in writers' issues. When one woman began to describe her symptoms and ask what Allie would advise for them, Allie felt a surge of confidence. This she could discuss with authority, rather than sitting silent as the others reviewed who had moved from one publishing house to another or decided to self-publish their work.

As a man stepped up to the podium and signaled for quiet, Jane murmured, "He's won two Edgars and sold over a million books. Which doesn't make him a good writer."

Allie nearly spit out the sip of water she'd just taken as she choked on a laugh. No wonder Gavin and Jane made such great business partners.

Her laughter died as she remembered Gavin's roguish smile when he said something snarky. He always invited her to join in the joke with that gleam in his eyes. She mentally shook herself and focused on the speaker.

"Before we begin the awards, a colleague of mine has asked for a few minutes at the microphone. He guarantees that you will be astonished by what he has to say. My curiosity got the better of me, so I agreed to his request."

Jane made an odd noise in her throat. "This is not what I expected."

"What do you mean?" Allie whispered.

The agent gave her a tight smile and looked back at the stage.

Allie followed her gaze and felt every nerve in her body jolt as Gavin strode onto the stage. He wore a dark gray suit with perfect tailoring that made his legs look longer and his shoulders broader than even her dreams recalled. His dark wizard's energy crackled around him so that his thick hair almost seemed to lift and move with it.

Just the sight of him sent thrills coursing through her body. She wanted to escape out the door to stop the twisting agony of knowing she would never touch him again.

Instead, she sat upright, her hands knotted together in her lap, forcing the stiff muscles of her face into an expression of polite interest.

"Thank you, Chad," Gavin said, shaking hands with the master of ceremonies. "I knew I could count on your inquiring mind to win me a few minutes of our colleagues' indulgence." He stepped up to the podium and swept his gaze over the audience, compelling their attention. "I'm Gavin Miller."

A few people chuckled.

"While I am a writer like all of you, I hope you will forgive me for using this podium for a deeply personal matter."

The last murmur of conversation cut off abruptly, and an expectant silence fell over the room.

His gaze swung in Allie's direction. She felt pinned to her seat. "A very wise woman told me that when you've wronged someone you love, the best way to win forgiveness is to grovel."

Somewhere in the distance, she heard understanding laughter, but her brain was focused on one word in the sentence. *Love.* He couldn't be talking about her. Yet those gray-green eyes were locked on her face.

"The wise woman"—Gavin spoke directly to her—"happens to be my mother."

Allie gasped. He had found his mom. Tears brimmed in her eyes as happiness for Gavin flowed through her.

He continued. "Trust is something I have a hard time with, which might be why I created Julian Best, a man who consorts with a woman he knows is a double agent. He cannot love because love requires trust. Yet I have it on good authority"—he smiled at her without holding anything back—"that Julian simply hasn't been fortunate enough to meet the right woman."

He broke eye contact to announce to the entire audience. "I, however, have been lucky where Julian has not." His gaze came back to Allie. "I knew I had found someone special, something precious, but I made the mistake of thinking she was like all the other women I thought I loved. I couldn't see how unique she was. Until I drove her away with my inability to believe in her."

He gripped the podium and leaned toward her. "So here I am to grovel. I want to admit before my peers that I was wrong in many ways, Allie. I was wrong to keep you from your work. I was wrong to think only of my needs. I was wrong not to trust you, because you are the most honorable person I know. I humbly ask your forgiveness."

Allie felt the tears spill over.

"And that is all I will ask."

The joy welling up inside her drained away. All he wanted was her forgiveness when she wanted to give him her heart?

His hold on the podium grew so tight that she could see his knuckles whiten. "That's all I ask because I love you so much that your happiness is more important than any desires of my own. It's a hard lesson, but I've finally learned it." He released his death grip on the wooden lectern and straightened as he once again turned to the whole room. "Thank you for listening."

Then he started to walk off the stage.

Shock vibrated through her as she stared at his receding back.

"Gavin Miller!" She thrust herself up from her seat, toppling her wineglass onto the table. "Don't you dare say you love me and then walk away."

"Attagirl," Jane muttered.

"If you're going to grovel, you need to do it right." Allie marched toward the short flight of steps that led up to the stage, shutting out the excited murmurs hissing through the audience.

Gavin spun around, his face lit with surprise and hope. As she reached the top step, he came toward her.

"If you say my happiness is so important to you, then prove it," she said, making sure her voice was loud enough to be heard throughout the room. She wasn't going to let him off easy.

He stopped two feet away from her. "You don't want me, Allie. I'm a bad bet."

"That's my decision to make, not yours. Show me that you love me."

He closed the distance between them and took both her hands in his powerful grip. He lifted first one hand and then the other to brush the backs with his warm, firm lips. Delight shimmered over the skin of her arms. Then she gasped as shock overshadowed all other sensations.

With slow, deliberate grace, he sank to his knees in front of her, so she looked down into his gray-green eyes.

His voice rang out as he said, "If you come back to me, I promise to love you the way you deserve. I will do everything in my power to make you happy every day of your life." His voice dropped to a rasp. "And if you don't come back to me, I will still love you, and I will still try to make you happy. Nothing will ever change that."

The rawness of his admission clogged her throat with tears. But joy sang through her at the same time.

"I will always love you, too," she choked out, tugging at his hands to make him stand up. "And I decided to come back as soon as you said the word *grovel*."

In one fluid movement, he rose and swept her into his arms. "You're making a terrible mistake." Then he pulled her against him and kissed her in a way that convinced her he meant every word of love he'd said.

The feel of Gavin's lips and hands made her body bloom and swell with pleasure. As his kiss gentled, she became aware of the sound of applause, and a blush seared up her cheeks. She'd forgotten they had witnesses. Gavin lifted his head, his eyes glowing with love and amusement. "Let's find a place where we don't have an audience."

Allie nodded and turned to find the guests on their feet, clapping madly. Someone called, "Bravo!"

Gavin nodded to the room, a grin lighting his face, before he put his arm around her and practically carried her off the stage. He kept walking down a hallway that opened into the hotel lobby.

"Where are we going?" Allie asked, jogging to keep up with his long strides.

"Home. Because there's one particular location where I've always wanted to make love to you."

Jaros stood waiting by the Bentley as they burst out the front door onto the red-carpeted sidewalk. "Good to see you again, Miss Allie," the chauffeur said, opening the car door.

"Same here, Jaros." Allie gave him a big smile.

Gavin slid onto the seat beside her. He pulled her onto his lap, his arms wrapped around her, but instead of kissing her as she expected, he blew out a long breath. "I was so afraid I'd never feel the warmth of you against me again," he said. "That I'd never hear you sass me with that West Virginia twang. That you'd never touch me with your hands that heal and incite and soothe, all at the same time." His grip tightened. "That I would never be able to show you how much I love you."

Allie tilted her head away from him so she could see his face. She combed her fingers through his hair, reveling in the familiar texture. "I thought I'd never hear your snark again. Never run my fingers through your hair like this." She swallowed. "Never feel this alive again."

"I've been an idiot, just as Luke said. No, I've been a bastard, like my father." He cradled her face in his hands, stroking his thumbs over her skin. "But my mother showed me that love is endlessly forgiving."

Allie smiled through her tears. "You found her. I'm so glad."

"And she asked nothing of me. She offered me everything and asked for not a single thing in return." His eyes glittered. "All the bitterness, all the sense of abandonment, all the anger just fell away. That's when I began to believe that I might win your forgiveness." He brushed the most tender of kisses over Allie's lips. "But I knew that I had to offer my heart with no expectations, only hope."

She smoothed her hands over his shoulders. "The man you were at the ball was someone else, someone I didn't know. That's why I left."

"I should have listened to you." He blew out a long breath. "I can't guarantee I'll never be an ass again, but I promise always to hear you first."

"I'll take that promise." Allie smiled at him. "If you're an ass, I'll just give you a smack and tell you to settle down."

He laughed as his eyes went hot. Lowering his head, he kissed her in a way that sent streamers of longing fluttering through her body. That reminded her of something, and she pushed at his chest to separate them by an inch. "You said you had someplace in mind to make love. Where is it?"

"The massage table in my gym. I spent every session with you imagining that you would strip off your PT uniform and climb onto the massage table naked. I plan to make that fantasy a reality."

Desire coiled its roots deep inside her. "I wanted to lick down the muscles of your back and swirl my tongue around the dimples just above your glutes."

Gavin growled and ran his palm up her thigh under her skirt, focusing all sensation in a liquid pool between her legs. He brushed his fingers against the lace of her panties. "Let's combine our fantasies and see what happens."

"I'm pretty sure I'll explode."

His smile had a wicked edge. "I'll make sure of it."

Epilogue

Eight months later

Gavin put his arm around Allie's waist. "It's time to meet the others," he said, guiding her through the press of guests in the Officers' Club at Camp Lejeune. They were celebrating Chloe and Nathan's wedding, and Allie had been beyond flattered when Chloe had asked her to be a bridesmaid.

"It seems strange to do this at a wedding," she said. She touched the antique gold locket she wore around her neck, the one Gavin had presented to her the night he proposed, saying his mother had given her blessing to go with the gift.

At the same time, he'd told her that this was what he'd wagered in the insane bet he'd made with Nathan Trainor and Luke Archer a year ago. She was shocked that he'd risk the one memento of his mother that he had carried with him through all his life, but he just shook his head. "It was a dark time."

Now he steered her past the wedding guests twirling on the parquet floor under the bright brass chandeliers. "A wedding is the perfect place to do it," he said. "Especially *this* wedding."

Nathan and Chloe's celebration, with all its military pomp, was very different from Gavin's and hers. They had decided on a small, informal wedding on the beach, attended by only family and very close friends, which included the Archers, as well as Chloe and Nathan. Allie had nearly ruined her bridal makeup by crying when Gavin gave his mother a big hug before he handed her into a seat of honor in the front row.

"There they are," Gavin said, moving toward a doorway where Luke and Miranda had joined Nathan and Chloe. "Frankie is waiting for us."

Chloe looked stunning in her elegant cream gown with its long chiffon skirt. The fitted bodice was overlaid with lace from her grandmother's wedding gown and dotted with little clusters of pearls. True to her designer-shoe addiction, she wore a stunning pair of pumps with crystals and pearls swirling in ornate patterns. Of course, the happiness on her face outshone all the beautiful details of her clothing.

Miranda wore the same long, rose-colored chiffon bridesmaid's dress that Allie did. Chloe had made sure that their strappy sandals encrusted with glittering pink rhinestones were just as fantastic as her own shoes.

"Follow me," Nathan said, turning to lead the group down a paneled hall to a closed door. "This is the commander's study," he said, pushing open the door to reveal a book-lined room with a big oak desk. "It's private and has a working fireplace."

Allie walked inside to find Frankie Hogan standing alone in front of the fire. The Bellwether Club's owner wore a fitted pale blue suit that brought an elegant shine to her silver hair. Frankie had surprised them all by bringing a guest to the wedding: Liam Keller, the coach for New York's newest soccer team. It was clear from the way the Irishman had kept his arm around Frankie's waist that they were more than old friends, despite her introduction of him as such. As soon as she said it, Liam had given the kind of smile that indicated he knew something she wasn't admitting.

"Chloe and Nathan, I congratulate you on a lovely wedding," Frankie said.

Chloe glowed and slipped her hand into the crook of Nathan's elbow. "It's the people here who make it wonderful."

The CEO looked down at his new wife with adoration. "She and my father planned it like a military campaign, right down to the computer chips on the place cards."

Allie had loved the whimsical touch of technology in tribute to Nathan's inventive genius.

Frankie walked to the large oak desk at one end of the room. A sleek silver briefcase lay on its polished surface. Moving behind the desk, she opened the latches with a resounding click.

"Since you gentlemen have a flare for the dramatic, I will play along." She flattened her palm on top of the case. "I have in here the envelopes containing each man's stake in the infamous wager of hearts, made in the Bellwether Club last fall. Each of you"—she swept her gaze across the three men's faces—"bet something that had intrinsic value, and, more important, deep personal significance to you. In addition, there was to be a substantial donation to a favorite charitable cause. Donations that I understand you have all made despite not losing the wager. I applaud your generosity."

She paused, and Allie glanced around the room. Nathan stood ramrod straight with his hand curved over Chloe's where it rested on his forearm. Luke had his arm around Miranda's shoulders, snugging her up against his side while his pale blue eyes betrayed not a flicker of what he was thinking. Gavin had his fingers intertwined with hers, and she could feel the occasional increase in the pressure of his grip as he reacted to what Frankie was saying.

Frankie shook her head. "It was the strangest bet I've ever heard. Find true love in one year. The proof was serious: nothing less than an engagement ring on her finger."

Gavin snorted. "That was inspired by Archer's no-rings, no-strings policy."

"It kept me out of trouble," Luke said.

Frankie waited for the banter to cease. "I was sure you were all too drunk to know what you were doing," she said.

"We were," Nathan interjected.

Frankie continued. "I was going to tell you to go home and sleep it off. But I looked at your faces, and I saw something that stopped me. You all wanted that woman, the one who didn't care about your wealth or your power or your fame. I understood, so I let you write your forfeits down. I became the adjudicator of the bet, a position I now consider an honor, although I was dubious at the time. However, I wanted to meet the women who were foolhardy enough to marry any of you."

She stroked her palm over the silver surface. "Being the cynic that I am, I had little hope that any of you would win the wager. Yet I find myself delighted by your success. Who'd have thought three rather . . . difficult personalities could convince anyone to take a chance on you?"

Allie choked on a laugh.

"Yet you found impressive women to love," Frankie said. "Amazingly, they love you in return."

Gavin's grip went tight, and he lifted her hand to kiss the back of it with a lingering touch.

Frankie made a show of flipping open the top of the briefcase. She pulled out three envelopes. Allie had seen Gavin's before, when they'd visited Frankie's office to show her the Paraiba tourmaline engagement ring to prove he'd won the wager. Of course, Gavin had wanted to give her a precious stone, but she loved the sea green of the tourmaline because it reminded her of his eyes. So he'd settled for surrounding it with big, honking diamonds.

Frankie laid the envelopes on the desk in a neat line. Allie could read each man's name and see Frankie's bold notation, "Wager satisfied," and her initials.

Frankie swept her hand over the envelopes. "In chronological order of being canceled. Gentlemen, these are now yours to burn."

The three men stepped forward almost simultaneously. They looked magnificent in their white dinner jackets. Nathan carried himself with that brisk military posture, learned from his Marine father. Luke's golden hair picked up glints from the flickering fire. But Gavin took her breath away. His dark hair and olive skin made the white jacket look more brilliant, and he moved with that magnetic grace that always made her think of a conjurer.

Gavin seized his envelope and held it up. "I confess to acute curiosity. Shall we share what we wagered?"

"Why not?" Nathan said. One corner of his mouth quirked up in a smile. "In chronological order?"

Luke's dimple appeared. "Which means Miller goes last."

Nathan slid his finger under the envelope's flap. "I don't remember exactly how I phrased it." He pulled out the single sheet of paper and unfolded it for a quick glance. "Simple but clear. The family sword."

"The antique one your father is wearing today?" Luke asked, his normally unflappable calm disturbed. "It's been in your family for generations. He told me about its history."

Nathan nodded. "Dad and I hadn't seen each other in two years. The sword represented all that was wrong between us." He took Chloe's hand. "Luckily, my wife changed that, as well as winning me the bet." He returned the paper to the envelope and offered it to Chloe. "Would you do the honors?"

"Gladly," she said, taking the paper in one hand and her floating skirt firmly in the other. She walked to the fireplace and flicked Nathan's wager into the flames. They all watched the edges turn black as it caught and burned to ash.

Luke ripped open his envelope but didn't bother to look at the paper inside. "I bet my Super Bowl rings."

"Rings, plural?" Gavin asked. "You were more desperate than I realized."

"He only had four rings then, so it wasn't such a big deal," Miranda said with her serene smile, making her husband's dimple reappear.

"Anyway, I always win, especially the big games," the ex-quarterback said before he handed the envelope to his wife.

Miranda tossed the paper into the flames. Once again they waited until the last bit disappeared in a curl of smoke.

Gavin slid his envelope back and forth between his fingers. "I wagered my mother's necklace, the one Allie is wearing now. I'm not proud of that." He brushed his fingertip over the sparkling locket where it lay at the base of her throat. Just having his hand that near made her skin tingle. "But it has brought two amazing women into my life, so I cannot regret it."

He held out the envelope to Allie. She walked to the fireplace, ripped the paper in half, and flung it into the fire. Turning, she saw the flare-up of the last forfeit throw flickers of firelight on the faces of everyone watching. It was strange on such a warm fall day, but fitting, like a festive bonfire.

Gavin stretched his hand out to her, palm up, his gesture both commanding and beseeching. She put her hand in his, feeling the power in the fingers he wrapped around hers before he pulled her close to him.

"You know, the three of you aren't the only winners," Allie said, turning against Gavin's side. "I feel pretty good about the results of this wager, too."

Chloe winked. "But we won't admit that to the guys."

Gavin chuckled and turned to Frankie. "I think it's time to break out the 1928 Dom Pérignon we brought down for the occasion."

Frankie bent down, and Allie heard the rattle of ice against metal before the woman held up two dripping bottles of champagne. Gavin took one bottle while Luke took the other, popping the corks almost simultaneously. Frankie moved the tray of crystal flutes from the credenza to the desk so the men could fill them.

When Gavin offered her a glass, Frankie shook her head. "This is a moment for just the six of you. I was honored to be the keeper of your wager, but now my job is finished." With a smile and a wave of her hand, she strode out the door before they could dissuade her.

When they all had champagne in their hands, Nathan looked at Gavin. "You're the writer, so you propose the toast."

Allie remembered the days when Gavin would have flinched and made a snide remark about his writer's block. But *Christmas Best* was finished, and being rushed through production for release this holiday season. Even better, he'd started the next book and had ideas for three more.

Now he slipped his arm around her waist and stood considering for several seconds before he lifted his glass. "First, I'd like to toast the surprising friendship that began that night at the Bellwether Club. I hate to admit it, but you, my fellow gamblers, have become important to me."

Tears welled up in Allie's eyes as the three men touched their glasses together. She'd come to understand the loneliness they'd all felt at a time when they had reached the height of their success. As they tilted their heads back to drink, she could find nothing of that despair in their faces. Instead, a deep contentment radiated from them.

Gavin swallowed his champagne. "And I will deny I ever said that."

"No one would believe it anyway," Luke said.

"Now," Gavin said, "let us drink to the women who saved us, not just from losing our bet, but from becoming cynical, joyless men who no longer believed in one of the most powerful feelings on earth. When we made our wager, we were bluffing, but our hearts called our bluff." He lifted his glass. "I most humbly salute Chloe, Miranda, and Allie, the only women in the world who could love us for who we are."

After they drank, he raised his glass once more, his face lit by a flashing smile. "A CEO, a quarterback, and a writer walked into a bar . . ."

Gavin waited for the ripple of laughter to die down before he said, "And they came out better men."

AUTHOR'S NOTE

If you enjoyed meeting Claire and Tim Arbuckle from Sanctuary, West Virginia, you might enjoy the book that tells their love story, *Take Me Home*. Their book is the first in my Whisper Horse series, set in the mountains of West Virginia, and each starring a special horse who will share your troubles to lighten your burden. Every book in the series stands on its own, but if you prefer to read them in order, here it is:

Take Me Home (Book 1)

Country Roads (Book 2)

The Place I Belong (Book 3)

A Down-Home Country Christmas (Novella)

By now you may find yourself humming the tune of John Denver's famous song about West Virginia, "Take Me Home, Country Roads."

I hope my whisper horses, and the people they help find love, will bring you much reading pleasure.

DISCUSSION QUESTIONS

1. Family is a strong theme throughout the novel, and yet it is seen very differently through Allie's and Gavin's eyes. Allie's mother wrapped her in love and warmth and instilled a love of reading in her, while Gavin's parents either abandoned or belittled him. How much do you think family shapes us? If Gavin and Allie had grown up in different situations, how would that have changed who they are as people?

2. Allie's cat, Pie, plays a key role in the novel. How do pets affect our daily lives? If you've ever had a pet, how has it helped you?

3. Gavin has an obsession with "making it right." While the concept is admirable, do you think this mentality has affected his life in a negative way? Are his Julian Best novels an outlet for his desire for a positive outcome?

4. All three billionaires strive to win their wager of hearts by finding women who love them for themselves, instead of

their money. What similarities do Chloe, Miranda, and Allie have that allowed them to win the hearts of their men? What draws certain people together, despite substantial differences in social station or monetary success?

5. Gavin's writing has made him rich, but his love of writing isn't only about the money. Do you have a hobby or creative outlet that you can't do without? Would you be able to give up your creativity?

6. The Julian Best novels are considered commercial fiction, not great literature. Are books like Gavin's an important part of our culture, or are works of commercial fiction, such as spy novels and romances, just for fun?

7. Gavin often misinterprets friendship for pity, and empathy for weakness, so he walls himself off from the people who care about him. What does being a good friend entail? Do you ignore your friends' flaws, or help them acknowledge them? Would you consider Nathan and Luke the right friends for Gavin?

8. Luke, Nathan, Miranda, and Chloe—main characters from the first two books in the series—are featured in this novel. Did you find that their presence enhanced the flow of the story and the series? Do you miss characters after you've finished their books?

9. Gavin almost loses Allie because he believes Troy and Irene's story over hers. Can a relationship succeed without a certain level of trust? Was Allie right to leave Gavin to discover the facts for himself instead of trying to explain?

Although Allie forgives him for jumping to conclusions and takes Gavin back, does a lack of trust leave lasting scars in a relationship?

10. The novel features several strong women, including Allie, Frankie, Jane, and even Irene. What does it mean to be a confident, successful, and independent woman in the world today? Is it considered a positive thing, or are there still some prejudices against take-charge women?

11. Allie is a very talented physical therapist, but she struggles to find work until she meets Gavin. Do you believe that "it's not *what* you know, it's *who* you know"? Or will talent eventually be rewarded, with or without connections?

12. Gavin and Allie bond over their less-than-ideal exes, both of whom are actors. Is it true that "artsy" types tend to be more difficult people to live with? Does Gavin fall into that category?

ACKNOWLEDGMENTS

This book is especially dear to my heart because Gavin is a writer, as am I, and as are so many of my closest friends. I understand him perhaps better than any other character I have ever written. Therefore, I am especially grateful to all the wonderful people who have contributed to Gavin's story in so many ways. My deepest gratitude is owed to:

Maria Gomez, my marvelous Montlake editor, who watches over my books with such care and enthusiasm. She sparkles in every way.

Jessica Poore, Elise Taubenheim, Kimberly Cowser, and the whole Montlake Author Relations team, who are the most brilliant support group an author could ever ask for.

Jane Dystel and Miriam Goderich, my amazing agents, who continue to encourage me and help me grow my career. I'm overjoyed to have them in my corner. Yes, Gavin's agent, Jane, is a tribute to my own wonderful agent (but fictional Jane's words and actions are all my own inventions, of course).

Andrea Hurst, my longtime and invaluable developmental editor, who always pushes me, in the nicest possible way, to make my books the best they can possibly be. She made Gavin a better man and Allie a stronger woman.

Sara Brady and Lea Ann Schafer, my incredible copy editors, who make sure I mind my commas, my antecedents, my timelines, and the thousand other elements that make my prose gleam brightly.

Jill Kramer, my meticulous proofreader, whose profound knowledge of grammar, spelling, and punctuation awes me more with each book. Her attention to detail is downright superhuman.

Eileen Carey, my gifted cover designer, who captured Gavin's dark, brooding—and sexy!—presence so perfectly, and who valiantly revised the design until it was absolutely perfect.

Martin Duke, PT, for answering my endless questions about physical therapy with such patience, precision, and thoroughness (especially since I originally buttonholed him while he was on vacation). His knowledge and passion for his work are hugely impressive. Any errors are entirely my own.

Patti Anderson, expert personal trainer and dear friend, who made sure I kept Gavin's posterior and anterior deltoids in the right place. Again, all errors are mine and mine only.

Ellen Gerstner, my much-appreciated fresh eyes, who read the first chapter of this book and generously answered my questions about what information needed to be included for the new-to-the-series reader.

Cathy Genna, my marvelous, expert assistant, who generously shares her profound knowledge of what readers want and makes my authorial life so much easier in many ways.

Rebecca Theodorou, sensitive reader, talented writer, and overworked vet student, who created this book's perceptive, thought-generating discussion questions in order to provoke a lively conversation, whether internal or external.

Pie, my little gray rescue cat, who graciously allowed me to include her in my story.

Jeff, Rebecca, and Loukas, who expand my heart in every direction. I love you all very, very much.

ABOUT NANCY HERKNESS

Photo © 2015 Lisa Kollberg

Nancy Herkness is the author of the award-winning Wager of Hearts and Whisper Horse series, as well as several other contemporary romance novels. She has received many honors for her work, including the Book Buyers Best Top Pick Award, the Maggie Award, and the National Excellence in Romance Fiction Award, and is a two-time nominee for the Romance Writers of America's RITA award.

Nancy graduated from Princeton University with a degree in English literature and creative writing. A native of West Virginia, she now lives in a Victorian house twelve miles west of the Lincoln Tunnel in New Jersey, with her husband, two mismatched dogs, and an elderly cat.

For more information about Nancy and her books, visit www.NancyHerkness.com.

You can also find her on:
Facebook: www.facebook.com/nancyherkness
Twitter: www.twitter.com/NancyHerkness
Pinterest: www.pinterest.com/nancyherkness/
Blog: www.fromthegarret.wordpress.com